For Amanda
In the hope that
and whatever
more smoothly t

Emma

Past Imperfect

Past Imperfect

Emma van der Vliet

PENGUIN BOOKS

PENGUIN BOOKS

Published By the Penguin Group
Penguin Books (South Africa) (Pty) Ltd, 24 Sturdee Avenue, Rosebank,
Johannesburg 2196, South Africa
Penguin Books Ltd, 80 Strand, London WC2R 0RL, England
Penguin Group (USA) Inc, 375 Hudson Street, New York, New York 10014,
USA
Penguin Group (Canada), 90 Eglinton Avenue East, Suite 700, Toronto,
Ontario, M4P 2Y3, Canada (a division of Pearson Penguin Canada Inc.)
Penguin Ireland, 25 St Stephen's Green, Dublin 2, Ireland (a division of Penguin
Books Ltd)
Penguin Group (Australia), 250 Camberwell Road, Camberwell, Victoria 3124,
Australia (a division of Pearson Australia Group Pty Ltd)
Penguin Books India Pvt Ltd, 11 Community Centre, Panchsheel Park, New
Delhi – 110 017, India
Penguin Group (NZ), 67 Apollo Drive, Mairangi Bay, Auckland 1310, New
Zealand (a division of Pearson New Zealand Ltd)

Penguin Books (South Africa) (Pty) Ltd, Registered Offices:
24 Sturdee Avenue, Rosebank, Johannesburg 2196, South Africa

www.penguinbooks.co.za

First published by Penguin Books (South Africa) (Pty) Ltd 2007

Copyright © Emma van der Vliet 2007

ISBN-13: 978-0-143-02527-6

Typeset by CJH Design in 10/13.5 pt Classical Garamond
Printed and bound by Paarl Print, Cape Town

For my mother, Virginia, funny and wise.
With love and gratitude.

My thanks ...

... to André Brink, supervisor extraordinaire, for invaluable advice and encouragement
... to Stephen Watson, Ron Irwin and UCT's Centre for Creative Writing, for the course and for their counsel
... to my first ever Gentle Readers (and proofreaders) Maria, Jo, Sarah, Katharine, Carey and Josi ... for their suggestions and reassuring noises
... to everyone at Penguin, for making this happen, and for doing it so splendidly
... to Penguin's Jane Ranger, for whom this book might as well have been written, for loving it in the first place and for her unwavering encouragement, astute editing and some delightfully therapeutic conversations
... to Jane and Lynne, for TLC all round
... to Welshie, for having us (on numerous occasions) and to Mom, for babysitting (*all* of us!)
... to my brother Robert, for nagging, and for the beer-fuelled photo-session
... to all my friends, family, colleagues and students for their love and support
... to Jack, for years of shared disgraceful humour
... to Laurent and Jeremy, for Paris
... to Mrs Askew, wherever you may be, and to Claudia Regnart and Lesley Marx
... to my late father, Eduard, for the love of language
... to Oscar and Leo
... and to Will, for keeping me in laughter and in curry

I

Gap year

Prologue

Every year, hordes of young Britons and Euros in white socks and sandals and baring their touchingly vulnerable pasty knees, desert their families, friends and everything familiar and head down to our continent to find themselves and help the starving Africans. We from the Southern Hemisphere have learnt and inverted that tradition. Those who can, head off on their own pilgrimages to the cultural and financial Mecca of the North. There, they find Europeans and help themselves.

The Brits call it a Gap Year. I fell into a Gap Year like Alice into the rabbit warren and came out the other end all grown up and ground down. After my catastrophic encounters with group healing (but more of that fiasco later), my mother Claude, and various other Well-Wishers convinced me that solo therapy was more my style. I might have been less inclined to listen if I'd been less desperate at the time ... and if Jack hadn't told me he'd never do his Barbra Streisand impersonation for me again if I wasn't nicer to myself. Clearly I had no choice. Everyone seemed convinced I could 'write myself well'. This is my attempt.

Clementine Fynn-van Zyl

Life in the soup kitchen
Shop: NB: lentils, milk, bread, feathers from Pudney's, plastic seagulls, mace spray, lentils

When I arrived home through the back door there were already four people in our grubby digs kitchen. There was Angus (my housemate) engrossed in a *YOU* magazine, some guy called Stuart (on guitar), an unknown girl with blue hair (on Stuart) and a complete stranger with waist-length dreadlocks making cream cheese from sour milk in the legs of an old pair of pantihose (mine). Stuart and the girl with blue hair were hopelessly stoned, and while he strummed on tunelessly she degenerated from singing along to fondling him ineptly and eating handfuls of cornflakes out of the box. I dumped my bags at the door, resigning myself to this company for the next few hours. Officially, Angus and I lived in the house, but a tenacious and ever-present satellite community had established itself there. Our digs was known locally as the Soup Kitchen, which was sometimes funny and sometimes (for instance the day before a crucial exam) intolerable.

Right now I had five fake crows to make for my boyfriend Kurt's Art Happening, and there was no escaping the fallout shelter in the kitchen since the rest of the house had just been gassed with noxious anti-flea poisoning and it was pouring with rain outside. A couple of days before, some hippy acquaintance of Angus's had suckered us into looking after a pitiful stray dog. Angus told me it would help him get over the death of his cat, Lobotomy, who had recently gone berserk and been run over after eating the leftover dope cookies at a Soup Kitchen party. Besides, as Angus said, dogs made 'great babe magnets'. We had shut the shivering creature in the house overnight, but he squeezed through an open window and escaped, leaving behind him a colony of fleas. After days spent scattering the house with mint, I'd managed to persuade Angus to consider a less eco-friendly option and nuke the place.

'Amazing,' said Angus, apparently apropos of nothing, his head buried in the *YOU*. 'Listen to this: Baby devoured by fat-eating virus. My Dad is actually my Mom. Teenage Satanists killed our Pets. Where do they get this shit? These housewives are the sickest people imaginable. Do they *want* to be freaked out and paranoid? I mean listen here: "Johanna was only away for three minutes when she heard the lawnmower go on in the back garden. When she heard her son's screams it was already too late …" '

Angus was morbidly fascinated with pulp media. He scanned the obituaries every day for their poetic and entertainment value, and hoarded masses of them in box files in his impenetrable study among the earnest tomes on African history he had used for his Masters. I grinned and continued to glue black feathers onto the plastic seagull I had just purchased.

'What are you doing?' Angus had sensed a lack of attention to his reading and lowered his magazine.

'Props for Kurt's Happening,' I told him, not looking up from my fiddly work.

Angus made a kind of piggy, snorting, derisive noise and picked up his magazine again. 'I bet you wouldn't be doing that if he weren't your boyfriend,' he mumbled from behind the magazine, his face oddly replaced by some soap opera heroine on the cover.

'Angus, it's for his Masters,' I said. 'It's very important.'

'To him, maybe,' Angus muttered. He sighed, and reluctantly began perusing the pile of unmarked undergraduate essays next to him. I hoped he might relent and read me a couple of howlers from the essays, always one of our favourite late-night games, but his grouchy mood lingered and he read them in silence.

I had known Angus for several years, most of which we'd been housemates. We'd met through my mother Claude when I'd just arrived in Cape Town from Grahamstown to start university. Angus had finished third year as Claude's Favourite Student and had recently moved to Cape Town. He was bright, provocative and charming, and Claude gave him a special place in her scheme of things. He was going on to do English Honours in Cape Town after a dreadful year during which he discovered that his housemate and close friend had been putting himself through university as a spy for the security police. Suddenly the dead cats in the letterbox, the strange noises on the other end of the phone and the feeling that someone was shadowing you and knew everything about you, had made sense to Angus. The paranoia was justified. He left Grahamstown and didn't look back.

After years of living as Claude Junior in the same university town where Claude had lived and taught since before I was even born, I too decided to move to Cape Town to study when I finished matric. Claude was not the most maternal of mothers, but she accompanied me to Cape Town to see that I was properly installed there, citing a crucial conference as her excuse. It was deeply frustrating. She'd insisted on trying to guide me down the runway into my new life like one of those men with ping-pong bats at the airport. While I traipsed from digs to mouldy digs looking for accommodation she attended the conference and secretly made enquiries of her own.

Angus and I met by accident on the afternoon of my humiliating first (and last) venture into the acting world. Claude had met up with an old university friend who had gone into film casting and the friend told her about an audition for a chocolate advert. They were looking for pale-skinned, dark-haired 'milkmaids' to take the lead in their advert. Since the milkmaid was required to utter a few words it had been suggested that they were looking for actresses rather than models. For one day of being a milkmaid the Chosen One would earn a ludicrous sum, enough for me to pay off a fat chunk of student loan before I'd even started studying. Finally, I would reap the rewards for all my amateur high school theatrics and be paid outrageous amounts of money for a day spent eating chocolate. I knew it was the role for me. For days I practised the seven words required for the part in my most milk-maidenly tones in front of the bathroom mirror in the university house where Claude and I were staying. The venue for the audition was almost next door, and I eyed the neat *Casting Studio* sign on the gate each time I walked back from the Spar, feigning nonchalance.

Claude came in one evening before the audition, and proudly presented me with a hired milkmaid outfit from some local costume place as a surprise. It verged dangerously on Little Bo Peep, but with some adaptation became the perfect outfit. I was amazed at my luck. That one could still find a milkmaid outfit only two days before the audition! Surely it would have been snapped up weeks before? Cape Town must be a bigger place than I'd thought if there were enough milkmaid outfits to supply the whole city's aspiring actresses.

On the day of the audition Claude helped me to curl my hair into ringlets with a hotbrush. This was a two-person job, as we both knew, since past efforts with hotbrushes on my hair had led to tears and almost to baldness as the brush stuck in my frizz and began to burn. It was also the closest Claude had let me to her in years and I realised she was actually going to miss me. With a pang of guilt I remembered how I'd run away from home all those years ago, not long after my father died. Ma's preoccupation with her students, and with the education of township children that she took on in her time off, left little time for me. I'd written her a note: *You only care about other people's children. I am running away.* I was found curled up asleep near the stream at the bottom of the vice chancellor's garden later that day. Half the contents of my mother's fridge – the half not already eaten in disgustingly inventive combinations before I fell asleep – was strewn all over the nearby grass by the vice chancellor's dog. Claude had said nothing, she'd just looked mildly annoyed. She pulled me up by the wrist when I was still half-asleep and dragged me home, apologising to the vice chancellor's wife for the mess all over the lawn and promising to come back later for the picnic basket. It was not quite the adventure I had planned.

The milkmaid audition was to be held between three and five. At three on the dot I pushed open the gate to the casting studio with the hand that was not holding the milk pail and went in, in all my milkmaidenly splendour. Inside I followed the tacked up *Casting* signs until I ended up in a huge room where rows of immaculate, emaciated girls sat looking at pictures of each other in photo albums and chatting. As I walked in, fifty pairs of perfect eyes looked up at me incredulously. There was not a milkmaid in sight. They were sophisticatedly decked out in the latest fashion. One particularly unlikely cluster of milkmaid candidates sported hotpants smaller than the average headband. Suddenly I was a deckchair on a beach full of bronze, flab-free thighs.

'Sorry,' I said, avoiding the urge to run backwards out of the room as fast as possible. 'I think I must be at the wrong audition. I'm looking for the chocolate audition – for the milkmaid.'

'This *is* the chocolate one. Those are the forms.'

'Oh.' Reluctantly I entered the room and took a form. For a moment all remained silent. I felt every pair of eyes on me. An angry blush crept over my face and I bent my head over the form to hide it, determined to go through with the audition after all the time and effort Claude and I had put into it. No one actually laughed out loud but I could hear a buzz of mirth and astonishment in people's voices.

When I finally got inside the inner sanctum of the casting chamber, the bored photographer's eyes lit up with amusement at the sight of me. He turned to the casting director and grinned openly. She shot him a withering look and eyed me with professional courtesy, asking me to introduce myself to the video camera and give a right and left profile.

'Is this your first audition?' she asked as she adjusted the camera.

I nodded miserably. Was it that obvious?

'It's just that people don't normally make much of an effort to dress the part.' She finished fiddling with the video camera and looked up at me, wilting in layers of nylon frock under the lights. 'Don't look so gloomy, no one enjoys castings. You'll get used to them.'

'*Never!*' I swore to myself moments later as I tore down the passage past the hotpants brigade, my face scarlet with humiliation. 'I will *never, ever* go to an audition in my life again!' I yelled at the amazed postman. I speed-walked down the road, burst into the house where Claude and I were staying and began ripping off my milkmaid outfit as I headed for Claude's study.

'That was the most humiliating experience I have ever had in my life,' I shouted, kicking off Claude's pumps, pulling off the milkmaid outfit and throwing it in a heap on the sofa as I rounded the corner. Sitting on a chair next to Claude's desk was a young man with a broad grin and curly golden brown hair whom I had never seen before in my life. He looked at me standing angrily in the doorway in nothing but knee-high socks and underpants, and burst out laughing. I let out a small yelp of shock and surprise and stood there, momentarily frozen in semi-naked horror, before I grabbed the outfit from the sofa and held it in front of me.

The young man continued to grin, unfazed. 'You must be Clem,' he said, coming towards me and extending his hand in greeting. 'I'm Angus Foot.'

We'd now been housemates for over three years. When I first moved in, Angus was already settled in Cape Town, though he hadn't yet shaken off the clutches of his recent past. He still woke up shouting in the middle of the night, still distrusted people, still broke out into a cold sweat in the presence of police and dreamt about being dragged off to do the army 'duty' he'd successfully managed to avoid. But it was already the early nineties then, and the darkest days of apartheid were over. By the time the first elections were held in 1994, and we'd stood together in the pouring rain in the endless snaking queue waiting to vote, glowing with optimism and *ubuntu*, both Angus and

South Africa had changed more dramatically than one could ever have imagined. Two years ago. It was hard to believe that Angus had ever been anything other than his present genial, humorous, generous self.

I was contemplating this, lost in thought and staring more through Angus than at him as he marked his essays, when the phone began to ring somewhere in the house. I looked around the kitchen for it, since it was supposed to have been brought through when the nuking began, but it was nowhere to be seen. I have never been able to ignore a ringing phone.

'Angus, where's the phone?' I asked. He'd promised to supervise the process, including this crucial detail. Angus too looked around the room then turned accusingly to Stuart.

'Shit. Stuart, where did you put the phone?'

'Oh fuuuck, bru, sorry. I forgot to take it out of the room.' He turned to me: 'Why don't you just leave it and not answer it.'

'That's a very fucking irritating suggestion, Stuart.' Angus glared at him.

I couldn't bear it any longer. Holding my breath, I raced into the hallway and got to the phone just in time. The flea spray was thick and nauseating. I tried to talk into the receiver without breathing.

'Clementine?' said the voice on the other side. It was my mother.

'Hang on, Claude, I'm just pulling the phone through to the kitchen,' I yelled at her.

'What *are* you doing?' Claude asked.

'Hold on.'

I had the phone in the kitchen now and had pulled the door shut behind me, but the vile smell of the poison had caused the dry heaves to mount from my stomach. I tried to suppress the waves of nausea but Claude barely waited for me. She soldiered on with the conversation.

'You know Mac had a little stroke a while ago? Well ...'

I was stunned.

'*What?* No, I didn't, Claude, I had no idea! Why didn't you tell me?'

'Didn't I? *Ag*, Clem you were never that close to her.'

Well that was true, but Mac still happened to be my grandmother. I looked up from the phone to see Angus, Stuart, the girl with blue hair and the cheese-maker watching me intently, like a sitcom audience. I motioned at Angus to take them away but I could hardly send them out of the only habitable room and into the rain, so I turned my back on them instead and curled into a tight foetal position over the phone.

'Claude, why are you speaking about her in the past tense? It's not as if she's ... gone.'

'No, you're right. But she's definitely not all here either. Anyhow, the reason why I'm phoning is that she seems to have taken a turn for the worse, and she really can't be on her own any more. I've had to bring her down to Grahamstown from Jo'burg and put her in a place here.'

'A *place*? What kind of *place*?' I asked, horrified. The idea of Granny Mac in an old age home was ridiculous. Granny Mac was indomitable. Probably immortal.

'She's in the frail care centre at Greenfields,' Claude said, intruding on my thoughts. 'I thought since you weren't doing much at the moment you might want to visit her. You know, just in case,' she added with ruthless pragmatism.

Despite myself I began to protest, mumbling that I was not actually doing 'nothing' at the moment. But she cut in on me again.

'Maddy's driving through from Stellenbosch tomorrow, so you could come with her.'

Maddy. My extraordinary half-aunt. My mother's half-sister and her perfect foil. Aunt Maddy of the preposterously red nails, dyed hair and sassy tongue – the only person who'd ever really stood up to Claude. In short, my hero.

'I can't come tomorrow ...' I began.

'I see,' said Claude acidly.

'That doesn't mean I'm not coming, Claude. Okay? I'll make a plan. I'll phone you back. How are you?'

But Claude was already saying goodbye and she rang off.

The smell and taste of the flea-poison was overwhelming. I went to the bathroom and heaved but couldn't vomit. When I came out everyone looked sheepish. Angus shot Stuart a menacing look from behind his magazine.

'Hey, like sorry we forgot about the phone,' Stuart said, on cue.

I stayed up till five the next morning in the kitchen, finishing the props and set design for Kurt's Happening. More visitors arrived and the Soup Kitchen was in full swing, everyone carrying on their Dionysian rites around me like a cross between the Brady Bunch and the Manson Family. I sat in agonised indecision: could I delay my trip to Grahamstown until after Kurt's Happening and risk missing a chance to see my grandmother again? Impossible. Could I miss my boyfriend's all-important Happening, one of the culmination points of his Masters (and around which his life revolved)? Impossible. I would just have to phone Jack in the morning for counsel.

Decision

'Darling!' Jack gushed into the phone.

After more than two decades as a drama lecturer and set designer his voice had mellowed into genteel camp perfection. We'd been friends since I first arrived in Cape Town, tentatively at first because he was my teacher and later wholeheartedly. For some reason Jack had chosen me as his protégée. I'd first got to know him one day all those years ago when he had swooped down the passage in his billowing full-length silk cape and intercepted me at force as I was running towards the women's toilets, desperate for a pee and late for a lecture. To my surprise it seemed he was headed there too. He strode up to the full-length mirror, sucked in his cheeks and instantly became captivated by his own reflection, unabashed in his vanity or by my presence.

'There's no decent mirror in the gents,' he said without taking his eyes off himself. I smiled awkwardly, and since he showed no sign of moving I slipped into the toilet cubicle and tried to pee soundlessly. When I came out of the toilet he was standing further away from the mirror, examining his profiles. As I washed my hands he caught my eye in the mirror and sighed.

'Tell me honestly: What do you think of my hair?' I was a little astounded, never having said a word to him in my life before. His hairdo was a kind of shoulder length pageboy special. I hesitated, trying to think of something polite to say.

'No, no. I don't want the polite version,' he interrupted with a flamboyant flap of the hand.

'I think you look like Prince Valiant,' I said, and instantly turned puce. How *could* I have said that? It had just popped out. Jack had spun around and stared at me. Then he'd burst out laughing and clutched my hand in his own Liberace-ringed fingers. 'All right, Poppet, you pass the test,' he said, and offered me a coffee in the cafeteria. I gave the lecture a miss and began an extraordinary friendship instead.

Jack was unequivocal about my present dilemma. 'Of *course* you must go and see your grandmother, Clementine, imagine how you'd feel if she shuffled off this mortal coil and you'd stayed behind to stroke your boyfriend's ego? Kurt's more than capable of doing that himself. Sweetie, he'll just have to understand.'

Sadly, Kurt did *not* understand. We met later that afternoon at the small Italian coffee shop near the art school campus where he frequently held court, and I couldn't help feeling that a lot of his sulky theatrics were for the benefit of the black-clad art students skulking around us. My boyfriend of two years, Kurt Hausmann was a Masters student in Fine Art who held Happenings of the most cerebral variety, thought out loud, and collected disciples who hung around him (when he allowed it) in admiring clumps. He had been sent to Germany on a scholarship for a year, taken one look at the art scene there and never looked back. Or forward. He remodelled himself entirely and came to Cape Town as that highly seductive creature, the Foreign Artist, speaking authoritatively about the Dokumente exhibition in Germany where he'd had an installation, and gaining instant superiority over local artists with their provincial and incestuous art scene.

I'd met Kurt for the first time at that same coffee shop two years before. Or perhaps I should say that, appropriately, I met his work before I met him. Ducking out after a drama seminar for a coffee and a bit of a read, I sat down at my favourite table at the window. On the table was a small black notebook, open on a page filled with ant-sized writing and drawings that looked like some kind of entomological record; tiny, scratchy, riddled with detailed notes. I didn't touch the book, just stared, fascinated by the mind that produced this intricate microworld, imagining the myriad creative thoughts and ideas such a mind must hold, thinking of my own notebooks which exploded with scrawled illegible handwriting and collected bits of stuff. And just as I was trying to decipher some of the writing, an excessively beautiful boy whom I'd never seen before rushed up to my table in a state of dignified and carefully controlled panic and picked up the book.

'Is it yours?' I asked.

'Yes.'

'I haven't looked at it,' I said defensively, 'just this page which you left open.'

'Thank you.' Then, 'I'm Kurt Hausmann.'

An art student, recently back from Germany. I was smitten … and became more so over the next few days as it turned out that, beyond any hopes or expectations, Kurt had chosen *me*. Despite my ignorance of obscure Russian performance artists and even despite my disobedient electrified-looking hair, I had somehow become his first lady. Flattered and ecstatic, I launched into a relationship with him and had been stuck there ever since.

Unlike most of his disciples, Kurt smoked no dope and worked in a CD shop to support his artist habit, eschewing offers of other potentially soul-threatening 'real' jobs like teaching. He was a purist. He was also, of course, extremely good-looking in a conveniently Teutonic way, with thick, straight blonde hair, blue eyes, and a mouth which curved deceptively upwards at the corners and gave the impression of an imminent smile. It remained an unfulfilled promise. If smiling was Kurt's natural expression he had trained himself out of it years ago. Kurt was an Angry Young Man. A Serious Young Man. And I now had to tell this Young Man (less than a week away from his final Masters Happening) that I would not be able to continue working on the set – and that I might not even be there for the Happening itself. I braced myself and spoke.

'Thanks a lot!' was Kurt's sarcastic response.

'Kurt, she's had a *stroke*. She is my *grand*mother.'

'You never gave much of a shit about her before. You always told me she was a racist old bitch.'

'She's still my grandmother. I'll try to be back before your performance, I promise.'

'Don't do me any favours.'

I left it at that. Instead, we talked about his anxieties over the piece he was working on, the struggle to keep his work pure … I tried to be consoling and equally enraged about the potential conservative backlash from the Art Department. 'No one understands this kind of interdisciplinary work,' he moaned, loudly enough to involve and impress the impressionable under-graduate art student couple sitting next to us. I shook my head sympathetically and surreptitiously looked at the clock on the wall. I still had to get to the shops, finish off the props, and pack.

A few hours later I was on the bus to Grahamstown.

The homecoming

Surely it was the same sky-blue Volvo sliding into the Market

Square towards me? I strained my eyes to see the driver, my legs unsteady after the long bus ride, clenched possessively astride my bag as I waited in the crowd. It was a Saturday morning and the square was crammed with jostling, shoving, shouting shoppers, dusty and irritable in the unseasonal heat. My sunglasses had vanished. So many times I had planned My Return, and as many I had put it off, convinced it wouldn't be long before I'd miraculously bloom into some stunning, sophisticated prodigal daughter who turned heads and started envious gossip. Instead I stood rumpled, sweaty, minus sunglasses, unkempt, unslept and acutely aware that I still somehow smelt of the bus's onboard toilet.

It had been a long ride. For hours I'd been pinned between the window and Wayne, a garrulous tour bus guide. I couldn't allow myself to fall asleep in case I ended up lolling onto his shoulder or (God forbid) his lap ... waking with a jolt to find that I'd been drooling in comfortable oblivion onto his beefy Polo shirt. After some abortive attempts at conversation on his part, he'd eventually fallen asleep, his comatose bulk on top of my jacket, trapping me in the seat. I turned my back to him, watching the landscape flash past in the early morning light, waiting to arrive.

The Volvo edged its way insistently towards me. It looked stately and dusty. Large as a boat. A relic. As it came closer I caught a glimpse of the driver. It was not Ma, it was Maddy, intently forging her way through to me. I could see her now, her short red fingernails impatiently gripping the steering wheel. I waved tentatively, unsure whether she'd see me, and she took both scarlet-nailed hands off the wheel, rolled her eyes and shrugged in a dramatic gesture of exasperation. Even from this distance Maddy looked sexy as hell with her big squashy mouth, green cat's eyes and longish-short auburn hair. She's as short, busty and voluptuous as I am long, willowy (at best), pale and titless. I stood there, dumbly planted over my meagre luggage. Eclipsed again. Maddy drove the car forward in impatient halting lurches for the last few metres, opened her door, left the car to idle and climbed out. She pointed at me, a lone honky girl in a sea of Saturday morning township shoppers and laughed.

'Dr Livingstone, I presume?' she shouted in a poncey English accent, and made her way over to me in one clear decisive motion. Always so bold. It was as though before she even started doing a thing her mind had already moved onto the next. She strode up to me, her hips sashaying with her naturally sexy gait. Hips that came straight from those girls in *West Side Story*. Unembarrassed, overt, uncompromising. Verging on predatory. She lifted her large dark glasses, scrutinising me shamelessly.

'Jesus, Clementine, you look dreadful.'

'Thanks.'

'Don't you ever eat?'

'Come on, Maddy, I'm just tired. I couldn't sleep on the bus.' I felt my face flush. Why the hell was I explaining myself, apologising already. Ridiculous.

'If one night without sleep made me that skinny I'd be a happy woman.' She scrutinised me at arm's-length, her eyes eventually resting on my downcast face. 'Don't look so miserable, Skinny-malinks,' she said, brushing the stray strands of hair out of my face, 'we're all just jealous.'

If Ma had been there she'd have scolded her for encouraging eating disorders. Unlike Claude herself, who rivalled Mother Teresa in her role as care-and-wisdom-dispenser to virtually everyone except me, her only actual offspring, my mother's half-sister never was very PC.

Maddy held the boot open while I hoisted my bag in clumsily. As I climbed into the passenger seat the most achingly familiar smell filled my nostrils. Mac's car. A smell of family outings, boredom, anticipation, treats, threats, only-childness and long conversations with Betsy, my imaginary friend. A lump of emotion rose in my throat.

'It's the same car,' I blurted out.

'You remember it?'

'Of course I do,' I said, feeling put out. Even if I was younger it was my history too.

Maddy steered the Volvo deftly, slicing a path straight into the past. Why had I stayed away for so long? Over three years had passed since I left for Cape Town. Now everything seemed clotted with memory, each wall or tree nostalgically significant. The town sped by. We passed the butcher who would spoil me with treats of free bright red polony – especially after Dad was gone and it was just Claude and me – a big, kind man with hands like his sausages, large and ruddy, generously plump. We passed Dullabh's sex shop, its cellar glittering with Mrs Dullabh's secret sari stash. Everywhere people carried on their lives, as if these things, this place, were nothing exceptional. They had laid claim to the town, clumsily, unknowingly, assigning things no particular value. A rock, a wall, a tree, a road. Nothing special. Infuriating.

'I suppose you're wondering why Claude didn't fetch you.' Maddy had never lost the habit of disguising her questions as statements. Actually it hadn't occurred to me to wonder. Pragmatic Claude, my infinitely capable mother, was a natural delegator. Always occupied and making sensible arrangements.

'Why?' I asked. More to satisfy Maddy's urge to tell than my own need to know.

'I insisted,' she smiled broadly.

I grinned at the compliment, shifting my bum in my seat. I felt as though I'd developed bedsores after that long bus ride and looked forward to the end of the journey.

'Besides,' Maddy went on, forthright as ever, looking straight ahead of her as she drove, 'Claude is far too busy martyring herself to *our* mother at the moment to be the perfect mother herself ... But I'm afraid Mac's past noticing most of the time.' *That* wiped the grin off my face. I braced myself for a gaga Granny Mac. Maddy pulled up at one of the few sets of traffic lights in the town and looked at me, very directly now.

'It's quite bad, Clem. This stroke was severe. She's paralysed down one side. And she's lost quite a few of her marbles.'

By the time we arrived at Greenfields I expected the worst. Greenfields. Such a lush, springy, beginning kind of name for such an ending kind of place. Maddy pointed me to the room and went in to talk to some of the nurses about Mac. I knocked on the door.

'Come in,' Claude called. I pushed the door ajar and looked inside. Claude was busying herself, briskly practical in the bright, offensively inoffensive little room. Mac was sitting propped up in a wheelchair like some ancient monarch on her throne, suddenly spectacularly bald.

'More visitors,' she said with an irritated sigh. I hesitated on the threshold.

'Madeleine?' she barked at me throatily. 'Stop loitering in the fucking doorway and come inside.' I stood there for a moment, absurdly flattered by her error – flattered and profoundly relieved that she had not lost her temerity along with the marbles. A mild, sweet-natured Mac would have been too great a shock.

'It's Clementine, Gran,' I said, approaching timidly. Mac frowned at me and said nothing. 'I'm glad you're here, Clem,' Claude said as if to make up for Mac's apparent lack of interest in my presence. She gave me a brisk, firm, practical hug and whispered in my ear, 'Try not to look so shocked.'

I leaned over and kissed the whiskery old prune. She was naked and vulnerable without her wig and I realised I had never seen her without it before.

'How are you, Gran?'

'How do I look?' I had a moment of acute discomfort, which provoked a chuckle from Mac.

'I look like shit,' Mac said. Another Rude Word, one of Mac's favourites, popped neatly out of her mouth like an olive pip. Claude had given up on Mac and her foul language, passed on to me as a child and a constant source of amazement and consternation at school. After Mac's stroke the dull but well-intentioned doctor had been very uncomfortable when he asked Claude whether her mother had 'always used such … strong language'. 'Oh yes,' Claude had said, undaunted and unembarrassed, 'that's nothing new, I'm afraid.' It was only when it came to Mac's outrageous racist slurs that Claude had always put her foot down, determined that that would not be part of my inheritance from her mother. I glanced at Claude for assistance but Mac interrupted before I could think of a reply.

'I look like shit and I feel like shit and it's all because I'm so busy entertaining guests in this bloody hotel that I never get out.'

Just like that she stepped into the unreal.

'Entertaining ghosts, more like,' Maddy stage-whispered as she came in past me. It was most disconcerting: I seemed to be missing a page in my script. Either that or Mac had a page from someone else's entirely alien script.

'You okay, Ma?' Maddy's statement-question technique again.

'Fine.' Mac stopped whingeing immediately. 'You don't have a cigarette do you, Madeleine? You're not smoking again?'

'No, Ma, you know I've given up.'

I raised my eyebrows. I'd never known Maddy to go for more than ten minutes without a smoke. 'Since when?' I asked her.

'Oh ages.' She shot a vile look in my direction.

I watched Maddy and Claude as they organised a tray of tea, their shared mother, unchallenged matriarch, dwindling before them. Each seemed more than ever a living incarnation of their own separate, long-gone fathers. For a moment, as they sat sipping tea at her bedside, they seemed absurdly more like husbands or suitors than daughters; drones ministering frantically to their shrinking regal queen. Mac opened one eye and darted a glance at me: 'Don't stare like that. I'm not dead yet.'

Maddy looked at Claude in distress, but Claude set her jaw stoically and ignored her. We all sipped our unwanted tea, awkwardly. The milk tasted slightly sour.

Suddenly Mac seemed to start and tried to stand up.

'What's the time?'

Claude and Maddy caught each other's eyes briefly and made a little pact: Maddy took this one.

'It's four-thirty, Mac. Why?'

'You see? Now I have a problem.' She seemed enormously agitated, trying to prop herself up in her Biggie Best-ish cocoon.

'What's the problem?'

'I've spent all day playing hostess around here and now I'll be late to fetch Leon. And it's rush hour.'

Strike two. Another blow to the world as we knew it. Another foray into scriptlessness. Leon, Mac's Jewish-businessman second husband and Maddy's father, had been dead for over ten years. Mac would never walk again, let alone steer the car through rush hour to fetch him even if he were still alive. The three of us looked at each other awkwardly. Claude looked sorrowful and dignified, as though she lacked the heart to reassure me in any way. I began to panic, realising with a pang of guilt that in my anxiety I was trying not to laugh, and looked away. It was just like the time I was about ten when someone told me their uncle had been eaten by a shark. I had laughed out loud and never got over the guilt. Nerves, I suppose, but also, somehow, it was just funny. For a few moments we all just avoided each other's eyes, saying nothing. Then Maddy shrugged, raised her eyebrows, made a decision and plunged straight in: '*Ag*, I wouldn't worry about that, Ma. Bugger him. Leon's a grown man – he can walk home.'

Four separate silences hovered in the room – Gran's unfathomable, unpredictable, Claude's mildly disapproving, Maddy's like a gambler waiting for the next card, and mine, anxious and astounded by Maddy's shameless fib. I held my breath. Suddenly through the silence came a sound like dry leaves crackling. From deep inside Mac's cocoon of blankets came a throaty cackle of wicked delight. For a second I thought she'd been having us on – playing a typical MacTrick on us. But no.

'I like that, young lassie. That's exactly what I'll do. Let the bugger walk.'

In that moment I knew we'd boarded the shuttle to the end of Mac's world: first stop Planet Dementia.

The three of us drove off silently in the early evening. Maddy applied some more lipstick in the rear-view mirror and lit up a cigarette.

'Are you *smoking*?' I asked stupidly.

'Looks like it, doesn't it? Why, do you want one?'

'No ... I thought you said you'd given up.'

'Of course I *said* that,' said Maddy. Claude drove in silence looking pained. Maddy put on the radio and started singing along tunelessly, the cigarette dangling from her mouth. The sun had started to set, bleeding an unreal magenta into the sky. We passed the Botanical Gardens with their prehistoric-looking plants, their fleshy leaves spiky in silhouette. Past the same buildings, same roads, new editions of the same knots of students talking conspiratorially on the corners. By the time we pulled up outside our house I was exhausted; saturated with memory, stunned by the encounter with the much-changed Mac. Our House, on the other hand, seemed unchanged, lurking secretively under a dark balaclava of dense ivy. Once, many years ago, my father (in a rare fit of domestic industry) had set out to cut back the ivy to a modest trim. A seven-foot *rinkhals* had slithered out at him and off into the depths of the overgrown periwinkle bank nearby. After that we had left the ivy (and the snakes) in peace. Jimmy called it mutual respect. I was assailed by familiarity. I put on my bravest face and voice, pleaded exhaustion and headed for bed.

My room was as I'd left it; a cluttered, eclectic monument to my past; a littered landscape of hoarded, untouched baggage and tacky memorabilia, some of which I'd had for so long I couldn't even remember where it came from or why I'd kept it. It clogged up the cupboards and all available surfaces. The room smelt of belonging. It had been mine since before my father died. Then one day he'd gone on a fishing trip with a friend and never come back. He'd gone out on deck for a last cigarette after an evening of hard drinking. When he was not around in the morning they looked all over for him, even in the pub where he'd made a nuisance of himself the night before. But he eluded them. In the early evening they pulled Jimmy's body from the water, just a few inches from the boat. He'd been there all the time. Full fathom five.

I stared at the photographs of Jimmy, of Claude. One cloudy Saturday afternoon after Jimmy died, Claude had made a bonfire in the back garden and started burning all my father's letters and photos while I stood by, stricken.

'I don't need these any more,' was her inadequate explanation, her expression wild and unreadable.

'Can I take the pictures?' I asked woefully.

'All right,' she said, 'take them.'

I took the photographs and went inside before she could change her mind. Soon it had begun to rain, and I watched through the window as Claude struggled with the trunk, dragging it towards the house like a corpse. She lugged it inside, hauled it into the bathroom and set fire to the remaining letters in the loo, blowing the entire toilet bowl out of the floor in her determination and laughing a horrible laugh that ended in tears.

All the photographs I had of Jimmy had been saved from that fire. I'd kept a clutch of them in a box in my trunk ever since, and I flicked through them again now, filled with a tired sadness. Here was Claude, smiling next to my father in another life. She'd grown hard and brittle so quickly after he died, like clay that sets too fast. She spurned sympathy. Maddy came down to help before heading overseas, but Claude treated her half-sister like a troublesome second child. She wouldn't talk to her, she wouldn't cry. Then Mac arrived from her plush Johannesburg home to check that her daughter was 'doing things properly'. She'd already lost one husband by that point and was a dab hand at widowhood. Mac stayed for three terrifying months. Daily, I invented imaginary illnesses to avoid being forced to take quasi-military brisk afternoon walks or take part in the bracing form of gardening Mac went in for. My grandmother was also a crack shot. She'd invite me up to the roof where she practised her perfect aim on the luckless starlings. I would then have to collect all the tiny shredded bodies for her and count them. For years I was convinced that she used these for culinary purposes and could not eat her food, reinforcing her notion that I was somehow soft or defective. She was also not averse to firing a few rounds to scare off any unwanted visitors and she was resolutely racist. Of all the houses in her neighbourhood, Mac's was the only one left alone by beggars. She would boast about this, though she toned down her shooting sprees after a couple of friendly visits by some 'charming young policemen' and promised to shoot only on 'special occasions'. Even the memory of that time exhausted me. I stashed the photographs back in their box, threw myself face first into my brown and beige seventies duvet, and fell into a dead sleep.

I woke again in the middle of the night, desperate for water, and headed for the kitchen. Maddy and Ma were sitting at the kitchen table. Maddy's eyes were red and slitty, her nose red. She held a cigarette absently between her fingers, its long ash drooping towards the full ashtray below. *Dronkverdriet*. A pair of empty wine bottles stood in front of her on the table. Maddy's glass was ringed with crimson copies of her mouth. Opposite her, Ma sat silent and tearless, sober and severe as I'd always known her since Dad left. Jimmy had packed her laughter into his fishing bag all those years ago and left her with none. He'd been the key to her happiness. They'd met at university the night he'd been thrown out of his residence for riding into the dining hall on a borrowed horse, steaming-drunk, wearing nothing but a kilt and reciting a poem by Kipling with ironic fervour. He had taken one look at the earnest young Claude and fallen in love. He lived to make her laugh and taught her about fucking. He used language almost as foul as Mac's and Claude felt right at

home, so when Jimmy proposed to Claude one moonlit Saturday
night when they were up to their knees in mud, pumping prawns
for bait in the river mouth, she'd said yes. Jimmy had brought
her out of her shell, and his death had sent her back in again.

Maddy patted the seat next to her and smiled sadly at me,
silent for a while. 'Maybe it's better that she doesn't really
know what's happening,' said Maddy to no one in particular,
presumably continuing their previous meandering conversation.
'The staff seem to be treating her very well. As if they really
like her. I caught her allowing Patience to do her nails yesterday.
Incredible.'

'Of course she does think they're all her servants,' said
Claude. 'A few days ago when I was visiting one of the nurses
came into the room. Mac sat straight up in her bed and shouted
at the top of her voice "What's that Af doing in my house?"
I apologised to the nurse but she seemed to think it was quite
funny. Poor old bigot. After all the arguments we used to have.
If she'd known she'd be dependent on Them ...' The sentence
trailed off, unfinished. Claude put her hands around the coffee
cup as if to warm them. She had allowed us a glimpse into the
locked box of her emotions, but just as quickly she snapped it shut
again. Again they seemed like Mac's suitors – dejected suitors
now, unified only in their loss. Two spurned lovers, I thought to
myself. Why did our men keep dying off on us? Maddy seemed
to read my mind.

'What happens to all the men in our family? Why are there
no fathers any more, no husbands?'

Claude stopped mid-sip but did not look at her. It was a
forbidden topic. I glanced anxiously from one to the other. But it
was Ma's taboo, not Maddy's, and Maddy insisted.

'Seriously, Claude. Think about it.' She had a good few
glasses down her by this stage and was spoiling for a fight ... a
small dog taunting a big dog. 'To lose several husbands looks like
carelessness,' she began, misquoting Oscar Wilde. It would have
been clever if we hadn't heard it before.

From what I'd managed to piece together over the years, the run of bad luck and incredible accidents had started when Claude's father, Mac's first husband, died when he was struck by lightning while pissing on a golf course. This seemed to have set a trend for deaths to come among the male members of our family. People called Mac the Black Widow after her second husband, Maddy's father Leon, also died under strange circumstances. In fact, he'd died in *flagrante delicto* in the flat he kept for his mistress. Mac had been called out of a business meeting, by his mistress, as it turned out, and had driven off to find him at a speed alarming even by her standards, her white knuckles grasping the steering wheel, crimson nails and lips. She did not cry when she saw him there, undignified in his state of elderly undress, his mouth drawn back in a grotesque smile. He lay on the bed, stiffly, frozen in a state of agony and ecstasy. The Mistress said nothing at first. She sat in terror, out of Mac's reach, staring at her with red-rimmed eyes and waiting in dread for her reaction. She was a far cry from the vamp in the slut-red dress, slit to the hips, who'd pitched up at Mac's Christmas-cum-Hanukkah dinner two years before, dragging her rodent-sized designer dog behind her. I had been captivated by this outlandish, extraneous creature, if somewhat perplexed by her role at our family dinner and by the effect she had had on everyone there.

Mac had stood frowning at the end of the bed, staring at Leon for a full minute without saying anything. Then she'd walked up to him and prodded him. When there was no reaction, she gave him a small push with her hand. Leon's corpse flopped stiffly back into position, grinning hideously. 'Dead,' pronounced Mac. 'Definitely dead.' The Mistress took this as her cue and began to wail. Mac shot her a curious look as if she had only just noticed her presence. 'And to think I once invited you for Christmas in *my house*,' Mac snapped at her. She crossed the room, assessing the love-nest with one devastating glance, and went to help the authorities fill in their report in the empty kitchen.

When Claude had arrived at Mac's just after Leon's death,

Mac's gardener had told her, not without pride, that 'Madam' had seen 'the Master' with 'that other Madam' and had put a hex on him. Claude scoffed at the idea, but particularly after my own father's untimely death it was a topic my mother refused to discuss. Finished and *klaar*.

Now, all these years later, she still refused to talk about it, but she kept her cool in the face of Maddy's insistent taunts.

'I don't *want* to think about that now, Madeleine. It's bad enough just dealing with Mac for the moment.'

'Especially for you, I suppose. You were always Mac's favourite.'

An unpleasant, petulant, childish tone had crept into Maddy's voice. It took me by surprise. Ma glowered at her and sat up even straighter in her chair. All wounded dignity and disapproval, she launched a counter-attack.

'You know that's not true. Mac always loved you most – despite your rebelliousness. In fact because of it. I was an impostor. I was the boring, bookish older daughter, a leftover. You were the light of her and Leon's life.' She laughed bitterly. 'Why do you think I spent my entire youth reading?'

I'd had enough. The whole scene seemed to be unravelling around me as two of the women I admired most in the world slipped back a few decades into their uneasy shared childhood and Mac, the only real link between them, clung tenuously to her life (and her remaining marbles) in some floral purgatory. Suddenly I felt exhausted. The thought of lying on the tatty sofa in the Soup Kitchen chatting to Angus seemed utterly appealing. Then, rather perversely, my mind conjured up images of unbridled sex with Kurt – clutching chunks of his thick hair as we sweated together on his digs bed ... I unclenched my hands and shook my head to dispel the fantasy. Maddy's voice whined on.

'You only did that to show me up, Claude. You were always the clever one.' To my horror Maddy turned to me for support, for complicity. 'She was such a goody-goody. Mac's serious, intelligent daughter who she could talk to for hours while I hung around on the sidelines trying to attract attention. I had to behave badly just so that they noticed I was *there*.'

I averted my eyes from Maddy's, flattered by her attention but unwilling to be conscripted into her side against my mother. I wished I'd never come. That afternoon with Mac I had tried so hard to feel part of what was happening but I knew I was in a different orbit, far from these seemingly indomitable women. Pathetic, really.

'I'm going back to bed.' I scraped my chair back and said goodnight. Claude looked wounded and embarrassed. Maddy looked puzzled and annoyed at the interruption; she was clearly just getting into the swing of it and her audience was leaving.

The next morning I woke disorientated. Dread filled my head like a hangover, as though something terrible had happened but I could no longer pinpoint what it was. Then I remembered. Mac all small and bald and sporadically bonkers, the scene in the kitchen. That nothing had changed but nothing was the same.

And then there was Kurt.

I dragged myself out from under the duvet and slunk towards the phone, hoping not to encounter Claude or Maddy *en route*. Then I dialled Kurt's number, hoping for some consolation. I woke him up.

'Thanks for phoning yesterday,' he sneered.

'I couldn't. We were at Mac's almost the whole day.'

'How was it?'

'Awful.'

'Well, you decided to go. I could have done with a bit of help around here, you know. I might have to rework the set because you've ducked.'

God, he could be a vile bastard. Why didn't I tell him to screw himself? Why? Why didn't I scream that I was only doing the sets and props as a favour, not because I had to?

'I did *not* duck! You know I had to ...'

'Whatever.'

Kurt was just about to ring off when he remembered

something.

'By the way, that screaming drama queen friend of yours has been had up for molesting one of his students. Wixley's suspended him.'

'*Jack?*' I virtually screamed into the phone, 'But he would never … How do you know?' I could hear Kurt's irritation on the other end of the phone. 'Everyone knows. Listen, I really don't know what you see in that passé old poof but clearly you're more interested in him than in me. My Happening is in two days and you don't seem to give a shit. I don't know why you even phoned me in the first place.' I mumbled a few apologetic platitudes as he rang off. I tried to get hold of Jack but he wasn't answering his phone. His normal inventive, frequently obscene phone-sex-inspired answering messages had been replaced with a frighteningly ordinary one. Jack's Polite Voice sounded strained and distant. I closed my eyes and concentrated on not panicking. I had to get back to Cape Town.

In the sitting room Maddy was watching a television interview with Naomi Campbell. She leaned forward in her seat with a frown on her face, scrutinising the TV and muttering oaths, as a seemingly endless variety of beautiful Naomi shots dissolved into each other across the screen. Claude was making organic dog food in the kitchen in huge vats. She put the bowls down outside the kitchen door, called the dogs, and went to perch on the armrest of the sofa next to Maddy to see what all the fuss was about. Naomi was looking indefatigably stunning. Over a series of Sealy-Posturepedic-advert shots of Naomi bouncing lithe and immaculate out of bed in the morning, the interview started. 'I never watch what I eat and I never exercise,' Naomi gloated. 'I guess I'm just lucky.'

'Lying bitch!' Maddy was shouting by now. 'It must be all the coke she shoves up that plastic nose of hers …'

'Morning, Clem,' said Claude, spotting me in the doorway. Maddy waved and continued to watch the Lying Bitch. I started to think I'd dreamt up the drama of the night before.

At that moment, Jessie, the geriatric Labrador, came ambling into the room and peed on the carpet.

'Jesus Christ,' said Maddy. 'I can't believe that's Jessie. Why is she still alive?'

Claude leapt up to clean the carpet.

'How many times a day does this *happen*?' Maddy asked.

'She's an old dog, Maddy. She's fourteen. That's very old for a big dog especially.'

'Don't you think it might be kinder to put her out of her misery?'

Claude shot her a look, her eyebrow raised questioningly. There was moment of discomfort and I knew they were thinking about Mac.

'Jessie's a *dog*, Claude,' Maddy broke in defensively. 'Sometimes I wonder if you take your attachments to your dogs a bit far.'

When Claude left the room Maddy let out a snort of derisive laughter. 'I tell you, Clem. One day we'll walk in and find Claude doing a *leetle* shit in the middle of the carpet just to make the dog feel at home.'

I don't think either of them was too surprised when I told them I had to leave.

Maddy insisted we eat at the motel on the hill. She was hung-over and swollen-eyed so we sat inside out of the light, she in her large sunglasses, looking out of the huge glass doors. You could see the whole town from there. Maddy and Ma were talking (well, mostly Maddy) but I wasn't listening. I was elsewhere. Even as I sat staring out of the windows a strange urine-yellow cast fell on everything. I knew this light well from all those years back. It was the light farmers prayed for, desperate for water in the arid decades of drought. Its meaning was unmistakable: storm. Each leaf, each blade of grass suddenly a distinct and vivid green. Utterly silent. A pregnant pause. I watched. At these times the sky is as fascinating as the sea. Dark grey and swollen as the fleshy belly of a fish, the clouds are the only thing moving in the perfect stillness, like waves in an inverted seascape.

The uniformed waiter moved the last of the cane furniture off the lawn and onto the patio just as the clouds broke. I caught his eye momentarily through the rain-streaked window but he quickly looked away. What must he think of this soundless Bergman movie on the other side of the glass?

Mac was the same that afternoon as she had been the day before; drifting between lucid and lost. I kissed her goodbye, hoping she'd remember I'd been there at all. The sweet, practical nurses assured me that Mac was tough and laughingly suggested she would probably outlast the rest of us. I told them I'd be back soon.

I'd found a lift with one of Claude's students and we left the next morning. I wore my new sunglasses, big Jackie O ones, black and plastic and bought outside the supermarket on my one brief and unfulfilling solo trip into town.

Somewhere past George we passed the bus on its way back to Cape Town. Near the back of the bus, staring out of the window, was Wayne the tour bus guide, in his Polo shirt. I'm convinced it was him. Maybe he was also heading home.

No muse is good muse

What's that screaming? A good many dramatic situations begin with screaming.
– Barbarella, *Barbarella*

The arrangement was perfect. I'd meet Jack before Kurt's Happening just to 'catch up' since he seemed reluctant to discuss his suspension over the phone. Then I'd surprise Kurt by managing to turn up after all, and earn some serious cred as his jet-setting but dedicated girlfriend. For a change the prospect of the performance seemed quite exciting, since I'd missed out on the run-up and for once didn't know exactly what to expect.

Jack had promised to come with me despite his suspension ('purely to scout for any new talent, of course') but my normally long-suffering housemate Angus dug his heels in and refused. He was resolute. 'I'd rather nail my dick to a burning building, as they say in the classics,' he had said to me. 'Why don't you just stay at home with the rest of us and we'll do a huge beetroot curry?'

'Come on, Gus, you know I have to go. It's Kurt's piece.'

He rolled his eyes back and snorted with frustration. 'What are you doing with that fucking jerk anyway, hanging around with him and all his friends in Pseuds' Corner?' He delivered this scathing and unexpected indictment in an affectedly casual voice. I frowned at him in surprise and he looked away and started chewing distractedly at the quick of his nails.

'Gus, he's a friend of yours!'

'He's a prick,' he countered, vehemently. I was amazed. It felt disloyal. It felt like sacrilege. It felt like the most refreshing thing I'd heard in a while. Angus flopped back onto the bed and picked up a horror comic.

'I can't *not* go ...'

'Go then. But I'm fucked if I'm going to be duped into sitting through an hour and a half of The Emperor's New Clothes.' And he was lost in the world of Gotham City.

I flew into Jack's Gucci-scented embrace when we met, desperate to talk to him. He pulled me to him and then held me out at arm's-length to inspect me. 'Darling, I must tell you, you look *so* gorgeous tonight. I swear one of these days I'm going to turn for you.'

'Heaven forfend. Now tell me, what's going on?' I broached the unpalatable topic immediately, but Jack put his finger to his lips theatrically and ushered me off to say hello to Cedrick.

It was Cedrick's deeply decadent bar that Jack and I always chose to meet in, Jack's home away from home. Cedrick himself was on top form. He was standing behind the brothel-red bar counter drying glasses when we arrived and talking animatedly to a languid young man who leaned on the counter from the other side, blowing elegant curls of smoke into the shaft of lamplight like a Beardsley silhouette. 'Darlings, you must meet Fritz,' said Cedrick. 'He's utterly gorgeous as you can see, but convinced he's straight! I just cannot get him out of the closet. I'm sure he's stuck in there waiting for the right boy to come along with the key, but the silly thing resolutely claims to be a hettie.' Cedrick rustled around behind the counter in his fussy silk shirt, gesticulating excessively and feigning exasperation. The languid heterosexual boy good-naturedly allowed Cedrick to continue the game as Jack and I took our drinks and retreated to a far-flung corner.

'Cedrick's a sweet old girl. So desperately trying to carry on as if nothing could rock our little boat,' Jack said. He looked stressed but buoyant. I was full of concern for his well-being but he just wanted someone to laugh with.

'Listen, darling girl, I've lost three kilos already this week. If I keep up this stress level for much longer I'll have such fabulous cheekbones I won't even have to have my back teeth out. Besides, you can't *believe* how exciting it was for a moment. I never thought I'd be butch enough to be involved in a public bar brawl. If it hadn't been for that bastard Wixley – who as I've told you is too scared to come out of the closet himself and can't bear anyone else to have fun – if it hadn't been for him and that boring young man whose treasured dick I only accidentally fondled in passing – well, if it hadn't been for that fatally unimaginative combination the whole thing would have blown over in five minutes. It's a most tawdry little saga, you see.'

If he was humiliated, if he actually felt like a sad old poof or outdated faggot or whatever Kurt had called him, he was concealing it masterfully. I played along for a while and then insisted.

'Come on, Jack, stop drawing it out for dramatic effect and tell me what happened.'

'Aah yes. The sorry tale. Let's see ... It all started during the mask-making workshop I was teaching with the second years. I couldn't help noticing that Neil Bertram was possessed of a decidedly above-average posterior. Late one night I bumped into most of the second years at the Slag's Heap. Perhaps I should have known better, but I reached out during a high point in a conversation about Fellini with Susan Klebb and gave Neil's butt an appreciative fondle. Fortunately or unfortunately he chose that precise moment to swing around so that I got a little more than I had bargained for ... including a punch in the jaw from the little turd.'

'Oh God, Jack. What did you do?' I found the scene hard to imagine. And totally absurd. With Jack's telling the whole thing turned into an entertaining little burlesque.

'Well ... it took a moment to recover myself and then I just left the bar.'

'You didn't even say anything?'

'Well yes, I did actually. As I turned to leave I looked him full in the face and told him "That's nought for *your* mask!" '

I burst out laughing and Jack looked highly gratified.

'Rather witty considering the circumstances, don't you think? And then the little bastard went and reported me to that rotten homophobic old fossil Wixley who, as you know, would stoop to any depths to get dirt on me.' For a moment Jack's smile faded. 'They expect me to make some kind of humiliating public apology to the school, Petal. I'm not quite sure I can. He's taken it up with the SRC, you know, and they're all in a tizz because they can't decide whether to take the side of the student or the poofter. Very unPC to come out against the *moffies*. Perhaps I'll just use the opportunity of the public apology to improvise and give them an entirely unexpected little performance of my own before fading graciously from public life and becoming a virtuous, asexual, fibre-eating, vegetarian hermit.'

'Don't be silly, Jack. How could you talk so irresponsibly? How would all the rest of us manage without you?'

He grinned and stroked my cheek. 'Well done, darling. At

least I can rely on you for immoral support. But the thing is, I'm actually getting desperately sick of being everyone's performing poof and living up to the public's expectations. One of these days I'll wake up and find I've turned into a jowly, flabby-arsed old fart and the performing seal routine just won't wash any more anyway. No one wants or even tolerates a fifty-year-old poofter *enfant terrible*.'

He nursed his drink for a while, swirling the whisky around in the tumbler, and took a big glug. Then he looked up at me and sighed.

'You know I think the main problem is that Wixley is just that worst kind of poof; a sad, frustrated old homo who's never been able to climb out of the closet. That's why he's such a dreadful homophobe. It's obvious. Really, I mean when last did you hear of a straight man doing drama?' Examples instantly flooded into my mind, but I decided it was more tactful to treat the question as rhetorical. One of my few running arguments with Jack was over the ludicrously high number of men he claimed were actually gay but in denial. Most often this was the result of wishful thinking on Jack's part and would inspire a great crusading pursuit followed by rejection by the pursued or eventual resignation by Jack. Admittedly, though, he'd 'outed' a good few in his time.

'Yes, I reckon Wixley's just a frustrated old poo-pusher,' Jack said provocatively, looking at me out of the corner of his eye and suppressing a grin.

'A shirt lifter?' I rose to his bait.

'A bum bandit?' he suggested wickedly, egging me on.

'A chutney ferret.'

Things degenerated from there. Our spirits revived by several drinks, and by this particularly tasteless little out-grossing game we sometimes played, the evening was looking up. After a few more minutes of front bottoms, back pussies and chocolate tea towel holders we were in childish hysterics.

Jack and I had become so engrossed in our pre-show drinks, secreted as we were behind the comforting labial folds of red velvet in our favourite 'faggot-friendly' Observatory meeting spot, that we were almost late for the show. We dashed down the dark road past the butchery and leapt into Jack's car. Above us a butcher's sign glowed palely: 'Pigs are not just for Christmas' the sign read, in mockery of the SPCA line, 'you can eat them every day'.

We slipped into the audience at the last moment, unseen. Behind Jack was one of his more timid students, who regarded the empty stage anxiously. 'This isn't interactive theatre is it?' she whispered to Jack, leaning forward slightly in her seat.

'Oooh yesss,' he answered wickedly. 'There's this little pile of costumes you have to pick from if you get chosen.' The girl looked as though she was about to bolt for the door and I smiled and shook my head to reassure her he was teasing. I settled into my seat, waiting anxiously.

A naked white light illuminating the stage signalled the start. From the first moment I wished I had not so diligently made a plan to get there. Kurt had pared the set down to the barest minimum. None of the crows I had so painstakingly glued into being featured on this blank landscape and I couldn't help feeling mildly hurt and angry. There was a strange sound of metal scratching metal over the speakers, then for what felt like hours after the show had apparently started nothing happened. Occasionally a small creak or murmur emerged from the speakers. I was in agony for Kurt. How could the sound system have chosen this of all nights to malfunction? People started shuffling uncomfortably, surreptitiously consulting their programmes. I cast a traumatised look at Jack, but he gave an ironic smile and thrust the programme into my hands. First: *Nach Dem Weltuntergang* (translated for us lowly groundlings as *After the Apocalypse*) – *Unaccompanied Sound Ensemble 10'15"* it read. Kurt was playing a new and alien game. In the three days I had been away he had moved on without me. I looked up, frowning at Jack, but he was grinning broadly, relishing the absurdly pretentious scene, loving every uncomfortable minute of it.

After precisely *10'15"* the speakers stopped hissing and were turned off. So that had been the first act. A clutch of black-polonecked and ethnically garbed students earnestly nodded their approval of this offering. Then onto the bare stage came Kurt, clad in a set of pristine white overalls and spewing forth Nihilist rhetoric. This part I had seen before, had experienced more intimately than I would have chosen to through each phase of its creation. Jack sat back in his chair, grinning with wicked delight, and fanning his face camply with the programme like the maiden aunt in a Restoration play. My attention began to drift. I stared down at Kurt and before I could stop myself my mind had wandered off and I began to fantasise, absently, about peeling off that pristine white overall, stopping his mouth ... Jack turned to look at me, his face alive with mirth, jolting me out of this unfortunate reverie and back into the even more unfortunate present.

The final act was a surprise. Simply entitled *Message, 7'34"*, we had no idea what to expect. More silence. Then Kurt once again strode meaningfully back onto the stage, his bare feet on the muffled boards making the padded sound I recognised so well from endless drama classes, rehearsals, and the few terrifying performances I had been involved in at university. A sound that has such potential. My heart beat faster in anticipation. For an eternity he stood on the stage, unmoving, silent. Out of the corner of my eye I could see Jack trying to suppress a giggle. I caught his eye and he turned his head away fast, his hand over his mouth, his face glowing redder and redder as the laughter threatened to burst out of him. On the stage Kurt carried on, oblivious. He stared fixedly ahead, immobile. Eventually, I noticed, he had started to make a tiny, no doubt deeply significant movement with his left hand once in a while. From somewhere higher in the stands came a sonorous snore. It was too much for Jack, who was now involved in some full-scale soundless laughter in the seat next to me, his body contorted away from me, racked with unstoppable guffaws, convulsive with the effort of silencing himself. I was beside myself with anxiety and gave him a sharp kick. He eased himself off the edge of the stand and, feigning a coughing fit, muttered apologies and headed up the aisle into the foyer.

Still Kurt stared straight ahead – pained, suffering, noble, arrogant and ... sexual? I followed his gaze and my eyes lighted on that most pathetic and dangerous of creatures. Tall, pale, shaven-headed, bonily androgynous and bum-less as a boy, she sat in the audience, smiling her skew, self-assured smile. The Anti-Oxidant. I called her that because she attached herself to any Free Radicals – and often just as readily to those who were not-so-free. She belonged to a group of painfully pious students that ripped their own jeans, pronounced Lenin Leneeen, and generally basked in the self-assured glow of their own political correctness. No trendy leftie or bohemian, male or female, was safe from her wandering sexual attentions. Until recently much of her time had been dedicated to her torrid relationship with a very good-looking leftie journalist whom Jack and I called the Press Stud, but she and the Press Stud had come apart and both were now ominously on the loose. I sat in a daze, feeling nauseous, my eyes gazing on their mutual gaze, oblivious now to the subtle increase of activity on the stage.

My attention clicked back to the Happening itself when Kurt snapped the catches on a pure white box on the stage. From this he produced and switched on a carving knife ... *my mother's* carving knife from our digs kitchen, I noticed, kindly lent to Angus by Claude when she discovered his interest in cooking. Kurt wielded the carving knife dangerously in front of him, brandishing it at the audience and causing justified concern among the people in the front row in particular. After fondling the body of the machine for a while he suddenly turned around and attacked the white canvas flats of the stage, ripping them to shreds and sending splinters of wood and sawdust flying into the luckless nearby audience. Feathers exploded from between layers of canvas and the shrill distress calls of birds screeched

over the speakers. When the hacking came to an end he stood
back to admire his handiwork, breathing heavily as though he
had just run a marathon, conducted a symphony or performed
a particularly strenuous miracle. The word *Übermensch* gaped
gorily from the destroyed flat. I made a mental note to myself to
buy a new carving knife blade before my mother found out.

It was all over. Kurt stalked arrogantly off the stage, ignoring
the applause. Near me some matrons and parents clapped politely, confused but well-meaning and clearly secretly relieved
that the show was over. Later the matrons would crowd around
their wicked industrial strength cappuccinos ('Ooh, I shouldn't,
you know, I'll be up all night') and hope for someone else to be
brave enough to admit that what they had just seen was totally
lost on them, that it was indisputably bullshit. From a dark recess
at the other end of the stand the cluster of black-polonecked
and ethnically garbed disciples clapped ardently, but the object
of their devotion remained resolutely offstage.

I walked 'backstage' behind the decimated flats concocting
a suitably flattering, appreciative and discerning critique of
the night's offerings as I went. With an admirable pretence of
confidence and a deep breath I stepped into the change rooms
to surprise him. There sat the Anti-Oxidant, full of praise and
smug self-satisfaction, smiling grotesquely. To the casual observer
they were 'just talking', but I saw it as it was. The two of them
sat locked in earnest discussion, their bodies radiating lust.
Had I been that quickly usurped? More sickeningly, had I been
humiliatingly betrayed and duped all along? Was I simply the last
person to find out? For a second I wavered, about to back out of
the door, unable to predict whether I could salvage my dignity
in this confrontation. But it was too late. Kurt detached himself
from the woman's mental tentacles and turned to face me.

'Clem!' He seemed genuinely caught off-guard. Suddenly he
was quite ridiculous. To my surprise, I burst out laughing.

'Oops!' I said feeling slightly hysterical. 'Oooh dear!'

'I thought you were still in Grahamstown,' he blurted angrily, as though I had deliberately tricked him into this uncomfortable position.

'Yes, obviously you did. I got back specially to make tonight, but I suppose I shouldn't have bothered.' I stunned myself with my boldness. This out-of-character sneering composure was most exhilarating.

'What do you mean?'

With some effort I managed a kind of feeble sneer. 'Never mind, I'll leave you to your fans. I can see you have your hands full.' Kurt walked up to me and lowered his voice.

'Listen, Clem, don't get hysterical, there's nothing going on between us. We were just talking about my work, which I notice you haven't even bothered to comment on. This petit bourgeois jealousy of yours is very disappointing, it's just herd mentality. I expect you to be above this.'

'You're telling *me* I'm fucking above all this.' I turned on the Anti-Oxidant but found that I was lost for words, so I settled for what I hoped was a look of unmitigated scorn. I stalked out of the room with as much dignity as I could muster.

Jack was waiting in the foyer, smiling and aloof. 'Where's the Thought Führer, Clem?' he asked. 'Is the Great Dictator happy with the groundbreaking art he has made here tonight?' The moment he smiled at me and stretched out his hand I felt the despair setting in and my resolve melted. The kindness was too much. Unable to trust myself to speak at first I shook my head, bit my lip and avoided Jack's eyes. He could see I was dangerously close to humiliating myself, and began to lead me though the foyer, away from the milling crowds who clogged the access to the coffee hatch.

When I felt more composed I told Jack about the Anti-Oxidant, her irresistible lure, but he flapped his hand dismissively.

'Oh puh-lease! She's like puberty, darling. Everyone goes through her at some stage or another, but you can rest assured that nobody *enjoys* it. Also it's so *terribly* embarrassing to think back to it in retrospect.'

I stared down at a rip in the linoleum, trying not to cry.

'Little asshole,' Jack murmured to himself. 'To think he gets away with exhibiting such inexcusable crap. He's our own home-grown Treplev, wailing on about new art forms and producing work which is "Cold, cold, cold! Empty, empty, empty! Dreadful, dreadful, dreadful!"' Jack threw his arms about as he recited, overacting wildly. Then he took a moment to recompose himself and gently put his arm around my back.

'You know this is silly, my sweet girl. You are not trapped in *The Seagull*, you know. You don't *have* to wear black and be in mourning for your life. You really don't have to take this.'

I nodded, not speaking.

'Oh shit,' Jack sighed theatrically giving me a squeeze, 'now we're going to have to go and get drunk *again* tonight. What a sorry pair we are! Let's go and sort our lives out.'

Jack smiled as he passed the comments book, which would be handed to the board of examiners (on which the dreaded Wixley sat) as part of Kurt's submitted 'artwork'. He had kept himself busy while waiting for me in the foyer after his laughing fit. In the comments column, in a carefully forged, neat, old-fashioned hand, were the words 'Not enough pussy'. Jack had paused for a moment to admire his handiwork before he signed the 'name' column: Roger Wixley. He chuckled with glee in anticipation. That was bound to irritate the old homophobe.

We went back to Jack's divinely indulgent apartment. His living room is designed like a Catholic church, complete with confessional – full of excessive colour and texture, secret nooks and chambers, and redolent of sin and decadence. I have always loved it. Jack topped up my whisky, found me two slices of cold cucumber to put over my tired eyes, and began to massage my shoulders expertly.

'Does this help just a little?' he asked me after a few min-utes.

'It's perfect. Where do you learn to do that so perfectly?'

God it was rejuvenating.

'It's all those years of piano playing,' Jack told me, spurred on by the flattery.

'Like hell!' I said, perking up. 'It's all those years of ambi-dextrous wanking.' Jack burst out laughing and hit me on the head with an exquisitely decadent brocade pillow. 'Ooh you are a disgraceful girl! Thank God there's only one of you, I don't think the world would cope with more.' I laughed. Then my mind strayed back to Kurt.

'God he's such a bastard!' I wailed drunkenly.

'*Übermensch* indeed. The only superhuman thing about him is the size of his ego! What a pretentious git! Next thing he'll be bottling his own bowel movements and passing them off as art.' I wrinkled my nose in distaste, imagining the turds coiled into Consol jars like foetuses in a lab. 'It's all been done before, darling. Dreadfully *passé*. He should be locked in the closet with Wixley and relentlessly tortured and forced to watch epic Russian movies set in Siberia where nothing happens except people philosophising and dying in snowstorms until he *begs* for reruns of *Friends* or *Thirty-Something*. You're the *Übermensch* for putting up with all his shit for so long.'

'You know who I am? I'm the fucking *Überwench*!'

We drank to that, and to a lot more after that. Eventually I fell asleep on Jack's sofa and he woke me and took me home.

It was illogical but the last thing I thought about that night as I lay in bed drunkenly replaying the evening's events, seeing visions of Kurt and That Woman, was that I regretted not having worn higher heels that evening. As I drifted off to sleep I dreamt of starting my own clothing range, workerist and hardcore, rugged and sexy like a cross between a pilot's uniform and a super-heroine get-up, all emblazoned in bold with the brand name: **ÜBERWENCH**. I dreamt I met Kurt in a warehouse surrounded by a posse of my favourite *Überwenches*. He was holding a carving knife without a blade and looked confused. 'What happened?' was all he said.

I think I laughed in my sleep.

The next morning I woke up with a hangover from hell to the gentle urban rustling sound of *bergies* digging in the garbage outside my window. When I opened my eyes, Angus was standing next to the bed with a huge grin and a glass of hissing, effervescent vitamin potion.

'I hear you had a hell of an evening last night ... told that fuckwit ex-boyfriend of yours where to get off.' The night before flooded back into my addled brain in inglorious Technicolor. I groaned and tried to sit up. The light streamed in through the window, obscenely bright, and hit me full in the face. I fell back, writhing, and pulled the duvet over my head to shield me.

'Oh dear,' said Angus. 'Jack phoned for you just now. Will you give him a ring when you're capable?'

I didn't get up until Kurt phoned much later that day and told me to meet him at the Curry Den. He arrived before me and was waiting outside, scrutinising some unfortunate busking juggler with undisguised scorn. He had once said that this particular form of begging was an insult to begging and to art simultaneously. The truth is, Kurt never could juggle.

I am sorry to confess that my heart had lifted momentarily when he phoned, anticipating an apology, some reassuring words. Instead, I sat pinned back in the tatty banquette at the restaurant as the invective poured forth with a vengeance. He gave some Nietzschean justification for deception but maintained (confusingly) that he and the Anti-Oxidant 'didn't do anything anyway'. He told me I was 'just being so petty bourgeois about everything'. Then he said he couldn't stay long, he was meeting someone who would help with the photography of his Happening, help get it into the press. The Press. Immediately I realised what he was saying. A lump of dread formed in my stomach and I couldn't eat. Still, I had to confirm my fears. 'Who are you meeting?'

'Does it matter?'

'No, I'm just curious.'

'Well, I'm meeting …' And he said her name. Great. Just as I thought. The Anti-Oxidant.

'Oh,' I said.

'Oh come on, Clem. That's why I didn't want to tell you. I knew you'd react badly.'

'Oh well, don't let me break your stride, you just go right ahead and fuck her. Somebody's got to do it.' I was sick of pretending to be sophisticated, of pretending not to hurt. And most of all I was sick of pretending that I didn't know what was going on.

'You see this is exactly the problem. You can be so unreasonable sometimes.'

'This is *reasonable*, Kurt!' I shouted, trying not to be shrill. Several of the patrons turned to look. I caught their eyes and looked away, staring at the table, then at Kurt.

'I don't know what you hope for, but I can't offer it,' I said sadly.

He hardly protested.

I walked home in a fog of confusion and misery, cradling a doggy bag of curry I'd left virtually untouched. In my distress, I opened the door of the basin cupboard in front of the toilet (*Place Nose Here For Best Sleeping Position* someone had scrawled drunkenly on the door) and with meticulous neatness I stowed the doggy bag for later. Then I shut myself into my bedroom to think homicidal thoughts in peace.

Angus found the doggy bag later while looking for a bog roll.

'Good God,' he said, emerging from the bathroom with the polystyrene box full of curry, 'look what I found!' He brandished the curry at me in astonishment. I was as surprised as he was – I'd been in such a dejected daze that I'd completely forgotten putting it there. Then he realised.

'Clem, did you put this here?' he asked, looking at me quizzically.

'I'm afraid I did.' I let out a sad little laugh.

I was definitely going off the rails. It was time for a breather. I knew that Kurt was a Bastard of Note, but much of my confidence stemmed from having won his approval in the first place, and it was hard to relinquish that. Kurt was a hard habit to break, and I knew that I wouldn't be able to get a realistic perspective on the situation unless I took myself far away from it all. Things had got so bad that I felt ready to throw my usual tedious caution to the wind and to do something rash. When Angus left the room I pulled an old atlas out of the bookshelf. I opened it to a map of the world, shut my eyes, twirled my finger around in the air, and stabbed it down onto the page. It landed somewhere in the middle of the Atlantic, but with a little subtle manipulation I moved it to rest on France. France! I clapped my hands in delight, convinced that my destiny had been revealed. I would polish up my high school French and live a different life for a while. 'It was written!' I shouted exuberantly, and flopped back onto the bed in bleary, hung-over bliss to dream up a flight plan.

II

Flight of the Überwench

Flight of the Überwench

To do:
- *Buy new blade for carving knife (Swift model SI-5) – useful even if Claude doesn't ask for it back as can use for sawing off Anti-Oxidant's giraffe neck.*
- *Air ticket, Paris Guide bk, Marvelon, undies*

The next day I went to the travel agent. Then I went to the chemist to get some ID photos taken. I made the patient and understanding pharmacist do four sets, each worse than the previous one, holding out hope for a set that suddenly, miraculously, revealed me for the international jet-set sophisticate that I actually was underneath this unfortunate drab outer layer. Eventually the pharmacist (and even some of her inquisitive elderly customers) started giving me tips on what I should do with my hair – 'put it like this' one said, draping it over my shoulders, and 'what about an upstyle?' I realised I might soon outstay my welcome, professed myself delighted with the fourth set, and left the shop.

Then I set off to make the announcement. 'I've booked my ticket,' I practised saying out loud as I walked. I was ecstatic. I was terrified.

First I told Angus, who I found at the kitchen table, clipping flowery obituaries for his collection. I said I was pissed off with Kurt and had finally decided to give it a break for a while.

'Well *finally* she's seen the light,' he exclaimed in a television evangelist voice, throwing up his arms in a dangerous gesture of triumph since he was still holding the scissors.

Then I told him I was going to France, and he looked perplexed.

'Why run away?' he asked me eventually. 'Why leave this country, especially now? That's not the problem. Why don't you just leave *him* and enjoy all the stuff you've been missing out on for the last God knows how long since you've been with that asshole?' I was taken aback by his disapproval.

'I'm not *leaving*, Angus, I'll be back. I'm just going to get away from things for a while.'

Angus looked away from me. 'Fuckit,' he said to himself. 'Suit yourself. Pack for Perth like all the other scared whiteys.' He reached for the newspaper and cut me out.

'This has nothing to do with being white. Isn't anyone allowed to have a personal life in this country?'

He ignored me. I didn't need this. After all his whining about getting rid of Kurt I'd hoped for a little more confirmation from him. If he couldn't be happy for me it was all the more reason for me to go. Irritation increased my sense of certainty and I set off to tell Kurt while I was still feeling fired up.

Kurt reacted dismissively, coolly. 'What ticket?' he asked, apparently unconcerned.

'I'm leaving for France in three weeks' time.' A nonchalance I had never known wrapped itself reassuringly around me. He struggled to conceal his surprise, reluctant to concede me any victories.

'Just like that? What about me? I suppose you didn't even think about that? If this is about … (the unmentionable Anti-Oxidant) you're being really silly. I told you, there is nothing between us. It's an intellectual connection.' I could feel his sly manipulations start their offensive but I held him at bay.

'This is not about you, Kurt, it's about me. You'll be fine without me, and it won't be for long. I just need a break.'

Only Jack congratulated me on the idea. Perhaps because he felt the most stuck and envious himself. 'Darling girl!' he said, smothering me in a fragrant hug. 'You'll be such a hit!' He smoothed back my hair and grinned at me. 'I have some appropriately decadent and fascinating friends in Paris. I'll put you in touch – they're just what you need. But just remember that I'm only letting you go if I can design your whole look, veto the wardrobe you take, and get exclusive first rights to any seedy and outrageous news about your gorgeous self. And of course you have to bring me more Gucci from duty free.'

'Promise!' I said lightly, knowing full well that the wardrobe project would forever remain a fantasy we shared. 'And you have to keep me up to date with news of your battle with the Closet Chutney Ferret. Jack, you don't mind me going when you're in the shtuck, do you? I mean I don't want to desert you.'

'Listen, Petal, you're long overdue for a break. I'd go too, if I could, I assure you. And they *do* have phones in France, you know. And a postal system.'

But to my shame other things were weighing on my mind.

'Jack, what about Kurt?' I asked, suddenly serious.

Jack raised an eyebrow and looked me in the eye. He sighed. 'This could only be about sex. God knows I've done some foolish things in my time to gain access to a good firm pair of buttocks, and I must assume his physique fulfils your requirements. But, sweetie, it's time to think of yourself for a while.'

I lapsed into reverie. What was it about Kurt that had drawn me to him? His hands, his mind, the sense that he was out of the ordinary, that he brought a bit of elsewhere with him. And, of course, the fact that he'd chosen me, something I still found hard to believe. I was in awe of him, convinced people all around us wondered why someone so beautiful and talented had ended up with gawky, frizzy-haired me. With every artistic coup he managed, in the face of the admiring crowds, I'd decided I must just have been lucky. So if I was so lucky, why was I so unhappy? Surely there was an adequate alternative somewhere out there, for whom you did not have to donate a pound of flesh? For whom you did not have to feign an interest in turgid German philosophy just to get through the day? For whom you did not have to suppress the occasional urge to binge on afternoon soaps or risk becoming an outcast? For whom you did not have to conceal that you actually *laughed* at Mel Brooks films? For whom you did not have to start an all-out battle with some freak-of-nature giraffe-bodied woman to keep your turf? But it was no good. I knew that if I stuck around I'd stay stuck with him. Jack interrupted my pondering.

'If he's still what you want in a few months' time and it was meant to be, he'll be around for you.'

'You're right. Maybe he can even visit me in Paris,' I added cheerfully, as if all my worldly problems had just been solved.

Jack's face dropped fractionally. 'Maybe he could, darling girl, maybe he could.'

I was on a mission. Now I phoned Claude. She barraged me with questions: 'Why Paris? What are you going to do there, just fritter away your time? How are you going to support yourself? Have you even thought about that?' But at least she listened to my answers. I told her about Jack's friends in Paris who would help me out, and she seemed quite impressed by my initiative. She even offered me a loan to tide me over, reminded me about the emergency credit card I had which was linked to her account, and didn't lecture me at all about choosing Europe, though I was sure she wouldn't have approved. I accepted the loan gratefully: between that and the meagre amount I'd managed to save in my props job I might manage to stave off starvation in Paris until I found a job.

It was gracious of Claude not to criticise my wanting to go to Paris, I knew that. Claude and my father had 'given Europe a try' when I was just two years old, and she'd hated it. It was the seventies, and things were getting really bad in the Eastern Cape. Activists went missing, academics were interrogated, and there were rumours of torture and death at the hands of the Special Branch. Then, the year after I was born, the Soweto riots happened and Jimmy persuaded Claude to leave South Africa with him. We lasted a year in England and were back, on Claude's insistence, when I was just four. Claude came home to the absorbing camaraderie of the Black Sash and spent more and more time dishing out soup and advice in the townships and less and less time at home. She felt needed. She had discovered her niche and was making up for lost time. But it had been hard to fit a hard-drinking free-spirited, hedonistic Irish husband

and a needy little girl into her new scheme of things. Claude grew more serious and Jimmy grew more drunk and a few years later Jimmy was dead and Claude was left with me. And now I was making my own journey to the worn-out old world she'd found so unbearable, just when the country had gone through its miraculous transition. My timing was all wrong. But there was something else bothering me.

'Claude, what about Mac?'

'What about her?'

'I mean ... well what if she ... dies when I'm away.'

'Clem, don't create obstacles for yourself ... and for that matter, don't create false nostalgia for a relationship with your grandmother that you never had.' I think Claude must have realised that this was unnecessarily wounding. 'Listen, your staying put is not going to serve any purpose and Mac could stick around for *years*. Anyway, you're far away in Cape Town, you'd hardly see her as it is.'

Then for a moment she sounded vulnerable, almost shy. 'You could come home, you know. Here. For a while. If you like. I hope you know that.'

I felt so touched by her awkward offer that I almost agreed to, but I knew it was a disastrous idea.

'I can't,' I said sadly, staring at my hands.

'I know. You're right. So go to Paris. Perhaps it'll do you good.'

And with Claude's sanction I was on my way.

Before I left we had a farewell dinner at the Soup Kitchen. It was quite convivial and even Kurt was behaving, but Angus was in a foul mood. He threw a curry together with none of his usual flair and good grace, complaining endlessly about having to find a housemate at such short notice, even though I had a list of at least ten people who wanted to apply and I had paid until the end of the next month. Couldn't he wait until tomorrow after I'd left to be in a bad mood and just grant me one final wonderful night?

As if Angus's mood wasn't bad enough to start off with, Tamara (his fling-of-the-year) was suffering from lack of attention and had decided to be her boring, ardent-vegetarian worst. They had an argument over the jelly in the trifle, which I started seeing as part of a play. The script went something like this:

T: 'Does this have gelatine in it?'

A: 'I presume so, or it wouldn't set.'

T: 'Do you know what gelatine is made from? It's made from hoof and horn, boiled up animal parts.'

A: 'Mmm. Delicious.'

T: 'Glue. That's what it really is.'

A: 'Do you want any dessert, Tamara, or are you just trying to spoil it for the rest of us?'

T: 'I just think you should know what you're eating.'

A: 'I know exactly what I'm eating. It's trifle. Very good trifle. Tell me, Tam, have you ever been to a tannery?'

T: (perplexed) 'No.'

A: 'Don't. Or with that attitude you'll end up walking around with plastic bags tied around your feet instead of shoes. Hell in the rain.' He took another big mouthful of quivering jelly. Tamara eyed it in silence, clearly dying for a bite. Then ...

T: 'Is it made with animal gelatine or agar-agar?'

A: 'I don't fucking know, okay? I bought it at Woolworths.'

The rest of us had started shifting uncomfortably in our seats by now. Angus was being uncharacteristically harsh. I frowned at him questioningly, but he looked pained and averted his eyes when they met mine. Tamara's hurt little voice ruptured the silence.

T: 'Where's the packet?' she asked, getting up from her seat.

A: 'I chucked it, for God's sake.' Angus saw how hurt she looked and felt a pang of guilt. It wasn't her fault. 'Oh leave it, Tam,' he said more gently. Please don't go digging in the rubbish bin in the middle of dinner. Just eat it or don't.' She sat down, wounded and sulking, and watched everyone eat.

After dinner, I walked Kurt to the gate. We stood outside, not knowing what to say. He spoke first.

'I suppose you won't spend the night at my place?' he asked me.

'I don't think that's a good idea,' I said, struggling not to give in. A bout of bonking would be unlikely to strengthen my resolve. He opened his mouth to say something, then shook his head.

'What?' I asked. He looked at me, unsure of what he was about to ask.

'Clem, it was okay, wasn't it?'

What did he mean? The sex? The relationship in general? I waited for a clue.

'I didn't make a fool of myself on that stage, did I?'

Ah. The Happening. I was astonished, and touched, by the question.

'No, no. Not at all. Of course you didn't.'

'You'd tell me, wouldn't you? Because I did something different, which was a risk, and it's not always easy to tell if something's really worked. It was supposed to be about the breakdown of communication and the isolation of the individual ... Did that come through?'

It was as though he were handing me his balls on a plate. And what could I do but reassure him? The next day I'd be thousands of miles away anyway.

'It was great, and you'll do brilliantly,' I told him. He always did.

He graced me with a boyish smile, took my hands and kissed me good night gently and (I thought) regretfully. I didn't feel victorious any more, I felt like I was deserting him. He seemed so vulnerable as he loped off down the street without his usual arrogant verve, and I stood waving next to the gate with a pain in the place where my heart should be.

In the middle of the night, when I couldn't sleep, I slunk down to the kitchen with my book. Angus was at the table polishing off

Tamara's untouched trifle. He laughed silently. Here we were again, wide awake in the middle of the night and whispering like thieves so as not to wake our assorted 'guests'. It was my last night in this house, possibly forever.

'You were quite hard on Tamara earlier,' I ventured.

'I know.' Angus refused to meet my eyes.

'Why?'

'She was just fucking irritating. Don't really want to talk about it. Anyway it's your last night here. *Vot's* on your mind?' he asked, breaking into a bad German accent and a Freudian interrogation style.

'I can't help feeling terrible about Kurt. Like I'm deserting him.'

Angus looked livid with frustration for a second, then just sighed deeply and looked in the other direction. 'What are you doing with a jerk like him? I just can't understand it.'

'You call your relationship with Tamara a model union?' I burst out indignantly.

'Come on. That's different. That's not serious.'

'And mine is?'

'Well ... taking a couple of years of ceaseless shit from that pretentious phony fuckwit must mean you're either serious or a total fucking masochist.'

'Well thanks for your support,' I said ironically.

'*Ja* well, it's probably a good thing you're going,' he said.

'It certainly seems so,' I said. His words really stung, and I busied myself gathering up my blanket and book and heading back to bed so that he wouldn't see my face. He didn't look up.

'Sorry, Clem, it has nothing to do with you. I'm just irritated with Tamara,' he said, not sounding sorry at all.

'It's fine,' I lied.

I sat miserably on my bed, staring at the room which had been stripped of all my things, turning Angus's words over in my mind. Angus was not alone in his criticism of Kurt, though it had taken me a long time to realise this. I'd started out so infatuated with Kurt myself, and so grateful for the privilege of being his lover that I was convinced I had no right to complain about anything, and since his disciples were so much in evidence I presumed everyone felt the same way as I did. When Jack had pointed out gently one day that some people found him just the teensiest bit pretentious and maybe a little chilly, I defended Kurt fiercely and with genuine conviction. They didn't know the secret Kurt that I'd been allowed to see; the Kurt who created an intricate parallel world in his journal. He seemed to dwell mostly in this other world himself, and I was graced with invitations to join him there. His was one of the most fascinating minds I'd ever encountered, and he shared his ideas with me unselfishly. He was *not* chilly. On the contrary, he was passionate about the wildly obscure art and ideas he exposed me to. Between that and the expert sex he provided I'd felt permanently thrilled. He had in fact perfected his sexual technique to such an extent that he could ponder (out loud) the contradictions of Brecht's Verfremdungs-Technik while pleasuring us both with admirable precision. I've never been able to talk about *The Caucasian Chalk Circle* since without blushing furiously.

Jack had listened to my impassioned defence patiently, trying not to interrupt.

'Hmmm. Nevertheless, darling,' he had said when my eulogy came to an end, 'I just thought you ought to know that his detractors call him The Horror. From Kurtz in *Heart of Darkness*, of course. Not saying I agree ... necessarily. I'd just hate you to be the last to hear.'

But I'd been in denial. It had taken almost a year for my ferocious infatuation to decline, for the first cautious tendrils of doubt and later scorn to creep into my mind and now, all at once, I was desperate to get away from everything, even from grouchy Angus, so that I could think in peace.

The next day I went to say a final goodbye to Kurt before I left. He seemed so much sadder and softer. He gave me his ubiquitous black Beatnik beret 'for France'. It was one of the most intimate gestures he had ever made, and I had to battle the urge to cling to him and promise never to leave. I blinked back the tears on the walk home, hoping to have a happier conversation with Angus before I left, but he was on his way to placate Boring Tamara, so we hugged each other warmly and both apologised for our parting feeling disappointingly rushed.

Thank God for Jack. He took me to the airport and we sat in his car discussing final details and trying to say goodbye. He'd already organised for me to look after the flat of a friend of Serge's, Jack's old friend (and one-time-lover), 'a set painter who wears white shoes with conviction and is not to be trusted for a minute. I mean it, darling, he's a sexual omnivore and he'll eat you up before you even know what's hit you. He'll try anything: man, woman, child or beast of the field.' Jack noticed my look of alarm. 'Oh look. Now I've upset you. Actually, darling, that's quite defamatory and unfair of me. Serge wouldn't lay a *finger* on a child. Now send him my warmest regards, keep your back to the wall at all times and never ever bend over when you're in his company – he has an insatiable predilection for buggery.' Jack kissed me avuncularly on the forehead. With this curious cautionary benediction he sent me off into the great wide world.

Crossing over

Michelle, the young woman next to me on the plane, was South African, returning to her French boyfriend in Paris. I listened to her chat comfortably about her life there, confident in her familiarity. Then she asked me about my plans. I must have sounded less brave than I'd intended to when I told her I was leaving my friends and boyfriend in Cape Town for an uncertain future in a city I'd never seen, because she frowned curiously at me.

'Why are you going then, if it upsets you so much?' she asked. The more I tried to explain the more I wondered to myself how long I'd manage to stick it out in Paris before I could reasonably come home. I hadn't even got there and some lurking, inarticulate fear had taken hold of me. I had made a terrible mistake. Why was I doing this? Heading out into nowhere all alone with no promise of a welcome, stubbornly avoiding the familiarity I might find with friends or family in England, or even Ireland? I'd tried so determinedly to avoid the classic 'Young South African In London' scenario that I had given up every comfort that went with it. I ate my aeroplane food dutifully, peeling back the packaging of each silvery box. Each mouthful tasted saltily of swallowed, unshed tears. I ordered another whisky. Ten minutes into the late-night movie I fell asleep, my head still attached to the armrest by my headphones.

When I woke up we were fifteen minutes from Charles de Gaulle. I tried to look out of the window but all I could see was my own sad reflection staring back. My hair was in a bad mood all of its own and stood out electrically from my head in a dry static fuzz. My skin managed to look simultaneously dry and shiny, and my ears felt punctured from having spent half the night hooked into the sharp plastic headset. Brushing my teeth was out of the question since the toilet queues snaked unsteadily down both aisles, occasionally tossed around by the turbulence so that less stable queuers lurched into the laps of slack-mouthed tenacious sleepers.

Michelle woke up, stretched in her seat, smoothed her straight hair with her hands, looked out of the window and regarded what was to her an increasingly familiar landscape below with casual contentment.

Sentimental education

Vocab: épicerie = *grocery shop;* un carnet = *bunch of métro tickets*
To do: Fax Angus and beg to return library books

'This way,' said Michelle. I followed her gratefully past a Babel of French direction signs, onto a seemingly endless succession of escalators and through various passages and queues, until we were finally disgorged from the airport with our luggage. It was a shock to arrive from winter into the sticky heat of French midsummer. The tarmac shifted queasily in the heat. Before long we were moving again, herded onto buses and métros on which we stood swaying in sweating silence, like refugees or lambs to the slaughter, in our wintry South African clothes. Initially the view from the bus was unspectacular – not at all what I'd expected from Paris. But slowly, as we drew nearer, the Paris I knew from photographs and movies was revealed, and as we emerged, mole-like, from the final métro we stepped thrillingly into the real thing.

Michelle and her boyfriend lived in rue Popincourt in the eleventh *arrondissement*. Reality was doing a creditable imitation of all the movies about Paris I'd seen, with its appropriately picturesque *places* and its little enamel blue street signs and its well-cast locals smoking and drinking in the cafés or sweeping debris into the gutters. I longed to shed my rucksack and some of my ill-chosen clothing.

'Here we are,' said Michelle, when we arrived outside the apartment in rue Popincourt.

I looked up at Michelle's window sill at the boxes of vivid pink and red geraniums, sturdy South African exports to the rest of the world, and realised how completely unprepared I was for this change.

Michelle led me up interminable wooden stairs and fed me tea in her apartment. I was pathetically grateful. She gave me a brief lesson in how to use the métro, pointed out a few places on the map, and showed me where we were and where I was headed. We were not far from my address in the fourth, since these *arrondissements* had apparently been allocated numbers in a sort of spiral snail shell formation. I knew I should feel excited, but I couldn't suppress the panic. I had never experienced such complete sensual bombardment and dislocation. My only claim to belonging here was a scrap of paper, clutched hotly in my hand inside my pocket, on which Jack had written a name and a phone number and an alien-looking address for Serge's friend's flat. Michelle dialled the number on my tatty little piece of paper and spoke in confident, convivial French to the stranger on the other end. Then she handed me the phone. I felt a rush of anxiety and stuttered forth into faltering, absurdly scholarly French. The person on the other end laughed, but not unkindly, and told me the code for the apartment door and where to find the key. I finished the tea and wrenched myself reluctantly from the comfort and security of Michelle's flat. Grasping the Galéries Lafayette map on which she'd circled the address, I headed alone into the sweaty streets laden like a packhorse.

As I got closer to the circle on the map my stomach began to flutter with excitement. I started to stride, despite the backpack, and I even greeted a shopkeeper who was arranging his fruit and vegetable display outside his *épicerie* and bought a bottle of his wine. Then I realised I had taken a few too many strides in that direction and had to retrace my steps, smiling sheepishly at the shopkeeper as we greeted each other again. When I still couldn't find my way I consulted an old lady whose small poodle-ish dog was depositing copious gouts of crap on the pavement while the owner feigned ignorance. It turned out we were standing right outside the building I was asking for, and she looked at me as though she couldn't work out whether I was mad or simply out to irritate her. I was too excited to care. I punched in the code I'd been given for the huge outside door and leaned with all my weight against it. It swung open and I half fell into an old stone courtyard. Bliss! I had the key to the kingdom! I belonged! I wanted to lie down on the comforting bulk of my rucksack and squeal with pleasure, but I recovered myself and located the postboxes instead. Inside box number three was a key, as promised. After wandering about in some confusion trying to work out which of the doors led to the correct stairwell, I managed to haul myself up another seemingly eternal set of wooden stairs and slid the key into the door of apartment number three. The door swung open and I stepped inside and shrugged off my massive rucksack. The room was large, with wooden floors and big wooden windows looking out onto the courtyard. I was elated. How miraculous that I should head off from Cape Town with nothing but some scrawled names and numbers and end up in a real old apartment in a real street in real Paris. Just then, it was the most beautiful place I'd ever seen. Shafts of afternoon sunlight streamed in through the tall windows, and a woman was calling in (real) French from a downstairs window to her son who was riding his tricycle in the stone courtyard below. It was warm and light and *mine*, for a while at least. And it felt safe, a refuge I could come back to if things outside became too unfamiliar.

Later, after I'd pottered around the flat for a while turning taps on and off and investigating the contents of the kitchen and bathroom cupboards, I sat next to the window reading in the last of the evening light, suffused with a sense of relief and well-being. I leaned out of the window and looked down onto a stone courtyard. I could smell the wet mint bushes under the guttering. A small yellow canary was singing tunefully from a cage just across the courtyard on the same level as me, and somewhere a child was blowing furiously on a kazoo. I was enjoying my second glass of wine, which was fine, if a little sweet, and it occurred to me that I might be okay here after all.

Yes, the wine was fine. I poured another glass. Tomorrow I would phone and meet Serge the set-painter, he of the rectal obsession. I would fit seamlessly into the Paris social scene, assimilated into the trendiest sets, hitherto unknown to any outsider, with unprecedented rapidity. I would become wise and knowing and able to drink an entire Bloody Mary on my own without vomiting ... and my hair would become miraculously straight and silky-smooth.

Awakening

To do: buy drinkable water, proper map book of Paris, top French fashion magazine (resolve 'wrong clothes' crisis immediately), miracle hair product

Thought for the day: (though sadly gleaned from guidebook – not very illustrious source)
Every man has two native countries, his own and France.
– Thomas Jefferson

The next morning I woke up with a mouth like a dank cave full of bat shit since I'd been too lazy to brush my teeth the night before. I tried to drink some tap water but it tasted vile. Then I remembered: I was in Paris! I tried to leap out of bed and throw open windows like Helena Bonham Carter in *A Room with A View*, but my head felt a bit tired (not surprising after the long flight) and it was unnecessarily bright outside. I thought I'd just try to recover for a while before making the call to Serge. Instead I lay in bed eating cheese, planning my Day-One-In-Paris outfit and practising my French telephone conversation. Adjusting.

After trying on several outfits, none of which seemed remotely satisfactory, I eventually settled on my customary summer ensemble – a floor-length Indian wrap skirt, a cotton embroidered shirt, clog-like slip-on shoes – and headed out to find a phone booth. The bastard things only took cards, but I reassured myself it was all part of the adventure and headed off to the nearest shop with a nonchalant capable-single-woman-abroad strut.

As I walked, I made mental notes of appropriate clothing items for Paris, and a critique of my own:

- Clodhoppers must go. I've always liked big reassuring shoes with a sense of humour, but in Paris in summer the joke falls flat – problem is women here wear funny little pump things I've always hated.
- Skirt must not trail on ground in manner of Victorian costume drama.
- Dresses must be very small and girly (yeah, right – probably not a realistic option for me since I feel naked unless I'm covered at least to below the knees and elbows).
- Hair must be pinned up elegantly in French roll type thing or fall in sleek curtain-like bob over face when nodding/looking coy – like little girl (long-forgotten fantasy).

The list was endless, the gap between what I was wearing and what I saw on the average *Parisienne* unbreachable. It was going to be hard work. Jack had tried on many occasions to persuade me into clothes he thought would suit my pale, awkward body. 'Pale is *interesting*, darling,' he insisted, 'and you just have to get used to wearing a little *less*. Only fat people should wear this much clothing.' But to me it would have been like going to lectures in a bikini: exposure was just not my style.

None of the shops in the area seemed to sell phone cards, so I bought an apple and some postcards instead and headed towards the river, eating the apple as I walked. *'Bon appetit'* a construction worker called to me, and his cheerful nosiness made me feel oddly elated. I loved this place. It was seedy, noisy, theatrical, and alive with little scandals. I walked on past the cathedral, and as I came up the Boulevard Saint Michel, I got the distinct feeling that something extraordinary was about to happen. The boulevard was packed with people in carnival mode. Around the fountain the homeless camped with their big dogs on bits of string, comfortably spread out in the sunshine. At a safe distance from that informal settlement, crowds of onlookers lined the roads in anticipation. I put my street map away and stood there for a while, waiting for something to happen.

I was about to ask the old lady next to me what we were waiting for when a ripple of laughter and excitement spread down to us from further up the road. For a moment the crowd grew silent, then began to cheer. I craned my neck forward to see. A flock of waiters in penguin suits came speeding towards us, bearing trays full of glasses and wine bottles. A race! The crowds whistled and cheered and one or two of the competitors laughed and lost the contents of a glass or paused momentarily to steady a wine bottle. In seconds they had passed and it was over, as if it had never happened – a surreal little Sunday afternoon interlude. The crowd dispersed noisily, exchanging comments on the spectacle.

I didn't meet Serge that day. By the time I had finally found a phone card (how in Christ's name was I supposed to know they keep them at tobacconists?) and squeezed myself into a phone booth, all glass and like a conservatory in the heat, I got Serge's answering machine and chickened out. When I ventured out to the phone that evening to try one last time there was a crazed-looking woman pacing in a perilously haphazard orbit around the phone booth. I stood a few metres away, waiting for her to leave, but she continued her speedy pacing and began to shout at the phone booth, wagging her finger at it, screaming and lecturing at the top of her voice. I came a little closer, hoping she'd snap out of it and leave. She noticed me out of the corner of her eye and shut up for a moment, examining me with a bulging eyes and a livid expression like a fairytale witch. Then she climbed into the phone booth, took out a little foil package, and became absorbed in her own little drug-preparation ritual. This was not good. Having had no experience of waiting outside phone booths while people indulged in serious narcotics it was hard to judge just how long it would take. A clock in the *place* told me it was almost nine at night and I decided to call it a day. Despite the lateness, the sun was still bright and people were strolling around in the streets, sitting on the pavements on assorted garden chairs drinking sundowners and contemplating dinner. I walked past a whole lot of these makeshift cafés and eventually summoned up the courage to sit down and order *une bière,* since it seemed the easiest thing to ask for in French. I suspected I'd be drinking a lot of them. Perhaps if I drank enough Kronenbourg I'd drown my sorrows and social inadequacies and go back home all carbo-loaded and voluptuous like some Bavarian barmaid. I hid my face behind my book, age-old tactic of single-woman travellers, and spied on all the people around me. Tomorrow I'd meet Serge, and before long I'd be painting sets and making props for the opera. Thank you Dad for the Irish passport!

But when I woke up the next day I couldn't breathe through my nose. Then I realised that one side of my hair was stuck to my face with sweat and I couldn't swallow either. I dressed myself (in a highly regrettable emergency outfit) and headed out on trembling legs in search of drugs. Being in a cold sweat in the heat is an unpleasant experience, so when I got back from the chemist and discovered what he'd put in the bag I was too exhausted to go back and change it. Instead, I bit the bullet (so to speak) and curled up with my journal:

Why am I the only person on the planet to have a streaming cold in midsummer? I am swaddled in most of my winter wardrobe from home while every other woman in this town walks around like sex on a stick, carefree and clad in dresses as small as handkerchiefs. Dismal. I managed to get to a chemist this morning, half-drowning in my mucus on the way (and blowing off most of my nose skin on the abrasive French bog roll I'd stuffed in my pocket). The bastard pharmacist sold me suppositories. Suppositories! Only in France would they give me something to stick up my arse when I have a runny nose – it's just not logical. Of course I only opened the packet when I got home and narrowly avoided trying to swallow this enormous waxy thing before I read the instructions. Then it was a matter of decoding the French pharmacy jargon – 'How to use an anal suppository' is not something they really get around to in school French. After several agonising minutes (I feared one false move might put me in a particularly compromising position) I managed to work out why I was having such trouble. Why they can't just write it in plain French, something like 'Stick it up your bum but don't forget to take the plastic cover off first'. God, I'm in a bad mood. I think I'll just have a little sleep and then go and contact Serge.

I woke up from a brief sleep, freezing cold but sweating profusely and throwing my head from side to side like they do in nightmare scenes in movies about Vietnam vets, and realised there was *no one to call.* I suddenly understood what it was to be alone and sick and spared a thought for all those grannies who die in their flats and are only found weeks later because they haven't paid their bills ... Then I put on every item of clothing I could reach while still sitting under the covers in the bed and went over the road to the café to buy something hot to drink and to try and phone Serge.

The café was crowded with people freshly released from their offices. I waited at the bar for my coffee, feeling a bit dizzy and very hot. Then I took one sip and somehow fell onto the floor in the middle of the cigarette butts that the French seem happy just to throw at their feet. 'Why don't they use ashtrays here anyway?' I pondered as I hit the ground.

When I came to, the elderly woman who ran the bar was holding my head up and smacking my cheeks gently, coaxing water into my mouth. A bar-full of people was leaning over me, concerned and curious. A fabulous intro into the neighbourhood! The woman shouted to the aproned young man who assisted her behind the bar and insisted that he take me home, despite my protestations. I mumbled directions and tried not to lean on him too much. Being me, I even managed to feel guilty that I hadn't paid for the coffee.

I slept fitfully for a while. Then at about ten o'clock there was a knock on the door.

'It's Jean, from the bar.' In my semi-delirium I was convinced he'd come to fetch the money I owed, but he only wanted to check that I was okay. 'Madame Rouillard' had sent him. So the gruff café owner had a heart (and a name) after all.

I finished a letter to Jack, giving him a detailed account of the ignominious incident at the café because I knew it would tickle him, and asked him to send me particulars about his 'Trial by Chutney Ferret'. At least I was starting to feel a bit better now. Maybe those bottom-plugs from the pharmacy were a good idea after all. Soon I'd go out and conquer the city, but in the meantime I'd see if I could make it to the post office without any more debacles. I sent Jack my love and a sprig of mint precariously picked from the gutter and fell asleep.

The next few days I spent in bed or at least in the apartment, still dressed in most of my wardrobe, going out only to buy the most basic supplies and thinking about how much more fun it was being sick in the Soup Kitchen where I had Angus to nurse and entertain me. After the fiasco at the café I was reluctant to go back. I dropped some flowers with Madame Rouillard to thank her but declined her invitation to stay. I made coffee at home and turned into a hermit, reading the Paris guidebook from cover to cover and glutting on novels. I vowed to contact Serge as soon as my nose skin had grown back.

Discoveries

* *Must eat real food – vegetables etc*
* *Intensify search for miracle anti-frizz hair product*

Thought for the day: [Only the French] can combine grossness and grace.
– Aldous Huxley

Over the next few days, while I waited for my cold to go, I took to making brief forays into the Parisian wilderness to acquaint myself, to acclimatise. I got to know the neighbourhood – at first, in the safety of the apartment, through the guidebook, and gradually, tentatively, in reality. And I revelled in it. Without Kurt or anyone else around to see me I could walk in the wrong direction and get completely lost, or spend twenty minutes staring into a shop window if I wanted to. I got used to looking in the wrong direction before I crossed the road and I almost got used to being surrounded by tall, grey and beige old buildings above which I could only see a narrow strip of jet-stream-striped sky. I developed my own habits and indulgences. When I discovered that the grand Hôtel de Ville was not, in fact, an extremely upmarket hotel but some kind of glorious city hall, I took it as a challenge to coax a smile out of the young guards who stood outside it, shouldering automatic weapons and taking themselves terribly seriously. When I was hungry, I cut across to the narrow little streets of the old Jewish quarter and bought myself a falafel at the takeaway hatch, where they even began to recognise me and remembered I liked my *sauce piquante*. I liked to eat my falafel on one of the metal park benches in the Place des Vosges, watching parents watching their children play in the early evening sunlight against the backdrop of spectacularly chichi designer shops and residences. Everything felt like a minor triumph and the days were outrageously beautiful.

Once I'd got over the humiliation of my introduction, Madame Rouillard's café became my regular haunt. I was expected and greeted and felt I belonged, and I could ask for *une assiette de crudités* or an omelette without needing to find out the price or fearing bankruptcy. I loved the café's tacky deco-green interior and the battered beige awning that was laboriously cranked over the entrance in hot weather when the patrons spilled out onto the pavement, unconvinced by the ancient fan which only stirred up the limpid air inside. Very quickly I grew fond of the Rouillards, who ran the café and, in the case of Madame, apparently ran the lives of many of her patrons too.

It was hard to tell Madame Rouillard's age. I presumed she must have been in her late sixties but she was a commanding presence, to put it mildly, and seemed to possess unbelievable physical and mental energy. She shouted orders in her deep smoker's voice at staff and customers alike from behind the bar, and henpecked the beleaguered-looking Monsieur Rouillard, who looked at least ten years older than her. I felt rather sorry for him at times. She functioned with daunting efficiency, extended no credit, and told people off if they irritated her. Madame was not likely ever to have been a beauty. She was short and broad with a hard mouth and a boxer's nose, which looked like it might have been broken in the past, but her eyes were soft and dark and contradicted her other facial features and her apparent toughness. She was also, unfortunately, given to the odd racist or xenophobic outburst, which I found difficult to come to terms with in someone I otherwise liked and was increasingly relying on. She let me send faxes home from her machine and I managed to avoid discussing politics.

Madame Rouillard was incorrigibly curious and liked to think of herself as having insights into people which they themselves didn't always realise. Occasionally she was right. She liked to know what was going on, and even though most of the time she couldn't have avoided it even if she'd wanted to, the situation suited her nosy nature. One morning I sat at the bar waiting for my coffee and opened an envelope from Angus. He'd doodled mischievously all over a photograph of Kurt in the university magazine and written a disgracefully rude and defamatory update about colleagues in the history department. It was another in the series of off-the-wall missives he had been sending, and I burst out laughing.

'From your boyfriend?' Madame asked inquisitively.

'A friend,' I replied, grinning broadly and continuing with the letter. She caught my eye again and raised an eyebrow.

'He makes you laugh,' she observed.

'Yes, he does.'

One day, perusing the hot pink fake fur and posh silks in the crowded hilly streets around the fabric market, I noticed a young man watching me. He was with a group of friends, mostly Arabs and Africans, and one white guy with his cap on back to front ghetto-kid style and his pants so low I don't know why he bothered wearing them. When the starer saw I'd noticed him he smiled disarmingly.

'Where you from?' he asked me.

This would have been an extremely easy question to answer except that I was white and came from South Africa and I had no particular desire to advertise this to such a group. It would require too much explanation and justification.

'Guess,' I said, playing for time.

'England?'

'No.'

'Australia?'

'No.'

'Germany?'

'Definitely not.'

He kept guessing for while, increasingly wildly, until finally he gave up and demanded an answer. I still hadn't thought up an evasion tactic, so I just told him the truth.

'I'm from South Africa.' I braced myself for insult, interrogation. I'd been through this before.

'Ah, Mandela,' he said grinning, 'Bafana Bafana.' Our new ambassadors. I hadn't realised how thoroughly they'd already done their job, hadn't bargained on being included as one of the globe's new darlings, having so recently been part of a pariah race. It was a thrilling and unexpected relief. I caught sight of myself, smiling, in a shop window. I looked pretty good actually. My cold was gone and my nose was no longer scarlet, which was a start. This realisation cheered me up no end, so I ducked into the nearest phone booth, dialled Serge's number, and actually got through to him. We arranged a rendezvous for the following day. I bought myself a bottle of acceptably cheap wine and headed back towards the apartment to celebrate. The next day I would finally meet the extraordinary Serge.

Rendezvous

Unfortunately our initial introduction was not quite what I had hoped for. I had planned to appear very casual in jeans and a long-sleeved T-shirt. Sadly I was sweating profusely by the time I arrived and had to walk with my knees together and my bum pinched due to my bursting bladder. I was desperate for a pee, but hadn't been able to bring myself to enter those space capsule toilets in the middle of the street. What if I got stuck in there and was found half-decomposed weeks later by the cleaners? Also, I had walked around in increasingly exasperated circles trying to find the place. The café, some kind of old pool hall, was clearly a place for those in the know. Chicly, discreetly, infuriatingly devoid of signage on the outside, it looked more like a community hall than any kind of café I'd ever been to before. I tried to check my hair in the window but realised swiftly that it was a lost cause and hobbled in to find the WC and do some damage control before I searched for Serge.

The toilet was an unsanitary-looking hole in the floor – a pity considering I was in no state to factor in any tricky bum-positioning logistics – but what a relief! Having helped myself to a handful of the pink sandpaper that passes for bog roll in Paris, I zipped my fly and pulled the chain. A torrent of water gushed out of nowhere, flooding my shoes and the bottoms of my trousers. This was not good. I grabbed another handful of pink sandpaper and rubbed my shoes vigorously. Then I went out of the toilet cubicle and stood under the hand drier. I slid a foot up the wall and dried the bottoms of my jeans under the drier for a while, wondering what I'd say if someone walked in while I was doing the splits against the toilet wall. Then I remembered: I was in a city where I knew no one and had nothing to explain. Most liberating. I clipped my hair back into semi-submission and smiled encouragingly at my reflection.

Still exhilarated by my anonymity I headed out of the toilet into the café and looked around.

'Clementine,' someone purred smokily. I jumped and turned towards the voice. Someone with white shoes was walking towards me. It could only be Serge. He looked like some fantastically sordid plumber or housepainter who'd fallen on bad times. No one back home looked like that voluntarily, not even the politically correctest of the white left. I had never encountered cultivated seediness on this level. Too decadent and too Arabic to be Eurotrash, he looked like he should be lying around the fountain at St Michel with an Alsatian, a guitar and head lice. With his dark complexion and eyes and his sordid demeanour he was deeply sexy in an ugly sort of way, and he had the most splendidly enormous nose I'd ever seen on an actual person. Granny Mac would have written him off instantly as a 'dirty sand nigger', which of course added tremendously to his appeal. He seemed to enjoy the fact that he'd caught me off-guard and breaking into a slow, post-coital sort of smile, took me by the shoulders. Miraculously I managed to avoid a clashing with his impressive proboscis as he planted an excessively succulent kiss on each cheek.

'I saw you walking to the *toilettes* and then you never came out,' he drawled, speaking English in what sounded to me like a caricature French accent. 'I was about to send someone in *et puis voilà*! *Bienvenue à Paris!*'

How had he known it was me? How had Jack described me? So much for seamlessly blending into the Paris social scene.

Serge ushered me over to one of the leather-upholstered benches and ordered Moroccan mint tea. It came in tiny glasses with the leaves still in it. It was sweet, and I took a big sip out of nervousness and scalded my mouth. We spoke in English with a smattering of my frantic school French. Then he gave me the bad news. There was nothing going in the set and props department for the moment, so I wouldn't be staging operas in Paris just yet, but he had a friend who worked in a language school and he was sure I'd get a job teaching English. He promised to speak to him and arrange for us to meet. It was a bit of a blow, but all was not lost; I'd just have to refocus on the idea of becoming a wildly exciting teacher in some glamorous Parisian international language school, inspiring generations of students who worship and adore me à la *Dead Poets Society* ...

When I said goodbye I left Serge chatting at the bar. With renewed confidence I began to stride out triumphantly across the length of the vast old hall, self-assured, full of promise, enjoying feeling everyone's eyes on me. Serge called after me from the other end of the room. He motioned towards my shoe. I looked down. Stuck to my shoe and trailing behind me was a metre of pink toilet paper. Just when I'd been doing so well! Did I have to come across like some vaudeville clown from the colonies? I detached the grubby streamer from my shoe with a sheepish smile and legged it.

Sex city

Thought for the day: Where do all these perverts come from? Why do they come to me? What am I doing wrong?

One morning I decided to empty my landlord's postbox and found a stash of post for me. There was a deliciously gossipy letter from Jack and a brief and sober note from Kurt defensively professing that he couldn't understand why I'd left. Kurt's note was attached to a sycophantic review of his work with a photograph of himself – the same photo that Angus had so irreverently defaced and sent me in his previous letter. There was also a series of delightfully bizarre and inconsequential second-hand postcards from Angus depicting places he'd never been to, and some clippings from *YOU* that he claimed I'd find 'uplifting'. I could almost hear his voice as I read. It was a feast, and I consumed it all with relish.

Then, still feeling great, I strode out into the Paris summer to send some postcards of my own.

Within five minutes I'd had my arse grabbed on my way into the subway, been propositioned by the man sitting next to me on the métro, and been treated to a sneak preview of another man's meagre and rather unhygienic-looking turkey wattles. I wanted to shout some witty retort at him, but by the time I had worked out how to say 'it looks like a penis, only smaller' in French, the man and his mini-penis were long gone. Not for the first time I wished I was more like Maddy: she'd have had some searingly witty comeback for him, no doubt. I tried to put the sight out of my mind, but the worst thing was that every time I blinked or shut my eyes I saw his unsavoury-looking offering all over again, like when you get the sun or a camera flash in your eyes and it won't go away.

Since I was feeling cheerful despite having willingly relocated to a city of sexual deviants, I decided to phone Michelle from the flight over. I mentioned the pervert overdose to her and she claimed it's just because of the heat and because 'they can see you're an impressionable foreigner'. She says the longer you stay here the less it happens. When I told Madame Rouillard she claimed it was 'the Arabs'. She said this without batting an eyelid while pulling the dead leaves off her ugly pot plant. Ha! Obviously she thinks it's fine to say such a thing to a white South African. I was going to pick a fight with her but I was waiting for a fax from Jack, so I just lied and told her (with an expression of pseudo-innocent amazement) that none of them was Arab. I love to imagine what she'd think of Serge! There was an old man in the café drinking *pastis* at the counter in the middle of the day and eavesdropping on our conversation. He said I should feel flattered by the attention. 'Berthaut!' scolded Madame Rouillard, flicking him with her dishtowel as she cleaned the counter. I stared at him with unconcealed disgust for a moment, wondering if he was joking, and then turned my back on him and read my book.

After a few weeks in Paris I was beginning to lay claim to parts of it. I spent much of my time alone, though I went with Michelle and her lover for a drink or to see a movie every now and then and had spoken to Serge several times on the phone. I really missed Jack and Angus, and once or twice I even found myself talking out loud to them in public places, but I was definitely falling for the city. I wished Claude and Maddy could see me looking happy and at home. Once I asked a stranger, an American tourist, to take a photograph of me so that I could send Claude some 'evidence' that I was fine and flourishing, but it was excruciating to approach him with this request and to pose cheesily while he fumbled with my camera, and the picture came out all blurry anyway. I tried hard to avoid thinking about Kurt since it confused me and made me miserable, and I was much happier just to live in the present now that I'd finally landed. And anyway, I had more pressing practical matters to consider. I had to earn some money, and I was getting anxious to meet Serge's friend and to start my career as the most sought after English teacher in Paris. Serge had promised to get hold of him. I made another pilgrimage to the nearest phone booth, dialled Serge's number, and he answered.

'What are you doing now?' he asked me. I tried to think of an inspired-sounding answer but gave up and opted for the truth.

'Nothing much,' I confessed.

'Come for lunch. Bring a baguette.'

He gave me his address and the code for the front door.

Serge lived in a small grubby street not far from Pigalle, a study in picturesque urban decay. Layers of posters and adverts for phone sex or live acts encrusted the walls of the old building, flapping sadly in the slight breeze where they'd come loose. A clutch of pretty, dark children, flourishing French-Arab hybrids, rode past me as if I was invisible. They pushed each other off their bikes, wrestled gleefully on the filthy pavements, climbed back on their bikes and rode off again. I could see Serge's attic flat right at the top of the building. I punched in the code and pushed open the heavy door onto a trashed courtyard piled with wheelbarrows, ancient pot plants, an iron bedstead, and some old shop dummies. At the top of the inevitable Escher stairs Serge's door was open. I knocked anyway.

'The door's open,' he shouted, 'come inside.'

The attic apartment was low ceilinged, minute and crammed with paintings, canvases and bizarre *objets*.

'You're early,' Serge called from the next room. I followed the sound of his voice, passing a painting that looked disconcertingly like a man in *flagrante delicto* with a chicken, and pushed open the door into the next (and I soon discovered the *only* other) room in the flat. There, in a zinc tub in the middle of the floor, Serge sat naked, washing himself with a big green sponge.

'Oh!' I recoiled instinctively at the sight and stepped backwards out of the room. 'Sorry.' I stood foolishly just outside the bathroom door.

'Was that such a shock?' he laughed at me. 'Come inside and talk to me while I finish my bath.'

'Oh, I'll just wait out here,' I said, affecting a casual tone. There was a sigh and a great deal of splashing from inside as Serge finished washing and I heard him lift himself to standing position in the bath. He emerged moments later in a small towel and a pair of leather slippers.

'I brought some bread,' I said, putting the baguette on the table and avoiding looking in his direction. 'I also brought some wine, but you don't have to drink it if it's terrible.' Anxiously I took the wine out of my bag and put it next to the bread. He examined the label.

'This is only a *bit* terrible,' he said. 'We will drink it.'

Serge pottered constantly while we talked, putting away paintbrushes, eating a slice of bread, scrawling something on a piece of paper and making me squirm with self-consciousness by sketching me casually while he made us some food. He kept a lit cigarette next to him and smoked while he ate, and the smoke, the surroundings and the drinking in the middle of the day, made me feel steeped in decadence.

When I left he handed me a scrap of paper he'd been scribbling on. It was a list of wines with comments next to them. I smiled up at him, surprised and touched. When I thanked him he just shrugged. 'How will you know if no one tells you?' he said. 'And anyway it's good for me. Next time you'll bring better wine.'

A few days later Serge left a message for me at Madame Rouillard's. He'd contacted the elusive friend, and I was finally going to meet him and Serge at a bar on the Place St Sulpice. I consulted my map book and planned to arrive early and then lurk around nearby until the appointed hour, avoiding a last minute panicky attempt to find the place.

It was a wonderful venue. Outside the café itself, rows of chained together dark green iron chairs and a scattering of tables were arranged to face the ancient church, like deckchairs facing the sun. I was just about to turn away and tour the shop windows until our meeting time when an unmistakable gruff voice called my name from the other end of the terrace. Another ambush. Serge and his friend were already there, relaxed and drinking Camparis in the glowing evening sunlight. 'Chérrrie,' Serge said, rolling the r like a purr, 'did you not recognise me with my clothes on?' I frowned, then laughed nervously when I realised what he was talking about. 'Oh, the *bath*!' I said, in an awkward bid to reclaim my innocence. The friend's face remained one hundred per cent smile-free. It didn't seem a good start. Serge got up to embrace me, slipping a hand proprietorially around my waist and planting kisses more on my exposed neck than my cheeks. I pretended not to notice. 'This is Yves,' he said, slipping an arm around the friend's waist as well as he stood up. He squeezed us both to him in a way that I might have interpreted as fatherly had I not known better, then motioned at us to sit down.

Yves was about the same height as me – about medium-size for a Frenchman, ie more or less a midget. He had a sturdy frame, more thick dark hair on his head than is necessary on one person, and a head and face that looked like a Roman emperor on an ancient coin. His posture was very erect and he held his head high and tipped slightly upwards so that he appeared to be looking down his nose at everyone. His hair was cut in a short version of the foppish style the French seemed to favour, and he was wearing a dark suit despite the heat. A *suit*! I couldn't think of anyone I actually knew back home who wore a suit – not a *friend* anyway. This was a language teacher and he looked like something out of *The Godfather*. I didn't know how to talk to people in suits. I searched surreptitiously for signs of one of those gentleman's handbags Serge had told me to look out for, and although he came out clean I couldn't help but allocate him a phantom one to complete the look. He caught me staring at him out of the corner of my eye and I looked away quickly. But Serge had clearly been watching me even more closely.

'Yes, he looks good but he is in a *sheety* temper. Yves has been talking to the lawyers all day,' he said, and left it at that. Yves looked every bit the mafia hood and I was distracted by wild imaginings of what he must have done to necessitate lawyers. Yves caught me staring at him, frowning. I smiled. He didn't.

The waiter arrived and I ordered a margarita and hoped that was an acceptable thing to do. I was so high on nerves already, so hopeful.

'Serge says you come from South Africa?' Yves said. He had a strange, deliberate quasi-American accent in English, as if he paid attention to pronouncing each syllable correctly. A businesslike accent and a sexy, lazy voice. It was a strange combination.

'Yes,' I answered, and went mute. ('Great, Clem,' I admonished myself, 'inspiring answer. Fill him with confidence!')

'So do you teach English in South Africa?'

'Uuuh no. Actually I design sets and props for the theatre.'

'I see,' said Yves, raising an eyebrow at Serge questioningly. Serge eyed me expectantly, encouragingly.

'But I studied English. And drama, which is apparently very

useful for teaching foreign language speakers.'

'Not necessarily if they are businessmen,' said Yves acerbically.

'Are all your students businessmen?'

'Mine, yes, but that's my particular field. Business French for foreigners. The school caters for many categories of students.' I was already starting to build up a picture of this place. God, I wanted this job. I needed this job. I had looked at my bank balance this morning and was appalled. Almost broke already and I felt I'd eaten nothing but baguette and cheese and the odd falafel since I'd arrived. I was going to have to try harder.

'You see, the thing is,' I burst forth, 'my mother is actually an English teacher so I've been surrounded by it all my life. I really know I'd be a good teacher.' I couldn't believe it. Here I was, begging to be Claude Junior all over again.

'And your father, what does he do?' asked the nosy bastard.

'He died when I was young.'

'I see.'

Yves looked at me curiously. 'You know it is nearly August?' he asked me, lighting a short, fat, smelly Gauloise. What did he take me for? An idiot child from the colonies who didn't even know what month it was?

'Yes?'

'Well in case you haven't noticed,' he continued in an infuriatingly patronising tone, 'Paris does not work in August. Our next term only starts in September. Also, I would obviously have to check whether there were any openings for less experienced teachers at the school.'

I chose to see this as positive. 'So you think it might be possible?' I gushed.

'It might be, but what will you do until then?'

Gloom descended once again. Clearly I had not taken into consideration that France spends several months of the year on holiday. This explained why the proprietor of the bakery down the road recently seemed to think nothing of closing at noon every day and going to play *boules* in the park.

'You must go to the American Church,' he ordered, 'they advertise jobs for foreigners there.'

'Yes,' I said glumly, 'I know.' I was being reprimanded for my idealism and my foreignness. Michelle had told me about the American Church, but I had thought I wouldn't need it since I was moments away from being offered a plum job as a female version of Robin Williams and would shortly be leaping around in front of a blackboard shouting, '*Carpe diem.*'

'It's only for a couple of weeks, don't look so depressed,' said Serge. 'And you neither,' he admonished Yves, who was staring, pained and imperious, down his nose into the middle distance. It must be an odd vantage point, I thought, looking down your nose like that all the time. Like looking down a runway at everything. Yves looked irritated but said nothing, and Serge continued in frustration: 'Do you think you are the first person ever to get divorced?'

Ah. Divorce. The lawyers fell into place. Yves finished his drink and threw some money on the table. 'See you at Patrice's,' he said down his nose at us and he walked off into the evening. I watched his departing back in consternation.

'*Chérrrrie,*' Serge purred again, stroking my cheek. 'Do not look so *triste.* Yves will find you a job,' said Serge. 'He's just a bit preoccupied at the moment. He's stayed married to this woman for ages to be with his child and now she's finally asked him for a divorce. They should have done it long ago. He'll be fine by next Saturday and you can talk to him then.'

'What's next Saturday?' I asked.

'It's Patrice's exhibition, *chérie,* you have to come. Free wine and free sex.' He beamed seedily at my consternation.

That night I felt unaccountably restless and confused, so I scrawled a quick account of the meeting for Jack, faxed it off, and climbed into bed early with Aldous Huxley.

Exhibitionists

The next Saturday morning, when I went to get my coffee and *pain au chocolat*, Madame Rouillard handed me a long fax from Jack. It was a perfect hot day, and I decided to save up the fax until I had walked all the way to Les Invalides. There I would lie on the grass in the middle of that glorified traffic island, pretend I was on an immaculate deserted beach somewhere, and treat myself to Jack's message.

By the time I reached Les Invalides I was tired of pretending I was the heroine of some French movie. The novelty had worn off, and so had most of the skin on my feet. I collapsed onto the grass, threw my shoes off (exposing my worm-white feet to the sun) and devoured the fax.

Hello, darling girl

Sorry I didn't reply immediately to your most intriguing fax, but I've been in the thick of it down here and you'll be very pleased to know that things are looking up for us poofters in the colonies. In the end the rest of the department decided that a humiliating apology speech was not only uncalled for but presumptuous. They therefore called together a kind of gathering of the clan and we had our own mini Wildean courtroom drama with moi *at the centre of it all! I made a speech about the error of my ways and looked meaningfully at Wixley when I suggested that we all had skeletons in our closet, had done things we might not be proud of. It was all fairly gratifying to the old ego, particularly since it ended up with the entire student body on my side and explaining that it had all been a misunderstanding, which of course it had. Even the dreary Neil came forward and explained that he had never meant it to go this far – I swear he actually looked tearful. A lot of free-flowing emotional catharsis among the drama contingent ensued, at which point I noticed Wixley escaping through a back door.*

The Chutney Ferret had bolted.

Everyone began giving each other (and particularly me) comforting, supportive little hugs. Naturally I didn't try and hug Neil for fear of accidentally starting off the fiasco all over again, but he did shake my hand in a typically square-jawed US-marine-movie-character way and all was well in the kingdom ... or would it be the queendom? I have now written formal letters of apology for the misunderstanding to all concerned and it looks likely I'll finish my days here as reigning queen of the drama school, just as planned. I've already even started on another mask-making workshop, which is going rather well, actually.

Since you ask, by the way, there is no sign of Kurt and Anti-Oxidant being together, nor any particular rumour on the grapevine. However, darling, I can't help thinking that this will not actually be what you want to hear ... that it won't be the relief or good news to you that I expect you want me to believe it will. If you know what I mean.

(I read this paragraph several times but became increasingly confused, so I carried on with the next one.)

No? You don't know? Okay, Petal, here's a clue. The man in the suit. Are you sure you're not just the teensiest bit in denial about him? 'Cause I have to say I detected a strong sexual frisson under all that garbage about Roman profiles and thatches of black hair. If you end up leaping into the sack with him without providing sufficient narrative build-up I will feel extremely hard done by. Lots of people have to wear suits, darling – they have to, for their jobs. Not all of us can have pretend jobs in academia. And you said yourself that he didn't carry a handbag, so surely that's one point in his favour? Many an irresistible bod has been concealed under off-putting clothing. Look at Lady Chatterley's Lover, *Sweetie, ambling around in muck-filled gardening gear. That didn't put the Lady off, now did it? You have to see past the clothing (though God knows, seeing* through *it would be infinitely more effective and save us all a lot of time). And give the guy a break if he's getting a divorce – even if it's been on the cards for ages it couldn't be fun for him. Just think of all the consolation he's going to need, hmm ...?*

I was reading Jack's fax for the third time when a soccer ball flew towards me and hit me on the shoulder. In irritation I took the ball and impulsively sat on it, laughing spitefully at my own joke, buoyed up and cheeky after my one-way chat with Jack. Predictably, a bronzed man in soccer shorts ran towards me.

'You okay?' he asked in English, his Australian twang virtually a parody of itself.

'I'm fine,' I said, then resumed rereading Jack's letter and ignored him as if I hadn't noticed I was sitting on his soccer ball.

'Okay, mate, give me the ball back and I'll buy you a lager.' I shook my head and laughed. He turned to his friends with an incredulous smile, then looked back at me. 'Okay, here's the deal. You sit on *me* ... and give the ball back to my friends instead.' I gave him an exasperated look and passed him the ball. Honestly, I think the sun brings people's hormones closer to the surface or something. He was quite nice though, and I might have considered going for that lager with him (a bit of English-speaking Antipodean camaraderie would have been comforting), but it was getting late, and I had to go and get ready to go to the exhibition with Serge that night.

As I walked home I chuckled to myself. Just when I suspected I was becoming a sort of social outcast, I'd had two invitations for the same night. I stopped in at a café for a quick coffee to celebrate being in such demand. I bought an obscene *fin de siècle* postcard and, nettled by Jack's presumptuousness re The Suit, wrote him a quick reprimand in tiny, prissy print:

Dear Jack

Thank God the Chutney Ferret Fiasco is now over. I wish you could come over here and play.

As for The Suit, I think you are projecting more than a little bit. I know you think you know my mind better than I do (and sometimes you've been infuriatingly right on that front) but I DO NOT have a crush on The Suit, okay? It's preposterous! And as for your insinuations about my wanting Kurt to be with the Anti-Oxidant: presumably you mean that's because it'll 'free me up' or something ridiculous? Let me make it clear that even if I were about to embark on some huge affair (which I'm not) I would never wish that unmentionable woman on him. And may I remind you that I am not out here on some gigantic sexual safari? The man wears a suit, for God's sake. He's a divorcee with a child and he specialises in business language. He's not even vaguely my type!

I put a large lipstick smooch on the card and dropped it in a postbox. Just as I heard it slide into the pile of letters it occurred to me: I had not really asked about home. It was the first time I'd omitted to do this and somehow it saddened me that the present was now my reality more than home was. I tried to take it as a good sign, an indication of having adjusted, but it made me felt treacherous. For a while I sat and wondered whether people from any other country in the world felt guilty if they enjoyed being away from their home country? Why did South Africans experience this peculiar sense of guilt if they 'deserted', even temporarily? I looked around to check that no one was watching, then tried to stick my hand into the box and fish out the postcard but the slot was far too narrow. Short of intercepting the postman there was nothing I could do. I walked back to the apartment in a pall of gloom. When Serge arrived in a taxi to fetch me and took my mind off those thoughts I was greatly relieved.

From Serge's description of the exhibition I'd expected live sex acts and women popping ping-pong balls out of their nethers on the bar counter, but of course he'd just been having me on – it was wishful thinking on his part. It was a 'normal' exhibition in a kind of dockland-ish warehouse area somewhere in Paris with some interesting work by a perfectly nice young photographer who Serge introduced me to. Most of the photos were of people squashed into glass boxes or leaning against panes of glass. There was one particularly obscure looking picture called *Portrait of the Artist*. I leaned really close to it to try and work out what it was and realised it was a close-up of his genitals squashed almost out of recognition (as genitals, that is, not as *his* genitals *naturellement*). Grotty. It looked like hairy chicken breasts and giblets squashed into cellophane. I felt momentarily awkward when a woman came and stood next to me and laughed at my expression.

'To think I came all the way from Sweden for *that*!' she said. Then she stuck out her hand at me, utterly forthright. 'I'm Inge,' she said. 'The Artist's Lucky Girlfriend.'

Inge turned out to be a Swedish yoga teacher, in Paris with Patrice for the summer, and that much-missed commodity in this city, a potential girlfriend. She led me round the exhibition at a pace, pointing out the people in the room who'd posed for the photographs and frequently passing the snack tray to refuel. I revelled in her company and the easy familiarity. I was wearing my long Batman coat-dress (a bit too hot for the occasion, but it was more important to look chic than to be comfortable) and she said she liked it. I glowed with the compliment. Once we'd done the full circuit and she'd provided a wince-worthy commentary on the Artists' Models, we sat down next to the gallery entrance and began consuming all the remaining complimentary schnapps and snacks and laughing at each other's comments on the passers-by.

'Jesus, I hate Parisian women!' she exclaimed vehemently. 'What a relief it is to meet a woman who actually eats and drinks.' This struck a chord: *Parisiennes* in general seemed the most unsisterly creatures I had ever encountered. Arch, coquettish and sulky, they apparently devoted their lives to pleasing men. Even the abominable Tamara was more of a sister than any of them. I felt a surge of well-being in Inge's company.

Everything was going fine until I started mixing drinks. Behind the bar. After evicting the barman. My hard-drinking father had turned me into a kind of living bar mascot when I was little, and by seven I was a dab hand at mixing a staggering range of elaborate drinks. I could whip up anything from a daiquiri or a diabolo to a sidecar. I enjoyed the alchemy of it, the colours, the challenge of getting cream to float on an Irish coffee, and the skills had stuck with me. Serge had inadvertently set me off on my drunken bar-tending spree by giving me a pathetic Bloody Mary. After one taste I'd jettisoned it discreetly behind a pot plant, hoping no one would notice. But Serge had sidled up to me in his usual sluttish manner and stuck his enormous proboscis into my business. 'You don't like your Bloody Mary?' he asked me in his throatiest pillow-talk voice.

'It's ... fine,' I said non-committally.

'Fine?' Serge bellowed. 'What kind of an English word-without-balls is that?'

'It's a Bloody Mary without balls, Serge, since you ask. It's all out of proportion. If you mix it right and add just a bit of sherry it makes all the difference.'

Serge wrinkled his considerable nose at me. 'Sherry is a drink for old English ladies.' But I was adamant, and buoyed up with the Dutchest of courage. Which is why I climbed in behind the bar to get at the rest of the ingredients. Then I saw Yves watching me surreptitiously, from a distance, looking amused despite himself and vaguely intrigued in much the same way (I felt sure) as he would have been by a performing monkey. I'd been dreading seeing him, uncomfortable still after the embarrassing job request scenario, but he looked a whole lot more relaxed and even a bit sexy out of his suit. I smiled broadly at him, but just as I did that a sulky-looking woman wearing too much make-up and an absurdly pronounced pout slunk up to him, followed his gaze and looked daggers in my direction. He looked away quickly and began talking to her but she was swinging into a full-scale sulk and looked wholly unimpressed. Was she his soon-to-be-ex-wife? If so, why was he still trailing her around to exhibition openings, pandering to her every pout? I returned to my cocktail mixing and resolved not to think about it.

I mixed a perfect Bloody Mary, tangy without being acid, savoury without being overbearing, and offered it to Serge: '*Now* taste,' I insisted. Serge took a sip and raised the glass at me.

'Not bad at all!' he announced smacking his lips sexually in approval and making all kinds of obscenely juicy noises inside his mouth. Then to my dismay he called Yves over and passed him the glass. Yves greeted me in a cold, polite manner and took a swig.

'Who taught you how to do this?' asked Yves. His question was so abrupt I was not sure whether I was in for a scolding or a compliment. Then he nodded approval to Serge, so I told him.

'My father.' Yves looked at me sideways, frowning.

'I thought you said your father died when you were young?' I looked at him full in the face, though after countless glasses of complimentary schnapps I found it hard to focus at this proximity.

'He did. I have a good memory.' And clearly so did Yves. I was amazed and rather flattered that he'd bothered to remember anything from our first meeting. Suddenly Serge grabbed Yves's hand.

'I have an idea. Why don't we take her?' Serge asked Yves enthusiastically. Yves looked suspicious.

'Take me?' I asked stupidly.

'I think Serge is inviting you to join us all at my parents' place in the South,' Yves explained in a sarcastic let's-all-suffer-the-idiot voice. Out of the corner of my eye I saw he was getting killing looks from the Unimpressed One. Yves kept his head turned resolutely away from that direction.

'Yes,' said Serge, 'you can make cocktails wearing a *verrry* small *tablier* (he did a quick explanatory charade of an apron the size of a fig leaf) and we'll drink them. You know other cocktails?'

'Of course. But it's Yves's house.'

'No it's not, it's his parents' house and it's *our* holiday, not just his. It will be Yves, Véronique (he pointed towards the Unimpressed One), Yves's housemate Robert, Patrice, Inge ... There's no point in being in Paris in August, Clementine, there's no work here now.'

Yves looked unmoved. He shot the Unimpressed One a glance. She turned her back on him and held out her cigarette like some film noir heroine. He ignored her and looked at Serge.

'I see I have no option – your decision's made. I'll book an extra train ticket,' he said, with an ironic smile.

I tried to protest, since I had no money and no desire to be invited to someone's house against his will, but Serge shot me a meaningful look to shut me up and smiled his roguish smile at me. 'Yves is a person who doesn't always say what he wants, *ma petite*,' he said cryptically, 'sometimes one has to guess ... or tell him.' And he demanded another drink.

I spent the rest of the night whipping up impressive cocktails and trying to contain my excitement about the holiday. Inge seemed delighted that I was coming and I couldn't believe my luck. With some embarrassment I broached the bank balance issue, but Serge pointed out that they'd feed me, and reassured me that the tickets were cheap because we were going on the sleeper train. He gave me a big meaningful grin and did an exaggerated set of inverted commas in the air with his fingers as he said 'sleeper' so I rolled my eyeballs at him in mock exasperation and gave him my best 'offended prude' look.

The birds were already up when Serge and I left the gallery in a taxi. 'Who was the Unimpressed One?' I asked him.

'Who?'

'The woman who followed Yves around all night, was that his wife?'

'Oh *no*,' Serge said emphatically. 'That is Véronique, his colleague. She's been trying to get him for years. She thinks she's succeeded now that he's getting divorced.'

His colleague. This was not welcome news. Perhaps I could make friends with her in the South of France, I pondered, but frankly this seemed unlikely.

'And has she?' I asked.

'Has she what?'

'And has she ... got him?'

'*Putain*, I hope not!' Serge growled. Then suddenly he stared at me with his eyes all screwed up and suspicious. 'You are very interested in my friend Yves tonight, aren't you?'

I denied it emphatically but Serge laughed at me and shrugged. '*Quelle pisseuse!*'

I was starting to wonder if Jack and Serge were in cahoots on the Yves issue and communicating secretly behind my back.

Serge walked me to the door while the taxi waited, his arm around the small of my back. Then he tilted my chin up with his other hand and looked at me lasciviously. '*Tu veux tirer un coup?*' he asked me. I looked blank and frowned. 'Do you want to fuck a leetle?' he repeated in English. I burst out laughing.

'No thanks, Serge. 'Fraid not.'

'*Tant pis*,' he sighed theatrically. 'Never mind.' He kissed me on the forehead in a fatherly manner, patted me on the bum, and headed back to the taxi, unfazed. I stood amazed and amused on the pavement. One moment Serge was playing fairy godfather and introducing me to the delights of Paris and the next he's proposing some quasi-incestuous liaison in the sack. It might have been really trying if I didn't like him, but I did. He was funny and caring and kind, and I was immensely grateful to him for uncomplainingly helping me out and dragging me into his social circle when I must really have been an encumbrance. He had been unfailingly good to me, even after he must have realised that the chances of getting any nookie out of the arrangement were less than slim.

Yes, he has a seedy sort of charm, I thought to myself as I climbed into bed, gloriously alone. Before I fell asleep I tried to imagine sex with Serge and found it difficult. It was a blessing he was particularly partial to buggery, I decided. Getting up-close-and-personal and face-to-face would be physically impossible with a nose like that in the way.

Journey to the centre of the world

- *Buy fake tan, sunhat*
- *Buy French slang dictionary*
- *Look up* pisseuse *in said dictionary*
- *Find out where Caramany is*

Serge had filled me in. So to speak. The idea was to travel by train to Perpignan, just about as far south in France as one could go and then to drive up to Yves's family's house in some place called Caramany.

'We're going to the centre of the world,' Serge had told me. 'That's what Dali called Perpignan station.' I nodded, trying to look impressed without looking surprised since I'd already pretended to know all about Perpignan. Then Serge had smiled, amused but kindly.

'He was not being serious, of course.'

Of course.

We would all meet at Le Train Bleu in the Gare de Lyon at half past seven the next evening for a couple of drinks before we set off on the 'slee-pearrr' train, as the ever-hopeful Serge pronounced it.

'Who is "we all"?' I asked him anxiously. He gave me the

low-down on our fellow travellers. I made notes when I got home so that I could contemplate them in private and reduce introduction anxiety the next day:

- Yves (meaningful interrogative eyeball roll)
- Véronique (pained apologetic shrug)
- Serge (exaggerated suggestive leer followed by much laughter)
- Patrice (*'le photographe'*)
- Inge ('girlfriend of Patrice')
- Robert ('lives in apartment of Yves' ... quick glance to check my reaction to mention of unknown male)
- Sebastian ('our other friend, the comedian ... he'll try, but he's not for you, *chérie'*)

So the only people I had not met were Sebastian and Robert. I lay in bed that evening and practised introducing myself coolly in French '*Salut, je m'appelle ...*' until I bored myself to sleep.

The next morning an altercation on the road outside my window woke me from a disconcerting dream. I pulled the sheets around me and leaned out of the window. Two men were fighting over a moped, pushing each other and shouting. Angry neighbours joined in and the noise level escalated as they shoved each other around in the gutter, foolishly macho and Latin – like characters from *West Side Story*. As quickly as it had started the dispute seemed to subside and I lay back on my bed trying to remember what I'd been dreaming. Moments before waking, I had been flitting about outside some vine-clad country house dispensing drinks in nothing but a French maid's apron. I knew who they all were – Serge, Yves, Véronique, Patrice ... but in my dream they were all variations on Yves: a gallery of supercilious Romans looking scornfully down their noses at me while I did the rounds in my embarrassing micro-outfit, dispensing lurid-looking drinks. I was relieved to be awake, sweaty and twisted into the sheets, alone in my narrow little bed.

I showered and headed down to Madame Rouillard's, still feeling rattled by the micro-mini dream, to drink a quick coffee and to ask her to keep my post while I was away. She waxed lyrical when I told her where I was going. Her family came from the area, she told me, 'They are good people there.'

I smiled.

'Very good people,' she said, her eyes clouding over nostalgically.

I nodded enthusiastically.

'But too many Arabs.'

I changed the subject.

I confessed to her that I couldn't actually find the place in my guidebook and in fact could not remember the town it was near. This was highly regrettable, particularly since I had feigned recognition of the name in a moment of weakness with Serge and really needed someone to tell me where I was going. Madame Rouillard pointed eagerly to Perpignan right down south on the map, then moved her finger up and stabbed insistently at the place my destination would be. Obviously a trip to a bookshop was called for. I was getting up to leave when Madame whistled to me and held up a letter. 'Photos Fragile Do not bend' was written in neat, authoritative letters on the envelope. No exclamation marks. And the handwriting was Kurt's. I thanked her, pocketed the letter without opening it, and started walking towards the nearest bookshop.

Near the FNAC I found a bench and sat down, heart speeding, to open the envelope. Inside was another envelope with a newspaper clipping on a recent exhibition by young installation artists stuck onto it. I skimmed the article automatically for Kurt's name. *Hausmann's ambitious exhibit is a video wall consisting of a dozen screens in front of which he performs in order to 'place himself within the frame'. But while he has scaled up his technological component, he seems to have scaled down his characteristic no-holds-barred style. This work, simply entitled 'Woman', suggests a mellowing of his approach.* Fumbling, I opened the envelope. Inside it was a photograph and a neat pile of small pieces of paper, each cryptically bearing a single letter: S, Y, O, I, S, M, U, I. Oddly Japanese. I looked at the photograph. It was a picture of Kurt in front of the video wall, in performance. I looked closer at the screens behind him. There were four screens across and three down, and on each of the twelve screens was the same image of me, a photograph that I remembered someone taking one happy Sunday when we'd been having lunch at an open-air seaside restaurant. My hair was clipped back, but the salty wind had lifted a lock free and it stood out quirkily like a curly aerial. I was smiling. I stared at the photograph: of me, of Kurt. What was he trying to say? Was this some kind of Kurtian apology? I checked the envelope again ... definitely nothing else, no actual letter. I picked up the pile of letters and tried to make sense of them, but there was no way I could do it on a public bench. I packed everything back for later and headed for the FNAC, filled with doubt but going through the motions.

I found Caramany on the detailed road atlas and read a few lines about the area, which would help disguise my ignorance. Languedoc was the cradle of the Cathars, a huge group of heretics who emerged in the eleventh century and who believed that Satan created the world, that Jesus was entirely divine and did not suffer or die on the cross, and that angels and demons walked among us in human guise. Languedoc had once been the centre of European culture and had had its own language and almost been an independent country. I armed myself with a dictionary of French argot in an attempt to educate myself beyond my current *'la plume de ma tante'* vocabulary. It was an enormous, horrifyingly expensive book and it would add several kilos to my baggage, but without it one could hardly expect to survive. It would be my indispensable first line of defence. If I went. Or perhaps even if I stayed. Because at that moment I had no idea what I was doing or why I'd ever thought of going on this trip.

Back in my room I spread the letters out in a long line on

the floor. S Y O I S M U I. Why couldn't he just write me a note, like other people would? It was just typical of him to send me a MENSA test. I stared at the letters. The Y and O stared back at me, and I pulled them out and followed them with a U, and suddenly it was obvious. I M I S S Y O U. It was impressively sentimental for Kurt, which was why he'd needed to hide behind the MENSA format. Still, there it was, however irritatingly evasive. And where did that leave me? What was I thinking, agreeing to go off with a bunch of strange Frenchmen on a holiday I couldn't afford while Kurt languished without me in Cape Town, pouring out his heart in public like a latter-day troubadour? Was this, these eight neat letters, this photographic evidence, enough to strand me in Paris, waiting for the next flight home to Kurt? If I didn't meet Serge at seven I'd miss the train and the decision would be made for me. Once again I put everything back into the envelope. Then I started to pack my bags.

I arrived at the Gare de Lyon at seven-fifteen. Le Train Bleu was grandly situated at the top of a sweeping (but unswept) marble staircase, which had seen better days and looked like Cinderella's ballroom after midnight. I began walking up towards it, but was gripped by a sudden fit of anxiety and sat down absurdly on the top step, overwhelmed by the feeling that I was not in control of my life. Did I really want to head off with a posse of virtually unknown foreigners on a sleeper train to a virtually non-existent town in the south of France? Inge would be with Patrice, everyone else knew each other ... what would I *do* there? Perhaps they were just being polite. Would they tire of me after the novelty wore off? Would I be dishonourably discharged from duty in my maid's micro-mini, penniless and alone?

After a few moments of anguished reflection, I decided I couldn't face it. I headed off across the station to a newsstand and started browsing through all the magazines in a confused blur, mentally debating whether I should just phone the Train Bleu, tell them something had come up and I was staying in Paris.

After I'd loitered indecisively for longer than was acceptable, the newsstand man began to look irritated so I sheepishly gave in to my frivolous desires and bought a *Marie Claire* and an *Elle*. That clinched it. I would stay in Paris, sit in the free sun, and read magazines in peace for the first time in years. If Kurt wrote me a proper letter and did a bit of begging, I'd consider going home – on my terms. The thought of doing nothing but reading magazines filled me with delicious contentment. Conditioned by years with Claude and Kurt into concealing my occasional consumption of pulp mags, I hid them under my clothes at the bottom of my bag as surreptitiously as if they were porn. Just as I was zipping up the bag I heard a voice behind me and started, guiltily.

'You are leaving your shopping a bit late.'

It was Yves. I turned around, my cheeks glowing.

'I'm sorry, I was just ...'

'Come upstairs,' Yves said, shouldering my hefty bag without asking. 'We are all waiting for you.' He began to walk rapidly in the direction of Le Train Bleu. Since he'd absconded with my bag I had no choice but to follow him, feeling rebuked and rather embarrassed. Once again the decision had been taken out of my hands.

The interior of the Train Bleu was quite startling. It was full of murals, polished brass and plush banquettes and must have looked much the same for decades. But I hardly took in my surroundings as I strode after Yves towards the waiting group. There they all sat, side by side, facing each other like teenagers in a fifties movie: all, that is, except Véronique, The Unimpressed One, who sat glowering at them at an elegant distance in the booth alongside theirs. There were simply too many personalities fighting for dominion in that small space. When The Unimpressed One saw me arrive with Yves she looked displeased.

'You remember Véronique?' he asked me.

'Of course.' I would have greeted her, but she was pouting into her handbag at her compact, ignoring me and applying yet another layer of perfect lipstick in the mirror. Her black hair was sleeked back into a glamorous chignon exposing her elegant neck. I suppose she had been hoping I wasn't coming – that I'd decided to stay or had conveniently fallen in front of the métro. It was pretty obvious that Véronique resented any female near her turf, even the scruffy, stray South African variety.

'Clémence, I think you know everyone else here ...' Yves gestured briskly at 'everyone' and left me to it.

'She doesn't know Robert or Sebastian,' said Serge, getting up to greet me with a big proprietorial kiss. Inge waved, smiling, from behind a tall man – well, tall for a Frenchman anyway. He was dark-haired and brooding-looking with big eyebrows and an endearing, incongruously goofy grin. On the other side of her was a well-tanned, slim, athletic-looking man with an alarmingly bouffant hairdo. Serge propelled me forward to greet them.

'Robert,' said the tall brooding one, standing to kiss me on each cheek. There was something lugubrious and Eastern European about Robert, despite his grin. 'And that is Sebastian.' Without warning, Sebastian the bouffant-haired stood up like an enthusiastic schoolboy in class and lunged forward towards me across Inge and Robert as if released on the end of a spring, his lips juicily puckered, his eyes closed. His body, small-framed, wiry, and clad in some rather naff-looking sportsclothes, held the position like a dancer or a discus-thrower as he waited for my response. I looked anxiously at Serge but he and everyone else (except, of course, the Unimpressed One) were laughing at Sebastian, the bouffant athlete, the self-appointed court jester. So I laughed too, and eventually Sebastian stopped straining forward at me, lips first, and settled for a conventional kiss on each side. Even this he did with such cartoonish exaggeration, surprisingly camp for someone Serge had insisted would 'try' me. Since I was in the swing of it (and because it seemed this was what was called for) I bent down to kiss Inge and Patrice. Which meant that the only people I had not kissed were Yves and Véronique. Which was not surprising.

I had arrived just in time to leave. Serge went off and returned with a trolley. Everyone packed their bags onto the trolley (except, once more, for Véronique, who watched while others did it for her). Serge shouted '*On y va?*' and we followed him downstairs, onto the platform and into the train with only two minutes to go before departure time. It was thrilling. The last time I'd been on a long train journey had been years before with Claude. We'd arrived cautiously early and had to wait in the stuffy compartment for at least half an hour before the train left, alternately bickering and sitting in gloomy silence. Serge and Yves had booked two cabins next door to each other but after dumping our bags everyone piled noisily into one of them. Patrice and Inge immediately assigned themselves the top bunk and climbed into it 'to have a little rest'. Sebastian snorted, and I detected a hint of envy in that snort. Then he opened up his bag, hauled out his Walkman, hung it around his neck without any apparent intention to use it, and continued to rummage around in his bag looking for something. As the train pulled out of the station everyone began to bring out their wares. Serge took out some wine, Sebastian stopped rummaging in his bag and produced a small chunk of hash with a triumphant grin, and Robert brought out a bottle filled with a liquid the colour of urine with bits of grass suspended in it. *Zubrovka* it said on the outside. There was a picture of a bison on the label. I eyed it suspiciously. Robert noticed my sceptical expression: 'Vodka,' he announced, and cracked open the cap.

As the train rattled through the outskirts of Paris, Robert sucked back a generous sample of bison-wee vodka.

'*Excellent*,' he said, smacking his lips with earnest approval, and handed me the bottle. I hesitated, but Robert insisted, so I tried some. It tasted potent and slightly herbal and it burnt its way pleasantly down my gullet. As a peace gesture I passed it (with a smile) to Véronique. She simply turned her head away as though I were a bum offering her meths in a subway. Inge had clearly witnessed this from her vantage point on the top bunk.

'I'll have some,' she said, leaning down and revealing a generous portion of her breasts in the process much to Sebastian's delight. He sucked air in sharply between his teeth as though he'd touched something hot, and sat on his hands. Inge gave him a withering look, chugged back some Bison, and passed the bottle to Patrice. Out of the corner of my eye I noticed Serge watching me attentively. He saw that I'd noticed and smiled at me; a slow, sly, curious smile.

We trundled on past garden plots, small towns, churches, fields, petrol stations. Sebastian passed around a joint. I discreetly handed it on without taking any, though the compartment was rapidly turning into a hotbox anyway. Town, town, church, town. Worlds flew by unnoticed. I saw a sign on a church: 'God takes no summer holiday,' I translated. Shops, garages, billboards bearing car adverts or package tour adverts with girls in bikinis ... With a pang of regret I realised I had forgotten my depilatory cream.

When the landscape outside was darker I could watch everyone, myself included, in the reflection. Yves and Robert were playing cards, Véronique was flipping aggressively through the pages of some tastefully discreet plain-covered novel, Sebastian listened to his music and rolled another joint, Patrice and Inge continued with their 'rest', muttering endearments to each other in French and Swedish.

'*Älskling*,' Inge said breathily.

'*Ma petite pute*,' responded Patrice.

We all feigned deafness and the Bison did the rounds. I stared again at our reflection in the window. It was like watching a film about a group of people including someone who looked like me: as distant, as curiously entertaining, as mildly disconcerting. I could feel the vodka slowly spreading through my veins and was almost surprised when I moved my hand and saw myself waving back in the reflection, as though I could direct the action in a dream. I was annoyed that I'd left my notebook, my intended 'holiday journal', in my bag, now squashed unreachably behind everyone else's baggage. Sebastian nudged me and offered me the joint, but I declined and stared out of the window. It was getting dark. Patrice and Inge had started making more boisterous noises from the top bunk, but no one else seemed to notice or care. They moaned and whispered loudly to each other above us.

'*Kanoola may!*' moaned Inge. Or that's what it sounded like, anyway.

'*Aaaah oui!*' replied Patrice inventively.

I closed my eyes and tried not to think of the turkey wattles in the *Portrait of the Artist*. The compartment really was becoming intolerably stuffy and thick with dope smoke. Véronique slammed her book down on the seat next to her and started shouting about everything being *insupportable*.

'Well why don't you just go and read next door?' Yves suggested quietly. She shot him a vicious look, snatched her book up off the seat and stormed out of the compartment. After an awkward pause, Yves got up reluctantly and followed her. For a while there were raised voices from the next door compartment.

'*Hho la la!*' said Serge and ducked in his seat as if cowering from a beating. Sebastian took his headphones off and listened too, his ear eagerly plastered to the wall. With his lupine hairdo and exaggerated expression he looked like the missing Marx Brother. Robert had passed out after the lion's share of the Bison and now began to snore loudly. Sebastian nudged him, but he kept on. Then he nudged him again – to no avail. Sebastian smiled, got out of his seat, sneaked up quietly to the sleeping Robert and bent over him, the cords of his Walkman almost touching Robert's face.

'WAKE UP! WAKE UP! WE'VE ARRIVED IN MOSCOW!' he shouted loudly. Robert bolted up with a look of complete confusion until he saw Sebastian laughing hysterically, clutching his sides.

'*Connard!*' Robert shouted, and lunged at him with a pillow, but Sebastian ducked deftly out of the way and he crashed into the opposite bunk. Sebastian laughed harder and goaded him: 'Ooh, now I'm frightened,' he wailed in a high-pitched voice, mincing around on tiptoe, infuriatingly out of reach. Then Robert spotted the dregs of the Bison. He picked it up, cornered Sebastian, and poured the rest of the vodka over his head. They were both laughing now, tussling with each other and swearing.

'I had to do it,' Sebastian shouted, 'we couldn't stand the snoring any more.'

Serge and I flattened ourselves against the seats, out of reach, giggling in the corner. We stopped laughing when Yves burst through the door, looking stressed, and took in the uproar, very much minus a smile. He looked at Serge and me for an answer, but neither of us managed to explain. Yves gave an obligatory scowl, swore at Sebastian and Robert, then settled down on the opposite seat, clearly grateful for the excuse to get away from the cold war in the next-door cabin. When Robert dozed off again and Sebastian, Serge and Yves started playing cards, I climbed up to the top bunk for some peace. With the help of the Bison I'd indulged in I quickly fell asleep.

When I woke up, the landscape we were passing was lit by the silvery light of the very early morning. Beautiful in its bleakness, it slipped by like a dreamscape, so different from the landscape up North. I was the only person awake. It felt like paradise.

A few hours later the train stopped outside a town I'd never heard of. It was my first real glimpse of the South and I wish I remembered its name. We had '*cinq minutes*' at the station, so when I saw Serge getting up I followed. I climbed down onto the platform, blinked and inhaled. The light was completely different here from in Paris, a different smell in the air. Bright, almost peppery, like dry pine. It was another France – the pale stone red-roofed buildings were squatter, more human after the imposing slaty buildings I'd started to get used to. I headed for the *toilettes*, intent on brushing my teeth. As I was bending over the basin to rinse my mouth out, a very fat woman in a cotton button-down dress came into the bathroom, remarkable in that she was the first non-petite, non-coquette woman I could remember seeing since my arrival in France. I smiled a sisterly smile at her but she ignored me and shut herself into a toilet cubicle, banging the door behind her and issuing forth a volley of the most extraordinary lavatorial trumpeting sounds. I grinned to myself as I beat a quick retreat. It was proof that I had left Paris, and it was welcome; frankly, I doubted whether *Parisiennes* farted at all.

Out in the sunshine, the light roared down from the sky at me. I took another lungful of air, then it struck me. The quality of the light, the spicy plant smells were not unlike being out in the sun in the *veld* at home. *Fynbos.* It smelt like *fynbos.* I wondered what the Cape would have been like if the French had made it theirs – if they had dotted it with *boulangeries* and *épiceries* and modelled it on France? What would they have built in Cape Town, presented with landscape and a climate so unlike that of England or Holland whose realm it became?

From down the track Serge called to me, held out a paper cup and a small packet, and jerked his head towards the door of the train. We were moving again: next stop, Perpignan.

Fugue

- *Buy: depilatory cream*
- *Defn.* pisseuse: *young girl, adolescent*
- *Defn.* connard: *stupid individual – from con (female sex – vulva and vagina; why le?)*
- *Bruschetta Capri: tomato, cheese, tuna, capers, garlic, olives*
- *Sicilienne: anchovies, garlic, cheese, olives*
- *Perpignan: big, hot dusty station out of movie about hot French countryside*

Yves's family owned not one, but two ancient-looking creeper-clad houses in palely plastered stone, picturesquely run-down and lovely like a well-designed film set with their blue shutters and thick, baked-orange roof tiles. One arrived at the larger of the two houses first: the smaller one was more secluded and almost hidden from sight behind the larger, and the two houses appeared strung together by the haphazard looking Johnny-come-lately wiring running from roof to roof that seemed to be the local norm.

I got out of the car as soon as it came to a standstill, having travelled in undesirably close confines with the ever-fondling Patrice and Inge on the back seat, weighed down by luggage, while Véronique and Yves sat unencumbered like the parents in luxurious splendour in the front of the hired car. Since Yves's parents kept a car at the house, Serge, Robert and Sebastian were taking the bus and we were only hiring one car. I'd been panic-stricken when I was told about this arrangement and had tried to stick with Serge, but my attempts had been foiled by their misplaced Gallic gallantry: *naturally* the womenfolk would ride in the car.

Inge whooped with excitement and ran to the front door of the big house, and Patrice followed, smiling indulgently, with their bags. Yves opened the car door for Véronique, who sat impatiently in her seat until he did so, and shut it for her again once she'd climbed elegantly out. I hauled out my bag and joined the party at the front door. Yves unlocked the door with a satisfactorily large and ancient-looking key, and opened the house.

It was shuttered and pitch dark inside and it smelt like cool earth and lavender and lemon. Yves fumbled with the catches and threw open the shutters, and we saw that the doorway led into a huge main room, enormously high and open to the rafters, with dark wooden beams. There was a large open fireplace, several comfortable looking sofas and armchairs, and a vast table, long enough for an entire boarding house. Patrice did an impressed whistle and Inge swore in Swedish. A grin spread over my face. Yves remained matter-of-fact.

'You're up there, the back room,' Yves told Patrice and Inge, pointing up the staircase. They picked up their bags. I shouldered my bag again, eagerly awaiting directions.

'Not you,' said Yves. 'You're in the other house.'

'Oh.'

For some reason, something really *bad* I did in a previous life perhaps, Yves had decided to put me in the smaller house with himself and Véronique, away from all the others. All I needed was a hurricane or a plague to prevent us from leaving the house and my own private Sartrean dystopia would be complete. No doubt Yves didn't trust Serge's infamous venery and was keeping me out of harm's way, but frankly, my money was on Véronique as the more dangerous of the two. It was clear that she hated me, and hated me even more than she hated the rest of humanity, which was a considerable amount of hate for one (fairly petite) person. If only she hadn't come I might have been able to relax, to work on Yves about the teaching job. I indulged in a momentary fantasy about Véronique coming out in plague-type buboes and falling off a cliff, and had to stop myself from smiling.

Yves hauled Véronique's massive suitcase out of the boot and turned to look at me, noting with what looked like disapproval that I was already carrying my own baggage. Véronique stood huffily in the doorway of the smaller house, her hands on her slim hips and one elegantly sandalled foot forward, like a bad-tempered mannequin, waiting impatiently for Yves to bring her luggage inside. I traipsed in after him with my baggage like an unwanted child.

From the layout and contents of the smaller house I gathered that it was generally occupied by the grown-up contingent of large family parties, which made it all the more confusing that Yves had chosen to put me there. Perhaps it was because I was a last-minute addition to the party and had foiled his initial accommodation plans? It was clear that most of the congregating and living happened in the big house. The kitchen was small and basic, and a kitchen table with only two chairs was the only dining area in the house. The living room was also fairly small, with a straight-backed sofa and two chairs arranged around the open fireplace. It was quite obviously a place the chosen few adults retreated to, to read or sleep. Slightly in the shadow of the large house, and more or less hidden from the road, the small house was cooler and quieter – and threatened to be a lot more intimate. I was to be installed in the smaller upstairs bedroom, Véronique had been allocated the palatial upstairs suite, and Yves was taking the large, comfortable-looking bedroom his parents usually occupied, downstairs at the back of the house. There was a separate toilet upstairs, Yves said, but I would have to share the royal bathroom with Véronique, or trek across to the main house to use one of those. I had no doubt as to where I'd be abluting; Véronique and her bathroom would be left in peace.

Yves told me to wait and carried Véronique's luggage to her room. I heard snatches of an altercation about the water not being hot yet, followed by much angry theatrical sighing from Véronique. Then Yves backed out into the passage and came downstairs again. He strode over to me, grabbed my bag, jerked his head towards the staircase and led me upstairs.

'This will be your room.' He guided me into the dark room, groped past me for the light switch and flicked it on. His face was about a foot away from mine and he was smiling an oddly intense smile. Was he waiting for approval?

'Thank you,' I said, 'it's a lovely room.'

He did not move away. He screwed up his eyes and looked down his nose at me as though intent on trying to read something written in very fine print. I felt a flush of heat spread over my face and throat. He laughed at me, and there was something wolfish in him momentarily which caused a peculiar sensation in my guts.

'*Pas mal,*' he said, turning to look at the room. Not bad. Then he turned his look on me. My face felt like it had developed an instant tic. For a moment it seemed that he intended to come in, and I was about to stand aside and unblock the doorway when he turned away and walked back downstairs instead. I flopped with relief onto the bed and lay staring at the ceiling, wondering why Yves's presence threw me into such a spin ... which somehow made me think about Kurt. What should I think of the puzzle he'd sent me, of the public way in which he seemed to be trying to apologise? Or perhaps it was even a Kurtian declaration of love? And what was this 'mellowing' that the journalist spoke about? Far from intriguing me, the cryptic nature of Kurt's message and the single photograph irritated me with its refusal to commit. Since I had no idea what the Woman Happening entailed I was probably more in the dark about his feelings for me than anyone who'd been in his audience. Perhaps Jack could enlighten me, but I resented having to have my lover's messages decoded by a third party. 'Oh for fuck's sake,' I groaned out loud. Couldn't he just be straightforward for once?

I got up and opened the window. The view was a postcard patchwork of terracotta rooftops with the hills in the distance. Highly satisfactory. I shoved my luggage into a corner and went next door to the main house to find Inge and Patrice. For a while I stood in the main room, listening, then calling their names, but there was no answer. They were probably already trying out their holiday bed. So I took a quiet unguided tour around the ground floor. Behind the main room was an expansive kitchen, at the centre of which was a big wooden table. All sorts of rustic-looking implements and artefacts were in evidence. Pots hung on the walls, the floor was tiled in terracotta, and the ceiling had the same dark beams as the living room. The kitchen was 'country' without being twee. I poured myself a glass of water, yielded after much initial protest from the tap in the old sink, and sat down at the table, willing the others to arrive. Without Serge around I felt even more of an intruder, a feeling which only got worse when Yves walked into the kitchen and looked surprised to see me there.

'Oh,' he said, stopping momentarily in his tracks.

'It's a lovely place,' I said. For the third time since we'd arrived.

He did not deign to respond.

'When do you think the others will arrive?' I asked, pseudo-casually.

'Oh much later. They'll have stopped at the bar in the village.'

'Which bar?' I asked. Perhaps I could find them somehow.

Yves ignored me. But I persisted.

'Have they been here before?'

'No.'

Oh dear God ... what happened if they never showed up and I had to spend the next few weeks with the Absent Fornicators, The Suit and his Psycho Sidekick?

'Don't worry, they won't get lost,' he said with a hint of scorn.

'I wasn't thinking that ...' I began, but my protest trailed off into silence. Yves regarded me, head tilted back and on one side as he looked down his nose as usual.

'Are you the oldest child?' Yves asked.

I frowned. 'I'm the *only* child.'

'Hmm.'

'Why?'

He shook his head infuriatingly. 'Just asking.'

'But why?'

'Because you worry about everything, all the time. I thought you must be the oldest child – but the only child is worse.' I was about to quiz him on this tenuous theory but I kept quiet and drank my water instead, and he soon left me in peace.

That evening we were all exhausted, so Inge and Patrice concocted a simple pasta dish for dinner. Serge and the others were still not back. It was quiet without them, and I was beginning to feel decidedly uncomfortable. Then, late that night, just when I was starting to get really worried, there was a call from Robert. He and Serge and Sebastian were still in the bar and insisted on being fetched. Patrice left to fetch them in high spirits (and full of local wine) and only came back an hour later. I hung out of the window in my room, looking very unlike Rapunzel, and watched them all weaving arm in arm in arm up to the front door of the main house, singing some schmaltzy French ditty until Véronique leaned out of her window and shouted at them all to *fermer* their *gueules*.

It was already bright morning when I woke up, and the sun shone down fiercely. I took my blank new journal-to-be and went outside to explore. In the dappled light under the trees, I imagined myself as some kind of nineteenth-century heroine. I walked staring up into the canopy of branches, trying out a Manon des Sources expression, and literally stumbled into Yves. I let out a yelp of surprise, deeply embarrassed because he must have seen me with my Manon face on. He was smoking one of his usual stubby cigarettes and reading the newspaper under a tree, slightly out of place in his urban gear.

'Sorry sorry sorry!' I said, my heart pounding with adrenalin. Yves seemed to find it particularly amusing and began to smirk very irritatingly as I struggled to recover my composure and stave off a coronary.

'So you like it here,' he stated, smoking contentedly and scrutinising me.

I was trying to think of something to say when I heard Véronique calling him from the house. He didn't answer her call.

'I think Véronique's calling you,' I said gratuitously.

'I know she is,' he said, with a lopsided smile, 'but I can't hear.'

Coullioure

The day we went to the sea I took a chunk out of my shin while attempting to shave. I'd found the razor in the muck at the bottom of my toilet bag, and despite being disgustingly rusty it managed to slice off my flesh as cleanly and thickly as a piece of julienned carrot. I groaned and looked down my larva-white body to where the blood gushed with impressive copiousness from my still-hairy shin. I removed the sliver of flesh from the razor with a shudder of disgust and threw it into the drain, cursing the lack of a nearby pharmacy. There was nothing else for it: I would have to swim in an ankle-length kikoi like those Indian women in the Ganges and pretend that was how we did it back home. I limped out of the shower, applied enough bog roll to the wound to last a dysentery victim for a week, and prayed that the French sea did not have sharks in it. Someone was trying the door handle, but I'd barricaded the lockless door with a wash basket and a chair.

'Are you coming?' It was Inge. 'Yves is waiting in the car.'

'In a minute,' I shouted back, pulling my clothes on with frantic haste and plaiting my mad hair severely into submission. Then I removed the bathroom door barricade and emerged to join the impatient party.

We were travelling in two cars. Serge and Robert, cigarettes dangling from their lips, had wheeled the old 2CV out of the garage and were already on their way. Yves was driving us in the hired car. We seemed to be heading rather fast towards the narrow front gate.

'Careful!' I shouted shrilly as we sped closer. I couldn't stop myself. Instead of slowing down Yves sped up even more, and as we drove through there was a terrible thudding noise. I flinched in my seat and let out a yelp. Sebastian burst out laughing, raised his eyebrows at me and gave the door another slap to demonstrate his practical joke technique. Then he brought his arm back inside the car through the window and chucked me under the chin patronisingly. I looked at Inge for support, but she was too preoccupied to notice. Yves looked at me in the rear-view mirror and shook his head.

'I told you, you worry too much,' he said, annoyingly. He smiled a slow, teasing smile at me. I sat in the back of the car like a sullen child, resentfully trying to relax. Yves made my skin prickle. With irritation. Or maybe it was just the heat. I shook my head as if to shake loose the sensation and bent down to tend to the toilet paper on my wounded shin. It would be safer just to ignore him.

On the stony beach at Coullioure I sat in the sun next to Serge, watching him smoke and sketch contentedly. Sebastian and Robert were swimming, Yves was rummaging in one of the cars trying to find a picnic blanket he was *sure* he had brought, while Véronique stood by, arms folded, looking on imperiously, refusing to sit on thé pebbles. Inge and Patrice were arguing further down the beach. Suddenly Serge stopped sketching and put his arm around me, sliding it down surreptitiously so that it rested on my arse. My long skirt pulled up slightly, revealing the toilet paper and blood-encrusted gash.

'What happened to your leg?' he asked.

'Cut it shaving.'

Serge raised his eyebrows but said nothing. He looked out at Robert and Sebastian in the sea, turned to look at Yves still standing next to the car. Then he lit a cigarette and looked at me with a little smile.

'Have you thought about why he's keeping you in a separate house away from the rest of us?' he asked me, gesturing towards Yves.

I blushed and looked away, wondering whether he knew I'd guessed that it was Serge's own sexual proclivities which were the cause of my isolation. He seemed to read my mind, and he laughed at my discomfort and patted my bum. 'No no. It's not because of me. He wants you for himself.'

'Rubbish!' I protested. If that was the case Yves had an extraordinary way of showing it.

'Rubbish!' He mimicked in a mocking castrato voice, and laughed again. 'No, it is not rubbish. I'm very lazy. If I have to try too hard I move on. Of course I would like to take you to my bed, but you are a *leetle* bit *coincée, chérie*. I might be a pervert but I'm not a rapist.'

I had no comeback to offer, but Serge didn't seem to expect one. He picked up his sketchpad and hummed while he drew.

Coincéé? Where was my dictionary when I needed it? When Serge went to swim I went over and tried, as casually as possible, to ask Yves what the word meant. He actually laughed.

'Who called you *coincée*?' he asked.

'I didn't *say* someone called me that.'

'You didn't have to. Was it Serge?'

God, I hated his games sometimes.

'What does it *mean*?'

'Was it Serge?'

'Yes it was, okay? Now what does it mean?'

'It means, *ma petite*, that he doesn't know you quite as well as he thinks he does.'

Extremely irritating. I was obviously not going to get any clearer answer from Yves, so I asked Inge.

'Do you know what *coincée* means?' I sat next to her, prodding at the pebbles with a stick to avoid having to meet her eye.

'It means you are ...' (she gestured with her hand, curling the index finger and thumb into a circle, like an okay sign only tighter) '... you know what I mean?'

'Oh.' I got the picture. Uptight, constipated, prudish, tight-arsed. Thanks a lot, Serge!

'Why?' Inge asked. Then she took one look at my glum expression and burst out laughing.

'Let me guess ...' She mimicked a fortune-teller over a crystal ball, attempting a Romanian accent and opening her eyes really wide as if in a trance. 'I see a man with a really biiiiig nose approaching a pale, black-haired young woman,' she began, fondling an imaginary glass ball. 'He is asking her a question. I see her shaking her head ... she is saying no ... she is walking awayyyyy ...' She snapped out of it just as quickly as she had started.

'So you refuse to fuck a man and he calls you uptight,' she

summed up briskly in her own voice. 'Was it Serge?'

'Who else?' I said, dully.

'Well, Serge is not the only one.' I felt a rush of heat spread up my throat and neck.

'What do you mean?' I asked.

Inge rolled her eyes with exasperation. 'Oh, God, Clementina. Even you can't possibly be that naïve. I mean Yves, of course. It's obvious he's after you.'

'But Yves is with Véronique. I mean, isn't he?'

'She *wishes* he was. Anyway, that man would keep a harem full of women if he had half the chance. He's always been like that, even before his marriage fell apart. No one stays special for that long.' There was an edge of bitterness to her voice as she said this. It was only later that I realised she must once have counted herself amongst Yves's women and spoke from experience.

On the drive home we stopped at a market to buy supplies. Robert, chief foodie and the tallest of the party by at least a head, led the fresh produce mission, moving swiftly and expertly around the market with the battered but capacious basket he'd found in the kitchen. I trotted obediently next to him while he fondled the fruit and vegetables expertly, eyed out the cheeses and the glistening piles of olives and sampled with evident relish the dubious-looking sausage. There were bright, floridly blushing apricots, scented melons (I know because Robert gave me one to 'sneef'), luscious-looking figs, artichokes the size of my head and a range of strange vegetables I'd never even seen before. I'd been to markets in Paris but had felt too ignorant, too ill-equipped and too poor to venture buying anything unusual. Robert linked his arm loosely through mine and propelled me around the stalls, gesturing with fanatical eagerness at the produce, demanding samples and earnestly discussing recipes and techniques with the vendors, smiling his goofy smile. Clearly he was intent on educating me. After listening to him discuss the right way to cure boar sausage for at least ten minutes I left him to it. I wandered around the stalls, stopping on the way to 'sneef' an

extremely seductive array of *savons de Marseilles*, and slipped
into one of the shops nearby in search of something comforting
like depilatory cream, in case there were any more unexpected
trips to the sea in store. I was offered whole grilled chickens
(perfectly bronzed), quail's eggs, more of the same dubious-
looking sausage and all sorts of other culinary delights, but of
course I found nothing remotely resembling depilatory cream.
It was a hopeless quest. I gave up and bought some ridiculous
postcards from the tatty collection of miscellaneous *anciennes*
postcards – Bienvenu en Espagne, Paris: Cité des Amants (badly
dressed couple in seventies clothes), Carcassonne, Nice – for
Jack and Angus instead. I contemplated getting one for Kurt,
but I knew he wouldn't find them funny, and anyway I had
no idea what I'd say to him or even what to *think* about him.
For Angus I chose a postcard featuring a fabulously outdated
Technicolor photograph of a girl with dark plaits and rosy cheeks
in Provençal garb and clogs, grimly reminiscent of my frightful
milkmaid get-up all those years ago, fondling a goat. *La Belle
Provence* it said above this picturesque mountain couple. I jotted
down a message about 'remembrances of things past' and hoped
he got the allusion to our first meeting. On a postcard of a camp-
looking local displaying his artichokes at a market I wrote Jack
a quick note:

*Mayday, Mayday! Send depilatory cream! Jungle encroaching
rapidly and the shops around here totally medieval – all sell
organic vegetables, ammoniac cheese and chunks of donkey meat.
Will soon have to surrender and hang up bikini for good – pity
because bloody hot and beautiful sea around here. Am cohabiting
with motley crew – Serge and numerous friends – will inform you
– maybe you even know them. HOW ARE YOU?*

I slipped the cards into the postbox and went back to join the
others.

La vie en rosé

Ingredients for Toulouse-Lautrec's cassoulet – as prepared by Yves:

1.3kg white Soissons beans; 1.3kg boned mutton; 1 goose, boned and chopped into pieces; 3 large onions; 6 shallots; 4 cloves of garlic; 100g bacon; 1 veal knuckle; 100g smoked ham; 1 calf's foot; 1 truffled pig's foot; 400g coarse pork sausage; 800ml bouillon; 2 tbsp tomato paste; 1 bay leaf; parsley; salt and pepper.

Couldn't help imagining what poor Tamara would make of this – the whole zoo in one pot! Would not want to be a domestic animal in France.

There were a few unexpected customs in this little village. One of these was the tendency to announce the arrival of the greengrocer or seller of *charcuterie* over a booming Tannoy system loud enough to broadcast the message to the entire population of France in one go. No one warned me about this. The first time I heard such a message I had sneaked back to the toilet in the small house after breakfast (the one advantage of having my room there) and had just shut myself in and taken a seat when a brutally loud voice bellowed in at me through the second storey window, shocking me nearly into orbit. At first I couldn't make out the words. I shot to the window to check that the house wasn't under police siege and that Sebastian was not standing hanging onto the window sill with a megaphone in his hand, watching me on the loo. When I'd ruled out both options I sat down again, waiting for the heart palpitations to stop, and listened carefully to the repeated message. '*Le poissonnier est sur la place. Le poissonnier est sur la place. Terminé.*' It was the fishmonger's weekly visit to the village. Within minutes I heard a noisy shopping party emerge from the other house and head down, presumably, to the *place*.

Other than that, it would have been remarkably peaceful if it had not been for the presence of Serge, Sebastian and Robert, who formed an exhaustingly restless (though admittedly entertaining) combination. They did a special line in teasing, constantly played tricks on each other, and generally behaved like hyperactive eight-year-olds on a school summer camp, much of which was recorded by Patrice with his ever-present camera. I criticised them constantly, feigning disapproval as was expected from me, but I'm quite sure they were all quite aware of how charming their antics could be.

Every evening the kitchen was a site of struggle. Robert reigned supreme, head and shoulders above the kitchen plebs, perpetually whipping up something astonishing with his legendary culinary flourish. To me, used to digs specials such as Tuna Surprise or the occasional beetroot curry *à la* Angus, the unwavering focus on the purchase, preparation and consumption of food and wine seemed to verge on obsessive, grateful though I was to be fed and watered. Inge and I were exiled during the serious process of meal preparation, or relegated to chopping and peeling duty, but even that we couldn't seem to do satisfactorily. After a while I gave up pretending to help with the cooking and stuck to making drinks, though never in that *leetle* apron Serge had envisaged. Véronique, completely exempt from any quotidian duties, stretched out on the sofa and read her book, undisturbed, for hours, luxuriously feline in her self-indulgence. Her prolonged absence was a great relief to us all.

When we weren't shopping, cooking or eating we did a lot of reading, card-playing, and driving to the dam at the old mill, where we spent whole days swimming and lazing in the shade, drinking gallons of local rosé *vin de cave* that poured like petrol from the hoses at the local *cave co-operative* into our five-gallon plastic containers. I was taking a welcome break from being me, with a group of very friendly and familiar strangers who happily accepted this holiday persona. It was almost impossible to imagine going home. It was hard enough to imagine going back to Paris, and I had to 'practise' by thinking about it sometimes (running through the métro map in my mind, walking the streets, ordering food) just to remind myself that that would soon be my reality again. Sometimes I volunteered to do the morning walk to meet the bread van at the *place* to fetch breakfast supplies so that I'd have to speak French out loud. I began to dream, and daydream, in French, and I justified reading my frivolous French women's magazines in public on educational grounds, though such justification proved entirely unnecessary. Sebastian entertained us all one afternoon, showing off his comic flair by reading aloud (and adapting) a sex quiz in one of the magazines, and Inge shared my pulp-reading with unapologetic enjoyment. I wrote letters home, though none to Kurt: effusive ecstatic letters often under the influence of a few glasses of rosé, or after a mid-afternoon trip to the local café where they served up a mean lime diabolo. But it wasn't just the alcohol. I couldn't remember when last I had been so happy, so relaxed. I had fled real life, and so had everyone else. No one seemed to care whether I'd read all the right books, attended all the right rallies, hung out with all the right people. It was a glorious state of suspension and I vowed, as one probably always does, not to return to the angst-ridden, preoccupied state I'd been in before this trip. I decided to take a holiday from thoughts of Kurt and succeeded in banishing him from my mind most of the time.

In fact, it was almost paradise. Except for one small problem. Well, perhaps two. Véronique's presence (and her dislike of me despite my rather unctuous attempts to befriend her) was the minor problem. The other problem was more alarming. The other problem was Yves.

August 16, 1996

14:45
What is it with Yves? I can't make it out. He veers from friendliness one minute to ignoring me the next. Not that I care. It's

just confusing. And then there's the unwelcome siesta-fantasy situation. On the few occasions I've managed to doze off over my book during the general late-afternoon rest, I've ended up having lurid half-awake daydreams about being ... visited by him. I try to dispel regrettable images in a very rational manner, eg imagining him having sex with Véronique (just watching him slavishly applying suntan lotion to her back every morning is enough to make me sick), or reminding self what Inge said about his harem-gathering tendencies. The fact is, he's really not my sort and his sort really doesn't turn me on. Sometimes, in real life, I find myself wanting to be near him, and when I am near him I find myself fantasising about being even nearer. Odd, because I DON'T FIND HIM ATTRACTIVE. I don't.

15:07
But now have begun imagining that he's encouraging it, too. That he's staring at me from across the table and holding my gaze longer than he needs to. That he's deliberately touching me in passing. That Serge and Inge may just be right and that he does find me attractive. (God, how embarrassing. All this throws me back to early adolescence – awful.)

15:23
And anyway, even if he did want me it'd only be because he's a collector, and he sees me (very wrongly) as available and to be had, which of course is not the case as I'm still technically going out with Kurt. Aren't I?

15:37
If only Kurt had written me a proper letter I might not be entertaining these thoughts in the first place.

Driving with the snake

Note: Day in hell, despite rosé-tinted glasses

About two weeks into our holiday, during a typical rosé-saturated lunch with the 'Three Brides for Twice-As-Many Brothers' crew, Véronique cheered us all up enormously by announcing that she was obliged to return to Paris early. She seemed surprised when no one leapt at the chance of accompanying her to the travel agent in Perpignan to organise her flight.

'Who's coming with me?' she asked uninvitingly. There was an awkward silence, and out of the corner of my eye I saw Sebastian trying not to laugh. Véronique looked pointedly at Yves and waited for him to volunteer, but Yves was staring grimly down at his plate, eating with rapt concentration, practising passive resistance. I wondered with a secret pang of regret whether they might not be good for each other. I imagined them lying in bed dismally on a beautiful Sunday morning, side by side like the couple in the American Gothic painting of the unsmiling pair with the pitchfork, unable to start the day because each refused to make the coffee. When Véronique asked again and got no offers, the silence and suspense became unbearable. Perhaps this might be my chance to try to make friends with her. It also occurred to me that it would also be a way of ensuring that she left.

'I'll come with you,' I offered eventually, in my cheeriest voice. She looked at me with an incredulous half-sneer, as though I had entirely missed the plot, and didn't even grace me with an answer. I looked down at my plate, obscuring my blushing face behind a thatch of hair, and continued to eat.

After lunch I headed to my room with the rest of my glass of wine, and a headful of barely suppressed fury. How dare that woman humiliate me when I was making a kind offer? Sebastian followed me into the other house and (too closely) up the stairs making sexual groaning noises. I spun around and glared at him. With his springy body and his bouffant hair he reminded me of Zebedee in *The Magic Roundabout*. He grinned from under his wiggy hair and continued to follow me to the door of my room. I was not in the mood for games.

'Piss off, Sebastian, I'm going for a siesta,' I said, and I slipped inside my room and shut the door in his face. Silence. Then after about a minute I heard him sigh. 'I wish you slutty dreams,' he said, and walked away. Was it just Serge and his friends, or was the whole of France populated by sexual desperadoes? I could hear Yves and Véronique arguing in the room below and suddenly I felt exhausted. I threw myself across the width of the unmade bed and wrote Jack a note, in a foul mood and unfinished sentences, my writing getting progressively bigger and angrier and ending in an illegible scrawl:

Okay, it's beautiful. Now if only certain Frenchmen would stick to the goats and goatherdesses around here and leave luckless foreign women alone ... Trying to make friends with Véronique is like trying to cosy up to a snake. I'm sure she must have had a sex change, she just can't be a real woman.

I'd come to the end of the postcard and downed the rest of my wine.

Wine here délicieux, though, I scrawled up the side of the postcard next to the address, thinking it churlish to produce such a negative postcard from such a wonderful place. I must write Jack another proper letter soon.

As I was rereading my scrawl someone knocked loudly on the bedroom door and burst in before I could respond, just as I was scrambling to hide the postcard in my bag. I was amazed to see The Snake herself standing there, car keys in hand.

'You coming?' she demanded. I frowned, not quite sure how to take this. 'I'm sorry for being rude just now,' she blurted out belligerently, her eyes looking everywhere except at me. I couldn't help smiling to myself. She was behaving so like a spoilt child, ordered to apologise by a parent.

'Okay?' she asked aggressively.

'Okay,' I said. She stayed standing in the doorway, waiting for me, so I picked up my bag, slid on my clogs and followed her downstairs.

Patrice and Inge had headed off in the hired car that morning so we had to go in the 2CV, a fact that did not improve Véronique's mood. Yves brought the ancient car back out of the garage and opened the door for her. She climbed in regally without a word of thanks, checked her lipstick in the rear-view mirror and turned the key in the ignition before I had even had time to get in and shut my door properly. The car made a high-pitched whinnying sound and died. She turned the key again, more forcefully, and the engine leapt into action with a hideous clanking sound. Véronique took off with a series of alarming lurches, swearing at the state of the car.

'Are you trying to kill me?' she shouted viciously at Yves. Of course there were two of us in the car, but that trifling detail did not occur to Véronique. I looked into the rear-view mirror. Robert and Sebastian were laughing uncontrollably, bent double outside the house. Yves seemed to be trying to suppress an amused smile. We drove out of the gate in uncomfortable silence. Véronique sat with her nose in the air and did her best to ignore me.

A few minutes away from the house we reached the first of a series of almost vertical hills. Véronique hit the brake but the car kept careening down.

'Merde!' she screamed, stamping frantically at the pedal. We sped on towards the bottom of the hill, gathering momentum. My stomach lurched up into my throat.

'Change down!' I shouted at her, watching the trees flying by and the turn at the bottom of the hill approaching rapidly. I began to beg, in true agnostic fashion, beseeching every deity and force imaginable to help us, seeing in my mind's eye a loaded truck, a crocodile of school children …

'Change gears!' I shouted again. 'Use the handbrake!' We sped on. Suddenly a viewing site appeared at the side of the road. Véronique stamped hard and pulled the handbrake and the car skidded across the road and came to a halt on the clearing. She flopped forward and lay there, hysterical with fear, clutching at the steering wheel with her white-knuckled, perfectly manicured hands. Then she sat up and turned towards me.

'Stay away from Yves,' she screamed. I was flabbergasted. A near-death experience and this was all she could think about!

'You're wrong, Véronique,' I said, as if to a child. 'I'm not doing anything ... he's all yours.'

'Yes he is!' she shouted back, her painted lips curling fatly as she started to cry. Patches of her usual thick lipstick were coming off, revealing the slightly purple inside flesh of her mouth. Her lips looked like blotchy, badly dyed polony. It was an ugly sight. She must have known, because she turned away from me and cried at the view instead. I tried to think of something to say, but couldn't. So I got out of the car and started walking home to fetch someone, leaving her to ruin her make-up in peace.

It was uncharitable of them to laugh, but they did. I told Yves where it had happened and he called for a tow truck.

'*La pauvre*,' said Serge, putting his arms around me and hugging me closer than was strictly necessary. Yves gave Serge a black look.

'You must be in shock,' he said, and I realised I probably was.

'Let me pour you a glass of wine. I *know* how *délicieux* you find the wine here ...' Yves continued, in a teasingly insinuating tone. I stared at him, feeling a bit sweaty. There was something I wasn't quite getting. He laughed at my confusion and held out the goatherdess postcard. 'You shouldn't leave your letters lying around, you know. They could end up in the wrong hands. Or is that what you intended?'

'Where did you get that from?' I couldn't believe he'd gone into my room and taken it.

'You dropped it in the doorway in your rush to join "The Snake",' he smiled, waggling the card like bait so that I had to come towards him and snatch to get it away from him. It was excruciating to know he'd seen my comments about sex-crazed Frenchmen. I didn't want to imagine what he'd thought of that. As I grabbed the postcard he caught my hand and held me there, staring at me and grinning.

'How you are tortured,' he teased. He released my hand a little, and as I was about to take it away he scratched the flesh of my palm with his middle finger. It was the tiniest, subtlest, most lewdly erotic gesture, a signal instinctively understood. I blinked in astonishment. But he was laughing.

Véronique laid into the lot of us that evening. She ranted at Patrice and Inge for taking the hired car in the first place. Inge pointed out that they had asked everybody if it was okay and that if Véronique only got up at midday she could hardly expect to be consulted. So she turned on Yves: he was totally irresponsible to let her drive in a car like that! Imagine if she'd been killed! Everyone fell silent, so when Sebastian failed to stifle a laugh it came out like an explosion.

'What is it?' Robert asked.

'Nothing.'

'Come on, Seb.'

And Sebastian couldn't resist enacting a quick sketch of Véronique speeding brakeless down a hill, complete with a brilliant imitation of her voice, sound effects and hilarious facial expressions. By the end of it everyone except Véronique was in hysterics. I tried to contain myself but it was impossible. Véronique went ballistic. She stood up from her chair, screamed her lungs out and threw her glass against the opposite wall. Then she ran, still screaming, out of the room. Yves glanced around the table at us, pulled the corners of his mouth down in an 'oh shit' expression and followed her upstairs to the bathroom. The rest of us sat in silence, listening. There was a lot of shouting and, intermittently, the sound of objects being thrown around or broken upstairs. Then, after a while, silence. Silence, then almost inaudibly initially, the sound of sex, detected (of course) by Serge, whose ears seemed to be especially tuned to pick it up. It seemed his nose was not his only overdeveloped sensory organ.

'*Ah oui, c'est la seule solution*,' Serge said philosophically.

'It's the only way.'

'You really can be disgusting, you know,' Inge said, scraping her chair back and standing up. 'I'm going to bed.'

So there it was. The Snake had 'had him' after all. And to think that for a moment I had flattered myself into believing that Yves had actually been flirting with *me*. It was deeply humiliating. Perhaps I had misinterpreted his behaviour towards me, which meant that Inge and Serge had both misread it too. Or perhaps they'd just been teasing me, and I'd secretly, vainly, taken them seriously? But that was too embarrassing to contemplate. I laughed wanly at myself, at my adolescent musings. Perhaps luck was on my side, leading me away from temptation … At least this way I was no longer a threat to Véronique and it might be more feasible to approach Yves about the job again. Yes, it was the best thing that could have happened, I reassured myself.

Later, safely alone in my bedroom, I began a quick letter to Jack.

Dear Jack

Ha! You were wrong! The Suit and The Snake just got it together noisily during supper today, so so much for your predictions … Anyway I'm very happy about it. Now I can get some peace …

There was a knock on the door.

'Yes?'

The knocker hesitated then came in. It was Yves.

'Hello,' he said.

'Hello,' I said in my coldest, most matter-of-fact bank manager voice, calmly turning the postcard upside down to conceal what I'd been writing.

'Véronique leaves the day after tomorrow,' he told me, apropos of nothing.

'Oh.'

'I thought you'd be glad.'

I shrugged and pulled a 'so what' mouth. I wasn't sure why he'd come. To explain himself? To apologise? To deny it?

'Do you have everything you need?' he asked, reverting ridiculously to playing the perfect host as if he hadn't been rogering The Snake in the bathroom a moment before.

'Yes, of course,' I said coolly, 'and now you do too, it seems.' He hovered uncomfortably. I relished it.

'Okay, *bonne nuit*,' he said.

'Good night,' I replied, and feigned a sudden and intense interest in the objects in my handbag. He didn't leave and I finally looked up. He looked as if he were weighing something up, trying to say something. He said nothing. Eventually he just did a strange little smile and left.

Once Véronique had left (and we'd all finished playing porter or maidservant in her own private little movie) the atmosphere became instantaneously festive. We had stumbled willingly under the extraordinary weight of her baggage as we carried it to the car, we had showered her with last-minute snacks and Badoit – out of relief and as offerings to the great god of the aeroplane who would soon bear her away – and now we were finally released from general flunkeydom in the Kingdom of Véronique. Inge whooped as Yves drove the car off, bearing Véronique to the airport, and I grinned guiltily.

'*Au revoir, les parents*,' Sebastian joked, smiling and waving frantically. There was an audible, communal sigh of relief. Once the car had driven out of sight Sebastian went to put some music on the sound system. The party had started.

Carnavalesque

As soon as Yves returned from the airport he suggested I move into Véronique's suite. But I had no desire to fill the space she'd so recently vacated.

'Why don't Inge and Patrice move in there?' I asked. 'It's such a huge room anyway.'

Yves looked nonplussed by this suggestion. 'They are fine where they are. And besides, Inge's only here for another three days.' I had forgotten she was leaving. She'd told me at the beginning of the holiday and it seemed so far away then.

'I'm fine where I am, Yves,' I told him. 'Unless you want the house to yourself?'

He rolled his eyes and looked away, snorting with derision.

Perhaps I'd speak to the others and swap with one of them. I had no desire to be alone in the small house with Yves. No desire at all.

But there was no chance for sober discussion when I went into the main house that evening. There was an awful lot of noise, and Sebastian was providing some pre-dinner entertainment for Robert, Yves and Serge, dancing suggestively with a broom in the middle of the room, occasionally crooning into it like a microphone and mincing about in a pair of skimpy black underpants. I laughed until I realised they were *my* underpants! The idea was not very palatable.

'Take them off!' I shouted.

'*Volontiers!*' said Sebastian suggestively, and tweaked the side of the underpants down stripshow-style to uproarious laughter and encouragement from the others. Even Yves was smiling.

'No!' Too late I realised the foolishness of my instruction. I ran laughing out of the room and Sebastian mounted the broom and charged after me through the house, an absurd French farce. He cornered me in the bathroom and brandished his broomstick at me suggestively.

'Enough!' I screeched, and ran back to the safety of the others.

'*Ah oui, la vierge sauvage,*' Yves muttered with a patronising look.

'What?'

'The wild virgin. That's your type.'

'It was a *game*, Yves.' For some reason I felt I had to defend myself.

'You like games, don't you?' he shot me a lopsided smile.

'No I don't, in general.'

Yves did a snorting laugh. I turned my back on him, flopped down on the comfortable sofa formerly dominated by Véronique, and pretended to be engrossed in Stendhal. It was too hot in there. I wished I could clear my head; it felt crowded with people, and thoughts, and sensations, all of which were unfamiliar and demanding.

Robert came over to the sofa and looked at me.

'Tonight we make *your* food.' I was puzzled.

'We make *bréflisse*,' he said, grinning. I still didn't get it.

'*Bréflisse, comme chez vous* in South Africa,' he said enthusiastically, doing a *braai* grid and tongs charade.

'*Braaivleis!*' I couldn't remember when last we'd had a *braai* at home, nor did I have the faintest idea about *braaiing* meat, but I was touched by his gesture. Of course with Véronique gone and Inge virtually grafted onto Patrice I was the only woman towards whom they could direct their gallantry and their teasing, this strange and unfamiliar breed of men. They began to stack wood inexpertly in a kind of artistic pile and tried to set fire to it. It was a pathetic excuse for a fire but their ineptitude was endearing.

'*Merde!* We need more wood,' said Yves, poking at the smouldering wood with a log. 'Which one of you drunken lazy bastards will come and help me?' he asked his dear friends. Predictably, everyone ignored him.

'Clémence?' he half-shouted. And I followed him out obligingly like a girl scout.

The shed was stacked to the ceiling with logs like some realist pastoral scene by Thomas Hardy. As I bent over to scoop up some logs I could feel Yves come up behind me. I ignored him and started stacking logs into my arms, but I could feel him looking at me. My body pulsed hotly.

'What?' I said crossly, too nervous to look around. Absurdly I pretended to be absorbed by my wood collection activities.

'You *do* like games, don't you?' He moved closer to me. He smelt of woodsmoke and Gauloise and some sort of limey men's cologne. I stopped pretending to gather wood.

'I don't like your games, Yves.'

'Yes you do.' He grabbed my arm, turned me around and pushed me up against the wall of the shed.

'Tell me you don't like this,' he said, kissing me fiercely on the mouth and neck, his knee pushing up between my legs, so that my loins rose up and shrieked for more. I pushed him away roughly and he stumbled over some logs on the floor and fell against the tool shelf. He rubbed his wounded back and stood there, fuming, then turned away from me and, rather absurdly, paced the one stride to the other side of the small room, his body tense with anger. Suddenly I found I was shouting.

'What is *wrong* with you? Véronique left a few *hours* ago! Perhaps you've forgotten? She was the elegant one with lots of lipstick who you've been fucking?'

'I *never* want Véronique,' he interjected violently. 'I had to. It was charity. Clémence, life is not so *seemple* ...' He walked up and down the room and then came back, calmer now, and stationed himself in front of me.

'You know I want you ...'

'I didn't, actually.'

'You lie to yourself, Clémence. You play games. And I know you always want me.' Passion did nothing for his grammar. Suddenly I had to stop myself from giggling. Yves misinterpreted my smile as encouragement and came over to me, fondling me with his voice.

'Why do you keep throwing things in our way? What are you scared of? I have a *préservatif* if you are not taking the pill.'

'That's not the *point*! I *am* on the pill as it happens and that's because I am *involved* with someone in a *relationship*,' I said insistently, my voice rising and falling emphatically with school-marmish righteous indignation.

'With who? With who you are in a relationship? Hmmh?' He gestured dramatically, searching the empty air around us with his outstretched hands.

'I told you. He is at home.'

'In South Africa? Then why are you here? No one's *bite* is long enough to reach you all the way from there, not even mine.' He fiddled with his lighter, shaking his head, then looked straight into my eyes.

'*Chérie,* you drive me mad. You are *farouche*. You know that word?' I shook my head. 'It means you are savage and timid at once.' He grabbed a pile of wood and turned to leave. 'Tell me when you change your mind,' he said with a cool smile. 'If you're lucky I may still be interested.'

It was not the most relaxing '*bréflisse*' I had ever been to. Yves clearly had no trouble pretending nothing had happened, and I tried to do the same. I suspected that for Yves the brief scuffle in the woodshed didn't even feature on the Richter scale of gropes, whatever he protested, and I felt humiliated. Did he think he could work his way through every woman around without encountering any resistance? I knew he couldn't want me, I was just leftovers now that Véronique had gone. The man was a walking dong, he'd settle for anything. He'd been nothing but scornful to me in Paris, where he was spoilt for choice by an oversupply of tastefully groomed and well-behaved potential fuck-things, and Inge had *told* me he was a serial bonker. Out here it was me or the goats, and most of the time he acted as though there was little to choose between us. I'd put back too much wine and my thoughts were getting maudlin. I wished I could confide in someone about the woodshed incident, but I suspected that Inge still had strong vestigial feelings for Yves, however much she might deny it. As soon as I could I went to bed.

Alone in my room, I lay thinking through the incident again, trying to work it all out. To my shame I discovered that however humiliated I felt, I was undeniably turned on. My hand roamed exploratively around under the blankets and I tried very hard to imagine it was Kurt's hand, but Yves's cynical smile kept intruding. This was not good. I sat up in bed, switched on the light to dispel the fantasy and gave myself a good talking-to. Then I invented a conversation between myself and Virtual Jack.

Clem to Virtual Jack: 'Not much to report,' I fibbed. But I knew I wouldn't be able to resist telling Jack about the woodshed, so I did.

'You'll be proud to know that I pushed him away and scolded him like a school marm,' I imagined myself saying.

Virtual Jack's response was not very helpful.

'Proud? Proud?' (he replied in absentia) 'You've been lusting after that …'

'Oh shut up,' I groaned out loud.

The conversation was getting me nowhere. I opened my copy of *Le Rouge et le Noir* and turned to the next chapter. The English quotation leapt out at me, initially for its Englishness but as soon as I read it, for its uncanny pertinence. It was from *The Tempest*:

> *Do not give dalliance too much the rein: the strongest oaths are straw*
> *To the fire i' the blood.*

A flush of heat spread up through my body. I felt as though I'd been found out. It felt like a personal warning. I must do something. I grabbed some paper and in my drunken state I started a mawkish letter to Kurt – an appeal veiled in endearments: *I miss you too*, I wrote, *There's so much I want to talk to you about …* It was all true, but the tenderness disguised a mounting sense of desperation. What I really was doing was making a last-ditch attempt at getting him to make a decision for me. 'Claim me!' the letter shouted. 'Love me. Stop me from leaping into bed with any number of permanently available and appealing foreigners who flatter me with their attentions as though I were the only woman in the world!' But deep down I think I knew it was too late for him to make us work, and my tenderness was a nostalgia for something that had already passed.

Yves didn't try to jump me again, and I didn't know whether to feel relieved or disappointed. He was the picture of hospitable politeness – impressively diplomatic and dignified. I wondered whether it simply didn't affect him. *Obviously* I was nothing special, but I thought he'd at least be slightly upset because he didn't get his way. Perhaps he was already planning his next conquest in Paris? One thing I never imagined at the time was that Yves could be hurt by my rejection. Humiliated, perhaps, or inconvenienced, but surely not hurt?

That Sunday Patrice, Robert, Serge and Sebastian decided to go fishing. Inge and I stayed behind to read, and Yves claimed he had to visit some neighbours.

'You coming?' Serge asked me a final time. I shook my head. Serge stared at me as if trying to read my intentions, then ran off to the car, whooping like a schoolboy. It could not have been a better arrangement. I had been longing to spend some time with Inge and also hoped to get an opportunity to discuss the job issue with Yves now that any romantic possibilities between us had been pragmatically ruled out. Inge and I were reading outside when Yves came down. He was smartly dressed in dark clothes – the picture of a good son from a good family.

'*Fy fan*, you look smart,' Inge exclaimed, lapsing into Swedish in her amazement. 'Are you going to a funeral?'

'Mass,' said Yves. 'I have to show my face.'

Inge drove us off in the 2CV (now more controllable after some time with the mechanic) and stopped on the dirt road some distance away from the church so that (as Inge put it) 'no one sees your loose foreign girlfriends'. It was a beautiful old stone building, lovingly tended and topped by a curly iron campanile like all the others in the area. I was curious to attend the mass, but this was clearly not an option.

'I'll walk home,' he told us. 'Enjoy your drive.'

Yves walked off towards the church on the dusty dirt road in his dark suit, a hero in some Spanish art movie. He didn't look back, which was a pity. It would have been a beautiful mental photograph. When he reached the door of the church, Inge started the car and we drove off.

Driving along a back road we passed on old hippy perched fatly on his moped. He had a big moustache, a faded psychedelic logo on the back of his leather jacket and a little helmet perched on top of his head.

'Getafix,' said Inge.

'I'm sure that's his intention,' I joked. I was thrilled by the liberation of being alone and unscrutinised with Inge, pottering along in the sunshine.

'All he needs is some horns on the helmet ... and maybe a menhir on the back of his moped,' I added.

We were both laughing, happy – a cheerful rural French take on Thelma and Louise. What a change from my last trip in the 2CV! I wondered what Véronique was doing in Paris and it seemed Inge was thinking about her too.

'Poor Yves. He's really in Véronique's clutches now,' she said, looking more amused than pitying.

'What do you mean?' I tried to sound quite casual.

'Working at her father's school and now fucking his daughter.'

'What do you mean, "her father's school"?'

'Surely you know? Véronique's father is the principal of the school they both work at. He's a real bastard, but she has him round her little finger.'

'I didn't know.' That partly explained why Yves tiptoed around her like he did, why she had such a hold over him. My spirits sank. It was dismal. If Véronique was the Snake in my fantastical Eden, her father had just turned out to be Satan himself.

That night the phone rang in the middle of a particularly animated game of Black Bitch. Yves tore himself away reluctantly, threatening a painful death to anyone who contemplated cheating in his absence. It was Véronique. The Black Bitch herself. Yves pulled the phone into the next room and spoke dully into it. He re-emerged a few minutes later looking decidedly more subdued and well-behaved. I thought about Véronique, comfortably en-sconced back in Paris, pulling the strings in my life even from there. I thought about the teaching job and the anger welled up inside me. Why had I not explored other options? The 'holiday' was nearly over. Inge was flying back to Sweden the next day. The reality of joblessness in Paris was looming. I knew it was stupid but the question was out before I could stop myself.

'Yves, does all this mean my teaching job is totally off the cards?'

'What do you mean, "off the cards"?'

'You know, that it's not going to happen … that there's no chance that I'll be able to work there?'

'There *is* a chance. I will personally speak to the director.' His bravura and his dishonesty irritated me.

'You mean Véronique's father?'

He looked at me, eyes narrowed. 'Yes.'

'Will you?'

'I said I will.'

'When we get back to Paris?'

'Yes,' he said, exasperated, 'I will speak to him.'

So I felt a little better. I'd done what I could.

In my mind I prepared for Paris. Yves seemed preoccupied, distracted, and I hardly spoke to him at all. Just once he seemed on the verge of speaking to me alone. Shortly after I'd gone to bed one night I heard footsteps creaking down the wooden-floored passage towards my room. My eyes shot open. The footsteps stopped outside the door, and as I lay there, rigid with anticipation, I heard him sigh deeply. I pulled the sheet up to cover me, expecting him to come in, but he walked away. When

I saw him the next morning he was as remote as before, and I wondered if the nocturnal visit had been part of a dream ... or a fantasy. Whatever it had been it did not happen again. Yves and I spent the last few days in Caramany being politely distant to each other. To my relief and disappointment, the danger was over. Sadly, so was the holiday.

Back to reality

Get: new top, new personality, new job (well, a job would do), new life

Avoir le mal du pays: to be homesick
No letters from Kurt. Trying not to care.
Have relented and written to Jack requesting intelligence on Kurt and his 'Woman' Happening. What is he up to?

'Your friend phoned,' said Madame Rouillard. 'He wants you to phone him back.' She handed me a note with Yves's number on it. It must be about the job, I thought, excitement mounting however hard I tried to suppress it. I raced off to a phone booth and dialled the number.

'Clémence. I was hoping you could meet me for a drink.'
'Sure. When?'
'This evening? Seven o'clock?'
'Where?'
'I'll meet you at Madame Rouillard's.'
I wondered how to ask him what it was about, without asking.
'Is everyone else coming?'
'No, just me.'
'Okay, see you at seven.'
'Okay.'
I hesitated, but I couldn't help myself. I had to ask.
'Is it about the job?'

There was an ominous silence on the other end of the phone.

'Yves?'

'Yes, well, that's what I wanted to talk to you about ...'

'Yes?'

'It's difficult. I spoke to the director about it, and he said he would think about it, but then he must have spoken to Véronique.'

I was plunged into gloom. I said nothing, just left Yves to state what was already obvious.

'Clémence, I'm sorry. Véronique confronted me, really angry. You see, she was hoping that what happened that day between us on holiday would carry on here and when she realised it would not ... Well, when she realised it was you I wanted her father to employ, she went crazy. She told him that you were totally unqualified and that if he employed you she would leave.'

Silence.

'Clémence?'

'I'm here,' I said in a really small voice.

'I'm really sorry. I tried.'

'I know. Look, don't come this evening. It's fine.'

'I want to come.'

'Please don't. I don't want you to. I'll see you another time, okay?'

'Clémence ...'

'I must go, Yves. Bye.'

I put the phone down while he was still speaking and managed to get back to the apartment before I started to howl with misery and anger. I'd done it again. I'd foolishly pinned my hopes on this one possibility and now it was gone. I had virtually no money, no idea what I was going to do. It enraged me that Yves obeyed Véronique in this pathetic way: that with one tantrum she could destroy my hopes, my well-laid plans. I was enraged – by her, by him, but especially by myself. I should *never* have allowed myself to depend on him in the first place. And through all the anger I knew I was still attracted to him, which made me angrier yet. I wept until I'd hardened my resolve: the next day I would go out and find *myself* a job.

But when I went down to get my morning coffee Serge was already there, waiting for me. I set my jaw and tried to be brave.

'You look so sad, *chérie*.'

'Bad night, bad news. But I'm sure you know that already. I presume that's why you're here.'

'Yves told me.'

I glared out at the passers-by over my coffee, being strong. I knew it was a bit unfair of me to speak to Serge in this mean-spirited way, but it was the only way I could hold myself together.

'Hho la la, *chérie*, you are a very angry woman.'

'Yes.'

'You know it's not his fault. He's really upset that he let you down. Really upset. The thing with Véronique only happened because ... well it was ... how you say ... *inévitable*?'

'Inevitable. Yes, well maybe it was. I just wish I'd realised that earlier.'

'He really likes you, you know. And I know you like him.'

I glared at him, astonished. 'I don't care about him and Véronique! I'm upset about the job, Serge. It's the fact that he's fucking the director's daughter and now my chance of a job is gone and I'm in the shit with no money. *That's* what bothers me. Jesus, all you guys seem to think about is sex – you'd swear it was the local currency.'

Serge ignored my protestation.

'What happened with Véronique was – a mistake ... a moment of weakness on his part, which he very much regrets. She has been chasing him for so long, *sans cesse*, and of course she has power over him through her father. Yves and Véronique know each other since high school, you know. I think their parents always expected they'd marry one day. There's a lot of pressure, important families. And then when Anne became pregnant Yves married her but the parents still didn't give up.'

It was strange to think of Yves even having parents, let alone being bludgeoned into a miserable shotgun marriage. I thought about him wandering off to Mass dutifully in his sombre suit and realised I'd had a glimpse into the other life of Yves. Perhaps he'd knocked this Anne woman up on purpose to save himself from The Snake. Who could blame him for that?

'That day in Caramany he was drunk and trying to calm her and it just happened.' Serge's insistence made me suspicious. Why was he selling Yves to me in this way?

'Did he send you here to say all this?'

'*Chérrrie!* It's not good for a person to be so angry. Of course he didn't send me. He's my friend and he made a mistake. He's very unhappy because he likes you very much. And I like him. And you. That's all.'

'Well thanks for telling me, but it doesn't really help.'

'I know that. I'm going to speak to a friend who has a restaurant ...'

'No don't. Definitely *do not*. If there's one thing I know after all this it's that I have to stop relying on other people.'

'We both look, okay? And I only tell you if it's definite?'

'Okay.'

Serge's persistent kindness floored me. I could see he felt really bad about my distress, which distressed me even more, but I was resolved: I'd sort myself out. When he left I went straight off to the American Church noticeboards to see what work was on offer, scolding myself every step of the way for not having done it when I first arrived. Still, when I thought about it, I'd experienced this place in ways I would never have expected by entrusting myself into the care of Serge and his friends. They certainly seemed to care about me more than Kurt did, I thought bitterly. Obviously his last missive had been nothing more than an apology after all, an olive branch, and he saw no need to communicate with me any more. Fine. So be it. Wasn't that why I'd left Cape Town and come here in the first place? I may not have a lover or a job, but here I was in Paris, walking towards the Church along the sunny Quai d'Orsay watching the passers-by. I allowed myself a smug little smile. Perhaps I'd gone through all my initiation rites; now it was time to take my place in the clan.

Yves on his knees

I suppose I must have been dreaming about him because when there was a knock at the door, later that night, I knew it was going to be Yves. I opened the door hesitantly and stood there as if I wasn't sure whether I was going to let him in.

'May I?' he asked me. He looked quite rattled. I said nothing, just stood aside to let him in, arms folded defensively in front of me.

Let him sweat.

And he did. For a while I denied my every good-girl instinct to offer a greeting, a drink, or even a chair. Eventually he went and perched on the back of the sofa and looked at me. I didn't say anything, just gave him what I hoped was a really aloof look and raised my eyebrows, waiting for him to speak. Eventually he sighed and smiled lopsidedly at me, teasing.

'I am very sorry I fuck her.'

'Fuck*ed* her,' I corrected him.

'Fucked her.'

'Yes. Past tense. Or so you claim. And I really don't see why you're apologising to me in the first place.' God. I amazed myself. I sounded just like Claude with that pompous marmish voice. Yves looked lost and confused and that was fine with me. I'd turned into Maggie Smith in *The Prime of Miss Jean Brodie*: hot pants under armour plating, prissy and prudish as hell.

'I am sorry not for fucking Véronique. I am sorry because I did it because of her father and because she insisted and not because I wanted to.' It was in the same kind of bizarre league of non-apologies I was used to hearing from Kurt and it got my back up.

'I told you, I don't even know why you're telling me this,' I snapped.

He looked at me and smiled.

'You would make a good teacher. Very *stricte*.'

'Yes, you're right. I *would* have made a good teacher. But you and your prick and that snake Véronique managed to fuck that one up for me, didn't you?' I turned my back on him and pretended to be absorbed by the laundry in the basin. He came up and stood just behind me, his hands on my shoulders, his lips nuzzling my hair. 'Let me make it better,' he purred, 'please?' I could feel the heat of his groin against me, and I'm afraid part of me screamed to be allowed to fuck his brains out there and then over that basin of soaking laundry, to fuck until I didn't have a thought in my own tired brain. Instead I pulled myself roughly out of his grasp and pushed him away, towards the door.

'Go away, Yves,' I said, struggling to keep my voice even, 'you and your overused prick would only make things worse.'

He kissed me on each cheek and left, reluctantly.

Serge arrived again the next day. We sat in the apartment with all the windows open and shared a bottle of wine. I'd found a potential waitressing job that morning, so it seemed I might be able to avoid complete financial ruin. I was also still glowing with pride after taking such a resolutely tough stand with Yves (and was midway through a triumphant letter to Jack to this effect), and between this feeling of smug satisfaction and the alcohol I was on good form – and kinder to poor Serge.

'I phoned my friend. He's still looking for someone to help in his restaurant,' he told me. 'One of his waitresses went on holiday to Monaco and never came back. He's had a lot of responses but he's looking for the right person.'

I must have looked unconvinced.

'He's very nice,' Serge assured me, *'très gentil.'*

'Actually I've seen one that looks good too. Someone who

wants a waitress either for short or long term, which means I could leave after a while if I found something else.' The word waitress stuck in my throat. I was embarrassed that I'd set out with such delusions of grandeur to start my set-painting career in Paris and was now reduced to begging for a waitressing job. I was just another English-speaking backpacker floating brokely around the city. In my letter I'd asked Jack to promise not to tell anyone – especially not Kurt – how things had worked out (or rather how they hadn't). I'd just have to reinvent that part of my story back home.

'My friend Thierry is also looking for someone temporary – or long term. It depends how it works out.'

Thierry. The name sounded familiar. I pulled the scrap of paper out of my wallet.

'Serge, is the name of your friend's restaurant by any chance La Rose Bleue?'

'That's it! La Rose Bleue. The same!' Serge turned to me in great excitement, put his hands on my shoulders and planted a kiss on my forehead. 'You will love Thierry, Clémence. He is a very good man, very kind. Tunisian.'

I was touched by Serge's enthusiasm, his obviously genuine relief that I was soon to be 'out of danger' and somehow still 'in his care'. Touched, but disappointed that I hadn't, just for once, done it all by myself. Still, it was a job. And with Serge's help I was more likely to get it. I had noticed how many of the slips with Thierry's number had already been torn off the page and hoped that he had not taken someone on already. Of course there was the minor drawback that I was an absolutely appalling waitress, even in English ...

Serge saw my wan expression and misread it.

'Don't worry, *chérie*. As soon as work comes up in the *décors* you will start there. It won't be for long.'

I went to meet Thierry at the restaurant the next day. La Rose Bleue was on a side road at the end of a steep trek up a cobbled hill near

the Notre-Dame de Lorette métro in the ninth *arrondissement*. I
lingered on the cobbles out of sight of the restaurant, waiting for
Serge to join me and take me in to meet Thierry. On either side of
the almost vertical road, merchants hawked their wares, noisily
trying to entice passers-by to their proudly laid-out produce. I
declined them all, smiling, and provoking from one young fish
merchant a comic, operatic charade of desperation, which made
me feel even perkier. I checked my reflection in a stationer's
window: not too bad, I thought, for a non-*Parisienne*. At the
turn-off into the road to the Rose Bleue, I stood looking around
me while I caught my breath. A fat old *dame* was reprimanding
a young child, her huge arms wobbling frighteningly with rage. I
laughed, then out of the corner of my eye I noticed Serge walking
towards me.

'*Salut, chérie,*' he said, planting three kisses on my cheeks,
and he led me into the side street towards the restaurant.

I liked Thierry immediately. He was a neat, compact, finely
built man, polite but kind-seeming. He spent most of his time
feeding his fluffy yellow-eyed black cat with finger-fulls of steak
tartare and quickly put me at ease. When something called him
away he moved with amazing speed and precision, avoiding
collision with the clients or his staff like a matador in the arena,
a skill mastered, no doubt, through years of being the perfect
inconspicuous host. With his tight bronzed physique he'd look
good in a matador's outfit too, I mused, or perhaps in an open
shirt on the cover of a dodgy Latin Love Song CD.

Thierry seemed unfazed by my assertion that this would not
be a long-term job for me and told me that he'd be happy to be
helped out until I found something more suitable. I was elated,
though it still struck me as rather sad that my expectations had
become so modest. That I should be elated about being deemed
fit for a waitressing job was something I didn't want to dwell on.
But then again, I would be a waitress *in Paris*.

I was to start the next day. Mission accomplished, Serge and I wove through the streets towards the Place Pigalle, peering into shop windows (increasingly disreputable as we approached Pigalle) jokingly in search of an 'outfit' for me for my new job. All around us there was cut-price sex for sale, and the streets were clotted with tourists bussed in to spend their money at the Moulin Rouge and the Folies Bergères. We rated some of the prostitutes in evidence, male and female, who were exhibiting themselves in the unglamorous daylight, and after violently disagreeing with each other's tastes we gave up on that and went to eat instead, to celebrate and to take advantage of the last of Serge's real free time before he started working in earnest on a new production. We ate what Serge insisted was authentic Parisian French food in some obscure and tiny restaurant near the Place Clichy. In a burst of touchingly patriotic sentimentality Serge described the 'sublime' music played here occasionally by a much-loved accordionist, who graced the faithfuls with nostalgic French songs. I nodded, straight-faced. Then we made rude jokes about the passers-by outside and smiled at each other a lot. It was not unlike being with Jack, I suppose, and I suddenly wanted to fling my arms around this unlikely fairy godfather in gratitude. Everything went into slow motion and some schmaltzy violins leapt into action. I stared through him, day-dreaming ...

'What is wrong?' he asked me, frowning at my expression.

'What?'

'You look strange.'

'I just wanted to say thank you ... to say how grateful I am for everything you've done for me.'

Serge looked at me with some concern.

'You sure you're all right?' he asked me, his hand on my arm. I put my hand on his and squeezed it. Then I leaned forward and kissed him on the cheek.

'You are a very strange girl, Clémence,' he told me, smiling and shaking his head. 'Maybe that's why I like you.'

When I got home that night I drank about twelve glasses of water and climbed into bed. I thought about the job I was about to start and the reality hit me. I was the worst and most reluctant waitress in the world and I was about to start a waitressing job in Paris. In French. I began to panic and wished I'd taken an *à la carte* menu home to study. Instead, I reached for my novel, crawled into someone else's life, and soon fell asleep.

La Rose Bleue

The first few weeks of working at La Rose Bleue revealed another Paris to me. A Paris of waking up each morning with a purpose, of reading on the métro and racing through the crowded pavements to get to work on time. Each weekday morning I took the métro from St-Paul to Notre-Dame de Lorette. I got so good at it I could walk down the underground and change métros at Concorde while still reading my folded *Libération* like any other real Parisian. Even though I could only understand about a quarter of what I was reading most of the time, it was worth it just for the thrill of belonging and feeling cool. The frantic summer had mellowed into something more autumnal, and the change in season suited my new mood of quiet contentedness. I loved the walk up the steep cobbled hill to the restaurant, loved buying twelve long baguettes and slinging them over my shoulder nonchalantly, loved playing the part. Despite the anxiety of speaking to the customers in French I was enjoying it – and learning quickly. Thierry was good to me, and although I missed Inge (and the wild antics of our holiday), I relished spending some time alone; alone and in control of this strange new life of mine.

One evening, after work, Serge arrived at La Rose Bleue with Sebastian and Patrice. Thierry welcomed them all, sang my praises (to my acute embarrassment), and brought out some excellent wine to celebrate. He shut the doors, put on his favourite Tunisian music and tried, unsuccessfully, to make me dance with him. It was an unexpected and festive night and we stayed up, talking, drinking and dancing, until I was virtually asleep in my chair. It was the best time I'd had since Caramany. It was bliss.

The next morning I woke up outrageously late. 08:55 the alarm clock said smugly. I dimly remembered defusing a bomb in my James Bond-heroine dream-persona and realised I must have switched off the alarm. I had no time to de-frizz my scary washed-and-slept-on hair so I pulled it up into a topknot and braced myself to confront the laundry crisis. After rifling among the discarded clothes on the floor and vainly searching the room for something clean, I gave up, threw myself into the same scary outfit as I'd worn two days before (entirely designed around said laundry crisis) and lurched out into the sunlight towards the métro.

I was decanting cheap wine from boxes into bottles just before lunch when Yves, with his usual immaculate sense of timing, arrived unexpectedly at the restaurant. I saw him talking to Thierry on the pavement outside and was instantly rendered speechless with mortification over my frightening physical appearance. It irked me hugely to discover that I cared about what I looked like in front of him. Perhaps it was just that my pride had already been wounded enough over the job issue, and it was just that I'd have preferred to be found glowing and triumphant rather than sweaty and badly dressed with hair like Struwwelpeter. Whatever it was, my insides were going crazy. For a moment I considered bolting out of the back door but it was too late. Yves walked in, looked me up and down in astonishment and said nothing. Then he blinked and shook his head.

'Never mind,' he said more to himself than to me. He held out his arms, pulled me towards him and kissed me on each cheek. 'I have a surprise for you,' he announced.

'I don't want your surprise, thank you,' I said coldly, but it seemed he had already charmed Thierry into letting me off early during their manly tête-à-tête on the pavement, and he managed to persuade me (too curious to resist) too. It was amazing. Yves seemed to get away with these things simply because he expected no contradiction.

He walked me through the hilly cobbled streets. It was quite exciting having been torn away from work on this warm afternoon and I began to imagine all sorts of wildly exciting treats in store for me. Then, all of a sudden, he said 'close your eyes'. He put his hands over my obediently closed eyes and led me through a door. When he took his hands away and I opened my eyes I was in the middle of a hairdressing salon. This was certainly a surprise. After my wild imaginings I was a bit disappointed, really. But it got worse. Once I had been straitjacketed in a chair under heaps of towels and plastic ponchos, the hairdresser approached me and inspected my hair, which was sticking out at wild angles after a day of being scrunched up in a topknot. She looked despondently across at Yves in the mirror above my head, lifted one lifeless, electrically frizzy lock and inhaled sharply between her teeth, as though the experience had caused her physical pain. Again she raised her eyes to Yves – in supplication, it seemed. Yves returned her smile, a raised eyebrow implying that she should get on with the job, and she walked off to prepare her scissors and potions.

'Yves, I'm not sure why you're doing this, but I can't afford it,' I whispered.

'Don't be such a Protestant,' he yelled at me. 'I told you this is my surprise. It is my *cadeau* for you. And I like to support my friend, she is a very good *styliste*.' He lowered his voice. 'I want also to say I'm sorry about Véronique. About the job. I made a *beeg* meestake.'

'That's fine. As you see, I have a job. I'm fine.' I stuck my chin out and tried to look proud and independent. It was difficult decked out in a plastic poncho and a deranged hairdo. Yves stared at me, frowning, then tipped his head back and grinned down his nose. The hairdresser-friend returned and ushered me off to a basin with a stagey sigh. While a depressed and downtrodden-looking woman shampooed my hair, Yves and the hairdresser-friend stood outside on the sunny pavement, smoking and chatting in a disconcertingly intimate way that made me suspect she had once been his hairdresser-lover rather than friend. I watched this out of the corner of my eye, my head still jammed backwards into the basin, then remembered that I didn't care about Yves or his love life, past or present, and concentrated on the head massage instead.

The hairdresser dropped her cigarette butt on the pavement and scrunched it underfoot. Then she came inside and shepherded me roughly back to the chair in front of the mirror.

'Pauline,' she shouted imperiously at the downtrodden one, who duly returned with a tray full of torture tools. Yves sat down casually in one of the 'husband's chairs', reading his newspaper and waiting. The hairdresser-friend stared expertly at my reflection in the mirror (and I stared nervously back at her), then took up her scissors and started to chop with frightening flourish. Hunks of my hair fell to the floor and I shot Yves a look of sheer panic. He shook his head, smiled, and put a finger to his lips as if to silence me.

Once she'd finished cutting she stepped back and inspected. I regarded my semi-shorn self dubiously, turning my head from side to side to assess the damage. Then she reached for the drier and a round brush, began to pull my remaining hair into some semblance of obedience and glued it into place with half a can of asphyxiating hairspray. So this was it. Instead of my usual A-frame thatch look, I now sported a short bob, cut just below the ears so that if framed my face like a pair of brackets. I looked stiffly frizz-free, sophisticated, glamorous and totally un-me. I felt miserable. At least Jack's wonderful René made me *feel* fabulous. I could sit in his arty antique barber's chair, drinking herb tea and looking like death, and René would prance around me, sucking in his cheeks, narrowing his eyes and looking at our reflection in the mirror: 'I'm thinking femme fatale, I'm thinking Juliette Binoche, I'm thinking Cher but *much* younger than she is now ...' Then he'd get to work, flattering me outrageously and *skindering* up a storm. It always worked: I'd walk out of there feeling as chic as a celeb. It was an infinitely more significant and long-lasting achievement than a mere hairdo, since hairdos degenerate after a couple of short-lived shampoo-advert minutes anyway.

The hairdresser-friend thrust a small hand mirror behind my head so I could see the back of the sleek helmet. The back was cut shorter than the front to leave my nape naked, and the heavily sprayed sides barely moved as I turned my head. I put my hand to it and it felt disturbingly crisp. I understood the effect they were trying to achieve – dark wings of hair that sweep forward over your cheek like a curtain titillatingly drawn – but I also knew that do's like this required maintenance, products, know-how and dedication that I was simply not equipped with. I smiled at the hairdresser and at Yves, who was looking at me approvingly, head tilted to one side, and tried to look grateful. Yves headed off with her to the till to pay and I overheard her mutter a kind of disclaimer: 'The best I can do.' She shrugged as if to say 'What do you expect?' but Yves smiled and told her it was perfect.

So there I sat, while Pauline the downtrodden relieved me of my plastic poncho, and I wondered how many such 'makeovers' Yves had organised in his time. Yves, this arrogant Pygmalion, this audacious Henry Higgins, wasn't interested in me. I was just his Doolittle, his raw material, his 'prisoner of the gutter' ripe for reformation. What I was looking at in the mirror was his creation.

We left the salon and stepped into the bright sunlight. I felt totally exposed and alien – who did people see when they looked at me?

'Now we'll have a drink,' he announced, leading me off down the street. 'I want to show off your new hairs.' Now that I was presentable. 'Hairs' indeed. Even his grammatical errors sounded obscene.

He eyed me appreciatively across the table as I sat there in my alien hairdo. 'Hmmm,' he said in a fondling tone of voice.

'What?' I asked snappily.

But he just laughed.

I carried on eating peanuts.

'How is Véronique?' I asked pointedly.

He rolled his eyeballs at me. 'Very happy fucking the son of her father's friend.'

'Hmm.' So this was news – if it was true, of course. I raised my eyebrows but made no real response.

'How is Robert?'

He looked at me for a long while, until I began to squirm. And then he spoke, not in his normal voice but in an alien, pillow-talk voice that sounded so strange that I thought he was joking – until I remembered the voice from the woodshed incident. The voice said:

'I think you should stop pretending you don't know I want to take you to bed. Come home with me.'

'No such thing as a free hairdo?' I asked him cynically. But Yves didn't seem to hear me. The presumption of the man! Did he think I would pay that dearly for this helmet?

'I have to leave,' I told him. I was exhausted after the night before and decided to stick to my principles rather than stick around. Besides, if I didn't tackle the laundry crisis soon I'd have to wear my sleeping bag to work. I got up and slipped some money for the drinks under my water glass. Yves frowned at me and shook his head, scraped back his chair and leaned forward to kiss me on each cheek.

Later, when I sorted the laundry, I found the drinks money in my pocket. He must have put it there when he kissed me goodbye.

The next morning I could no longer stand the rigidity or the smell of my new hair. I washed it and stepped out of the shower to be greeted in the mirror by an apparition in a semi-afro. I tried to pull the afro back into a topknot but it was now too short and layered and it sprung out of the clip defiantly. I looked like a rabid bouvier. This called for desperate measures. I pulled on

Kurt's beret and drew up a shopping list.

- clips
- hats
- scarves
- helmets/paper bags
- industrial strength hair gel

Alternatively: cut off head or die of embarrassment anyway.

But a few days later Yves pitched up again, before I'd even had time to go shopping. He looked at me in some confusion, noting that the recent hairdo was now unrecognisable and plastered back with a riot of clips, but sat down at the table and said nothing. He ordered a carafe of rosé and relished the fact that I had to serve him. When I could no longer avoid it I walked up to the table to take his food order. He looked me up and down, taking in my long-sleeved shirt and trousers.

'Why don't you ever wear nice little dresses like other women?' he asked me.

'The specials today are lamb tajine and dorado,' I responded.

He laughed at me.

'Is the tajine good?' he asked, and tutted when I told him I hadn't tasted it. Thierry was watching me and I wanted to get away, but Yves continued his interrogation.

'Is the fish served with a *brandade*?' he asked me. I frowned, panicking inwardly as I tried to work out what he meant, then gave in.

'What's a *brandade*?' I asked. He looked at me incredulously. 'You work in a restaurant and you don't even know what a *brandade* is?'

'Well so what? I mean you don't even know what *bobotie* is!' I countered ridiculously. Yves laughed.

'But we're in France, remember?' he said, amused by my

crossness. Then he just sat there looking at me for a moment while I got more and more uncomfortable. 'Maybe you can make me a *beau-beau-té* when I come to South Africa one day,' he said suggestively.

'Do you want the fish or not?' I spat.

'Not. I have come to invite you to dinner at my apartment on Saturday.'

I eyed him suspiciously.

'Don't look so worried, my little overdressed virgin,' he said in a patronising tone. 'Everyone you know will be there. You'll be safe.'

When I went for coffee, Madame Rouillard gave me a fax from Jack, and I nestled into a remote seat in a corner to savour it. He provided some highly satisfactory gossip about various students and staff, and then, inevitably, there was news of Kurt.

'The Thought Führer,' wrote Jack, *'appears to be having some form of midlife crisis. Of course I was compelled to attend his most recent artistic contribution in order to give you feedback, and I was all geared up for a giggle and a scoff but he was disappointingly sedate and even comprehensible. He called it* Woman, *though* Women *would have been more appropriate, and it was a bit of a tribute to all the women he's ever had the hots for, starting with his mother and passing through a miscellany of misses, ranging from Marlene Dietrich to some little girl called Olwyn who he seems to have interfered with in the treehouse when they were in nursery school together. He said some flattering things about you, extolling your virtues as a "thinking muse" no less, and splashed a rather adorable photograph of you all over the screens. He had the gall to call the Giraffe* Woman *a madonna, which I thought was a bit rich, I mean we're not even convinced she's a woman at all …'*

So it was 'women', was it? And I was referred to in the same breath as the Unmentionable One. Fuck fuck FUCK him for that! Perhaps he'd fired off cryptic little MENSA messages with the appropriate photographs to all the women he'd used. Suddenly I didn't care what he'd meant with his Hallmark message. I didn't care even if it was an attempt at an apology or a declaration of love. It was just too little, and way too late.

Prawn surprise

Brandade: *salt cod purée. That's it? Why do I constantly feel like the subject of some particularly erratic and challenging educational experiment?*

To do: search whole of Paris for miracle hair product
Failing that, buy wig.

That Saturday morning I cruised every cosmetic shop within a four-kilometre radius of the apartment for something to address the hair crisis and came away from the comforting Body Shop clutching something resembling superglue. The rest of the day I spent trying to apply this alarming substance to my hair and trying on various unsatisfactory outfits. I should have been revelling in the indulgent frivolity of my day off, but I was sick with anxiety. Everyone I knew in Paris would be at Yves's, and I looked forward to seeing them all again, but I couldn't help feeling restless. Nothing I did relaxed me. I lay on my bed trying to read but found I was rereading the same words perpetually, so I got up and went for a *citron pressé* at Madame Rouillard's. When she brought me my drink it was a lemonade, and when I politely told her she'd made a mistake she insisted that I'd ordered a lemonade and gave me a strange look. I shut up and drank it, unable to shake off the inexplicable feeling of unease.

Despite setting out early that evening I managed to arrive late at Yves's apartment. An hour late. He had given me his new address in a typically casual manner as though I had been living in Paris all my life and knew every back alley. *Beeeg* mistake. Once I got to the neighbourhood I spent at least three quarters of an hour retracing my steps, staring increasingly frantically at métro maps, and asking passers-by for what was surely the most obscure fucking address in all of Paris. The only number nine in this road was a hair salon. I started to feel a bit paranoid when I saw this. Was this his idea of a sense of humour? Was it a second attempt at remedying my disastrous hair? Was I the butt of some huge practical joke? Perhaps the whole road was rigged with cameras and I was being filmed for some dreadful French equivalent of *Candid Camera*. I pressed the button of the hair salon at number nine and walked away, deeply relieved, when there was no answer.

I finally found the place by mistake. I had given up and was about to head home when I was sidetracked by the clothes in a lit-up shop window. Next to the shop I noticed a small lane with the same name as the road I had been trudging over for the past half an hour and from then it was, as Yves had told me it would be, *très simple*.

Yves greeted me at the door and asked me with a teasing smile why I was late.

'I felt like walking,' I told him nonchalantly.

'You were lost,' he said loudly, with a big grin.

'I was *walking*,' I insisted, irritated now.

He looked at me curiously. 'You are very stubborn, my little *pisseuse*,' he said laughing. 'Do you know what that means? It means you are a leetle girl ...'

'I know what a *pisseuse* is, Yves, I found out. I was *walking*.'

'You English and your walking. Here people walk to get from one place to another. *Simple*.'

I didn't even bother to remind him that I wasn't English. By then I knew too well that he only called me English to provoke me.

Before I could greet anyone I was dispatched to the Chinese

supermarket with Robert, on prawn-buying duty. Since I was not allowed to carry the basket (and was hardly in a position to offer much advice on what to buy) I trailed along behind him investigating all the strange, unidentifiable merchandise on the shelves. It reminded me of curry shopping with Angus and I suddenly missed the familiarity of that friendship with an almost physical pain. Tomorrow I would phone. I longed to get the low-down on The Soup Kitchen, its scandals and intrigues. I longed to talk to Angus, to have a comfortable conversation about familiar things, without the constant jousting and teasing Yves and his friends seemed to go in for.

When Robert and I returned to the apartment he lamented the poor choice of music playing and decided to play DJ, thrusting the prawns at me and bounding urgently towards the music system to change the CD as if what was currently playing caused him untold suffering. The party was already in full swing. Sebastian had removed most of his clothing and was clumsily attempting to seduce some sweet-looking petite foreign girl with a gamine hairdo on the sofa. Yves floated around, proffering drinks, and I went through to the kitchen to watch Robert cook. I thought back to my cocktail-making spree with Inge and missed her terribly.

I remember little about the evening except a succession of glasses of red wine (increasingly bad as the night wore on) and plates piled high with Robert's *piquant* prawns. I woke up alone, fully clothed, in a strange bed in the middle of the night. It took me a moment to work out where I was, and as I did I realised how ill I felt. There was a demon in my stomach, trying to claw its way out, and in my head a symposium of Hare Krishnas chanted and clashed their cymbals in a religious frenzy.

'Bastard shitty French wine,' I groaned, but I couldn't understand how I felt so sick. Surely I hadn't drunk *that* much? I climbed out of bed and headed towards the bathroom, groaning with nausea. Yves and Robert were still sitting on the sofa, drinking and talking.

'*Ça va?*' Robert asked, catching sight of me as I passed. I shook my head and headed more swiftly for the bathroom, hand over mouth, reaching the toilet bowl just in time. I sat down on the edge of the bath, trembling and exhausted.

'Oh *Jaysus*,' I moaned. For a fleeting moment I wondered whether Yves had deliberately poisoned me, but I quickly dismissed that as too paranoid, even for me, and tried instead to work out what to do. How was I supposed to make it out of the bathroom, let alone home? This was ridiculous. After a while I heard the door to Robert's room open and close. I listened to the footsteps up the passage, the knock on the bathroom door, Yves's voice: 'Are you all right?'

'Yes,' I lied in an absurdly cheerful voice. 'I'll be out in a second.' I checked the toilet seat frantically to make sure I hadn't left any evidence, flushed it again for good measure, stuck some toothpaste in my mouth and tried a smile. A dull-eyed sick-looking leer came back at me from the mirror. 'Disappointing effort, Clementine,' I admonished my reflection. 'Must try harder.' I opened the bolt of the bathroom door and wobbled into Yves.

'*Putain!*' He swore. '*Chérie*, you look like a very sick person.'

'Mmm hmm. I'm sure I'll be fine. Do you think you could get a taxi for me?'

'Don't be silly, Clémence. You cannot go anywhere in that state. You are staying here.'

I started to protest and looked about for the phone but he gently turned my head to face him. 'What are you worried about? You will stay in my room ... I will sleep there on the divan. *Chérie, franchement* (he laughed, infuriatingly) at the moment I don't think you would *survive* any French lovemaking. I will not ... disturb you.'

Yves kept to his word. I woke up the next morning expecting to feel much improved after a night's chundering, but my head was in agony. Next to the bed Yves had put a glass of water and some headache tablets, and a note to say that he'd gone to do some work and I should stay as long as I wanted. I sat up in bed to take the pills and immediately felt a violent need to be sick. Throwing off the duvet I headed back to the bathroom, making it as far as the basin. I then spent a further twenty minutes with a plumber's mate and a chopstick trying to unblock the ridiculously narrow drainpipe in the basin, cursing French plumbing and terrified that Robert would need to use the bathroom and find it awash with prawny vomit. I had had hangovers before, but nothing like this. I felt as though the top of my skull might blow off any minute like a lid, and I was desperate to take one of the pills Yves had left me. I returned to his bed, hoping that if I lay very still for a long time the nausea might abate. After a while I wrenched myself into a sitting position. I took two of the headache tablets and (by force of habit, I assured myself) popped the 'Sunday' pill into my mouth and swallowed it too. Slowly I eased myself down into a sleeping position and managed to fall asleep.

I woke again some time later feeling like the Black Death was upon me. I stumbled into the bathroom in my undies and T-shirt, ricocheting off all the furniture as I passed, and was sick *again*. Thankfully there was nobody around, but I did not want to push my luck. For safety's sake I took a plastic washing tub and a toilet roll back to bed with me and eventually fell into a sweaty, fitful sleep.

Yves came back that evening with armfuls of supplies. He stood there producing baguettes, cheeses, Badoit and salad from his shopping bags: a retail magician. I tried some baguette (tentatively at first, as I did not want to vomit on Saviour Yves), then with gusto. Yves watched me, grinning with satisfaction, as I demolished half a baguette. 'Now some Badoit,' he said, passing me the bottle. 'Perfect remedy for *la gueule de bois*.' I thought it unlikely that a bottle of water could cure *this* hangover, but I was willing to try anything.

When I had finished eating he took a new toothbrush from one of the bags and passed it to me. I took it gratefully, shyly conscious of the intimacy of the gesture.

'Tonight I invite you to dinner with some friends,' he announced magnanimously.

'I don't know ...' I began, but he put his finger over my lips and shook his head. 'You can not live on baguette. You will feel much better in a few hours' time and it's a good restaurant. Now, I have a surprise,' he said. 'Shut your eyes.' Jesus. For a moment I feared his frightening hairdresser made house calls. I heard him walk down the passage and return with a paper packet. 'Open,' he instructed. I opened my eyes. Yves held out a square paper packet from a boutique. Inside was a long brick-red cotton dress with unfeasibly thin spaghetti straps and a plunging back tied skimpily together with the same thin straps. I was amazed. I had never received such a present in my life. From Claude I had received books for as long as I could remember. Kurt seldom bought presents since it conveniently contradicted his stand against the consumerist mentality of the herd, and Jack bought me beautiful, tasteful, practical presents such as lamps or wall hangings. The only gift I remembered ever getting from Angus was an inflatable sheep with a hole in the arse ('the ideal pet, don't you think?'), which he thought was utterly hilarious. My other university friends, all strapped for cash, exchanged pot plants or bottles of wine. This gave a whole new meaning to gift-giving. It was so thoughtfully, so sexily, so embarrassingly intended for me. I had not worn something so skimpy and insubstantial since I was about six!

'Thank you ...' I began refolding the dress, but he wagged his finger at me, tut-tutting.

'Put it on.'

There was no point in protesting. I got out of the bed and went through to the bathroom to change. I pulled the dress gingerly over my head, and as my head emerged from the red cocoon of fabric I saw him in the mirror, standing behind me in the doorway, watching shamelessly. I gave a small shout of fright but it didn't even seem to faze him that he had been watching me dress. He was absorbed in the dress itself, scrutinising the fall of it, the line of the fabric, the colour ... I looked at my reflection. The red straps across my pale back made it look like I'd indulged in a serious flagellation session: no doubt that would be an unexpected bonus to Yves. A day of puking had done little for my complexion, which was paler than ever, and the black rings under my eyes looked like an amateurish attempt at heroin chic, waifish, waxy and sad. An overgrown Orphan Annie looked back at me. To my horror, that's who I'd become in that beautiful, sexy, grown-up red dress that would have turned any other fucking woman in the whole of Paris (and possibly the world) into a Carmen, a Beatrice, at *least* a Lolita. This was my chance and I was failing miserably. Without my usual layers of anonymous black garb I was a shell-less snail. Shucked.

'Pity about the English shoes,' Yves said to me, glancing disdainfully down at my clogs. They sat neatly and obediently next to each other beside his bed.

'They are not English, Yves, and nor am I. They are Swedish and I ...'

'Same thing,' Yves said, with a dismissive wave and characteristic national arrogance. Same thing – not French, not *Parisienne*. He pulled my drooping shoulders back and slid his fingers under the thin straps to straighten them.

'Aah!' he exclaimed, looking down at the straps across my back. 'It looks like you have been wheeped with a verrry tiiiny wheep just here.' He began to trace the lines of the straps slowly with his finger. I tried to pull myself out of his grasp, but his hands on my shoulders simply swivelled me around to face him now.

'Already better,' he said to himself in French, half under his breath. He scrutinised me unabashedly.

'So much better. Why do you never wear such dresses – like other women?'

It was the second time he'd asked me the same question and I was beginning to get irritated.

'I don't feel right.'

'But why not? It looks so good.' He looked genuinely per-plexed. No doubt if Yves were a woman he'd parade around in as little as possible at all times.

'I feel too exposed ...'

Yves made a dismissive gesture and exhaled through his nose.

'You are so English,' he scoffed.

'And you are so French,' I retaliated.

'*Touché*,' he conceded, impressed.

I gave him a sassy look.

He kept his hands on my shoulders and it felt like way too long a time to be standing there saying nothing, just being stared at. I felt myself flush with embarrassment and ... something a bit more awkward to own up to. Ah yes, entrapment, the age-old stimulant. Yves was smiling wickedly now. I narrowed my eyes at him and was sure I could see images of unbridled lust and erotic pleasure spin past in front of his eyes like fruits in a slot machine. I pulled away and he laughed, relishing my awkwardness.

'You'll want to wash,' he told me, 'there's a ...'

But I was already pushing him out of the bathroom and closing the door.

A few minutes into my shower there was a knock on the (locked) door. 'Hang on,' I shouted, irritably finishing my shower. He could wait. I scoured the bathroom and then the cupboards for a towel. Shit. Just my luck. The only towel was a hand towel the size of a bloody face cloth. I went dripping to the door opened it a crack while attempting to hold the face cloth over my vitals, and looked out. No one there, but on the floor was a towel, a big fluffy towel, and on top of it another paper packet. I slid out a hand and pulled them into the bathroom, wrapping the generous towel around me luxuriantly. In the paper packet was a G-string – the smallest undergarment I had ever laid eyes on. Such garments I had only ever given the most cursory of glances. I'd regarded them, flaunting their lacy minimalism on their tiny hangers in the shops, as a man might regard a rack full of assorted tampons; as curiously intimate objects one would never oneself use. But they were brand new and (despite feeling rather curious between the cheeks, as if something were stuck there) they fitted. Then I put on the dress and surveyed the scene. This was not the usual me, dressed in the ubiquitous quasi-Victorian-Russian-peasant-Bavarian-bar-slut style favoured by drama graduates and based loosely on the principles of a Russian doll: peel back the endless identical layers until you find the innermost core, the nugget, snuggling deep down inside all of that. Here was the nugget, exposed for all to see, naked to the world save for a flimsy piece of red fabric held on by a shoestring and a virtually non-existent undergarment purchased by a Frenchman. I found something resembling hair gel in one of the cupboards and smoothed back my wet hair into a cross between a chignon and a pineapple – not quite the radiant sleek-headed Spanish wonder look I had hoped for, but passable, definitely passable. I examined my profiles in the mirror: actually not too bad at all if you overlooked the deathly pallor. I felt a small, secret thrill at seeing myself so transformed. I searched the cupboards for possible discarded lipsticks from discarded girlfriends who were no doubt better organised and equipped than myself. Sadly it seemed the discarded girlfriends had taken their lipsticks with them, so after a few minutes of furious bottom-lip biting and cheek-pinching to lessen the corpse effect I stepped out of the bathroom.

Yves emerged from the kitchen and affected a double take.

'Hho la la!' he exclaimed, parodying an Arab accent and looking me up and down. He stepped closer and sniffed, smiling when he recognised the smell of his hair gel. Really, the sniffing was a bit much. It was excruciating enough being looked at like this, knowing that he had chosen and touched everything I was wearing, without being sniffed at as well.

'You like?' he said grinning, pointing with his elbow in the general direction of the virtually non-existent undergarment. I was annoyed to feel another childish blush creep over my cheeks: I was in my twenties, for God's sake, why did this still happen to me? And how could I allow this virtual stranger to be making overtures, to be leading me in directions I knew were dangerous, that I knew I was enjoying, that I ...

'Shall we go to dinner?' asked Yves, breaking into my mental self-flagellation session. 'My colleagues will be waiting.'

'Okay,' I said. I knew it was a bad idea to go out while I was still feeling so weak and queasy, but I could hardly bale out on him now, kitted out in my brand new dress and my minute underwear. And I didn't want to bale out either. I'd just have to avoid alcohol at all costs. I was quite enjoying the pampering, but now that the momentary frisson had passed and he was back to his businesslike self, I wondered whether I'd been imagining that there was some special significance to the way he was treating me. Perhaps he was only trying to make me presentable for his colleagues. I tried to pretend I didn't feel mildly disappointed as I followed Yves out of the apartment.

We went on Yves's bike. Both of us. I tucked the red dress under my rump as we rode, scrunching my toes to keep my clogs on, and shut my eyes as Yves swerved fearlessly into oncoming traffic and skimmed past pedestrians. The air was warm, the bicycle (if you kept your eyes shut) seemed to move with ease, sliding effortlessly through the streets. It was as close to Lady Godiva as I'd ever get, riding through the streets of Paris virtually naked. I was doing the Ballad of Lucy Jordan on a bike and I could hear Janis Joplin crooning on about the warm wind. After a day of hurling my guts out and thinking I'd never feel normal again, it was glorious.

The restaurant was fairly modest. The interior had wood-panelled walls and looked like it had once been a steakhouse. Of course I did not mention any of these thoughts to Yves. Clearly this was the latest 'in' place, one of his 'finds': to comment on the steakhouse walls would be to give yourself away as a hopeless provincial who lacked discernment and couldn't tell the difference between these and other mass-produced wood-panelled steakhouse interiors. I had learnt this lesson well with Kurt, who possessed the dubious distinction of having had a spree in Germany which, despite being Germany, was still part of the 'Europe' we felt obliged to bow down and pay homage to at home.

Everyone was already at the table when we arrived. To my horror I saw Véronique sitting there. I suppose I should have guessed when Yves mentioned that we were going to see his 'colleagues', but I still automatically stepped back as if to run out of the door until Yves put a firm hand in the small of my near-naked back and nudged me forwards. Véronique failed to conceal her surprise and suspicion under her haughty expression. Despite the obvious charms of the trendily dressed beautiful young black man she was sitting next to and fondling in her usual lazy feline fashion, her attentions to him flagged in Yves's presence. There was a moment of deafening silence, quickly broken as the greetings began with much chair scraping, standing and kissing. This was something I had by that stage still not quite perfected, and did with great awkwardness and occasional highly embarrassing accidental ear-or-neck-kissing of strangers. This form of greeting is like dancing, and I have Paris to thank at least for eventually teaching me this particular dance.

Some of the people at the table had been at Yves's the night before. I battled the impulse to apologise for my behaviour just in case I had done anything diabolical, and concentrated on manufacturing an air of silent sophistication instead, denial being the better part of valour. There was much scrutinising of me by everyone at the table, particularly the women, who sat straight-backed and stared at me, overtly and unsmilingly, from under their perfectly plucked arched eyebrows. Véronique shot me a poisonous look, pointedly swivelled her back to me and struck up a conversation with Yves. I stared blankly at the unfamiliar dishes on the menu and was overcome by a spasm of Order Crisis: my usual total inability to commit to ordering one particular thing. I waited for Yves to finish what appeared to be a highly engrossing conversation with Véronique. Her low, purring phone-sex voice was really beginning to get on my tits when her new lover (no doubt more annoyed than I was) butted in and distracted her.

'What do you think I should have?' I asked Yves.

'I order for you,' he said, taking it for granted. 'I order a surprise.'

Yves ordered honeyed prawns for both of us. They arrived glistening and immaculate. I took one bite of the delicate golden prawn flesh and instantaneously felt the contents of my stomach rise swiftly up my throat. I got up with my hand over my mouth and ran to the back of the restaurant searching blindly for the toilets and unable to take my hand off my mouth to ask the way. When I finally saw the WC sign I burst into the toilets, leaking streaks of stray vomit. The door of the toilet cubicle was closed and a desperately chic young Parisian woman stood outside it, waiting. I knocked frantically on the toilet door and then felt another warning wave spread up from my stomach. I spun around on my clogs and puked into the basin. I felt faint and dizzy and no longer cared that the chic lady was watching. I pressed my head against the cool mirror and tried not to slide down on the floor. It felt black inside my head, and in front of my eyes were small dots like light or dust swimming around like an experiment in Brownian movement. Then suddenly I realised. It was the prawns! It was not the wine but some kind of vicious food poisoning that had had me turning my guts inside out. I had to get home and I didn't think I could do it without Yves's help. 'How perfect,' I groaned out loud. When I felt I could stand again I began to make my way unsteadily as a drunk across the seemingly vast expanse of floor towards Yves.

'I'm really sorry, but I am very sick and I have to leave immediately,' I announced, staring biliously at him from my dead white slab of a face. Yves looked up at me in amazement.

'I'm sorry everyone,' he said, with some embarrassment. He did not conceal his reluctance to leave and with a brief goodbye and to the astonishment of all, we did.

Outside the restaurant the bicycle awaited us. Too weak to protest I climbed on and tried to tuck the dress under me. We set off less steadily than before but the fresh air seemed to help. I no longer felt nauseous. We were gliding along perfectly when I blacked out again. It was only for a moment, but in that split second, while my defences were down, the flowing fabric of my dress spun itself furiously into the elaborate cogs of the bicycle. I was jerked back into semi-consciousness and thrown onto the ground, joined at the hip to the bicycle by my dress. Surely this could not be happening? I lay on the ground under the bike and started to laugh slightly hysterically. Yves had managed to fall on the road to the other side of the bicycle, cleverly avoiding crushing me. He was not laughing. He sat up, tried to take the bicycle off me and realised it was attached.

'*Putain!*' he swore, when he saw the nest of chewed up fabric wound into the cogs. He pulled it, trying to unwind it. It was hopeless. He left the bicycle on top of me and leaned down to look at me. '*Ça va?*' he asked.

'Fine,' I answered. I was barely conscious and had fuck all idea of why I was lying in the middle of the road under a bicycle.

'I told you to keep the dress away from the wheels,' he said, pointing at the mess of fabric and metal teeth.

'I know,' I said.

Thankfully it was a very small side street that we had chosen for this interlude. We were still in the middle of the road when a tall, skinny Dutchman, apparently well-versed in every potential hazard associated with bicycles including this one, miraculously arrived on the scene. He examined the cogs thoroughly like a doctor with a patient. 'I live very close to here,' he then announced. 'I'll go and get the scissors.' He loped off again on his long Dutch legs and I realised what was happening.

'No, don't let him cut my dress! I don't want him to cut it!' I wailed incoherently at Yves, trying pathetically to extricate myself from the bike. Yves's voice had acquired an edge of irritation.

'He has to, Clémence,' he said, sounding like a long-suffering parent. 'There is no other way. We are very lucky he found us.'

The Dutchman returned and cut me free from the metal teeth, removing half the dress in the process. Why had this happened? Why? Here I was, standing in the middle of a Paris street in a shredded red micro mini. It hung off me asymmetrically like some freaked-out forest sprite costume from an am-dram dressing-up cupboard. We thanked the Dutchman for his assistance (well, Yves did), and began to walk home, carrying the wrecked bicycle between us. I thought it better to say very little for the moment. Instead, I concentrated on breathing, and the night air lifted the nausea a little. Yves walked along staring down his nose ahead of him, square-jawed and stunned. Occasionally he looked down at the destroyed bicycle, pursed his lips, and kept walking. I had blown this one comprehensively.

And then there was the small matter of getting the bicycle upstairs in the lift. Why do the French insist on making lifts just big enough to fit one medium-sized ten-year-old child in any comfort? Two adults (one semi-conscious and suddenly busting for a puke) and a dysfunctional bicycle proved decidedly problematic. I travelled most of the way up to the third floor with Yves's elbow jutting into my breast and his bicycle tyre causing rubber burns on my near-naked thigh. It was a relief to get back into the apartment. My mouth tasted vile and I went to the bathroom to brush my teeth with my newly donated toothbrush. When I came back Yves was kneeling next to the bike in the middle of the floor, pouring something like meths onto the cogs of the bicycle. The smell made my stomach turn, but I managed to suppress the urge to be sick. Yves lit the meths and tried to burn the fabric out. I watched transfixed as the cold-looking flames flicked around the metal, regressing momentarily to my childhood pyromaniac self. The fabric burned briefly but remained stuck in the gears. Yves's face bore a suffering martyr expression.

'No, no hope! You really fucked my bicycle,' he announced.

'You cause me much difficulty, you know.'

I hung my head. 'I'm sorry. I really am.'

I *was* sorry. I was remorseful. I was a big African bull in a small French china shop ... and a very small French dress ... Oh God. The dress. I groaned inwardly. What more in this catalogue of disasters?

'Yves, I'm really, really sorry about the dress.'

He stood up and looked at me suddenly, broke into a slow grin and walked towards me. 'That's okay,' he said merrily. 'I prefer the outfit without the dress.' He put his hands out as if he were about to pull the remains of the dress off over my head. I pulled away from him, caught in a riot of conflicting impulses, the id and the superego in a full-scale war.

'Tssk tssk,' went Yves from between his teeth. 'Silly girl.' He pushed me towards the wall and began to kiss me hard on the mouth, biting my bottom lip. God, it was good. Was it possible to kiss like this and not do anything further? Did it count if he didn't go below the belt? My limbs felt slack and I thought of those small buck in nature documentaries which go all floppy when they're caught. Perhaps if I thought about nature documentaries and didn't respond he'd leave it at this ... this delicious ... Oh God. He moved his mouth to my neck now. My nethers were in uproar.

'Come on, you know you want to,' he said, his hands pulling my hair, his teeth grazing my neck. This had to stop. I ducked and pulled away.

'Even if I *did* want to I can't,' I said as primly and firmly as possible.

'Why not?' he asked.

'You know.'

'Oh come on, this is ridiculous.' He went over to the sofa and flopped down on it, rearranging the contents of his trousers as he did so, I noticed to my perverse satisfaction. I pondered how many Hail Marys would buy me absolution for being a cock-tease. Yves was dismissive. He seemed (infuriatingly) to think it was an inevitability that I'd give in sooner or later, that it was just a matter of time. He looked up at me standing in the doorway in my Freaked-Out-Wood-Sprite outfit and laughed at me. 'Silly girl,' he said again. 'You're such a Puritan ... such a Calvinist.'

I leapt to my own defence. 'Actually I'm half Catholic,' I said snottily.

Yves raised his eyebrows, his eyes laughing. 'Which half? Certainly not your bottom half!'

'Very funny!' I had nowhere to flounce off to so I stood rather foolishly in the doorway for a moment, armed with nothing but a fixed scowl of disapproval.

'And one more thing,' I went on, in my school-marmish tone. 'I'm sleeping on the sofa tonight.'

'Oh good! You're coming to join me,' he said cheekily. 'But wouldn't it be more comfortable for two of us on the bed?'

'*Alone!*' I persisted.

'*Chérie*, don't be boring. I made a leetle joke,' Yves said wearily. 'You will not sleep on the sofa. I will sleep on the sofa and you will sleep on my bed with your boring Puritan conscience.'

I climbed into Yves's bed, *alone*, and fell asleep almost immediately.

I woke up in the middle of the night with the most acute feeling of pleasure. It took me a while to locate it. It was a moist, swollen, throbbing, intense kind of feeling, like in a dream, somewhere down ... I lifted my drowsy head. Yves, the source of this intense arousal, was lying with his feet and legs off the end of the bed and his face between my thighs, his tongue hungrily exploring every intimate fold of me, like an incubus. I was being eaten alive, from the oyster out. I made a supreme effort and sat up in the bed. Yves sat up from his exertions and grinned at me.

'You're awake,' he said.

'I can't do this!' I said.

He leaned forward and pulled off the T-shirt he'd lent me and lunged mouth-first towards my breasts. 'You are not doing anything,' he mumbled through a mouthful. '*Chérie*, you know I would not do anything you didn't want to do. I want to give you *pleasssure*,' he said, rolling out the s's so that he sounded like the sibilant snake in a Jungle Book play I once saw singing 'Trusssst in me ...'

'Is that all you ever think about? Don't you even *think* about AIDS?' I asked, noting the lack of condoms around. He sat up and looked at me.

'I am safe. I have done the test. I'm sure you are safe. Don't be silly, Clémence, can't you see how much I want you? I want you so much I'm prepared to take you in this sickly state.' The fine art of pillow talk. It worked.

In the words of another Failed Southern Lady, Reader, I fucked him.

Aftermath

To do: stick pins in eyes, flagellate self, confess to Kurt

The next morning, alone in Yves's bed, I hoped for a split second as I became conscious that having rampant sex with him the night before had been a dream – a wonderful dream, certainly, but hopefully nothing more. Then I reached down tentatively to check. Not even the most erotic dream in the world could have produced quite that result. I lay terribly still, racked with guilt, worried that I'd been foolish in making myself even more vulnerable than before, filled with remorse: it must *never* happen again. I should get up immediately and leave ... But just as I was having a final second of lying down semi-paralysed and thinking it through, Yves returned from the shop with bags of croissants and *pains au chocolat* and took all his clothes off.

'You are beautiful, you know,' he said, trailing his hand up my belly to my breasts. A wave of anger against Kurt filled me. Had he *ever* said I was beautiful? He had certainly never made me feel as desired as this. Anyway, I thought to myself as Yves rolled me over and began stroking my buttocks, it was too late to take back what had happened, and once more wouldn't make much difference. It seemed pointless to resist.

I woke up again sometime after two o'clock, alone again except for a packet of untouched *pains au chocolat*, and fumbled in my handbag for my diary. Perhaps if I wrote it down I'd be able to believe it had happened:

Appalling that have slept until now. Will get up immediately, eat pains au chocolat *for sake of energy, and make meaningful life plans for way forward.*
Oh.
Yves here and bringing more coffee. Can't be ungrateful – must extricate self diplomatically.

I slipped my diary back into my bag as Yves put the coffee down next to me. There was no sense trying to pretend that this was not what I wanted, desperately, to be doing, or that there was anything to be gained by stopping when it had already got to this point. Yves climbed into bed and I read his newspaper over his shoulder (a habit I soon discovered made him seethe) until he handed me a portion of the paper and continued to read his in peace. Obliged to read something I perused an article on some scary-sounding French folk singer who was in town. I forget his name, but how they tell them apart in the first place was a mystery to me. Then I interrupted Yves again.

'I have to get home soon, you know, Yves. I have to be a waitress tomorrow.' He lowered his paper and turned to me.

'We think about that tomorrow,' he said, licking my earlobe so that my resolution (and other parts) melted.

Gaming with Yves

'Oh Paris, you magnify me in my own sight!'
– Restif de la Bretonne

'You and me together!'
– Balzac's Rastignac on Paris

> *Dear Jack.*
>
> *You win. I accidentally had sex with The Suit and it was bliss. He woke me out of a deep sleep (I'd had food poisoning and was not at all well) and I kept slipping in and out of consciousness while he was slipping in and out of me. I say this to you, Jack, NOT as an excuse or to suggest that it was all his doing, but to say that I experienced the true meaning of ecstasy as you described it in a lecture about Greek theatre: the experience of being outside of oneself. Beside yourself, I'd say. Please don't tell anyone – I'm still suffering acute morning-after guilt and shame.*
>
> > *God, it was great though.*
> > *Delicious, in fact.*
>
> *Love*
> *Clem*
>
> *PS – don't gloat, just because you knew I would all along. It's very irritating.*
> *PPS – and don't you dare tell Kurt even though you think he deserves it. He's probably fucking his way through his whole fan club and I couldn't care less, but just DON'T TELL HIM! I'll do it myself when the time is right.*

Eternally cautious, I gave Jack Yves's number for emergencies but told him to keep writing to me at Madame Rouillard's since for all I knew this might be a very temporary address.

Of course I never moved back to the apartment in the Marais. Serge's friend was due back in a week anyway, so the timing, though completely unplanned, was perfect. Instead, Yves and I took a taxi to the apartment and Yves looked tactfully in the other direction as I gathered the scattered detritus from around the flat and stuffed as much as I could back into the horrendously un-chic backpack. Throughout this performance I was terrified that one look at the way I'd been living might make him change his mind about letting me move in with him, but he must have been feeling charitable since he did take me home with him again afterwards. Back at his apartment, he watched with impressive forbearance as I loaded my sad and motley collection, like the leftovers from a cheap jumble sale, into his wardrobe. They hung apologetically next to his immaculate suits. His *underpants* looked more presentable than anything I had on offer, but I reassured myself that there was a city full of *Parisiennes* out there to choose from if he'd wanted to fuck someone for their taste in Capri pants or evening bags.

Yves liked to expose my ignorance. I think it made him feel powerful. He liked to devise impromptu quizzes for me and snorted and rolled his eyes in theatrical disbelief when I didn't know the answers. There was, for instance, the time when he gave me the code to the front door of his apartment.

Yves: 'It's the year of the French revolution.'

Me: 'Okay.' I avoided his eyes. I could feel a test coming on.

Yves: 'You know in what year was the French Revolution?'

Me: 'Yes.'

Pause. Then Yves could no longer resist.

Yves: 'So?'

Me: 'I'm not playing, Yves.' I felt sweaty. One false step and I'd be into a full-scale quiz show.

Yves: 'Just tell me the year the Revolution started. *Simple*.'

Me: '1789, but I told you, I'm not playing.' I thanked providence that he'd miraculously picked one of the very few historical facts I knew – and had recently read about in my guidebook. But this did not satisfy him.

Yves: 'And which famous character from that time died in

his bath?'

    Me: 'Yves,' I said, 'I-AM-NOT-PLAYING!'

    And so on.

    I never worked out whether this habit of his was pure sadism or whether it was genuinely born out of a desire to enrich my pathetically weak grasp of history. I have, despite a few truly noble efforts, never managed to retain any relevant historical information and I stick with Our Jane when, in *Northanger Abbey*, her character explains that history is incomprehensible to her, that '... history, real solemn history, I cannot be interested in ... it tells me nothing that does not either vex or weary me. The quarrels of popes and kings, with wars or pestilences, in every page; the men all so good for nothing and hardly any women at all – it is all very tiresome: and yet I often think it odd that it should be so dull for a great deal of it must be invention ...' The long-suffering Angus, himself an extraordinary encyclopaedia of historical knowledge (and some dubious and extraordinary historical trivia) had come to accept this shortcoming of mine years before. After one too many of my blank-faced stares, he had confined himself to feeding me the oddities he thought I'd find amusing – about Rasputin's enormous willy or there only being one toilet in the whole of Versailles, a fact which Yves categorically denied as filthy English propaganda. Since Yves's jousting sessions generally ended up in a stand-off, a hard-on and fucking of the most thrillingly quasi S&M nature, I suspect his intentions in creating these little Trivial Pursuit quizzes were not strictly speaking educational.

    I confess it was strange that after someone like Kurt I should end up with a man like Yves, who was neither an artist nor a philosopher, and who wore a suit to work without seeing the need to make excuses for it. Very swiftly I came to the conclusion that several aspects of artists' reputations were vastly overrated. Sex was one of them. Sex with Yves was scintillating – an intriguing and delectable potpourri of minor perversions. I discovered that the fact that he spent his days dressed as a businessman teaching foreign merchant bankers how to speak Boardroom in French rather than spouting poetry did not detract from his sexual performance. On the contrary. This was a great revelation to me. I had spent my youth watching far too many movies and reading far too many books which featured sensitive passionate creative types having it off in screaming splendour and climaxing in democratic unison to believe that there might be greener fields elsewhere. Perhaps, though I shudder to confess it, I just liked a man in a uniform.

Yves liked to have sex in at least partial view of the neighbours – either that or he just didn't care that the woman over the courtyard could see us while she vacuumed her floors. I got used to it after a while – even grew to enjoy it, I have to admit, being so far from home and anyone who knew me. Initially, visions of Kurt troubled me at crucial moments. Despite my strong suspicion that he was an incorrigible polygamist, and my certainty that we'd never be lovers again, those three encrypted Hallmark-card words made me feel guilty that I'd still not come clean and told him about Yves. Now I'd procrastinated for so long it seemed pointless to contact him out of the blue to tell him. Whenever I felt a pang of guilt coming on I quashed it with anger, conjuring up images of him *in flagrante* with the Anti-Oxidant, convincing myself that I was only retaliating for his actions. I confessed my feelings of guilt to Jack and he wrote me a brief message on a postcard. 'Manipulation is a three-word letter,' it said. 'Get over yourself!' My rational self reassured me I was under no obligation to tell Kurt. I'd heard nothing from him for months, and I owed him nothing. In my darker moments I knew it was cowardice.

Yves was a dramatic fucker, prone to talking very dirty right until he came with much shuddering and wailing, reduced to a state of abject vulnerability and emitting multilingual protestations of love. I found this all quite delicious once I got over the initial prissy squeamishness. He called me *pute*, *salope*, *chatte* as he bit me and left marks in embarrassing places. I discovered I liked being called slutty names and having his hand up my skirt in public. On the whole, Yves could have dirtier and more scintillatingly perverted sex just by looking at me than Kurt could by actually rolling onto me in the middle of the night. Sex with Kurt, which had initially felt so thrillingly precise and accomplished, had gradually come to feel as formulaic and unsatisfying as a predictable one-act play. Despite all Kurt's avid and public reading of De Sade or the *Kama Sutra*, he still insisted on showering thoroughly before and after sex. He got to know what worked and approached the act with a controlled, goal-driven earnestness that ruled out any playful exploration. So while I can't say that Kurt was a careless lover, his attention to my needs often felt overly deliberate and sometimes even impatient.

Yves went everywhere by taxi now that I'd 'totally fucked' his bike, as he frequently reminded me. We did so much of our snogging and our social admin in the neutral territory in the back of taxis that we were on first name terms with a couple of the drivers, and secretly I found it quite thrilling and sophisticated. Anyway, Yves was incongruous on a bike. Somehow bikes were not sufficiently masculine for his haughty Roman Emperor self-image, but then that was something that fundamentally set European men apart from South Africans. Frequently I saw European men sporting gentleman's handbags (poofter bags, as Jack called them) and they'd look like a practical accessory, unremarkable. They could get away with outrageously camp hairdos and could hug and kiss each other in public without any of the hearty, reassuringly heterosexual backslapping that most South African men went in for, if they ever felt compelled to touch each other. I tried to discuss it with Yves once, after he'd kissed a man in greeting in a bar. He gave me a look of confusion and mild outrage and told me that everyone knew all Englishmen were *pédés* anyway and they must be trying to hide it, so I left it at that. When I thought back to Kurt I was chilled in retrospect by the frostily unphysical way he treated his friends.

Of course it wasn't unadulterated bliss with Yves. He was

prone to filthy moods and tormented by the situation with his ex-wife and his son. Walking the streets with him at night, I came to know the geography of his Paris with Anne instinctively. I could tell when we were near a place they'd often come to or where he expected he might find her by his sudden caution, his rigidity, and the fact that he'd stopped pinching my nipples as we rounded the corner into that block. It had little to do with Anne herself – I was convinced there was no abiding love there – it was about his son, Antoine.

My first meeting with Yves's son quickly revealed just how unprepared I was for the complications that being his father's lover would entail. Yves had arranged the meeting with grim determination and a look of martyrdom to some kind of impending doom that I didn't understand. As the appointed hour grew closer I found myself filled with an absurd sense of anxiety, even going through agonies about what to wear. Could this really all be over the approbation of a toddler? I was instructed to meet Yves and Antoine in a café near the house one Sunday where they would already be comfortably installed with their Sunday brunch. I stood for a while outside the café, watching Yves help a lovely dark-haired little boy with a spoonful of food, quite transformed with tenderness. Then I breathed deeply, pushed open the door, and walked in. Yves's head shot up to look at me and he stood up, visibly tense now, and introduced me to his son. Antoine greeted me, perfectly civilly for a two-and-a-half-year-old, then carried on eating his omelette and ignored me entirely. It was rather an anticlimax. I hovered next to the table, waiting for instruction as though the little emperor would suddenly, Buddha-like, motion to me to seat myself.

Really, it had much more to do with Yves's approval than Antoine's. Yves simply needed us to meet so that he could see me through his son's eyes, through the eyes of the public in relation to his son, to check whether I passed yet another test. But what role was I being tested in? I didn't know whether he wanted me to be a nanny or a stepmother or simply invisible. Was I a call girl, a child bride or some sort of virgin niece? It was impossible to tell, and the requirements seemed to change, exhaustingly, from one minute to the next. Yves adored his son to distraction and was proudly making him in his own image, only prettier and more delicate like Anne. The one weekend he spent without seeing Antoine he went into a deep decline. I sometimes wondered who was dependent on whom when I watched the two of them – generally from a polite distance.

Antoine's visits involved complicated rearrangements. For the sake of appearances, I was exiled into the spare-room-cum-storeroom across the passage from the actual apartment every weekend when Antoine came. There I was often joined in the middle of the night by a desperate Yves, who sneaked into me swiftly and unceremoniously, half an ear across the passage, like a man possessed. I found his urgency flattering, and he never apologised for the brevity of these encounters. He liked me to wake up when he was already inside me, delighted when I was finally conscious so that I'd hear his smutty words of appreciation before he sneaked back to be the perfect father in the room across the passage. He seemed to read my needs perfectly. Life was remarkably free and easy for me and sex was better than I could ever have imagined it to be.

In short, I was in lust.

Grasse matinée

Mot du jour: faire la grasse matinée: *to stay in bed late, to have a long lie-in*

One Saturday morning Yves and I were enjoying our last moments in bed before Antoine was dropped off and I was sent into exile overnight, when I heard a noise at the door. I started and sat up, frozen, alert.

'What?' asked Yves, not stopping.

'I heard something at the door.' I held myself up rigidly, head around, trying to listen. Yves protested and tried to pull me to him.

'Maybe it's the woman from next door. Should we invite her to join us?' he taunted.

Then we both heard it. Yves leapt up and ran naked across the room to the door, opened it a crack, and looked out. It was Anne, early, with Antoine. She'd let herself into the building because Antoine had insisted on punching in the door code himself. Yves muttered to her to wait and closed the door again, pulled on a pair of pants and threw me his dressing gown. I put it on and sat down at the table, resisting the impulse to run into the bathroom and hide like a character in a third-rate French farce. I tried to pretend I'd been reading the paper (yesterday's) and was acutely aware that the room smelt unmistakably of sex. I wished I'd thought to open a window. Anne came in, hesitatingly, and greeted me with downcast eyes when Yves introduced me, curtly, his jaw set. She was a beautiful, delicate creature who looked like she expected, and got, nothing but disappointment. How many times had she sat there, probably in that same gown, the smell of their sex still lingering in the air? I wanted desperately to reassure her, to comfort her somehow, but saw the absurdity of the impulse. She and Yves exchanged a few words, details of the arrangements with Antoine, and then she left. She did not look at me. Yves turned to Antoine and cut me out.

'It's not my fault, you know,' I mumbled, humiliated. But Yves was talking to Antoine and he didn't hear me. It was take it or leave it, I knew that. I couldn't pretend Yves hadn't warned me, and I tried to enjoy being unfettered and unconventional instead of feeling hurt and needy. I did try.

Yves barely spoke to me that day and was absurdly over-solicitous with Antoine, unhealthily indulgent. Left alone with so much time to think, I realised that most of Yves's more peculiar behaviour came out of a terror of losing his son. This vulnerability made me look more kindly on his idiosyncrasies, but I was glad to climb back into bed with the whole of Yves when Antoine went back to his mother the next evening.

Not long after the fiasco with Anne's arrival, I was still lying in bed early one morning while Yves showered when the phone rang. I had learnt not to answer any calls by now, but its insistent ringing made me tense and I hoped Yves might leap out of the shower to answer it before the machine kicked in. He didn't. Yves's voice message started and finished, and an oddly familiar voice began leaving a message in South African English. His voice was so utterly out of context that it took me a moment to work out who it was. It was Angus! I shot up out of bed, tripping myself in the coiled sheets as I raced for the phone.

'Angus!'

'Clem?'

'How did you get my number?'

'From Jack.'

'Of course! How are you?'

'Okay.'

Angus sounded glum. I desperately wanted to speak to him, to hear about home, but as desperately I wanted him not to be glum, not to cast a shadow on this fragile paradise I was inhabiting even for one moment. I made Angus do all the talking. He had a lot to say.

'Clemmy, she burnt all my cuttings.'

'What?'

'My obituaries. That bitch Tamara and I split up and she burnt the whole fucking lot.'

'Well, maybe it's a good thing. Maybe it's never struck you, but it's a pretty morbid occupation.' Hollow reassurance. I listened to the shower with one ear, wondering how I could end the conversation before Yves came through.

'They were for my PhD. I've been saving them for years and she burnt the lot.'

'God, she certainly knows how to kick you where it hurts.'

'Hmm.' He paused for a moment as if reluctant to say what he was about to say. 'She was fucking other men all along, Clemmy, and you know I didn't even guess. I feel so stupid.'

'Oh?' My voice went wavering down to the Southern Hemisphere, as I stood there naked in Yves's flat feeling disconcertingly wanton. 'I'm sorry ...'

'That awful little vegetarian slut. I can't believe I didn't guess ...'

I flushed guiltily and was awkwardly silent. I could hardly join in this particular verbal stoning session under the circumstances.

'Gus, I wish there was something I could do ...'

'*Ja.*'

There was silence at the other end of the line. Yves had turned the shower off and I wanted to put the receiver down before he came out of the bathroom with his loud Frenchman voice and blew my cover.

'Listen, Gus, this is an expensive silence. Go and do something wonderful and forget about Tam. It was a bad scene anyway. And you'll find more obituaries to work from.'

Silence.

'Gus?'

'When are you coming home, Clem? You said yourself you're not sure why you're there.'

'That's changed. I like it here. I *need* to be here. It feels right.'

'Does it?' He sounded tired, sad.

'Yes,' I answered in a small voice.

'Not to me. And Jack tells me you're being pursued around Paris by a bunch of sleazy priapic Parisians with their dicks poking out like baguettes sticking out from their shopping bags ...'

I laughed uncomfortably. 'You don't need me there. You've got masses of great friends who'll put you out of your misery in no time. Go and see ...'

'That's not the point ...' he began, but at that moment a truck drove by at Angus's end and drowned him out. He must have pulled the phone out into the garden in hearing distance of the street. I waited till it had passed.

'What?'

'*Ag* nothing,' said Angus. He sounded as exhausted as if he had crawled through a desert to make this phonecall. 'Go back to your day.'

It left a bad taste in my mouth. The moment I put the phone down I wanted to phone him back, tell him everything about what I'd been doing, how I'd been feeling. About Yves. But sexual euphoria was the last thing he'd want to hear about now and I knew I couldn't confess even to Angus. Yves emerged from the shower and asked me accusingly who I'd been speaking to on the phone.

'A friend from home.'

'A man?'

'Yes. A friend.'

'This one you think about when you fuck me? The one with the *sexe* long enough to reach you here?'

'*No*, Yves, a *friend*.'

He snorted in disbelief and eyed me suspiciously, drying himself roughly with the towel and standing in front of me like a Roman statue. I smiled up at him, grateful to be amused by his childish jealousy, and he dropped his towel and came back to bed.

On sunny afternoons over the weekends, Yves and I went out with Antoine in his pushchair. Yves was hard on most people but Antoine could get away with anything. He was besotted, and happiest with him, indulging in this acceptable form of self-worship. With Antoine, he dropped his guard and changed completely. He reverted to a playful childhood Yves I would never have expected. Once when we were bowling along the pavement with the pram (I felt just about forgotten as I staggered clumsily along behind them on the narrow pavement, trying to keep up) a stranger stopped to point out that Antoine's legs had come free of the pram strap and were threatening to get dragged along the road. She was a proper French matron and announced this in a proper French matron voice, rather like the woman who had once told me, pointing madly at my grocery bag and jabbering repeatedly when initially I didn't understand '*votre lait dégouline ...*' (your milk is leaking) as though telling me I'd forgotten to put on a shirt that day and hadn't yet noticed. Yves stopped careening along the pavement for a moment to listen to the woman's reprimand. He looked at her with an insolent smile.

'Oh don't worry about that,' he told her, 'he always does that. And anyway, he's only adopted.' The matron looked after him, horrified, as he continued jauntily and at a dangerously swift pace down the road. When we rounded the corner a few metres on, Yves turned to see that the woman was out of sight, bent down, and lovingly adjusted the straps of the pram.

Yves also encouraged displays of mildly disgusting behaviour from his son. Antoine's public snot-eating and Yves's vile stories put people off their food in the endless stream of restaurants we frequented, and both the stories and the reactions were a source of delight to father and son alike. I trailed along in their wake, shaking my head in an 'Oh these boys!' manner but secretly I hated feeling excluded from their pranks – and from their intimacy. In self-defence, I liked to make Yves jealous too. It was not very difficult. The first time I did it, it was by mistake. One evening I had been waiting for some time for him to meet me in the Petit Fer à Cheval, drinking out of nervousness, when a pleasant-looking young man came up and asked if he could sit at my table. He turned out to be an English journalist writing arts reviews for *Time Out*. He was funny and self-deprecatory and he reminded me of Angus, and after a couple of minutes and several glasses of wine I had relaxed into enjoying a mild mutual flirtation, assured of my own desirability. He told me what has since become my favourite joke (and the only one that I remember) and he told it with supreme comic flair. It was the one about a man walking past an asylum. The man is intrigued to hear all the inmates in the asylum shouting 'Thirteen! Thirteen!

Thirteen!' Curious, he bends down and looks through a hole in the fence, whereupon one of the inmates sticks a finger through the hole and pokes him in the eye. The rest of the inmates change their cry: 'Fourteen! Fourteen! Fourteen!'

We were laughing hysterically when Yves appeared out of nowhere, thrust my bag at me angrily and pushed me out of the bar.

'What's your problem? We were just *talking*,' I protested. Yves said nothing, squared his jaw angrily, and walked on.

'You don't *own* me, you know,' I shook one arm from his grip and tried to walk next to him instead of in front like a dog on a leash. Despite my indignation I had to admit that I enjoyed the sensation of having decisions taken out of my hands, of being propelled along without thinking (and mildly pissed) through the teeming Paris streets. But I longed to laugh more at the Englishman's jokes and Yves's quasi-Fascist attitude to me, oddly stimulating though it might be, was starting to chafe like an ill-fitting bit.

Jealousy enhanced Yves's sexual performance most effectively and was the one way of ensuring his complete attention. My only regret was that I never even found out the Englishman's name and in all my trips to the Petit Fer à Cheval I never met him again.

Home truths

The few hours before Antoine arrived on Saturday mornings were the most precious of all to me, which was why reading an article on the Truth and Reconciliation Commission early one Saturday was particularly bad timing. It pulled me roughly out of my mental exile and made me think about things I'd avoided confronting for months. It took me to a place where Yves couldn't reach me.

Yves had gone out early to knock back a quick espresso and had arrived back, as usual, with *pains au chocolat* and newspapers, and climbed back into his kimono in preparation for some pre-Antoine nookie. He brought me an English paper that morning (as a treat as well as to discourage me from reading his *Le Monde* over his shoulder) and I scoured it automatically for news from home. I did not have to search for long before I found a headline: Apartheid's Litany of Woes. It was an article about the Truth Commission hearings – about a woman who'd lost her child, about a boy who'd had electrodes attached to his genitals and been tortured to death. I felt sick and my throat ached with tears, but I couldn't stop reading. Somehow I felt I had no right to cry – that I had surrendered my right by going away. And surely I should be grateful to be away rather than homesick for such a place? Yves saw me blinking suspiciously.

'What is it?'

I explained, trying not to sob.

'It's not the only reality, Clémence. This' (he gestured at our semi-naked bodies on the bed) 'is as much a reality.'

He may have had a point, but it seemed so callous, him lying there glossy and complacent in his wildly expensive kimono while people were confronted with such misery. I began to realise that after just a few weeks of being together, Yves's charms, his appealing arrogance, his sexual mastery, were starting to wear a little thin. A shudder passed through me, but Yves mistook my distaste for distress.

'You are upset?'

It was an absurd question. I nodded like a child, unwilling to talk. Yves shook his head.

'I know you, Clémence. I think it is guilt. You should not feel guilty for being happy.' I looked at him in astonishment, wordless. How dare he presume he knew about this part of me?

'Guilt is just another vice. You should not indulge so much in it.' He pulled me to him, and I let him, but I wasn't really there any more. I think in that moment I started to despise him.

The next day, Yves announced that he was going to New York. On business. For a month. Alone.

Yves cooks his goose

The way he told me was cowardly in the extreme. We were having drinks on a terrace somewhere on the Ile de la Cité with some friends I'd never met before and whose names I couldn't even remember. When I came back from the *toilettes* a strange hush fell over the party.

'*Carissima!*' said Yves, in an uncharacteristically flamboyant and demonstrative manner clearly intended to impress his friends rather than to express any genuine affection for me. I thought he might even be slightly drunk, which was something I'd never seen before and which I noticed all the more since I was soberly sticking to *jus d'orange* that day. He held his arms out to me theatrically and I smelt a rat.

'You don't mind that I'm going to New York for a while, do you?'

Did I *mind*? I didn't even *know*. Was this another test? Was it for real? I shot him a look to see whether he was joking, but he looked tense and serious despite his self-assured smile.

'Yves, are you being serious?' I asked him eventually. I was on trial in front of these stranger-friends of his.

He nodded: 'Business.' As if that explained it all. Some of his friends began to look particularly uncomfortable – it was clear that he was using them as a human shield.

'How long are you going for?'

'For a month.'

'A *month*? When?'

'In a week.'

A week. What was I supposed to say? Surrounded by his friends he was safe and affirmed. I was nothing. I tried to hide my distress and developed a vicious headache from smiling at everyone to prove I was not a nag, that I was the French equivalent of a 'good sport', and waited in desperation to leave.

I broached the subject again on the way 'home', despite the fact that my headache was now inducing nausea. Yves affected an infuriatingly casual manner and tried to make me feel completely unreasonable for protesting about the way he'd told me. I wished so desperately that I didn't have to go home with him, that I had my own place where I could curl up into a foetal position and lick my wounds in peace. But as it turned out there was a more pressing reason to find my own place. Anne and Antoine would be staying in Yves's apartment while he was away. I stopped dead in mid-step when he told me this, as though I'd walked into a wall. I couldn't breathe. Yves looked at me with a flat, impenetrable expression in his eyes, as if he couldn't understand what the fuss was all about.

'I would let you stay there but I promised Antoine's mother three months ago that she could stay here because she needs to have some changes made to her new apartment.' I stared at him, stunned. Three *months* ago? So he'd known since before we'd even got together and he'd never mentioned it.

'Don't look so worried, Clémence, a friend of mine will be away too and you can stay at her apartment ...'

I didn't want to listen to this. 'Why are you only telling me now?'

'I didn't want you to worry for nothing. I've organised it all for you, Clémence, it's just for a month.'

I was sure he'd not told me because he didn't think I'd still be around. I was temporary and dispensable and I hated it. I did not feel independent or free or sophisticated, I felt used. And Yves seemed to think that he'd done me a great favour by controlling my life for me. He butted into my thoughts again.

'Don't look so upset, *chérie*, you will move back in as soon as I return.'

'Oh *will* I?' I screeched sarcastically. Yves looked genuinely surprised, which was rather satisfying, but the humiliation was overwhelming. I had to admit that if I looked beyond the sex, the signs had been there for some time. It was never meant to be a long-term arrangement, this crazy, precarious patched-together relationship, and I'd known it was coming to the end of its natural life. I was sick of putting up with his minor abuses – his quiz games and pedantry, his scorn at my barbaric ways, his contempt for my cooking, his 'You can not put *that* (perfectly good Colman's mustard) in the salad dressing! It is totally the wrong taste. Hho la la!' I was sick of it. I longed to open a can of baked beans and eat them out of the tin while reading a good book (or perhaps a really bad one). And now *this*!

'I've gone to a lot of trouble to arrange a place for you to stay,' said Yves.

'You shouldn't have bothered,' I said viciously. There was no point in pretending any more.

'She's the mother of my son,' Yves whined. 'I can't just leave them with nowhere to stay.'

'It's really fine, Yves. I was going to find another place anyway.'

'Ah, *ma petite*, I think you are perhaps a little jealous of my ex-wife?'

'Perhaps not,' I snapped at him. I snatched up my keys to his apartment and strode out into the grubby Paris streets in search of a room of my own, so seethingly angry I didn't even want to cry.

I found a room with Madame Rouillard from the café the same afternoon. It was the first lucky break I'd had in a while and it added strength to my anger. Now that I knew I had somewhere else to go I flounced back to Yves's and began ostentatiously to pack, sulking dramatically and stuffing things back into the same grotty old backpack like a film on rewind. He tried to 'reason' with me, then gave up and watched me superciliously over the top of the newspaper he was pretending to read. I had clicked into fast forward and nothing would stop me now.

III

Lift-off

Lift-off

I left Yves's flat at speed, excessively clothed in various non-matching black garments that wouldn't fit into the rucksack and carrying several plastic-bagfuls of accumulated crap with me. I knocked a picture frame off the wall with my rucksack as I went and didn't even apologise as I squeezed out of the front door like an overloaded bag lady. I refused to tell Yves where I was going and he seemed surprised, upset and even regretful to see me leave. He didn't try to convince me to stay, just hung around in the hallway looking wounded but superior. Perhaps he thought I'd change my mind and come running back. But he was wrong.

The lift cage closed and had just begun to descend when I felt my back jerk. I tried to turn around to see what it was, but I couldn't move. The buckle, the 'Unbreakable Quick-release Snapper' of the rucksack waist strap which I'd left undone in my haste, was caught in the door of the lift. I pulled frantically at the strap, but the clip was firmly wedged in, and while the lift was going down, the strap was stuck on the third floor. The rucksack started to pull me up off the floor as the lift descended. In desperation I managed to struggle out of the straps, but the bag continued to rise unstoppably towards the roof of the lift. I dropped the remaining plastic bags and clung to the rucksack, pulling it down with all my force, and I was still clinging to it when it reached the ceiling. This called for desperate measures. I turned upside down and braced my legs stiffly against the roof of the lift, pulling at the rucksack with my full weight, hanging there absurdly bat-like in my flapping black clothes. Eventually the lift slowed down and ground to a halt with an unhealthy-sounding gnashing of cogs. I hung in the corner and laughed so hysterically I began to cry. I could picture it: the *concierge* would be summoned by an irate Madame to see to the lift and they'd find me, incoherent with laughter and grief, clinging to the roof like an enormous spider, the floor littered with my untidy white plastic bag eggs. I could hear my taxi hooting impatiently in the distance, its meter ticking. I braced my legs against the roof again and pushed away. Nothing. One final attempt, and the 'Unbreakable' buckle on the waistband gave way. I fell with a thud onto the floor on my back, temporarily winded amongst the plastic bags, and the lift continued its descent. When the lift door opened I picked myself up (to the amazement of the woman and child waiting on the ground floor) and jammed my foot into the door to keep it open while I gathered my scattered belongings. The woman pulled her child behind her. I shouldered the heavy rucksack, the broken waist strap dangling uselessly, picked up all the bags, and walked out of the building to the waiting taxi.

Fortunately it was not one of the taxi drivers I knew. He loaded my tatty collection of bags into the boot, drove me wordlessly to Madame Rouillard's, and looked highly relieved as he drove away. I hovered on the pavement trying to gather my baggage, until Madame herself came out of the bar to give me a key. I tried to look brave and grateful but in control – anything but like the madwoman who'd emerged from the lift at Yves's moments before. This was the New Me, angry and independent. I punched in the code she gave me for the apartment, shepherding the ridiculous collection of plastic bags with my feet, and went inside. The foyer smelt of urine, the *lift* smelt of urine. I pushed the 'up' button and stood far back from the lift door, making sure all rucksack straps were out of the way, and waited to ascend to my new home. But somewhere inside me a button had been pushed and illuminated just as clearly as the button in the lift. I was sick of France and its urine smell. It made me feel sick – so sick, in fact, that I was amazed I hadn't taken one sniff at the airport and turned away. It stank more by the day, as if something was rotting – intolerable. I got out on the second floor and walked down the flophouse passage to *chambre 3*. I squeezed all my belongings into the minute room, lay down on the bed, which sank rapidly underneath me like a deflating soufflé, and howled with rage and abandon into the lumpy pillow.

A little while later, all howled out, I felt drained and slightly distanced from everything but astonishingly strong. I looked at myself in the stingy little mirror above the basin: eyes all red and puffy and a nose like a beacon. It was not an attractive sight, not the kind of look you wanted to make public, but I'd hardly eaten all day and was starving after all the exertions, so I washed my face in the basin and headed downstairs to the café. Madame Rouillard eyed me out and summed me up in a second: '*Ça va?*' she asked gruffly.

'*Ça va*,' I answered, quite truthfully.

She nodded sceptically and grunted. Madame Rouillard knew a sad case when she saw one. She shuffled off to the bar and returned a moment later with a large tumbler of red wine.

'*Merci, Madame*,' I said. But she shook her head and jerked it in the direction of the bar, and more specifically in the direction of Berthaut, the old man who'd once told me I should be flattered by the attentions of the seedy Parisians who harassed foreign women. I looked at him, momentarily unsure whether to accept his offer, and my distaste must have shown because he looked back at me and shook his head, making a tssking sound between his teeth.

'I'm only a man,' he said, with a kind of patient sigh reserved for idiots. Not a devil, then, just a man.

'*Merci, Monsieur.*' I gave him a watery smile and put the glass to my lips to drink, feigning appreciation, but the smell was enough to make me feel sick. I lifted my book up in front of my face like a shield and became instantly engrossed.

Jack and the crêpes

And so began an orgy of overeating and seclusion. Most of the time I couldn't remember why I'd come to Paris in the first place, but I enjoyed spending so much time alone. There was no one I wanted to see, not even Serge – he was too close to Yves for comfort. Serge was going to work on an opera set in Prague and he phoned to offer me his apartment when he found out about Yves and me. I thanked him, but declined and then felt dreadful because he seemed so hurt. I left a long message on his answering machine trying to explain that he shouldn't take it personally, that I wanted to be away from anything that reminded me of Yves. But when he left another message for me at the café I didn't phone back.

Yves came to the restaurant once before he left for New York and I hid in the toilets and begged Thierry to send him away. I was making an increasingly desultory pretence at working, arriving late and calling in sick far too often. I knew I was trying even Thierry's patience and taking his kindness for granted, so I decided to look for something else before he was forced to ask me to go. I scoured the newspapers for anything promising and visited the noticeboard in the American Church like all the other hopefuls, still pretending I was somehow superior and more local than they were. There were several false starts. Once I came across an ad for a job teaching English in an industrial town somewhere further south and was momentarily convinced that was the answer. When I asked Madame Rouillard what she thought about the idea she looked at me sceptically and shook her head.

'Not a good place,' she said, wrinkling her considerable nose in distaste. 'Not for you. No charm. Full of factories. And Arabs.'

I gave in, too tired to argue, and turned despondently back to the job ads.

I was sick of waitressing. Literally sick. Whether or not it was psychosomatic, I felt nauseous constantly – at the prospect of going to work in the mornings, at the smell of the rich food I served. I forced myself to go, but one morning I threw up onto the métro tracks and phoned in sick from Madame Rouillard's. On one of the increasingly rare days that I was at work Thierry took me aside and gave me the inevitable Talk. He didn't fire me, but he left the way wide open for me to go, talking sensitively about my being 'unfulfilled' by this job and suggesting (without putting any pressure on me) that I find something that interested me more. The truth was, as I foolishly told Thierry, that I could hardly do this job, let alone find the energy to pick up and start another. Perhaps it was the cold, Thierry gallantly suggested. He told me he'd suffered constantly with the onset of winter for his first years in Paris. We Africans weren't used to it. I nodded solemnly in agreement, knowing full well that winter had always been my favourite season.

Thierry's kindness was more than I could have hoped for, and I was determined not to abuse it. One Saturday afternoon I traipsed off to the American Church yet again. It was an unusually cold day, and although I'd already eaten two *tartines* at Madame Rouillard's that morning I was hungry again. My walk took me past several crêpe vendors and far too many phone booths and eventually I gave in on both accounts. I dialled Jack's number with my fingers still sticky with crêpe and had barely finished swallowing the last mouthful when he answered.

'Jack?'

'Hello, my gorgeous girl. How are you?'

'Dismal. I've been dumped. Or I dumped him, I'm not sure, but we've dumped each other. He's gone to New York for a month, and his ex-wife has moved into his apartment, which used to be *their* apartment, so I'm living in a flophouse above the shop where you send the faxes. It's just so fucking cold. I ate four *crêpes aux marrons* just as a snack on the way to phone you. I'm now not only imminently unemployed, I'm an imminently unemployed spendthrift blimp. If I stop phoning you it's because I can't fit into the fucking phone booth any more. How does that sound?'

There was an impressed exhalation at the other end of the line.

'Okay, sister, hold it. Firstly, are you premenstrual? Hmm? Because I've seen you do a lot worse than four meagre crêpes in that condition.'

'I suppose I must be. I hadn't thought about that, I thought it was just sheer misery in this instance.'

'Don't beat yourself up, darling.'

'Jack, how's Kurt? I feel a bit *kak*, you know, I never even told him about The Suit.'

'Oh do me a favour!' Jack exclaimed sarcastically. 'Forget about Kurt, Clem, why should you tell him? He's so far up his own arse he wouldn't even hear you. His midlife crisis is over, incidentally. He's started work on a new offering for some German competition – three installations and a Happening. It's called "Triptych with Wanker and Four Violins" or something.'

I giggled, and it felt like the first time in ages.

'Now go and have a coffee on some gorgeous pavement café and think of me,' said Jack cheerfully. I realised that, in my rush for consolation, I had not even asked him how he was.

'Nothing unusual, my darling child. I sell my soul daily for a pittance to a bunch of boring Philistines. I spend my nights searching for that elusive pearl of a man among the hordes of swine. Tragic, really.' I laughed, then I was silent for a moment. I couldn't bear to end the call.

'I wish you were here,' I said in a small voice.

'So do I, darling. So do I.'

When I hung up I stood smiling in the phone booth for a moment, trying to hold onto his voice, grinning at his excessive familiarity with my domineering hormones. And then it hit me. I had been premenstrual for a very long time. My period was late. I leaned against the side of the phone booth and tried to breathe, thinking through dates and events. Things blurred in my mind in fast and slow motion, slipping from my mental grasp, as if I had just been in a car crash and was trying to piece together what had happened. It could not be possible.

I got home and checked the previous month's pill packet still lying discarded on the side table. All the pills had been popped neatly out of their foil packaging. I had taken them all! Hah! Relief! I threw myself onto the bed and started breathing again.

It was a freak missed period. Nothing to worry about. It had happened before despite my ridiculously paranoid and diligent pill popping. The previous time, all those years ago, I had sat on the phone in a tearful heap in the hallway of the Soup Kitchen while some kindly auntie at the local Cape Town family planning clinic built up an elaborate picture: what the pill did to one's reproductive bits, why one sometimes missed a period, and eventually where I could go to get the final reassurance of a test. I checked the foil packaging again. Yes, here was the evidence in front of me: I had taken them all. I was safe. Flooded with relief, I kissed the empty packaging, clutched it firmly to my heart, and slid onto the grubby floor into a sort of foetal position.

Still, missing a period completely made me anxious, and the next morning I padded down the passage hoping for the reassurance of what Jimmy's Aunt Kathleen always used to call 'the red telegram'. No such telegram had arrived. A month. I was a whole month overdue. How could that have happened? Despite the empty packet I began to worry again. I went back to the room and read through instructions and side effects on the package insert, hoping to find some reassurance there. Instead two sentences struck me with such force that I sat there paralysed, my wide eyes swimming repeatedly over the words in terror: *If, within four hours of tablet intake, you have vomiting or diarrhoea, the tablet may not have been absorbed properly by your body. Continue taking your tablets as normal. In these circumstances your partner must use an additional method of contraception, such as a condom, either until your period or for the next fourteen days, whichever is longer.* My vision telescoped so that all I saw was these words, illuminated, glowing and suspended in the oily blackness. *Vomiting.* My mind raced back to the prawn poisoning. Surely it was not possible to have such bad luck? When there were people who blithely bonked away after repeatedly neglecting to take their pill? It seemed incredible, paranoid, unfeasible. And absolutely obvious. I had ignored all the signs – the heightened sense of smell, the insatiable appetite, the intolerance of alcohol, the tiredness, my strange moods ... I had blamed residual food poisoning, lack of sleep, abundant sex, and of course I had blamed Yves, but never this!

I got dressed quickly and ran out without stopping for my usual coffee towards the pharmacy for a test kit, hoping it might prove me wrong. As I rushed into the shop I could feel frightened tears spouting in my eyes and caught a glimpse of myself, distracted and pasty with dark rings around my eyes, my hair still unbrushed and ungelled in my panic and standing up in an Einsteinian frizz. Not a pretty sight. I searched the shop, head down among the shelves of unfamiliar articles, until the elderly pharmacist approached me.

'Can I help you?' I turned sharply to face him as if caught in the act and tried to explain what I was looking for, forgetting my French in the panic. He took me to the baby section and discreetly handed me a box without saying anything. How many similar hollow-eyed frightened young women this elderly pharmacist must have sold these kits to in the past.

I rushed past Madame Rouillard on the pavement on my way up.

'No coffee this morning?' she frowned, gruffly maternal.

'Later.'

She looked after me curiously and I was convinced she knew what was in the packet.

I creaked up to the third floor in the piss-smelling lift, locked myself into the toilet, and ripped the kit out of the packaging. I peed into a little see-through plastic container as accurately as is possible when your whole body seems to be shaking uncontrollably. Then I squeezed a few drops into the eyedropper and dropped them into the little test kit. I didn't breathe. Nothing happened. I almost smiled. I was about to throw the tester away when a thin bright pink line stained its way up the tester. I sat there for ages, unable to move. Something was constricting my heart and lungs and I could hardly breathe. Footsteps came towards the door. There was a knock, a pause, the handle was tried, then the feet shuffled off again. I just sat there. A while later the feet came again, quicker this time. The handle was jerked impatiently and someone swore bitterly outside the door in a voice that sounded like too much *pastis*. When the feet departed again, I opened the door and miraculously made it to the basin just before I was sick.

I told nobody. There was nobody I could tell. Inge was in Sweden, Madame Rouillard would have been appalled (and I was reliant on her for the roof over my head) and getting help from any of Yves's friends was out of the question. I went back to my room and sank down on the lumpy bed. From the lockable top compartment of my rucksack I pulled out the plastic travel pouch and looked at my air ticket. I would have given anything to go home. I imagined my friends assembled at the airport to greet me, gathering me to their communal bosom. Then the mental movie rewound and a different vision played out: I saw myself stumbling off the plane as a big-bellied joke, or emerging as a hollow-eyed failure, pale as a Panado, to be driven straight to some dubious doctor for a backstreet abortion. It was unbearable. I contemplated the alternatives. Could I ask Yves for money? Could I tell him I was expecting his child? Unthinkable. I could almost hear Yves lecturing me about how he would never have another child, almost see his imperious nose stuck in the air for emphasis. What an absurd figure. I thought of sad Anne, no doubt trawling the apartment for traces of our liaison, and I hoped she knew Yves and I were over. I felt an odd sort of kinship with her, as if we'd both survived relationships with Bluebeard, and was sad to think she'd never think that way about me. I fingered the piece of paper with the clinic details I'd found. Tomorrow I would go and get a proper test, just to make sure. And if that came back positive I'd use Claude's emergency credit card off Claude's account and do what had to be done.

The clinic

The bland hopelessness and Eastern bloc atmosphere inside the clinic reminded me of *Sophie's Choice*. I sat tearless, nauseous with apprehension, skinny as a runt despite my recent bingeing. A big peasant-looking woman with a girl of about fourteen were in front of me in the queue of women, who waited with bovine, obedient patience, resigned to their fates. The girl was explaining the form to the peasant woman in a strange accent, and I realised the woman could not read and that she was the first white woman I had ever met who was illiterate. A uniformed woman emerged from the consulting room and barked a name, and the young girl got up and went in alone, despite the older woman's protestations. What was this young girl's story? Rape? Incest? Ignorance? I was seeing a side of life I saw little of at home, though it happened all the time. Here, I was an immigrant, just like most of the other women in the grim room, poor and dependent. How many girls in how many towns at this moment …? If I cried now I might never be able to stop. The Peasant Woman leaned over and handed me one of her sweets, smiled at me, and tears sprang into my eyes but I quickly wiped them away. I'd have liked to have flung myself into her ample black crêpe lap and bawled my eyes out, but at that moment the door to the consulting room opened and a matter-of-fact doctor ushered the woman in to the desk where the girl was putting on her shoes, little girl's shoes, buckling the buckle with such a girlish, childish, gesture it was intolerable to watch.

Then I am in a dream state, in a nightmare. The doctor tells me what I already know. I am pregnant. He throws out the rest of my pee and hands my blood samples to the unsmiling nurse who is scribbling down everything we say in an illegible code on an official form. I must come back for the results of my HIV tests and 'to talk' in two days. I am numb. My mouth and throat are so dry I can hardly greet the doctor. I am out in the street in the bright light, outside the clinic. Although I feel so heavy

I seem to float outside of my body. I can't feel my legs. I keep walking somehow, but my vision grows blacker and blacker and tiny motes of light flit around in the deepening blackness. This is all I see as my legs buckle under me.

I come to with a crowd of construction workers looking down on me. My mind rages. It resists the growing consciousness, craving a return to oblivion. This is how a failed suicide must feel. My skirt is rucked up to my waist in the fall. One of the workers takes pity and pulls it down to cover me as they carry me back into the clinic and deposit me on a sofa to recover. The clinic staff tell me it's just low blood pressure. I lie on the tatty sofa studying the cracks and the posters on the wall for half an hour. Then I get up and walk back to my tiny room above Madame Rouillard's. I sleep for thirteen hours.

A few days later I found out that I was HIV negative. I wondered gloomily whether it might not have been simpler if I'd discovered I was positive. Then I could just have given up and thrown myself off the Eiffel Tower and let someone else clear up the mess. It seemed like quite a good idea. I was desperate to talk to someone, but the brief 'counselling session' at the clinic had only proved that talking to someone whose job it was to calm the desperate, someone who spoke bad English and didn't know the first thing about me, was not going to help. I had never felt more friendless. I would have phoned Claude but I dreaded a lecture about irresponsibility and how people had bigger problems to deal with. I tried to phone Jack, but every time I hung up before it went through. Death seemed like a remarkably appealing alternative.

In all of this, I did make one adult decision: I told Thierry I would only work until the end of the month and he seemed guiltily relieved. After telling him, I walked like a somnambulist down through the eighth to the rue de Rivoli and stopped at the WH Smith. I spotted South Africa in one of the stories in *Libération* and turned automatically to the page. I found it among a collection of other 'women's stories' which just happened to be about reproductive health, next to a photo of a woman in a clinic in Gauteng not unlike the one I'd recently been to. I felt a hot surge of adrenalin as I translated the headline: *Brave new abortion bill for South Africa?* It was unbelievable. In just a few weeks South Africa was likely to pass the Termination of Pregnancy Bill, 'one of the best reproductive rights laws in the world' in the view of the *Libération* journalist. There had been protests from the various religious groups, but in general the support for the bill was 'overwhelming'. This could mean an end to all the horrific life-threatening abortions Claude always told me about, an end to the unexplained trips overseas for the wealthier South African women and girls who 'got into trouble'. Claude would be triumphant. And here I was, alone in Paris, 'in trouble' just a few weeks too early. Somebody up there had a very dark sense of humour.

I shoved the newspaper back on the rack and went in looking for some cheerful fiction to hide in, but the baby section lured me towards it and I ended up glutting miserably on the facts of life. First, the facts on abortion – 'after twelve weeks termination is strongly discouraged' – then cheerful tracts (clearly intended for expectant parents) on how the baby grows. I flipped back to the first month. The book told me I'd probably be experiencing 'mood swings, nausea, food cravings and aversions, breast changes ...' No kidding. How could I not have guessed immediately? I couldn't help reading on: 'By the end of the first month, your baby is a tiny, tadpole-like embryo, smaller than a grain of rice ...' 'Your baby ...' I read again. It was real. My eyes brimmed and I bit my lip and sat on the floor with the book, out of sight of the suspicious-looking shop assistant. Would I start measuring everything in days and weeks? Would I leave it until it was too late? Could I run home and make history as the first South African woman to have a legal abortion in her own country? Unlikely. I stuck the pregnancy book back in the shelf, bought a bad-looking frivolous English novel and went 'home'.

The next day I spent in bed, immobile. I lay in bed staring at the cover of the bad-looking English novel and having fantasies about sticking Yves's cock in a blender and other violent phallus-mutilating activities.

But there were more rude shocks to come. That evening Madame Rouillard pushed a piece of paper under the door. It was a four-line fax from Jack, alarmingly brief:

Clem
I thought I should let you know that Kurt has been granted some arts funding from the Krauts. He's already left for Germany and intends to come via Paris and pay you a surprise visit on the way. Please, darling girl, be wise about this and don't be bullied. Phone me whenever you need to, and don't forget you can tell him to fuck off.

Jack

Dystopia

... we are indeed drifting in to the arena of the unwell.
– Marwood in *Withnail and I*

It was the cruellest timing. If only I had known he was coming I might have resisted Yves's advances without a regret and avoided this descent into hell. When Kurt finally phoned to tell me when he was arriving I felt absurdly like it was some kind of reprieve from reality, an excuse to delay the inevitable decision. Basically it was full-blown denial. I deluded myself into thinking that if I ignored this thing growing inside me it might go away ... I deluded myself into thinking that if I kept my secret Kurt might be a friend. I really believed it might be possible. I longed to have a real friend here, a friend from home. Might his familiar presence not be comforting? I could imagine it: I would forgive him for bonking the Anti-Oxidant and give him my blessing and he would be overcome with friendly gratitude. We could loiter brokely and companionably together in cheap cafés and live off falafels from the rue des Rosiers. I would not be alone.

Clearly I was delusional, but Kurt had been surprisingly nice on the phone, so nice it had almost dispelled the gloom and panic that Jack's fax had caused. Without telling him anything about Yves (and without referring directly to the Anti-Oxidant) I'd said I hoped we could forget the past and just enjoy being together. He'd agreed enthusiastically, said he was so excited to be seeing me. I wanted us to be friends. Now, as I stood in the chilly station in Kurt's black beret, waiting for the train to deliver him and trying to delude myself into a state of calm, anxiety coiled my guts into knots. I had succeeded in throwing up the coffee Madame Rouillard had given me that morning (though this was not so unusual in itself) but I had also succeeded in persuading her to let Kurt stay in Berthaut's room while he was away on holiday. In short, I had arranged it all, still operating under the delusion that Kurt would happily agree to sleep in a separate room. Just to make sure there was no cause for conflict I stashed my diaries in the empty rucksack in my wardrobe and locked the most recent and incriminating one into the top compartment with a padlock, patting the bag down until it looked empty. Perhaps it was paranoid – a journal-keeper like Kurt would respect others' privacy – but I felt much better for doing it. I was fully prepared.

The train pulled in but no Kurt waved frantically out of the window. I watched the other passengers climb off and be greeted on the platform – joyously, cordially, officially, rapturously – until finally, through the crowds, he made his way down the platform towards me. He was wearing a new black beret, identical to his old one which I was wearing, smiling a cool smile, pale and strained and gorgeous. I was aware that we must look rather foolish in our matching wannabe-Parisian headgear and I tried not to be upset that he had simply replaced the beret he had given me once I'd left. I gave him my most familial hug but he squeezed me to him and laid into me with an urgent and very un-friendly kiss. This was not quite the dynamic I had imagined. I disengaged myself from his grasp and accidentally patted him on the back as I did so. A foolish error of judgement. He stepped back from me and eyed me suspiciously.

'What is it?' he asked.

'Nothing. It's just a bit ... well it's a bit overwhelming.' I tried to smile. Had I not made myself clear on the phone? Had he wilfully misunderstood me?

'Let's get out of here,' I said.

I had planned a grand tour of pauper's Paris: we would stop at a café near the Gare du Nord, which (with its pug-faced cat and matching owner) radiated authenticity. We would climb into a bus (I had researched the route, thinking it would be more impressive than the métro) and take a stroll towards Madame Rouillard's, while I pointed out some lovely little shops along the way. I would be a nonchalant, knowledgeable guide. I would show him what a wonderful place I'd been living in.

'Isn't the métro that way?' he asked pointing to the M sign in the opposite direction.

'Yes, but I thought we'd go via a café near here and take the bus.'

'We can go out later. I'm exhausted and I just want to be alone with you.' He looked at me meaningfully, fixing me with his gorgeous eyes in a way he knew I'd always found irresistible. But this was no longer the case. I would have laughed if I hadn't been so frightened. He suddenly seemed so young, so obvious ... I had never felt less like having sex in my life. This was going to be a lot more complicated than I had hoped.

Once we were back in my room and alone together the confrontation became inevitable. Kurt brushed his teeth and washed his hands scrupulously in my basin and I knew he meant business.

'But why don't you want to?' he asked, when I tried as subtly as possible to resist his advances.

'I've told you, it's all just too much.'

Kurt flopped back onto the soufflé he'd clearly taken for granted we'd be sharing. From the moment he'd arrived I knew he'd never agree to stay in Berthaut's room. He held my face in his hands. 'I thought you said you'd forgiven me, that we were going to forget the past? I've spent the last few months thinking it over and I realised we're supposed to be together.'

I felt ill. I'd known nothing about this 'realisation'. Nothing. If he'd once written or phoned to apologise or asked me to forgive him I might have weakened and agreed to take him back, but he had not.

'I *have* forgiven you,' I said in a small voice, 'it's just that I can't ... I don't want to ...'

I turned my head away, and he took his hands from my face and sat back suddenly on the bed, staring at me in shock.

'There's someone else, isn't there?' he asked, staring up at the ceiling. My heart froze.

'No, there is not. I can promise you.' That much was true. There was definitely 'no one else' in my life now – no one at all, let alone a lover. I tried in vain to prise him out of the stuffy, suffocating room.

'Let's not spend our precious time in Paris bickering about nothing. Come, let's go for a walk.'

'Fuck Paris, I came to see you.' Kurt glowered at me.

'Well I'll be *with* you, silly. Let's go.' I was full of cheerless cheer.

'I know something's wrong. I'm not going to go out until you tell me what's going on,' he insisted.

I could feel my false courage disintegrate as the tears came.

'I just don't want to have sex ... ever since the Anti-Oxidant ...'

'The *what*?'

'Ever since I found you with whatsername after your piece I just ...'

'Clem, I should never have done it, but at the time I felt like you were just not interested in me or my work and she really was. She was there for me.'

'So you *did* fuck her! I *knew* it!' I wanted to scream.

'Actually only after you left. I don't regret it, but I didn't enjoy it.' He looked at me defiantly; chin up, daring me to challenge him. I laughed a bitter ironic laugh. He put his hand on my arm but I shrugged it off. I wanted to hurt him.

'Isn't that odd. 'Cause it's quite the opposite with me. I enjoyed mine thoroughly and I regret it more than I've ever regretted anything in my life.'

Kurt looked at me in silence. Then he got up, retched drily into the basin and sat down on the bed again a little further away from me.

'So you lied. There is someone.' He spoke in a small, cold voice.

'Was.'

'Why didn't you tell me?'

'Why didn't *I*? Why didn't *you* tell *me*? I was actually *there* when you were busy seducing her! I hardly felt the need to tell you when you were thousands of miles away fucking someone else.' This was not true, of course. I had felt a tremendous need to tell him but I was not exactly going to admit that. I noticed that he no longer bothered to deny that he'd screwed her when I was still there. I turned away from him. It seemed we had simply dreamt up different and utterly irreconcilable realities in our separate hemispheres. Now we sat on the same bed, worlds apart, adrift on an ocean, signalling frantically at each other in a semaphore which no longer made any sense. Kurt stood up and stared at me sitting there, hovering absurdly since there was nowhere else to sit.

'I can't sleep in the same bed as you knowing you've been fucking someone else.'

'You mean because I admit I enjoyed it?'

He gave me a disgusted look.

'Don't worry,' I sneered, 'I've booked you another room.'

'Did you fuck him right here?' he jabbed a finger at the bed.

'No I did not.' Thankfully it was the truth.

'You planned it this way, didn't you?' Kurt looked tortured and hateful. He acted as though I'd lured him here under false pretences.

'I wanted us to be friends. I thought you understood that when I spoke to you on the phone.'

'I understood something else entirely. I think you're deluded.'

'Maybe.'

We lapsed into silence again.

'Was it really worth giving everything up for this? Living in a dive and being a waitress?' He gestured around the room to the fly-spotted prints in their cheap frames and the peeling wallpaper. I'd tried to talk up my job, but he'd seen through that immediately.

'This' – I gestured around me – 'is not what it's all about. And if I have to explain that to you you're less enlightened than I thought.' I spoke more bravely than I felt. My courage came from sheer terror. I turned over on my side and shut my eyes. I thought if I ignored him he might give up and leave me alone, but he didn't. He didn't move at all.

Kurt did not go to his room that night. I woke up in the middle of the night to find we were sleeping head to toe on the sagging soufflé and there seemed no point in moving him. I watched him sleeping, his red lips slightly parted and curled prettily like a spoilt child's, and wondered why I once allowed myself to feel tyrannised by him. I stroked his hair but pulled away when he stirred.

I woke up with a start a few hours later. Kurt was standing next to the bed, still fully clothed. He had opened the window and a freezing cold draught was blowing into the tiny room. He stood in the icy blast in front of the open window like a tortured Heathcliff.

'What are you doing?' I asked. 'Shut the window and come back to bed, it's bloody freezing.'

Kurt continued to stare out like a mad person, his eyes as round as frisbees.

'I had a dream that I jumped off a high tower to my death. It was beautiful.' I think he thought he was gazing in the direction of the Eiffel Tower. Then he stepped forward to the window sill (unfortunately he had to stretch forward over the basin to do this, which made things a little awkward) and leaned precariously out.

'Maybe I should just do it,' he said. I pretended not to be frightened.

'Kurt, please come back to bed.'

'Why? You don't love me.'

'Yes I do. It's just that things have changed. I love you in a different way.'

'I don't *want* to be loved in a different way.'

'Please. *Please*. I'm so tired and cold, can't we talk about this in the morning?'

I had to get up and work in two hours' time. The thought filled me with dread. I had thought it might be a useful escape route. Instead there was now the extra fear of leaving Kurt alone in such a state.

He woke me up again before dawn.

'How many times did you sleep with him?' he asked before I'd even properly woken up.

'Please, Kurt.' I was hardly even conscious and already I felt nauseous.

'No really. I want to know all the details. I do.' He looked slightly crazed.

'Well I don't want to tell you.' I looked at the clock. Six thirty. I might as well get up.

'What did you do with him? Did you suck his cock?' I threw back the blankets and got up, rubbing my arms with my hands as I grabbed my bathrobe.

'Shut up, Kurt.'

'Did you?'

'I don't ask you these questions about you and ... her. Leave me alone.'

'You don't ask because you don't care. Where are you going?'

'I've got to get ready for work. I told you.' Queasiness was taking hold of me.

'You don't give a shit about me, do you? I have come all this way to see you, spent all this money, and you're going to spend most of my time here grinning at morons and serving them food while I float around aimlessly.'

'You came to Europe for an art exhibition, Kurt, and I have to earn a living. Most people do, actually.'

I stormed down the passage to the bathroom, hugely relieved to be out of that stifling space.

While I was washing my hair I thought I heard a strange sound that seemed to come from my bedroom. I opened my eyes wide as though it might help me hear better. They filled with shampoo but I heard nothing unusual. What if he had decided to throw himself out of the window while I was out of the room? Frantic and half covered in soap and shampoo I ran back and found him sleeping contentedly in my bed. I just managed to make it back to the bathroom for my first morning puke.

I was relieved to find Kurt in one piece and reading on my bed when I got home that evening. To avoid the inevitable inquisition, I suggested we go to a movie in my favourite old cinema in the fifth. Neither of us needed to be overtaxed so we decided we'd opt for something English. It was a fresh, clear cold evening, clean and bright. It felt full of promise.

'So what did you do today?' I asked Kurt eventually as we trudged along, our breaths making clouds in the cold. He looked at me contemptuously like a belligerent teenager might regard his hopelessly out-of-date mother and we walked to the cinema in silence.

Ironically, the only English movie on that night turned out

to be an old Mel Brooks comedy, which I found hilarious despite myself. Kurt sat scowling through the whole film so I tried to limit my laughter. He seemed determined to hate it. By the time we came out he was seething: 'They call this a fucking art house cinema? It's a scandal.'

'It was a comedy, Kurt. It's not pretending to be high art. I thought it was quite funny.'

He sneered.

'Can't you ever just enjoy something? Didn't you find it funny at all?' Before I would never have asked him, I'd never have exposed my bad taste. Now I couldn't be bothered to hide it.

'It was insulting.'

Suddenly I felt very tired and hungry. I didn't want to argue about the merits of Mel Brooks or the benefits of laughter.

'What about a falafel?' But Kurt was determined not to be lured out of the doldrums so I ignored him and started walking towards the falafel joints anyway. What would he say if he knew I was pregnant? I wanted desperately to shout at him, to point out just how selfish he was being and how other people actually had worse problems than having ex-girlfriends who no longer worshipped them as a sex-gods. Of course I felt guilty, but he really was beginning to drive me berserk.

'Why don't you just leave, if it's so unbearable for you here?' I blurted out.

He looked at me as though it were the most idiotic question he'd ever heard.

'Because we belong together.'

I said nothing. It was too late. They put too much tahina in my falafel and its thick milky smell made me feel sick. I had to throw it away half-eaten and remained ravenous.

That night brought no relief. No sooner had we hit the soufflé than he began his interrogation and emotional manipulation tactics all over again. And again, after a few hours' fitful sleep, he woke me to assault me with still more questions.

'Where did you do it? Did you think of me? What did you do?' Never ending.

Why I didn't turf him out and save my sanity I don't know. He pushed the guilt button and ground me down until I felt it was all my fault. I was defenceless. A few hours later, when morning broke, I was desperate to leave for work. I could hardly wait. As I threw up my morning coffee I decided I no longer cared whether he jumped out of the window or not. If one of us was going to survive this, why shouldn't it be me?

The ninth circle

... it is not without fear that I bring myself to speak, for to describe the bottom of all the universe is no enterprise to undertake in sport.
– Dante Alighieri, *The Divine Comedy, Inferno*

Once I'd endured almost a week of this I began to lose it. Kurt was relentless. It felt like he had been with me for months. His was a particularly effective form of torture: the sleep deprivation, the constant inquisition and accusation ... I couldn't even *pretend* to cope at work any more, that much was obvious. I was sickly pale, I shook constantly, I cried all the time for no apparent reason. My hormones had gone on the rampage, but nobody understood or sympathised because I couldn't even tell anyone I was pregnant. One lunchtime, when a customer pointed out that I hadn't brought her *pommes frites*, I burst into tears in the kitchen. Thierry took me aside.

'What is wrong, Clémence, are you sick?' His kindness set me off again. I blew my nose copiously into a pile of paper napkins.

'No, I'm not sick.' I *wished* I could tell him what was wrong – I so wanted someone to confide in – but Thierry was my boss and Serge's friend and it would have been a disastrous step.

'Is it drugs?'

'No!' I was very surprised by this question but I suppose I must have looked pretty bad at the time.

'It's … my boyfriend has arrived. My ex-boyfriend. From South Africa.' More nose-blowing. 'I'm just having a hard time.'

He frowned at me with concern. 'Does he hit you?'

'No no.'

Though secretly, in the middle of the night when Kurt persecuted me with his questions, I had begun to wish he *would* hit me instead. I thought it might even be a relief to escape the mental torture for a while, to endure something more physical and direct. I actually believed it might lessen the burden if he beat a confession out of me. It would have been less complicated to have been so obviously the victim.

To my embarrassment and immense gratitude, Thierry said I could leave that afternoon if I wanted to. I accepted with relief, though I dreaded spending any extra time with Kurt. How many more of these intolerable days could I endure? Thierry paid me out until the end of the month and made me promise to come and visit him. 'I'll make you a special *tajine de poisson*,' he called as I left, clutching a handful of paper napkins.

'You don't need to bribe me with food,' I called back to him, trying to smile, 'I'll be back.'

I never saw him again.

Booth

The next day Kurt and I walked to the bank. I had a second credit card off Claude's account, which she had said I could use in dire emergencies. I decided this definitely qualified. If I survived the next few days I would dispatch Kurt to Germany on a train, cash any money I could get my hands on and make some urgent plans. I left Kurt waiting outside the bank.

'I'm afraid you cannot draw any money from this account,' the over-coiffed teller told me, smiling a winning service smile (mouth only, no eyes) as though he had just been really helpful.

'What do you mean? It's *my card*,' I wailed.

There was no money in the account, no more credit available.

I tried to retain some composure. My throat burned with the desire to cry as I asked him to check once more. Kurt was pacing outside looking irritated. The teller gave me a supercilious 'suffer the idiot' look.

'Please,' I began, forsaking all dignity. 'It's a credit card, there must be some allowance? I'll pay it back!'

The man shook his head. 'I'm sorry,' he said simply, and began to fiddle with the papers on the desk in front of him. Our discussion was clearly over.

'This is ridiculous!' I wailed. I could no longer control my voice. All around me the immaculate matrons and businessmen averted their eyes. 'Petty bureaucrats!' I veered off in the direction of the door, half-blinded by the spouting tears.

Kurt was leaning against the fence outside with his usual casual nonchalance. He barely moved as I came bursting out of the bank.

'What took you so long?'

It could not go on like this.

'Why don't you just fuck off?' I screamed at him. 'I can't get any money.' I felt I had broken some barrier. I was too far gone to care. It was the most terrifying liberty. For a moment I managed to see myself objectively – a young woman screaming hysterically at her boyfriend in the middle of a quiet Paris street, a less than minor episode in the perpetual soap opera of Parisian street life. What would Claude say? Claude! Perhaps she would be able to help me get the money! I grabbed onto this feeble hope and looked around for a phone booth.

'I'm going to phone Claude,' I announced cryptically, and headed off at great speed to get away from him. He watched me coolly from his fence. He didn't move.

I dialled Claude's number and got her answering machine, which made me weep even more. Oh God, I could hardly leave a message like this on an answering machine. Then I tried Jack's number ... and reached *his* latest answering machine offering. Thousands of miles away from home and here I was being treated to porno groans and sexy moans on the other end of the line. It was just what I least wanted to hear. I sobbed distractedly into the mouthpiece.

'Jack, where the fuck are you?'

No answer.

There was no option. I'd have to phone Claude and leave Madame Rouillard's number so that she could phone me back. For the third time I put my much-depleted phone card into the slot and dialled my mother's number again, breathing deeply to control my voice so that my message wouldn't sound too hysterical, but all my defences dropped when I heard her voice on the answering machine again. 'Hello. We're not in at the moment ...' I began to sob so convulsively I could not speak. This was insane. If I carried on weeping like this I'd end up in the hospital with dehydration. I held my hand over the receiver so that I wouldn't bawl into the answering machine and struggled to get my breath back. It was like a Superman scene in reverse. The moment I climbed into the phone booth I lost all my strength and dissolved into tears. I lifted the receiver to my face again and tried to say something intelligible.

'They won't give me the money,' I howled. There was a click and a squeal and a lot of swearing at the other end of the line as the receiver was picked up.

'Clem? Is that you?' It was Maddy's voice. I was so taken aback I stopped crying and shut up momentarily.

'Maddy. What are you doing at Claude's?' I asked.

'Keeping an eye on Mac and feeding Claude's fucking awful menagerie while she's at a conference and touring around Australia. That bloody awful black Labrador of hers just pissed on the sofa. I took them all for a walk two minutes ago, and the others pissed but she held it in to wait for somewhere comfy to do it, on the fucking sofa in this case. Is this normal?'

'Did you put soda water on it?' The minor domestic crisis

was so comforting.

'Yes. Okay, now what the hell is going on with you? Where are you?'

'In Paris.' My voice wobbled all over the place again.

'Jesus, sweetie, you sound fucking terrible. If that's what a holiday in Gay Paree does for you ... shall I phone you back? It's Claude's phone bill anyway.' I gave her the number and perused the phone sex ads stuck up in the booth while I waited for the phone to ring. By the time she called me back I had managed to stop wailing.

'Hi. Okay, what's this money situation?' she asked with her usual directness. I explained.

'That's simple, Clemmy, I'll get some money into your credit card and you can pay me back, okay? Or Claude can.' I gave her the details.

'Is that all it is? Huh? I hear that pretty Kraut boy of yours is over there on some art thing. Is he making you miserable again?'

'Yes, but it's all my fault. I ... I ...' I hesitated. I was not sure I could tell anyone the gory details.

'You *what*?' she persisted impatiently.

'Well I had a bit of a fling ...'

'Ye-e-e-es?' Maddy asked slowly, as if trying to coax the information from someone mentally defective.

'And now Kurt's here ...' I blundered on.

'And Kurt found out?'

'Mm hmm,' I mumbled.

'Oh shit. How?'

I said nothing.

'Oh Clem, you didn't *tell* him did you?' she asked incredulously.

Sheepish silence.

'Hmmm. What a great pity. You live and learn, I suppose.'

'I couldn't carry on lying, Maddy. I felt so ... stressed all the time.'

'And you feel better *now*? You certainly don't sound it. Why don't you just tell him to leave?'

'I can't just do that!'

'Why not? It's only making it worse. You're just turning it into a guiltfest.'

'I can't. He's come all this way to see me and I've cocked it all up.' I told her about the suicide threats.

'I'll believe that when I see it,' she said. I kept quiet for a while.

'Maddy, it gets worse.' I stopped, bracing myself to confess. 'You promise on your life you won't tell anyone – not even Claude?'

'Of course I promise, for fuck's sake. What is it?'

There was a violent outbreak of barking in the background and Maddy swore viciously into the receiver, a talent she'd learnt young from Mac and subsequently perfected.

'*Ek is swanger,*' I said absurdly, breaking into 'not-in-front-of-the-children' Afrikaans just in case Kurt's hearing was miraculously sharp.

'What?' The canine cacophony continued in the background.

'I'm knocked up,' I announced more loudly, battling against the noise. 'You know, up the spout. I'm pregnant, Maddy.'

I looked around, paranoid that Kurt could read my lips, but he seemed oblivious.

Silence for a few beats from Maddy's side of the line.

'Aah. Oh fuck,' said Maddy as the penny dropped. 'Yes, that does make things a bit tricky. Just how pregnant are you?'

'I don't know. I think I'm about a month overdue.' I wiped tears and snot onto my sleeve and slumped against the side of the phone booth for support. Telling someone was such a relief it was all I could do not to lie on the floor, sucking in the nourishing familiarity through the umbilical phone cord and blubbing. Maddy said nothing for a while, no doubt digesting the fact that her niece was clearly further off the rails than she'd initially realised.

'Maddy, are you there still?'

'Of course I'm here, silly. I'm thinking. Do you have any plans?'

'What do you mean?'

'I mean are you planning to keep the baby? Do you know who the father is?'

'What? Of course I know who the father is! You make it sound like I've been whoring around Europe with every …'

'Well date-wise it can't be Kurt, so it must be the other guy.'

'It's the other guy.'

'Does this guy know?'

'No.'

'Does Kurt know?'

'No.'

'Well thank God for that. At least that makes it your decision. You know they're just about to legalise abortion here?'

'I know. I read.'

'*Kak* timing.'

'Mmm.'

Maddy's voice became softer, less strident. 'Have you thought about what you're going to do, Clem? If you're planning to get rid of it you will have to act quickly.'

I said nothing.

'Listen, Clementine, do you want me to get hold of Claude in Australia?'

'No, please don't.'

Maddy sighed irritably on the other end of the phone. Then, reluctantly, she made a suggestion.

'Okay, I've been talking about going over to see my brother in Cambridge next month. Maybe there's some way I can come earlier and fetch you on the way.'

'Can you? Maddy, you're a saviour.'

'No, I'm fucking well not, I'm … God! Down boy, drop that! Get away from the sofa!' There was a volley of oaths and insults and a smacking sound in the distance at the other end of the line.

Then Maddy was back.

'Bastard mongrel tried to eat my cellphone! Aggh, shit! If I come over now I'm going to have to bribe or blackmail someone else to look after your mother's bloody dogs. Perhaps I'll just drop them off at the SPCA.' Maddy chuckled to herself, suddenly cheered by the idea. 'Now tell me where I can *reliably* contact you over there.'

'Okay.' I gave her the number at Madame Rouillard's.

'And for God's sake, whatever you do, get Kurt to leave.'

'Okay.'

'And Clem, don't do anything *else* stupid.'

I hung up the receiver and stood motionless in the booth, flooded with relief. Maddy knew. Maddy was coming to sort it all out. I realised guiltily that I hadn't even asked after Mac. If Maddy came over Mac would be alone while Claude was away. Maddy had shown surprising tact in not mentioning it. I caught sight of myself in the glass. My sorry reflection stared back at me: swollen red nose, swollen slitty eyes, blotchy skin. My sleeves looked like they had been attacked by a pack of giant snails. Practice had not perfected the art of glamorous weeping in my case. I would have hidden behind my Jackie O's right there in the freezing semi-darkness of mid-winter if I'd only had them. Bracing myself, I stepped out of the phone booth and headed back to Kurt, clutching onto this secret new hope.

That evening Jean from the bar called me to tell me there was a call from Jack. I ran downstairs to the phone.

'Are you all right, gorgeous girl? You had me really worried with that message of yours.'

'I'm a mess actually, Jack, but I think I've found a solution.'

'Is it Kurt?'

'Torture.' This was not the time to tell him the whole truth.

'Oh God. I'm sorry. I tried to warn you, but he'd already left. I hope you got my fax.'

'I did. Thank you, Jack.' I tried to squeeze myself behind the wall where the phone hung to get some privacy. 'He told me he'd fucked the Anti-Oxidant so to spite him I told him about The Suit.'

'And he went ballistic?'

'Mmm hmm.'

'Hmmm. Oh dear.'

'Kurt wanted to kill him, of course. But since Yves was in New York he threatened to kill himself instead. He keeps threatening to jump out of the window ...'

'Well, tell him not to forget to point his toes, darling, someone may be watching. Maybe you could even film it as his last Art Happening.'

'Jack, I'm making light of this but I'm really scared. What if he does it?'

'Darling, I think the likelihood of him actually doing himself in is extremely slim.'

Kurt was coming into the bar, looking for me.

'I must go. There's ... some other stuff I want to talk to you about, but I can't now.'

'Anything, darling. Any time. I'm so sorry I was out when you called.'

'Miss you desperately.'

'Think of you constantly.'

'Love you madly.'

'Bye.'

I hung up, took a deep breath and went back to Kurt.

The next afternoon, while I was buying a single one-way train ticket to Germany, Kurt read my journals – all except for the most recent one, which I had locked away and hidden. When I got back in the evening he thrust the locked rucksack at me violently as I opened the door.

'What's in here?' he demanded accusingly. His face seemed out of control. Behind him a pane of glass in the window had been punched in. Clothes, books, papers and toiletries were strewn across the bedroom as if an explosion had occurred. In contrast to this chaos, my diaries were stacked neatly on the bedside table. So that was how he had spent his day.

'What have you done?' I asked. I could barely breathe. He walked towards me, lifted his hand to slap my face, then pulled his arm away as if with immense effort and roared with pain and frustration.

'I know what's in there,' he said. 'It's everything you didn't have the courage to tell me. Everything about how you fucked that guy ... Which one was it anyway, little *pisseuse*?' I winced as I recognised Serge's nickname for me. Kurt had read carefully. He always did.

'You had no right to do that!' I lunged past him and tried to grab the neatly stacked diaries from next to the bed, but he snatched them up and pushed me aside so that I fell onto the bed, hitting my head on the wall. Then he just stood there, holding my diaries to his chest, shaking his head at me. His face started working in a peculiar way, and to my horror Kurt began to cry in loud roaring sobs. He stumbled forward onto his knees, dropped the diaries and fell into my lap like a child. I pulled him up onto the bed and we lay together, respectively howling and silently numb, curled into spoons, lamenting our own separate sadnesses.

That night, after Kurt had finally drifted off, I managed to extricate myself from him and crept downstairs with the diary, still locked inside the top of the rucksack. Thankfully there was still a light on at the Rouillards'. I knocked tentatively on their door, hoping it would be the distant incurious Monsieur Rouillard who came to answer, but a few seconds later Madame Rouillard padded down the passage in her *pantoufles* and stared through the spyhole at me.

'Oh, it's you!' she said, pulling back the chain to open the door. Her hair was in pins and she looked quite frightening without her make-up on. She did not seem overly pleased to see me.

'I was worried earlier. I heard a lot of noise and then glass. I sent Jean up to check. He says your friend made a big mess in the room and the window was broken.'

'Yes, I know. I'm sorry. That was an accident. I'll fix it.'

'Don't bother. Jean will fix it and your friend can pay.' Madame Rouillard regarded me suspiciously. 'There isn't any trouble between you two is there?'

'No, no. No trouble.' I tried to look blithe but it was difficult, standing there trembling in the middle of the night.

'I am happy to help you, but you know that room is only meant for one person ...' she trailed off, disarmed by my pitiful state, no doubt, but I knew what she was building up to. It was a warning. Kurt might be a respectable-looking white boy, but he still looked like trouble, and Madame had a phenomenal early warning system when it came to detecting that.

'I know that, Madame Rouillard. You have been so kind to me, and I promise there'll be no more trouble. He's leaving tomorrow – I bought his train ticket this afternoon. Actually, I was just wondering if you'd keep this for me.' She eyed the locked parcel suspiciously.

'It's okay,' I reassured her, 'it's just some private stuff I've written and I don't want anyone to read it.'

She took the bag, handling it as though it might explode any minute. She stared at it then looked into my imploring eyes.

'All right,' she said.

'Thank you.'

I started up the stairs. Just as she was about to shut the door she turned to me again and whispered my name. I paused mid-step.

'Madame?'

'Don't let him cause you any trouble,' she said with gruff concern.

'I won't,' I said, touched and suddenly tearful. Then I made my way up the stairs before her sympathy made me cry.

Exit the nemesis

'I've bought you a train ticket. It's for today,' I told him.

'I can't leave like this.'

'You must.'

Kurt and I were sitting in Madame Rouillard's staring out at the freezing cold November day and pretending to eat breakfast. Both of us were wearing our sunglasses. We were worn out. Kurt had noticed that morning that the top compartment of the rucksack was missing from my wardrobe but he had said nothing, just turned to look at me with an expression of sad resignation. I had steeled myself against his look, stared back defiantly. Neither of us had the strength to fight any more. I thought back over the last few days, fiddling with my teabag and sinking it into the water to draw out the flavour, trying not to think about my future.

'Did you really believe we could just be friends?' Kurt asked me suddenly.

'I really hoped.'

'Did you really miss me?'

'I did.'

We stared out of the window in silence while Madame Rouillard shuffled around picking up coffee cups and shouting orders at Jean.

'I wish you'd written to me ... let me know how you were feeling,' I told Kurt. 'We could have saved each other a lot of suffering.'

It was my last offering. He turned to look at me briefly but of course we couldn't read each other's eyes.

At the station we took off our sunglasses to kiss each other goodbye. He said nothing more about the diaries, I told him nothing more than he had read. He thanked me almost meekly for the ticket.

Then he was gone.

Maddy and the hollow reed

Maddy had insisted on the phone the last time I'd spoken to her that she would find her own way into town, and I'd given her Madame Rouillard's address. I'd been counting the days till she came, and the great day had finally arrived. She was due at about nine. At quarter to nine I went down to wait, seized with anxiety. I would have to confront reality now; there was no more space for evasion. But at least I wouldn't be doing it alone.

I was sitting at the window, nursing a cup of hot chocolate, when Maddy's taxi arrived. I watched her step out and wait while the driver passed her her neat, wheeled suitcase. She scanned the window of the café, waved, and (pulling her case behind her like the Parisians lead their dogs) headed towards me. She was wearing high heels. When she opened the door it felt as though there was a communal intake of breath, like when the baddy walks into the bar in a Western. Berthaut's already bulgy eyes looked like they were in danger of leaving their orbits in his skull completely. Maddy, oblivious to the impact of her entrance, ditched her suitcase at the bar and made her way over to me just as I was getting up to meet her. I couldn't help looking at her incredibly high-heeled come-fuck-me shoes. Maddy saw me looking.

'Rule number one of travelling,' she said by way of greeting. 'Always travel in heels or you end up having to carry your own luggage. What *is* going on with your hair?'

I shrugged. 'Malicious hairdresser?'

'Well why don't you just cut it short?'

'That's worse. At least this way it'll soon be long enough to put up again.'

It was an oddly irrelevant discussion considering the purpose of her visit, but I suppose that was the point. I was quite willing to play along. I wondered whether I should do something like go up to her and hug her, but somehow Maddy just didn't seem up for that.

'So where do you stay?' she asked me.

I led Maddy into the building next door and towards the lift. She sniffed the air with a look of distaste. 'Smells like piss,' she said unequivocally.

I nodded. ' 'Fraid so.' We were going to leave her baggage in the room while we organised tickets to England. The door scraped the end of the bed as I swung it open and revealed the room. It looked worse than ever now that I saw it through Maddy's eyes. She raised her eyebrows, dropped her suitcase and did an amazed little whistling sound.

'Jesus, this is a shithole!' she said, staring incredulously. 'How do you *live* in this place?' She walked in and looked around, taking in the mean little mirror, the ancient unwashed-looking crocheted bedcover, the postcards and pictures I'd stuck on the wall in vain attempts to cheer it up.

'It's not that bad,' I said, slightly defensively. 'Not much worse than any digs at home.'

'Jee-zizzzz! I think I'll skip the shower. Let's go and see if we can get tickets for today.'

'Today?' Suddenly I dreaded having to rush, overwhelmed by the prospect of having to pack up my life here and leave within hours. Besides, I'd really hoped I could show Maddy around Paris a little, to prove to her that I wasn't a complete loser.

'*Definitely* today ... if we can.' Maddy looked at me curiously, as if trying to gauge me. 'How are you, I mean *actually*?' she asked.

'I'm okay. I'm feeling a lot better.'

'But you're still ... I mean you *are* still pregnant, aren't you?'

'Obviously I am.' I found the question insulting. As if I'd use something like that as a ploy to get her over here. 'Why?'

'It's just that you haven't mentioned it once since I've arrived. It's as though we were just going over to England to visit family and there was no problem at all. Have you ... thought about it?' What she said struck a nerve. I knew I'd been avoiding it, as though Maddy's mere arrival would resolve the situation.

'Of course I've thought about it,' I blurted out, trying to disguise the panicky feeling that was taking over. 'But what's the good of *thinking* about it?'

Maddy sighed and looked at me. Then she spoke to me in her best Rational Parent voice, which she'd no doubt been practising for days: 'As I see it, it's your choice whether you want to keep the baby or have an abortion, Clem. That's one decision I'm not prepared to make for you. I'll help sort out all the shit whichever way you decide, but it's still your choice.'

I sat still and concentrated on not cracking up. Maddy went on speaking, softening her voice a little but refusing to let me off the hook. 'Keeping the baby might not be a good idea under the circumstances, but perhaps you feel differently. If you choose to go the other route, it can be easily arranged in the UK. In fact if you'd waited a couple of weeks you could probably even have had it done legally at home.'

'I didn't exactly plan ...' I started indignantly, but Maddy shook her head and smiled.

'I'm teasing, silly. I'm going downstairs for a coffee. I'll leave you to pack and think about it, Clem, because you're going to have to decide very soon. Join me when you're ready and we'll go and find out about tickets.'

How was it that Maddy could casually saunter off for a coffee in Paris after being here for all of ten minutes when it had taken me ages to summon up the courage to do that when I first arrived? I watched her walk towards the lift, then turned away and examined the unpromising state of the room, feeling mildly hysterical. To avoid 'thinking about it' I squared up to another potential crisis: packing. I opened my backpack on the bed and started piling everything next to it in preparation. It was ridiculous. How was I supposed to fit this entire room into a backpack? Where had all this shit *come* from? I mean this box of watercolour paints, these theatre programmes and posters, this absurdly heavy Russian military-issue coat ... I was throwing things around now in desperation. My voice box had started making a strange little grunty panicking noise all on its own and I had to wipe my nose on the back of my hand. I sat on my haunches and breathed. Then I piled most of the stuff into the backpack and tried to get it closed. A space about a foot deep remained between the top and bottom sides of the zip. 'Do not get despondent,' I instructed myself. I got myself into a knee-threatening lotus position on top of the backpack, wiped my nose again, and tried a little chant, which my ditsy New-Age friend Lindsay had taught me once when we were cramming for an exam. 'I am a hollow reed. I am a hollow reed.'

'A *what*?' asked Maddy, suddenly reappearing in the doorway. I gave a little shout of fright and swung around.

'I thought it'd go quicker if there were two of us,' she said. One glance proved she was right.

'I can't shut it,' I said, undoing all the good 'hollow reed' work and dangerously close to hysteria again.

'Christ almighty, Clem! Of course you can't shut it. There's enough shit for ten backpacks in there. We're going to need a team of fucking Sherpas.' She knelt down next to me. Unfortunately I had not yet concealed the paints and other not-entirely-essential items from view. Maddy went straight in and pulled out the watercolours. 'What *is* all this?'

'I'm going to use them, I just haven't had time yet,' I mumbled defensively. Maddy gave me a laser look.

'No. No, no, no. Okay, get off the case.' I got off reluctantly, bracing myself for a fight if she tried to make me leave anything behind. She took out the paints, the posters, postcards, magazines as well as other less vital items, including some free offer hair dye, which promised to 'wash away the grey'. The latter she inspected with complete incredulity, shaking her head and giving me her typical 'Jesus wept' long-suffering-aunt-of-crazy-person look where she rolled her eyeballs up to look at me and raised an eyebrow archly. I pretended not to notice. When she had taken about a third of the stuff out of my backpack she put it into a separate pile. 'Now sit again,' she said, pointing to the backpack: Dr Woodhouse for problem teens. She managed to get the zip shut after little effort. 'For your own sake, Clem, we are going straight to the post office with the rest of this.' I sat on top of the closed backpack and nodded. She regarded me curiously for a moment, looked as though she was about to say something, then just closed her mouth and shook her head again, exhaling a small snorting laugh.

At the post office we wrestled my excess baggage into two large boxes. It was the first time I'd heard Maddy speak French and she did so depressingly fluently, once again triumphing in my domain. Although I knew she spoke a few dozen languages for her tourism job, somehow I'd always secretly fantasised that her French wasn't actually that good – that for once she might stumble and need my help. She charmed the man behind the counter into lending her his permanent marker and wrote Claude's address on each box in her rounded slightly childish handwriting, clutching the marker firmly with her red-tipped fingers. Then she paid the postage and I watched the parcels disappear into a back room, bound for home.

To Maddy's utter frustration I refused to go on the Eurostar.

'Oh for God's sake,' she virtually spat. 'Why not?'

'I just can't go under the sea,' I mumbled sheepishly. 'Claustrophobia.' Maddy wrinkled up her face into an expression halfway between amazement and disgust. 'You really are one fucked up kid,' she said reflectively, 'completely *farmisht*.' She made a mixed up circling motion around her head to translate the Yiddish. We soon discovered that flights to London would cost a fortune so it would have to be the ferry. At the Gare du Nord, Maddy asked for directions to the information booth and I hung around next to her like a backward child. The information booth window had one of those little *We Speak English* signs pasted into it with a British flag. Someone had scratched obscene graffiti into the booth next to the attendant's head. The words *Nique ta mère!* hovered over him like a speech bubble. I wondered whether he knew that he was offering to fuck people's mammas as an extra service. I stared gloomily at the booth, my eyes glazing over as my thoughts came back into focus. I thought about what I was doing and felt sick. My guts had been in turmoil since that morning. All I wanted to do was to lie down, but lying on the floor in the middle of the station was not an option. Miserably, I tried to concentrate on staring at the people in front of us at the booth to take my mind off it. They were an elderly German couple. I had a close-up view of his tufty ears and dandruff and her over-dyed coiffure. Her hair looked like it had been slept flat at the back and she was now walking around unknowingly with her bald patches exposed. I suddenly felt terribly tender and sorry for them. We waited while the German couple ploddingly concluded their business, asking the same question over and over again just as we thought they were about to leave. Maddy eventually rolled her eyes, hit her forehead with the palm of her hand in frustration and incredulity and said to me in an embarrassingly audible stage whisper: 'Jesus Christ! They need a special fucking window around here for the mentally handicapped.' I winced, convinced that the couple had heard this unkind aside, and smiled extra hard at them when they eventually bustled off to show that I Came In Peace. By now Maddy was aggro and spoiling for a fight. She greeted the little man behind the glass booth in French and asked him about the ferry times and prices. He reeled off a list of numbers at a ludicrous speed and shut his mouth like a trap once this litany was over. The series of numbers in French confused us. 'Would you please repeat the last few departure times in English,' asked Maddy, while I, the slow child, hung sullenly back.

'*Non*,' said the man behind the counter imperiously. 'You speak French.'

'What the fuck does this say then?' Maddy thrust a short scarlet fingernail at the *We speak English* sign. 'That's false advertising. Or are you just too scared to speak our language? Give me the times in English or I'll call the managers, you wanker,' she said levelly, in French. The man dropped his eyes to consult the timetable. Revved up by the aggressive interaction and noticing everyone's eyes on us, Maddy went into attack mode, suddenly all teeth and nails and scarlet lipstick. She turned to me and announced in a loud voice: 'Now you know why they put these fuckwits behind glass; it's so that you can't hit them.' The travellers around us, overhearing this exchange, twittered like a flock of excited little birds. The man looked at her curiously, handed her a pamphlet containing every bit of information we could have asked for, and greeted us civilly, in French.

'Thank you,' said Maddy sweetly. We consulted the timetable and were duly issued with tickets for that evening. No harm done. A normal transaction.

'I need a stiff fucking drink,' said Maddy, as we walked away from the ticket booth. She was still shaking with anger, though I suspect she rather enjoyed over-revving like this occasionally. 'How about you?'

'I could murder a milkshake,' I said, managing a laugh despite the fact that the tension was now really wreaking havoc on my guts. The truth is I was feeling kind of empty and sick and sore all at once and I was hoping a milkshake would help. Maddy looked at me and sighed and we headed off into the crisp, still afternoon air in urgent pursuit.

I sat down with relief on one of the plumply cushioned chairs at Terminus Nord just over the road from the station, surrounded by authentic-looking Parisian waiters and the tasteful authentic Art Nouveau ornamentation that forecast a very expensive milkshake. I tried not to be reminded of the restaurant at the Gare de Lyon and listened instead to the snatches of excited pre-journey conversations, which floated enticingly towards us from the other tables. It would have been such fun if there hadn't been the real reason for her being there. So this was how it could have been, I thought to myself as I drank my milkshake. This was why people came to Paris. How had it gone so wrong?

We took a taxi back to Madame Rouillard's to fetch my bags and to pay her for the room, and I was overcome by sadness as I said goodbye to her. She hugged me roughly to her ample bosom and wouldn't let me pay for Berthaut's room where Kurt was supposed to have stayed.

'I know you never used that room,' she said in her throaty Gitanes voice, enjoying catching me out. 'Why should I charge you for something you never used?'

I asked her not to tell anyone my new number until I said she could – especially not any man. She swore on the grave of her mother.

'I told you he was trouble,' she said, nodding at me.

'You were right, Madame, he was a lot of trouble,' I agreed. Weren't they all?

I was about to leave when she suddenly hit her forehead with the palm of her hand. She bustled over to a cupboard and pulled out the top part of my rucksack with my journal inside it.

'Don't forget this,' she said, as she handed it to me.

'I'll never forget any of it.'

I kissed her again, and I left.

Most of the way to Calais on the train Maddy and I sat in silence. Once I'd asked after Claude and Mac and found out that nothing at all seemed to have changed it seemed irrelevant to talk about anything unless it was the one topic I did not want to broach. The milkshake hadn't helped. I felt even more nauseous and my stomach was in a permanent cramp. Climbing the gang-plank to the ferry, laden with the accumulated shit from the last few months, it finally hit me. I was going to England to kill this baby. My baby. I went numb. My body felt floppy and I barely had the strength to stand upright, let alone walk. I was not even sure I was conscious until Maddy's wheeled case ran over my foot and brought me sharply to my senses. What I really wanted was to lie down and sleep forever. At that moment, a coma or perhaps a sudden painless death seemed like attractive propositions.

IV

The crossing

The crossing

I enter the ferry on autopilot. I am convinced my mind and body have separated; if they had a choice they would go their own ways, but they have reluctantly agreed to cooperate for the moment. Most of the chairs are full of noisy English yobbos returning after their day trips, shit-faced on cheap French lager and clutching crate loads of duty-free booze and Marlboro. Maddy and I settle down in the ferry bar, an oasis of calm by comparison with their DIY liquor fest. I sit glumly on a corner pouffe, which looks like it had been upholstered with English carpet from the seventies, occasionally sipping my tomato juice, staring out of the grubby, oil-streaked window. At the bar, a Frenchman in a white poloneck zeroes in on Maddy and buys her a double vodka. Clearly his intention is to get her blind drunk (Jesus, you'd *have* to be blind, I think queasily) so that he might have a chance of getting into her pants. Little does he know that she could drink your average Cossack regiment under the table. For a while I watch this exchange of sexual signalling from a distance. Just seeing Maddy match him vodka for vodka turns my stomach. The perpetual rolling motion of the ferry has my innards writhing and I think I might soon need to be sick. I think Poloneck Man catches sight of me and is embarrassed that he is being watched, because all of a sudden he seems to feel compelled to include me.

'You sure you won't have some vodka in that tomato juice?' he calls from the bar.

I shake my head and try to squeeze out a smile. 'I'm fine.' But I'm not. I have a sharp pang in my stomach and clutch my hands more firmly around it. I can feel my mouth stretch itself against my will into an odd sort of writhing expression.

'Excuse me,' I hear Maddy say. She strides over to me.

'What is going on? You're being even weirder than usual, Clem, you're acting like some kind of poltergeist kid. I'm getting really worried about you ...' She does look rather worried, actually. Very worried indeed. 'And another thing; I've noticed you're not drinking and I was wondering whether you ... were having a change of heart about ... *things*,' she asks, nodding towards my aching belly in case I don't understand.

'Thank you, Maddy, but I haven't changed my mind. I've told you before, it's just that I can't even *look* at drink without wanting to throw up. I'm just a bit seasick.' It was true about the drinking. I'd take to the bottle with a vengeance if I could, but it seems that the more pregnant I become, the more my body mutinies, ignoring what my brain and heart had to say and preparing for this little half-French baby. Maddy gives me a laser look, her bullshit-detectors in overdrive and quivering like an out-of-control polygraph. Then she returns to the Poloneck Man at the bar.

The pain in my stomach grows worse. Perhaps it is constipation. Perhaps it is imminent diarrhoea. Perhaps it is par for the course. A French-looking waiter walks by carrying a plate of lunch – a fine specimen of British cuisine in the form of soggy grey slices of roast beef accompanied by grey peas and an afterthought of salad. He holds it at a disdainful distance at the end of his outstretched arm, as if to disassociate himself from it. The food smell assails me. I lever myself up out of the concave chair and make my way to the bathroom, ensuring that I smile reassuringly at Maddy and Poloneck Man as I pass.

In the bathroom I lean with my head against the cool mirror. Painful spasms clutch at my guts. I propel myself rapidly into the toilet cubicle and pull down my jeans and discover that my underwear is wet with blood. I have a fiendishly intense pain in my abdomen. I sit for a while, staring at the blank white door, incredulous and frightened. Suddenly a blade of pain slices through my belly. I brace myself, biting my lip, my hand pushing against the door handle ... and feel a warm gush from my nethers. The pain obliterates the rest of the world for a few seconds. Then I turn around on the seat and stare, bewildered, at the contents of the toilet bowl. Irrationally, I believe I have somehow passed that whole glass of tomato juice straight through my system. But as the pain subsides it strikes me. That was it. My baby. It has just decided to leave of its own accord. I am stupefied. Without stopping to think I flush the chain, stuff half the toilet roll into my gusset, leave the toilet cubicle, wash my hands (staring at myself all the while in the mirror to ensure that this is real, and really me), and go back into the bar.

In a daze I walk up to Maddy at the bar where she sits with Poloneck Man.

'It came out,' I announce cryptically. Maddy is still smiling from something that her hopeless admirer had just said to her, but her face falls as I say this. She frowns in incomprehension.

'What do you mean, Clem?' she asks, looking me straight in the eyes. I look straight back.

'Just now, in the toilet. It just came out.'

Poloneck Man's face shows a hint of distaste at the direction this conversation is moving in.

'Excuse me just a second,' Maddy says to him again, and ushers me back towards the floridly upholstered corner pouffe, gripping me firmly by the arm.

'Clem, do you mean the *baby*? Are you sure?'

I nod and break into a grotesque nervous smile.

'I don't ... Are you all right?'

I nod again.

'Should I find out if there's a doctor on board?'

I shake my head. 'I think I can wait. I feel better now.'

I am trembling violently as we walk to the bar to fetch Maddy's bag.

'Well, good to meet you,' Maddy says to Poloneck Man. 'I'm afraid we have to go and get some air for a moment.'

'Wait! Wait two seconds! I'll come with you.' But Maddy has already started for the door. The man fumbles desperately with his wallet to pay the barman, loath to miss his chance with Maddy. As he pulls out some franc notes, a photograph flutters down out of his grasp, eluding his frantic clutches as it floats to

234

the floor at Maddy's feet. It is a picture of a sweet-looking, sadly smiling woman. Maddy looks down at the picture then her eyes dart back to his.

'Do send my regards to your wife, Monsieur,' she says archly.

'Wait! I swear, she's not my wife, she's just an old friend.'

'Don't worry, I'm actually a man,' smiles Maddy.

We walk off, leaving the Poloneck Man floored.

The Weiss squad

The taxi drove us out of Cambridge, towards the village where Ben lived, through countryside that was beautiful in a gentle, comforting, domesticated, mild sort of way – perfect for my needs.

'It's so calm,' I said to Maddy.

'Placid,' she replied, smoking out of the window to the irritation of the driver. 'Just look at all those rolling fucking green hills,' she said glumly. 'It's just undulate, undulate. Nothing going on. Makes you seasick.' She turned and looked at me, or rather at my stomach.

'You still okay?' She looked freaked out.

'Fine.' In fact I couldn't feel anything. At all.

'You're very pale.'

'I'm *always* very pale, Maddy, I'm okay.' I was still totally disconnected, numb and incredulous, waiting for the reality to hit.

We pulled up outside a huge old house. One wall was covered with wisteria, just like Claude's *stoep*. Now the vine was a skeletal sketch spreading over the wall like a Munch painting, but it must be magnificent in summer. We rang the doorbell and the shouting and general noise level from inside escalated, like a pre school class released by the break bell. Ben opened the door and leapt forward to hug Maddy. I'd last seen Maddy's brother almost twenty years before, and he'd since come to resemble a medium-size, good-looking bear. A manic halo of unsuccessfully tamed curls surrounded his jovial, ruddy-cheeked face. Ben wouldn't have looked out of place in a red suit in a shopping centre yelling 'Ho ho ho' and dispensing gifts to children.

'Greetings and salutations!' he shouted, his arms raised dramatically. At least ten small children threw themselves around his legs, laughing, refusing to relinquish the victim of their recent game. He still managed to kiss Maddy, greet me warmly, and pick up most of our bags, which he lugged into the hallway, bellowing like an ogre and wading through his Lilliputian captors. I'd walked out of a grim Realist novel into a fairy tale. Maddy and I stared down at the squirming giggling mass.

'Jesus Christ, Ben, don't tell me these are all yours!' Maddy exclaimed.

Ben shook his head. 'Sally's ... she collects them, but most of these are only on loan. I can only lay claim to two of them as far as I know. Which two I'm not always sure, but it's the matching pair, Davey and Sarah. And then there's another slightly older one somewhere, Rachel, who you may remember. Tuesday is Midget Day, and today happens to be my turn. Sally has discovered feminism so now I have to do my share even though she volunteered in the first place.'

'Give them an inch ...' Maddy teased. Ben snorted.

'God, it's good to see you, sister mine, and with Clem as a bonus too. Come and have a drink immediately.' Ben dragged himself inside on his encumbered legs, swatting the kids away with mock ferocity, which only delighted them further and sent them into new fits of giggles. This was possibly more *en-masse* children than I had ever been exposed to in my supposedly adult life. A wave of sadness went through me. The irony of the situation was not lost on Maddy, who caught my eye and gave me a sympathetic, apologetic little smile, her eyebrows raised, like the facial equivalent of a shrug.

Ben eventually managed to detach himself from the crowd of midgets and ushered us into the enormous kitchen. He commanded the children to go and amuse themselves at someone else's expense and shut the door on them, muttering oaths. Then he held out a bottle of whisky and thrust it towards Maddy with a flourish.

'Bog standard Irish,' he announced, as though it were something to be proud of.

'You lying snob! It's Lagavulin!' she shouted. 'Since when did you get so poncey?' Ben plonked three glasses and half a tray of ice on the table, cracked open the lid, and didn't put the ice tray back in the freezer.

'What's news, Mademoiselle Weiss?' he prompted.

Ben was just pouring another round for himself and Maddy (to his chagrin I had declined the whisky offer and was sticking to water) when the kitchen door opened to reveal a very pale and lovely woman, wrapped in numerous exotically coloured scarves, her hair scooped back in a messy blondish bun. It was Ben's wife Sally, whom I'd never met, back from yoga. Two of the mini-people had broken away from the rest of the crowd and clung to her.

'Hello,' she said from the doorway, serenely undisturbed by the children's demands as she unwrapped the succession of scarves and hung them at the door.

'Wait a second,' she said to the children, who obeyed immediately. Sally stepped lithely forward, kissed Maddy on either cheek and hugged her warmly. 'How *lovely* to see you,' she said. Then she turned to me and took my hand. I wasn't quite sure whether she was going to kiss it or shake it, but in the end she just held it lightly and smiled at me. 'And you must be Clem.'

I attempted a smile. 'Thanks for letting me come and stay,' I said, feeling a bit like Orphan Annie as I said it.

'Don't be silly, you're *family*,' said Ben. He sidled up to Sally for a fondle. 'May I pour you a drink, my beloved?' he asked her.

'Yes, you may indeed. A big one. And refill the ice tray while you're at it.'

Pale, beautiful, and definitely the wearer of the pants. Here was another dauntingly impressive woman in the family, and she wasn't even a blood relative.

Maddy knocked loudly on my door the next morning and woke me up. 'How are you feeling?' she asked, standing in the doorway.

I'd hardly had time to check yet. For all I knew all my insides could have fallen out in the night, but I seemed to feel all right. Physically. Everything else was a great void. I'd howled for so long the night before that I'd become a hollow-eyed automaton, hardly able to think. All I wanted to do was lie in bed and aim for oblivion. I couldn't face the idea of getting up and facing the real world.

'Maybe I won't need to go to a doctor,' I ventured.

'Of course you need to go to a doctor ... *this morning*,' Maddy said emphatically. 'It's all arranged.'

I flopped glumly back into bed, miserable at the thought that Sally must know, and tried to face the insurmountable task of dressing myself.

Breakfast was a chaotic affair. Sally managed, miraculously, to eat, cook and shove platefuls of egg soldiers at the twins. I had barely succeeded in dragging myself downstairs at all. I was installed next to Rachel at the table, watching her spoon mouthfuls of Coco Pops inexpertly into her mouth and all over the table while she read the back of the cereal box. I eyed the Coco Pops enviously.

'It's disgusting stuff, but virtually all they'll eat,' said Sally, misinterpreting my stare. 'Have some muesli.'

'No thanks. I'm not really a breakfast person.' This was of course entirely fictitious. I'm an absolute slut for breakfast buffets, but Maddy had told me it might be a good idea not to eat since the doctor might need to do a D and C.

'You see, Sal, almost no one actually *likes* to eat muesli. At least no one in *my* family,' said Ben. He turned to Maddy and me. 'A friend of mine once said that muesli was the only way of getting morning sickness without being pregnant.'

I tried to smile. He guffawed at the joke, but no one joined him. Maddy rolled her eyeballs and scoffed and Ben stopped laughing and frowned at us. 'Why the long face, sister mine? Someone steal your biscuit?'

Maddy and I took the car into town to 'do some shopping'. She drove, as always, at high speed down the country lanes as though we were in a rush – as though I were in labour rather than had miscarried. Lines of trees flashed by us on either side of the road like an epileptic's nightmare, making me feel decidedly unwell, and a clump of sturdy, German-looking cyclists loomed up ahead of us. The cyclists were all women and wore nothing but bikini bottoms and tank tops. Maddy drove so close to them I could see the back woman's cellulite. The woman turned around and glared at us and cycled on.

'Fuck off, weirdos!' shouted Maddy. I looked at Maddy, thought of the impression the two of us must make. As if we had a leg to stand on, calling perfectly ordinary, wholesome cyclists weirdos. Maddy drove swiftly on, oblivious.

Enter Doctor Donaghue

'Hello, I'm Doctor Donaghue,' said the man in white, 'and which of you is Clementine?' Dr Donaghue's accent was pure Irish. He pronounced my name so beautifully, his accent so like Jimmy's, that I would have wept if I hadn't already cried myself numb. He was about forty-something, medium height and slightly stocky, with dark, attractively messy hair and a very un-Irish dark skin lined to macho perfection. His eyes were outrageously blue and their outer corners stretched to an almond shape towards the side of his face, as if he'd had a facelift or was constantly smiling with ironic self-assurance. Dr Donaghue the gynaecologist looked like a racing car driver. Like he would dash down to Monaco at the weekends to play with his racing car. And I was about to lie there with my bonnet open. Would he reach for my breasts to do a check and call them 'hooters' by mistake? He wore the standard garb of his trade, white lab coat and stethoscope, with theatrical flair so that he looked like a pretend doctor dressed up for the part, too cheerful by half. He swept off into the next room to fetch something, gesturing towards some chairs. We sat down obediently opposite the receptionist in the neat, bright little room, so strikingly different from the packed soulless holding bay I'd been in at the Paris clinic.

'Jesus,' Maddy stage-whispered when it seemed the doctor was out of earshot, 'did we come all the way to England to find an Irish abortionist? Sounds a bit unlikely, doesn't it? Isn't it supposed to be the other way around?' I didn't respond, just stared unseeingly at a sign on the reception desk, barely moving. Maddy put her hand on my shoulder and gave me a little push, perhaps just to check that I was still conscious. When I turned to look at her she crinkled up her eyes and scrutinised me so I turned away, and scanned the magazines on the table. I picked up a *Country Life* and automatically flipped through the pages in search of the Deb of the Month. Sorcha, daughter of Lord and Lady Stuart Worden, smiled out of the page at me with horsy confidence. I bet *she* wouldn't end up in a doctor's room waiting for an Irish gynae to sort out the results of her Parisian misdemeanours. Angus would have relished her. He'd once returned to the Soup Kitchen after spending the vac at his parents' in Natal with an enormous stash of *Country Life* back copies to use for a tutorial. For hours that night we'd perused the pictures of the eager-to-please debs, debating their relative merits. He'd have had a lot to say about Sorcha.

I was brought back to the present when a nurse with a broad Irish accent came in to ask the receptionist about some files.

'Unbelievable,' Maddy exclaimed in a loud whisper when the nurse left. 'What is this, do you think? A covert operation?' At that moment a filing cabinet slid shut in the next room. The door was open and it became apparent that Dr Donaghue had been standing there all along, quietly consulting notes in his filing cabinet only inches from where Maddy and I sat waiting. He walked up to us with two definite stocky strides and addressed Maddy, his accent heightened for effect.

'I couldn't help overhearing your discussion,' he said, his permanently smiling eyes smiling even more as he took in Maddy's discomfort. 'Do you think all Irishmen sit around drinking Guinness and dream of kissing the Pope's ring? So to speak?'

I decided I rather liked Dr D.

'D'ya think all Oirishmen spend their loives sooking back Guinness and fooking the local altar boys? Some of us have actually come out of the bogs, don't ye know?'

It was the first time I had seen Maddy's confident composure knocked. But she recovered quickly.

'Sorry, Oi'm sure.'

'Will we go through then?' he asked me. I got up to follow him.

'I'll just wait here,' said Maddy, slightly at a loss.

'Please do,' said Dr D with more than a hint of flirtation. 'Colleen,' he called to the receptionist, 'won't you get contact details for Ms Fynn van-Zyl (he stumbled over this and pronounced it van Zile) from ...' he gestured towards Maddy as if to conjure her name out of her.

'Ethelrude,' Maddy said, without a flicker of a smile. Dr D broke into a grin. 'Get Ms Fynn's contact details from Ethelrude here,' he said. 'And perhaps Ethelrude would be so kind as to give us her details as well, as the next of kin?' I couldn't help feeling a bit put out by this flirtation. I would have preferred to steer clear of sexual thoughts of any kind before having my bottom drawer examined by a stranger.

There was a little brass name thingy on Dr D's desk, which said Dr Sean Donaghue. I eyed this, and the multitude of certificates stuck on the wall proclaiming his proficiency in various dreadful-sounding practices, while he opened the folder on the desk, took out a form and picked up a pen. We went through my medical history briefly and he made notes on the form.

'So are you doing okay?' he asked me.

'Yes, as I said, apart from the stomach and ...'

'I mean here as well.' He poked a finger at his skull.

'Oh.'

'Not so well?'

'I'm okay.' For which read numb, stunned, devoid of any feeling at all.

'So do you want to tell me what happened?' he asked.

I was surprised at his question. 'I accidentally went to bed with a Frenchman,' I confessed.

He laughed, taken aback, and his eyes stretched out so widely that they were almost closed. 'Well that wasn't quite what I was asking about, but thanks for telling me nonetheless.'

I blushed at my foolish mistake, and told him about what had happened on the boat. He listened attentively, jotting down a few notes and raising his eyebrows when I mentioned having flushed the evidence down the toilet. He warned me that I might feel pretty miserable, offered me a counsellor (which I declined) and told me they were going to put me under general for a D and C and I might feel groggy afterwards.

Then I was up on the table with my legs splayed and half a cutlery canteen inside me.

'Relax,' Dr Donaghue ordered. Really, it was a bit much to expect women's privates just to flop open conveniently to allow any old stranger to pop his head inside and take a look. He did a brief inspection and reassured me that all seemed well. Then he snapped his gloves off and went out to 'change for the theatre'. The word 'theatre' made me think of Jack. I closed my eyes and pretended I was elsewhere.

Dr Donaghue returned looking more like a racing car driver than ever in a stylish light green all-in-one jumpsuit made out of slightly shiny, rustly fabric. I was convinced he had his outfits tailor-made for exactly this effect. He took me through to another room where I was kitted out in a nasty nappy-liner fabric papery nightie that didn't close at the back and showed my bum. It made climbing onto the trolley-bed a rather tricky affair, and for some reason everyone insisted that I should lie down and get pushed to the operating theatre rather than walk there myself. My legs were shaking madly as they tried to put my feet in the stirrups and Dr Donaghue joked about this, not unkindly, with the nurses. It was all pretty amicable, considering. Then they gave me an injection and sleep flooded in.

When I came to, I felt like someone who has fallen asleep at the dinner table and woken up with a start midway through a conversation. I had a horrible image of myself lying there like a spatchcocked chicken. The only way to salvage my dignity was to deny I'd been asleep at all, to deny that I'd so totally relinquished control.

'I wasn't asleep! I wasn't asleep! I felt everything,' I heard myself shouting through the fog in my head. A middle-aged woman in a bed nearby who was waiting for her turn in theatre looked disturbed by my behaviour.

Then Maddy appeared next to me. 'So if you felt everything, what was it like?' she asked. I frowned and shut up, aware that I was being teased. She looked at Dr Donaghue.

'Some people react to general in unexpected ways,' he explained. He hovered above me in his boiler suit like a slightly disreputable angel. It was as though he'd absolved me.

It was over. Or so I thought.

Threnody: the lamentation

Thought for the day: None, due to suspected accidental curettage of brain during surgery.

Unfortunately Dr D was right. Things did come home to roost. I had never been this miserable in my life. For a while the grief was so intense it felt as though I had miscarried my own heart. I became sullenly tyrannical, lurking like a troglodyte in my darkened chamber and only grunting monosyllables when forced to communicate at all. I didn't get out of the ancient men's pyjamas I'd bought in a factory shop years before, and I gave up the fight with my hair, which stood out maniacally at right angles from my head. I wouldn't have been surprised if I'd suddenly grown horns or a third eye. In short, I was ghastly. Maddy, whose tastes didn't run to being locked up for hours on end in a stuffy room with only a book for company, occasionally stuck her head in 'just to check that I wasn't dead yet' but she didn't hang around. I think she was even a little scared of me.

Sally was not. When she 'invited' me to come around the garden with her a few days later it felt more like an instruction than an offer. She made me put on her spare wellies and I followed her around rather pathetically, trying to focus on something, *anything*, other than myself. It was a bit like trailing behind Granny Mac all those years ago, when she'd waded through her waist-high spinach, lecturing me about the 'evil and untrustworthy nigs'. I watched Sally bend with impressive yoga suppleness over the flower beds, her long, smooth, pale ponytail rolled carelessly into a bun on top of her head, dead-heading plants in the winter garden and poking around in the freezing undergrowth. By comparison with my rather botched-up self, she seemed full of serene wisdom. I groped in vain for something entertaining to say and ended up saying nothing at all, but it didn't bother her; she was happy just being quiet and she asked no questions.

Maddy joined us, following gingerly behind Sally in her inappropriate shoes, awkwardly out of her element in this natural setting of soil and plant debris and swearing in Yiddish about being nearly *farfroyen* to death in the *farkakte* cold. She smoked and chatted as Sally worked and I let the soap opera waffle of Maddy's narrative flow over me comfortingly like warm bath water. Some days, quite a few in fact, when I couldn't face even this level of sociability I pretended to be asleep when

Sally knocked on the door. I skulked about silently behind the closed door like a dysfunctional teenager.

'Why do you never talk?' Rachel asked me in her forthright way one evening when we were all sitting in the lounge listening to big band. She had clearly grown tired of dancing coquettishly in the centre of the Persian, keeping Ben neatly wound around her little finger with her girly wiles, while the twins ignored us all and plotted over their Lego blocks in the far corner of the room. I opened my mouth to reply but Ben got there before me.

'Mind your own business. She's a quiet sort of person, you nosy little madam, unlike *some – of – us*,' he said, prodding her ticklish belly on each final word to emphasise who he meant and causing a riot of giggles and squirming from Rachel. I was already regretting coming down out of hiding.

'Right, bath time,' Sally commanded. The children whinged, but allowed her to herd them upstairs.

Ben let out a deep sigh. 'Narrow escape,' he muttered. 'I thought I might be expected to do the bathing tonight.' He settled into his chair and swirled the whisky around in the glass contemplatively. Then the phone rang.

'Aaaarrggh shit,' he said, and dragged himself out of the chair to answer. Ben came back with raised eyebrows. 'It's for you, Clementine,' he said brightly. Then under his breath, 'Another narrow escape for me.'

I was struck by a sudden anxiety. Who could be phoning me here? Nobody even knew where I was. I picked up the phone reluctantly.

'Hello?'

'Hello, Clementine, it's Sean Donaghue.' Relief. Then a new anxiety that something might be wrong. Maybe they'd discovered that there was a twin inside me, hanging on for dear life. Or that I had cancer or some dread French STD.

'Is something wrong?' I asked, trying to keep the panic out of my voice.

'Nothing at all. How are you?'

'I'm okay. Fine.' But surely he wasn't phoning for a chat?

He must have mistaken the anxiety in my voice for reticence. 'Is this a bad time?'

'No no.'

'I just wanted to phone to say I've got the tests back and everything is okay.'

'Thank you. That's great to hear. And ... the future?' I asked cryptically. I could hardly ask him detailed questions about my dodgy breeding equipment with Ben sitting a few metres away. Fortunately Dr D understood.

'Miscarriages aren't uncommon at all. There's nothing to suggest you'd have problems having children in the future – if and when you want to.'

'Okay. Well ... thanks very much for phoning.' But he didn't seem to want to hang up.

'Um ...' he said on the end of the line. 'Er ... is Madeleine there by any chance?'

'Yes.'

'Could I have a word with her?'

'Sure. Well, thanks again. Bye.' I put the receiver down on the table, strongly suspecting that my gynaecologist had just phoned me as an excuse to speak to my aunt.

'Maddy, Doctor Donaghue wants to speak to you.'

'To *me*?' She got up and strode over to the phone.

'There's nothing wrong, is there?' Maddy asked, without even saying hello. She was silent for a while. Then a nasty tone came into her voice.

'No, I can't make it on Friday,' she said coldly. 'No, not Saturday either, or any other day. I'm with my family every night until I leave and I really don't have time.'

The poor man. Did Maddy have to be so rude? I sneaked a look at Ben.

'Who is it?' Ben mouthed at me.

'A guy we met in town the other day,' I semi-fibbed.

'Poor guy,' said Ben quietly to me. 'What's he like?'

'Really nice, actually. I thought Maddy liked him.'

'She may well. But you know what she's like with men. Ever heard the expression "nice from far but far from nice"? Ever since the Brazilian guy snuffed it, any guy who comes too close ends up with a knife between the shoulder blades.'

'*Snuffed* it? Which Brazilian guy?'

'Some guy she fell for when she first came over to work in Europe. It was years ago, but I don't think she ever quite got over it.'

'How did he die?'

'I'm not sure. Drugs maybe? He was Maddy's bit of rough.'

Just then Maddy put the phone down and walked towards us and we fell silent. She eyed her brother suspiciously.

'What? What's it?' she demanded. 'Do I have a booger in my nose or something?'

'A huge one, just hanging out there ...' She wiped at her nose quickly and then took a swipe at Ben when he laughed at her. 'God, you are a *shmendrek*.'

'Tell me, Maddy, do you eat your mate after you have sex with him?'

'What do you mean?'

'Well you were pretty vicious to that poor guy, whoever he was. Was he that awful?'

Maddy's face clouded over. 'I don't see what that has to do with you, Ben,' she said. She looked remarkably like Rachel standing there sulkily with her hands on her hips.

'Nothing whatsoever, my dear sister. Keep your hair on.'

Maddy made a little huffy noise and I guiltily avoided eye contact.

When Maddy and I were alone later that night I nervously brought the subject up.

'Why did you never tell me about the Brazilian guy?' I asked her. Then immediately wished I hadn't.

'About whom?'

I kept quiet.

Then it dawned on her. She looked at me fiercely: 'Listen, Clem. You never *have* to tell anyone anything. I certainly wish now that I'd never told Ben.' I had hoped for some closeness from her side, some indication that she too had been vulnerable once. I yearned for some exchange of confidences after I'd gushed out the most intimate and compromising details about my recent exploits. But Maddy and Claude were not sisters for nothing. Maddy snapped shut just as Claude did when things came too close for comfort. I didn't ask about it again, but that glimpse of Maddy the Human gave me a greater insight into her workings, the origins of her sassiness and hardness, than anything else had in all the years I'd known her.

A *fête worse than death*

A few days later I woke up to hear Maddy and Sally whispering excitedly outside my door. It felt suspiciously early, and I rolled over to consult the alarm clock: 07:26. It was unheard of for Maddy to be awake at this hour. Something must be up. There was a brief knock and the next second the door swung open to admit Maddy, followed by a more hesitant Sally who called to me first to see that I was 'decent'.

'Guess what? We're going to the Cambridgeshire annual Winter Festival of Organic Living,' Maddy announced with a flourish, pulling back the duvet mercilessly. I smelt a rat. Maddy was so unorganic she probably went out of her way to buy nylon-gusseted undies. Claude had once told me that she and Maddy had decided to make soup one day at Mac's when Maddy was about fifteen and Claude about thirty. Claude had come back from answering a phonecall and discovered Maddy carefully picking pieces of the red wax covering off the outside of the cheese and scattering them over her soup. Claude, who hated wasting food, flew off the handle: 'What are you doing? You'll ruin your soup!'

Maddy looked at her, totally mystified. 'But it's the best part of the cheese.'

So her sudden interest in some organic hippy fest was suspicious, but it seemed I had no choice but to go with them. I'd hardly had time to shove some dry toast into my mouth when we were climbing into the station wagon, bound for the fair. We'd only just arrived when we met up with Biddy. She was a friend of Sally's with big coarse springy blonde hair like a terrier, which rioted around her head, so that her tiny face looked like a button in the middle of an exploded coir mattress. She was wearing a kind of maroon Bedouin tent outfit and those ridiculous gnome shoes that curl up at the end like you've just come out of Aladdin's lamp.

'Shanti,' she said by way of greeting, and did a strange little bow.

'Shanti to you, Biddy,' said Sally (minus the bow) and introduced us. I looked at Maddy out of the corner of my eye. She was standing absolutely still. She seemed to have developed a facial tic but perhaps she was just trying to smile.

'Isn't this *fantastic*?' Biddy gushed. 'Such a sense of community spirit ... I've sold twelve bottles of cider already this morning. And there are some really *amazing* stalls here today. I've been wanting to go and see the palmist all morning, you know, Sal,' said Biddy confidentially. 'Pam says she went and it was *uncannily* accurate.'

'You mean *Anne* the palmist?' asked Sal, frowning.

'Yes. Apparently she's brilliant. Spot on.'

'But doesn't she live next door to Pam?'

'Yessss ...?' said Biddy, not quite getting the point.

'Well I mean she's got a bit of a head start on her then, hasn't she?'

Biddy looked momentarily crestfallen. 'Come on, Sal! It's not just the material things, it's the spiritual and psychological – things you couldn't know just by living next door to someone!'

Maddy began to look unwell. She patted her pockets to locate her cigarettes and seemed to get some consolation from finding them.

Foolishly, Biddy put Maddy and me in charge of her organic cider stand while she went off with Sally to consult Anne the palm-reader. Maddy consumed several bottles of the dubious-looking substance and then threatened to piss in a nearby teepee when she couldn't find the portaloos, alarming a didgeridoo-bearing maiden in front of the teepee who quickly pointed her in the right direction. When she came back she lit up a cigarette and dragged deeply, staring with amazement and disgust at the passers-by in their ethnic garb and their big velvet 'look at me, I'm barking' hats. A bunch of ill-looking health food specialists walked by in earnest conversation with a group of radiantly happy-looking Hare Krishnas. Clearly they'd just discovered that Nirvana is actually earning a living doing nothing but chanting and a bit of occasional cymbal-clashing and never having to get agitated over what to wear because you just stick on the same old curtain every day. I watched them enviously, briefly flirting with the image of myself in a saffron robe dispensing karma-friendly food.

'They're all fucking *meshugeh*,' Maddy pronounced suddenly. She looked like she wanted to bolt.

'Why are we here?' I asked her.

'Thought you'd like it,' Maddy lied blatantly.

When Biddy and Sally came back, Sally led us off for a tour. I made a mental list of some of the horrors on sale, intending to send an account of the day to Angus who would no doubt appreciate it for his 'Pseud's Corner' collection.

- sheepskin slippers (unwashed wool, still smelling of sheep sweat)
- healing crystals of all shapes and sizes (large stock of which rather un-magically wrapped up in Jiffy bags under table)
- Reiki massage tent (fronted by sad-looking pale person of virtually indeterminate sex)
- Shiatsu massage tent (intriguingly closed up and occupied)

- aromatherapy stand
- hemp clothing stall (with extremely mellow salesperson apparently asleep in hemp hammock)

We passed stall after stall manned by ill-looking people selling ugly dreamcatchers, home-made tofu and something even more sinister that looked like pots of ear wax. I was just reaching breaking point when Sally suddenly looked at her watch and announced that we were going home, and we left as swiftly as we'd arrived.

All the way home, Maddy and Sally twittered away in the front of the station wagon, occasionally shooting each other conspiratorial little looks, little smiles. I wondered whether some elaborate hoax was being played, and retreated into paranoid silence. They looked absurdly proud of themselves, as if they'd just each crapped out a solid gold egg. Eventually I couldn't bear it any more.

'What's going on?' I asked aggressively.

'Nothing,' they chorused, giggling like schoolgirls who've put a fart cushion on the teacher's chair and are waiting for her to sit on it. I was beginning to lose my sense of humour.

'Actually I don't really like surprises,' I muttered ungraciously.

'You'll like this one,' said Maddy.

Arrival

From inside the house came the familiar sound of toddler mayhem and a man's voice revving them up to a fever pitch. No doubt Ben was masquerading as Gulliver again. There was a volley of shouting and swearing as we approached the door. Sally rang the doorbell, which was odd, since I knew she had her keys, and we all waited in the freezing cold while she and Maddy continued to grin at each other like sly, smug idiots. After a momentary interruption in the swearing and some high-pitched giggling, we heard adult footsteps coming towards the door. Then the front door swung open.

'Surprise,' Maddy and Sally shouted.

Standing on the threshold of Sally and Ben's house was Angus. I stared at him in disbelief. He looked the same as always, except that he had a wind-up toy car stuck in his curly hair, the engine still whining on like a trapped insect.

'Clemmy!' Angus said. He too was grinning his head off. It was too much to take in, too much of a surprise. I yelped in amazement and leapt forward, clamping myself onto him, hiding my face and inhaling the smell of his familiar prickly olive jersey. It smelt of *veld* and curry and smoke and home. We all stood in the doorway for what felt like a terribly long time – we had to, since Angus and I were blocking it with our embrace and I was desperately trying to pull myself together and rearrange my thoughts and my face before anyone looked at me. Eventually Maddy decided she'd had enough gratification out of this particular scene and gave me a sharp prod forwards.

'Okay, okay, it's bloody freezing out here. Can we continue the moment inside?'

So we did.

'Horse! Horse!' yelled Rachel and the twins, rushing at Angus as soon as he was inside.

'Absolutely not,' said Sally. 'Into the kitchen, all of you, and stop abusing the guests.' Her gesture included Ben, who'd been hanging back from the main drama, watching and smiling avuncularly. He leapt into action and obediently herded the children out of the room. Sally turned to Angus.

'Sorry about my children,' she said. 'Perhaps Clem could remove their toys from your hair,' she said, gesturing towards the car on Angus's head. 'Why don't you sit down and I'll get you a drink?' We sat down obediently on the sofa and Maddy flopped into Ben's armchair. 'What would everyone like?' Sally asked. 'Whiskies all round?' It was ten thirty in the morning.

'Perfect,' Maddy answered for all of us.

Sally must somehow have intimated that I should be left with

Angus, because Maddy suddenly changed her mind. 'In fact I'll do the drinks and you do the fish fingers.' She pulled herself up out of the chair and headed purposefully towards the kitchen with Sally. I looked at Angus. The car was winding down in his hair. He looked charmingly absurd. It was so wonderful to be sitting here on the sofa next to my real live friend.

'I can't believe you're here,' I gushed.

'It's amazing, isn't it? You go six thousand miles away to escape all of us and we all just follow you. First your boyfriend, then your aunt, now me.'

I smiled weakly. I had no desire to think about Kurt; he sullied the trio. 'I suppose you think I should be flattered that no one can live without me?' I joked weakly.

'Well you know ... it was getting a bit boring running the Soup Kitchen all on my own.'

'What exactly *are* you doing here, actually?'

'Well actually I'm talking to people at a couple of universities over here about doing my PhD. It seems some fools think I'm worth a fat scholarship and I thought you might be missing the Cape Town *skinder*, so it seemed like an excellent excuse for a visit. I changed my thesis topic after that herbivorous slut Tamara burnt my obituaries, so she did me a favour after all.' He tried to look brave as he said this and was suddenly a little undignified with the toy car stuck on his head.

'Hang on, put your head down so I can liberate you,' I said, and started picking the hair out of the wheels. Angus looked up at me from under his hair.

'Go on,' I insisted. I couldn't believe I was sitting here in Ben and Sally's lounge removing a car from Angus's hair as if it were completely normal. I was blissed out.

'I came to find you in Paris, you know, once I knew that asshole boyfriend of yours was safely in Germany,' Angus continued.

'Oh?'

'*Ja*. I arrived with an address for you and I think I really upset this *dame* in a café who got angry when I refused to believe she did not know where you were. I had the whole café translating for me. I told them I was desperate and they really entered into the spirit of it, especially one old guy called Bertie who didn't understand a word I was saying but kept pressing me to drink more foul *pastis* with him. But the *dame* was a one-woman French resistance. I walked from one end of Paris to the other clutching feebly at the hope that I might see you. I had almost no money and I was exhausted.'

'What did you do then?' I asked, delighted by Angus's no doubt embellished narrative.

'Well, I went on a Paris tour on one of those topless buses, still hoping absurdly that I'd catch sight of you somehow. The tour guide went on and on about Notre-Dame in German and I fell asleep and nearly froze to death. I tried Claude, but she was away, and Jack didn't know where you were. Then I tried to get hold of Maddy when I finally remembered her surname, got this number for her off her answering machine, discovered you were already somewhere near Cambridge, a few miles from where I was actually headed, and I realised I'd come to Paris by mistake.'

I stared at Angus, listening to his story of how he walked straight out of the phone booth and came across to England with nothing but baguette and *pastis* in his stomach, but my mind was wild with images of what might have been. If Kurt had come a few months earlier and I'd never slept with Yves or got pregnant. If I'd never eaten that bad prawn or got my dress caught in Yves's bicycle. If Angus had arrived when I was still in Paris and I could have shown him all the bits of the city that I'd loved and which had now been so eclipsed by the bad stuff I thought I'd forgotten them all. But Angus had come to the end of his picaresque narrative.

'Your turn,' he said, grinning. 'Dish me the dirty.'

'What?' I asked, anxiously.

'Give me the low-down, Clemmy. The narrative.'

'Tell me more about home first.' I was scared that if I pulled out any thread of my story for Angus the whole messy fabric of the last few months of my life would unravel in a heap in front of him.

Angus obliged me with a dose of scandalously mean-spirited invective about Kurt. Then I asked him about Jack, about Tamara and about all the transients who passed through the Soup Kitchen. With desperate cunning, flattering Angus's ego as raconteur, I drew out his stories of home until it was time for dinner.

Sally put Angus between her and Maddy at the table and he sat there, chatting like a beloved brother, instantly part of the family. I watched him, envying his confidence, his ease. Rachel was annoyed that she'd been put at the other end of the table from him and was sulking indignantly next to me. I stared down at my plate while she had a mini-tantrum, trying not to feel too insulted. Sally had cooked quails to celebrate Angus's arrival. I looked at the poor little things, trussed up bondage style with little bits of string. Quail was not my favourite food and I would gladly have shared the twins' standby fish fingers instead.

'What's this?' asked Rachel petulantly, prodding the bird on her plate with a finger.

'It's a quail, darling. Let Daddy help you cut it up,' Sally replied.

'Julian has a pet quail. He keeps it in his kitchen,' said Rachel, picking off bits of quail with her fingers and sucking them into her mouth. She addressed her words to Angus, aiming to impress him with this typical Weiss-family dinner table titbit. Dinner table conversations in this household were generally replete with sin, sex, scat and sanguinity. It was not for nothing (or without a hint of envy) that Claude had dubbed them The Weiss Squad.

'Who's Julian?' asked Angus.

'My music teacher,' said Rachel with a mouthful of quail.

Ben turned to Sally. 'You see what you get when you send your children to a bloody muesli school. Poultry running wild in the kitchen and no bloody respect for adults.'

'Don't you think it would be nice to have a pet quail in the Soup Kitchen?' Angus asked me.

'Don't be silly. You'd have eaten it a long time ago.' He'd have cooked it up along with everything else in the kitchen in a curry to feed the five thousand. I eyed my quail without enthusiasm.

'No, it'd be nice,' Angus persisted. 'Pets we could eat before we go on holiday. And just when I thought our inflatable sheep was the perfect pet for us.'

'My dad has pet birds,' said Rachel.

'What kind of birds do we have?' Ben tested.

'Pheasants.'

'And?'

'Waterfowls.'

'And?'

'Egyptian geese, swans, knob-billed ducks, white-faced ducks, Ferruginous ducks, ruddy Shelduck, and Golden Eye Ducks.'

'Clever child,' praised Ben, patting her head with slightly quail-smeared fingers. She smiled up at him, basking. Really, it was a bit much, this precocity of Rachel's. I wouldn't have been able to tell one end of the duck from the other when I was her age.

'Peter Tudhope at my school has a pet tick,' Davey added helpfully. 'It's called Jason. He keeps it in a bottle.' I skirted around the sultanas in my salad.

'Charming,' said Sally, and continued to eat. Since no one seemed to object to the topic, Davey went on in a singsong children's TV presenter voice: 'When Peter Tudhope gets a scab, he picks it off and feeds it to Jason.' Clearly this was a source of great fascination to Davey. Sally lowered her cutlery noisily onto her plate. 'Could we talk about this some other time?' she asked levelly. Davey shrugged as if he didn't care either way and continued to eat his food quite happily, unperturbed by the subject matter of his story, as if he'd just let us in on something quite fascinating. Then he came up with another question: 'Is it true that crocodiles don't eat you while you're fresh?'

'Do they really drag you down under the water and keep you in a lair till you rot and fall apart and *then* they eat you?' Sarah continued.

'Oh, God. Not again,' groaned Sally. 'I think I've had enough of this line of conversation.'

'It's their obsession with nature documentaries,' Ben said in an explanatory aside. 'Clem comes from Africa,' he told them. 'She's seen real crocodiles. You should ask her.' Sweet Ben; he must have noticed I felt overshadowed by Angus, a little unloved by his children, and felt a little PR for his rejected niece was in order.

'But only when we've finished eating,' said Sally firmly.

After dinner, Davey and Sarah listened to my paltry animal tales in awe. Angus told Rachel a story and watched me out of the corner of his eye without interrupting. The twins became wildly enthusiastic about my stories (filled, no doubt, with all sorts of regrettable factual inaccuracies) and were gratifyingly reluctant to be taken off to bed.

'How are you? Really?' Angus asked me once everyone had gone upstairs and we were finally left unchaperoned. Oh God, did I really have to face the dread topic?

'I'm fine.' My answer sounded tinny and false. I squeezed out a smile and feigned light-heartedness, but a barrier of awkwardness sprung up between ús. Angus raised his eyebrows, expecting more.

'*Ag*, you know. A bit of a mess but what's new?' He screwed up his eyes and stared at me, as if he was literally trying to see past my saccharine jollity. He looked pained.

'I've missed you,' he said, suddenly so serious that I wanted to laugh out of sheer nervousness.

'I've missed you too.'

He laughed hollowly. 'Yes, of course you have. But it's not the same.'

'What do you mean?' Did he think it was different for me

because I was the one who had left? Because it had been my choice?

Angus snorted and looked at me with a sad smile. 'Never mind, Clemmy. It doesn't matter.'

I would have pressed him to explain but something made me reluctant to understand. The whole conversation was uncomfortable. I just wanted to go upstairs to my bed and start all over again the next morning. I *had* missed Angus, terribly; I wished I could convince him of that. But six thousand miles seemed like nothing compared to this sense of apart-ness.

'You're tired,' said Angus, suddenly looking quite deflated himself. 'And I have an interview at the university in the morning. Will you meet me afterwards for a cup of disgusting tea? Sally says there's a place in town called the Copper Kettle which specialises in exactly that.'

I couldn't help feeling a little resentful that my life was being stage-managed; that behind the scenes people were planning a series of teas and surprise visits from friends to get me back on my feet again and pretending that everything was okay. For one paranoid moment I wondered whether Angus even *had* interviews to attend. Perhaps he'd been flown over as part of an elaborate scheme to 'reintroduce me to normal life' without eliciting any resistance from me. Had I become a charity case? Did everybody know all the gory details of my recent blunders? Had I gone certifiably bonkers without even realising it? Of course I agreed to meet Angus for tea. I resolved to be bright and capable and to steer clear of any talk about me – or rather not to diverge from a witty adventurous retelling of my life over the last few months, which I would make up as soon as I had space to think. We would talk more about Angus and the Soup Kitchen. I would sate my lust for news of home. And for now I would have a reprieve. For now I would escape to the safety of my bed with Evelyn Waugh and forget that I had anything to hide.

Evasive action

When I arrived at the Copper Kettle Angus was already sitting at a table reading a paper.

I put on my cheerful face: 'How was the interview, Mr Foot?' I asked.

'Rather vile, actually. The whole conversation rapidly deteriorated into a discussion about rugby and I bluffed my way through so well they were all slapping me on the back and congratulating me by the time I left, saying repulsive things like "they breed them tough in the colonies".'

A waitress came over, chewing gum incessantly like a cow busy with its cud, and reluctantly took our orders. We lapsed into silence for a moment.

'Listen, Clem, it seems you want to talk about everything but yourself. I'm not going to keep blathering on about the same old shit, I want to hear about you.'

And suddenly my well-rehearsed story wouldn't come. To my horror I found myself wishing that Angus, my beloved friend Angus, would leave. I blustered forth unconvincingly with cheerful irrelevancies about Serge, about Véronique and my lost job, about travelling in the train to Perpignan with a bunch of strangers and a bottle of vodka made out of bison wee. Angus smiled sadly at me across the table, his chin in his hand, patiently waiting, while I indulged in a wild and somewhat hysterical pantomime of evasion. He didn't push me. Not yet.

When we got back to Ben and Sally's, Maddy was waiting to talk to me about our tickets home. She was due to leave in a week and she wanted to know whether I still intended to come back with her.

'I think I must,' I said. But as the words came out of my mouth I felt a surge of panic.

'You don't have to, you know. You could always make a plan to stay here if you wanted to.'

'What, at Ben and Sally's?' The idea seemed impossible.

'Or you could find another place to stay, get a job, come back when you're ready.'

I contemplated this for a moment, but while the idea of going home filled me with dread, the idea of trying to start all over again in another foreign and potentially hostile place was too awful to contemplate. I was too flustered to decide.

'Can I think about it and tell you tomorrow?'

'Of course.' She paused for a while, as though she were trying hard not to say something but couldn't resist. 'It's a pity that Angus has come over here now,' she said suddenly, 'isn't it? Seems like a bit of bad timing.' She slid me a little look. I met her look, eyes narrowed.

'Maddy, you didn't tell him anything, did you?' I asked suspiciously. 'I mean about ... what happened in Paris?'

'No. Didn't you?'

'I can't yet.'

'But aren't you two ... really close?'

'Yes, but I don't want to go through it all again.' I didn't want to mention the failure thing to Maddy – I couldn't say it out loud. 'Actually there's another thing. He's being a little strange to me too, awkward. I can't understand why.'

Maddy sighed out deeply through her nose and rolled her eyes at me.

'Surely you can't be that dumb, Clem. Or maybe it's just false modesty.'

'What do you mean?'

'I mean that he's totally besotted. It's absolutely obvious to anyone else.'

A big red flush spread over my face and neck at the mere thought. 'I really hope you're wrong,' I said grimly.

Maddy scrutinised my glowing crimson face and shook her head. 'My God, you are a truly weird girl,' she told me.

I couldn't face anyone so I slipped into my room. The curtains were still drawn and the room was dark and silent. I sat pondering in the gloom. It was deeply comforting and I wished

I could stay like that forever. Then, inevitably, there was a knock at the door.

'Yes?'

It was Angus. Of course.

'May I come in?'

'Of course.' I grabbed a book, flung open the curtains and tried to look normal. Outside the day was so dark the room remained almost as gloomy as before. Angus came in and sat next to me on the bed.

'So, Clementine, are you effa going to tell me vot's wrong?' Angus did his silly Freud impersonation, feigning lightness to disguise his obvious frustration. But I knew his tactics and I wasn't going to be drawn in.

'What do you mean? Nothing's wrong.'

'I hope you're not miserable because you're missing that pretentious prick boyfriend of yours.'

'Ex-boyfriend. And I'm not missing that prick or any prick whatsoever.' It was a daring experiment. If I could blame it all on Kurt, on men, perhaps he wouldn't realise how much I'd fucked things up, how inadequate I felt. Angus raised his eyebrows and looked slightly cheered by my comment.

'The fact is, I've gone totally off pricks altogether, actually,' I went on, 'they're far more trouble than they're worth.'

He smiled at me in a disturbingly unbrotherly fashion. 'Not *all* of them. You get some quite friendly pricks, you know.' It struck me that he might actually think that lack of sex was the root of my problems ... that he might *actually* be volunteering his services. I was incredulous. I was irate.

'Excuse me ... you wouldn't be offering me a charity fuck, by any chance?'

'Not charity. It'd be my pleasure.' Angus grinned.

'Fuckit, I don't belie-e-eve this!' I shouted. 'Why do men always think they're the Second Coming?' Angus had a glint in his eye that suggested he was about to make a predictable weak pun, but I was shouting now, flooded with unexpected rage.

'I'm serious. You don't have the faintest idea of what I've gone through recently! I didn't invite you here, but you act as though I promised you something and now I'm letting you down. You arrive here with your own agenda thinking you're the answer to all my problems and you don't even know what they *are*!'

I tried to storm out of the room as I felt the tears spouting, but Angus caught me by the wrist.

'Well *tell* me what's wrong! You've been moping around in silence ever since I got here, completely rejecting my offers of a friendly … er … ear?'

I rolled my eyes in exasperation.

'I'm sorry, Clemmy, but it's really frustrating. You're just so angry and aggressive and guarded all the time it's impossible to talk to you. Everyone is under strict instructions from Maddy to treat you like some kind of invalid who doesn't know her own mind, and she won't tell me what the hell's going on. You can't even look me in the eye any more …'

I felt ashamed. How could I be like this to Angus, of all people? Suddenly, after all my painstaking attempts to keep everything secret, I couldn't hold it in any longer. 'I fucked up,' I confessed. Again. 'And I was too proud and too humiliated to tell you.'

So I told him. Everything.

My eyes were still swollen and pulpy by the time we came down, late, for dinner. But although Maddy raised her eyebrows inquisitively as we sat down, no one asked any questions. The children had already eaten and been put to bed and everyone was unusually, inconveniently quiet.

'I got a call from Rachel's school today,' Sally said, breaking the awkward silence like a perfect hostess. 'Apparently she had volunteered to tell the class a fairy story and proceeded to tell them all the story of a wicked gnome called Rumpled Foreskin. The teacher is very PC and thought this was something suspiciously anti-gentile, so she phoned me and asked me to collect Rachel from school. I asked Rachel who had told her the story – I mean

I just presumed it was Ben – and twenty guesses who it was.'

'Well it wasn't me,' I said, since she seemed to be addressing me. Bravely I attempted a smile.

'No, I didn't think it was, actually. It seems your friend here is quite a raconteur.' Sally was grinning. I felt rather boring by comparison to wicked Angus, who seemed once again to be the main attraction of the evening. How come when some people do naughty things they pay in pounds of flesh and when others do it, it makes them a character? Angus apologised, though he was obviously pleased and proud that his little story had made such an unexpected impact. But when he caught me looking at him I saw the shadow of our recent conversation fall over his face again, and for the rest of the meal he was more subdued than I'd ever seen him. The others consulted each other with furtive glances and soldiered forth considerately with stories of compost and colleagues and discussions of the latest developments in the greenhouse. I think everyone was relieved when it was finally time for bed.

That night I had a disturbing dream about Angus. I was bent over Sally's kitchen table next to the Aga while he rogered me wildly from behind like something out of *Tom Jones*. It was rapturous. I was screaming for more when I woke up with a jerk, as from one of those dreams where you fall off a precipice, and sat up sweaty and disorientated in bed to check for the presence of my friend the intruder. No one. But the dream lingered there like an incubus on the end of my bed. How could I be doing that with Angus? Even in my sleep? *Especially* in my sleep? I couldn't help playing it back in my head, and despite my resolution never to have sex again my newly renovated privates refused to be ignored. Every time I relaxed or shut my eyes I felt the slap of his thighs on my buttocks, the thrust of him inside me, his hands on my breasts. But you could hardly control your dreams, could you? I resolved to forget all about it. I would just lie down again and go back to sleep. Right. Now.

Rude awakening

Shortly before dawn I finally slept for about two hours. When I woke again the first (and only) thing I thought about was the dream. It was proving impossible to get it out of my mind, but I would conquer it with logic. As I saw it, there were three main problems with the concept of fucking Angus, namely:

1. I had given up sex and intended to become a secular nun-cum-hermit.
2. It would be tantamount to incest.
3. I wouldn't be able to run to my best friend Angus if anything went wrong – or laugh with him if the sex was really dreadful.

For some reason I felt amazingly cheerful. I almost hummed as I got dressed and stepped lightly down the stairs. But when I got to the kitchen I discovered Angus was gone. Ben had had to go into town early to do some chores, Sally explained, busying herself so that she didn't have to look me in the eye, and he'd taken Angus to the station to catch an early train to Oxford. My legs felt all shaky and I sat down hard on a chair.

'He didn't want to wake you,' she said, 'but he left you this.' She handed me a tightly folded note from the shelf above the Aga, and as our eyes met I could see how disappointed she was in me. I looked away and unfolded the note.

Clemmy

I'm sorry. I'm sorry about everything, but mostly I'm sorry because I behaved so appallingly and I think I may have destroyed the most important friendship I have in the world by greedily trying for something more. I'm deeply ashamed of myself and intend to take cold baths and eat only English food as penance. This morning I felt that the best thing for it was to pack up the pieces of my shattered ego and leave

– because I don't know how to make things better and I can't risk making them worse. I will miss you more than you can imagine.

Your (over)loving friend, like it or not,
Angus

PS: You accused me of offering you a charity fuck. May I just tell you that that would be impossible? But if you are ever feeling charitable do let me know ...

I tried to get hold of him in Oxford but got no joy. I phoned the student office at the university to try and track him down. The poncey woman on the other end of the phone couldn't (or wouldn't) help me. 'I'm afraid I am not in a position to disclose that information,' she said in her smug, dirndl-skirted accent. I burst into a rage and told her to 'take the hot potato out of your mouth and shove it up your arse!' and slammed the phone down: satisfying, if not altogether effective. Then I realised that I should have tried to get a message through to him so that he could phone me back. I waited an agonising ten minutes and then phoned back in a disguised high squeaky voice and left a message for him with the same hot potato bitch. I made a pot of tea and sat foolishly next to the phone, waiting for him to phone me back. He didn't. I mooned about the house, jumping whenever I heard the phone ring, but it was never him. When he hadn't phoned by the end of the second day I felt my heart close up and I stopped waiting. I was angry all over again.

Breather

Maddy eventually gave up waiting for my decision on the ticket and booked both of us back on the same return flight. The day before we were due to leave, panic set in. I was holed up in my room, reading and rereading the same paragraph of my book without understanding a word, when Sally came in.

'Oh sorry,' she said, starting to back out, 'it was so quiet in here I thought you must be out. I was just going to leave you these,' she said, gesturing at the bathroom door with a few rolls of toilet paper. She lobbed the toilet rolls onto the bed and was about to go out when she turned to ask me a question instead.

'Are you excited to be going back?'

'I can't believe it yet. I can't imagine it ...' And I can't imagine it without Angus, I thought. Besides, what if he came back to Cambridge and I'd left? He'd think I didn't care at all. What if he hadn't got my messages? He'd never know I'd made those desperate phonecalls to the snotty bitch in the postgraduate student office who seemed to think she was working for MI5. A secret part of me wanted to stay until Angus came back; to sort out the whole misunderstanding and get things back to normal.

'Why don't you just stay?' shrugged Sally.

'How do you mean?'

'Just stay. For a bit, until you're ready to leave.'

'Well I can't just ... I mean the ticket's booked, Maddy has to go back for work ...'

'Your ticket can always be changed if you want it to be. Why not take a breather, get your head around things in peace?'

'I don't want to impose ...'

'Oh don't worry about *that*, it's an entirely two-way thing. You get to hide out here and be fed, and in return I exploit you mercilessly as a babysitter. It's an entirely mutually exploitative deal, if you think you can bear it.' The thought horrified me. In all likelihood the children would stick their fingers into plugs and electrocute themselves or drown in the bidet the moment Sally left them alone with me. I couldn't even keep a foetus alive; how could she possibly trust me with living, mobile children with wills of their own? I shook my head miserably.

'I'm sorry, was that a bad idea?' Sally looked mortified. 'Did I get it all wrong?'

'No, no. It's just ...'

Sally hugged me, then sat back and regarded me with concern. God, she must think me a basket case.

'Have you ever thought of some kind of therapy, Clem?'

Bingo! So she *did* think I was a nutter.

'I'm not really keen on shrinks,' I said, immediately trying to pull myself together.

'It needn't be a shrink ... why not do something therapeutic that would cheer you up? I'm amazed that your doctor didn't suggest some kind of counselling, actually.'

'Well he did, but I thought ... I was hoping not to need it.'

Sally sat down on the bed and started fiddling with one of the loo rolls she had thrown there.

'A friend just happened to tell me about a woman who runs an encounter group in town.'

Oh my God, it was probably Anne the palm-reader. I had a sudden vision of myself sitting around in a circle of greasy-haired hippy rejects, weaving our own hessian underwear.

'What exactly is an encounter group?' I felt squeamish even asking.

'Well this one seems to be a kind of art-therapy-based group. Women only, which is a blessing in itself. A bit touchy-feely maybe, but I don't think they're pushing any kind of psychological party line. How does that sound to you?'

'Scary,' I confessed.

'But you'll think about it?' Sally insisted gently. I nodded.

Downstairs that evening I still hadn't made up my mind, but the normal, comforting state of chaos made me more inclined to be open-minded and non-judgemental about it. Rachel was refusing to watch educational television and instead was riveted to a programme about an angel who went around moralising and interfering in everyone's lives. Davey and Sarah had created an elaborate city out of kitchen implements and were completely absorbed. We watched them for a while then retreated to the kitchen.

'Sometimes I wonder whether those two are ours at all,' Sally said once we'd ensconced ourselves in front of the Aga. 'They're just in a world of their own. Sarah hardly even speaks except to Davey. They have their own language.'

'Now, now,' said Ben, beating eggs deftly with the whisk. 'Don't mythologise them, Sal, they're only twins.' He looked up towards Rachel, who remained entranced by the squeaky clean angel on the TV.

'I wish Rach wouldn't watch that obscene programme. It's really filthy stuff.'

'Can you suggest something better for her to do? Why don't you go and read Homer to her instead of moralising?'

'Because I'm busy beating eggs for their omelettes, my princess. But it really is crap. Filling children with unrealistic notions that some kind of benevolent missionary woman, backlit to the hilt so that she looks like she has a halo, is watching our every move …'

Sally carried on grating cheese. 'Be careful you don't inadvertently turn into an old fart, Ben. Truculence in adolescents is one thing, and even then it's only partly acceptable. Nobody loves a cantankerous old fart.'

Maddy walked in barefoot and sat down next to the Aga with her feet up on the edge of the table. She had painted her toenails a pale blueish white colour in preparation for her return to summer, and was now displaying them to us all. It suited her sallow skin, even if they did make me think of the toenails on a corpse. Ben took one look and wrinkled his nose up in disgust.

'What have you done to your toenails? They look like cataracts!'

'Fuck off, Ben. Who needs fashion tips from a cantankerous old fart?' She grinned at Sally, but she took her feet off the table.

'You'll miss me when you're gone,' said Ben.

And at that moment I realised just how much I'd miss them too, how unprepared I was to go home, and a few therapeutic encounters seemed a small price to pay. I decided to take Sally up on her offer and stay for a while. I just had to break it to Maddy, which for some reason made me feel terribly sheepish.

After dinner I sat with Maddy while she packed. She opened her case on the bed, took all of her clothes out of the wardrobe and spread them out next to the case, then stood back looking at the pile with her hands on her hips.

'Have to have a cigarette first,' she said. She strode over and threw open the window. An Arctic gust blew in. Maddy lit up a cigarette and inhaled deeply, exhaled with a heavy sigh and looked over at me.

'God, I wish I didn't have to go back to fucking work. More arse-licking and babysitting adults who whine about missing their strudel or espresso all the time … Jeeeezuz it's boring.' She looked up at me and seemed to realise for the first time that I didn't seem to be preparing to leave. 'You already packed?' she asked doubtfully.

'Sally suggested I stay for a while; get my head right before I go back,' I admitted, unable to look her in the eye as I said this.

'Oh?' she said probingly. 'And *are* you going to stay?' Her eyebrows were raised in amazement.

'I think I am,' I said.

'Well you'd better think fast. We are supposed to leave to-morrow, you know?'

'I know. I'll stay. If that's okay with you.'

'Come on, Clem, it's not remotely up to me and you know it. I'm glad it's worked out.' She took a last deep drag, blew the smoke out of the window into the freezing air, then flicked her cigarette butt out of the window, craning her head out to check its descent, shut the window, and came over to the case again.

'It's just that I feel a bit awkward, because they're your relatives and everything …' I mumbled.

'Clem, you wouldn't know what to *do* with yourself if you didn't feel awkward. Loosen up a bit, for Chrissakes.'

I laughed.

'I wish you could stay too, I really do. Maddy, I don't know how to thank you enough for everything you've done. I *really* wish you weren't going.' Everything I said felt inadequate. Frankly, I felt as if I might not be around if it weren't for Maddy. She flapped her hand dismissively.

'Okay, okay. Don't lay it on with a trowel now, for God's sake. You'll just have to look after me in my old age when I'm a lonely spinster with emphysema.' She was cramming things into the suitcase, her mind elsewhere. Then she turned and looked at me. 'It's been quite a time, hasn't it, these last few weeks?' She grinned at me.

I nodded. 'I'll miss you,' I told her, feeling absurdly shy.

'*Ag*, you'll be back soon,' she said, waving away my sentimentality once again.

'Won't you?'

Paris calling

The same day Maddy left there was a call for me. I had a jolt of anxiety and excitement when I thought it might Angus, phoning to apologise and begging to be my friend again, but it was not. To my surprise, it was Madame Rouillard, the 'one woman French resistance' who'd almost kept him from finding me in the first place, phoning for a status report.

'*Tout va bien?*' she asked huskily.

'*Très bien*,' I could truthfully reply for the first time in ages.

I asked how she was and she brushed off the question and gave me some news of her patrons instead. Then she told me that my friends had been looking for me but that she hadn't told them how to get hold of me.

'Which friends?' I asked.

'Yves,' she replied. My stomach jolted. 'And the other one,' she somewhat grudgingly added.

'Serge?'

A grunt of assent.

'And you met my friend Angus? From South Africa? He says you refused to give him my number.'

'You *told* me to give it to no one. Especially not a man.'

'You're right, I did say that. But that was in the past. You can give people this number, I'm fine now.'

'That's good to know. I'll tell people then, if I see them.' She paused for a moment. 'He was very determined, you know, your friend from South Africa. Did he find you in the end?'

'Yes.'

'I thought he would.' She sounded cheered and relieved to hear this. But I didn't want to talk about Angus any more, and Madame was far happier holding court in her café than talking long distance on the phone, so I promised her I'd phone again and we said goodbye.

I was amazed that afternoon when there was a second call for me. Perhaps *this* time it was Angus.

'Who is it?' I mouthed, but Ben shrugged.

I took the phone with some trepidation.

'Hello?'

'Clémence?'

It was Yves.

'Where are you?' he demanded in a strained voice. 'I got back from New York early and you had run away. That old bag at the café wouldn't even give me your number before. I knew she had it but she just refused, even after I started to get mad ... Then today I go there again and she finally gives it to me.' He sounded genuinely aggrieved, as though I had played an excessively mean trick on him.

'I had to get away.'

'Clémence, I know you were angry about the apartment, but I had to let my son stay there. And I was coming back ...'

'It wasn't about the apartment, Yves,' I interrupted, irritated. 'It wasn't even really about you.' I hesitated. Should I tell him? I knew it would upset me again, perhaps more than it would upset him hearing it for the first time, but it would give me a cruel sense of satisfaction to make him realise just how bad a time I'd had and how useless he'd been.

'I was in trouble,' I said tentatively.

'I don't understand. What kind of trouble?'

'I was pregnant, Yves, with your child.'

He said nothing at first, but I could hear his breathing grow heavier.

'You have my baby?'

'I had a miscarriage.' I mistook his silence for incomprehension. 'I lost the baby. On the boat coming over to England.'

Yves made a strange animal cry. It was pitiful, but I could feel myself harden.

'Please come back,' he said in a strangled voice.

'I can't.'

'I beg you.'

The whole of that night I lay awake thinking. What would it be like if I went back? I could start again and make a success of my time there with the benefit of the experience I'd already had. Yves and I had had some good times together and this would surely put our relationship on a different footing. A succession of romantic, sun-filled images filled my head like the sappy montages in chick flicks where the characters are taking windy walks together and getting to know each other. Then I came to my senses. Men chucked you out of their apartments and fucked off to New York leaving you pregnant. They pretended to be your friend then tried to bonk you, and when you said no, they left you with nothing but a cheeky note and didn't even phone you back. They fell in love with themselves and fucked bumless giraffe-women when they were supposed to be in love with you. When I finally fell asleep in the early hours of the morning my resentful dreams made me grind my teeth so badly I felt like I had lockjaw when I woke up.

The session

I'd never have considered it if I hadn't been far away from home with a bunch of foreign nutters who I was unlikely to run into at the supermarket. I'd inherited from Claude a deep distrust of psychotherapists, who appealed only to the flaky and self-indulgent, but where had that got me? Besides, the art therapy part of this encounter group sounded like it could be quite fun. I missed mucking about with paints, and since Maddy had made me send back the watercolours I'd optimistically bought, the opportunity for some creative catharsis was quite appealing.

A small sign on the door bearing the stencilled words Holistic Healing Session directed me down the sick-house green passage to a light, cold room with high windows and wooden floors, rather like my junior school gymnasium. There were about eleven of them in total, including me. As advertised, we were all women, me and these unlikely soul sisters of mine. It felt like a meeting of dysfunctional adult Brownies. I almost expected someone to ask me to dance around the giant mushroom and deposit my Brasso'ed two-cent piece, like we had in the few brief weeks I'd flirted with Brownies as a child. As it turned out, there was no giant mushroom, but we gathered in a circle nevertheless. Brownie memories filled my mind: memories of getting a badge for being able to light matches (hardly a challenge for a juvenile pyromaniac who'd set fire to the carport only days before) and of chanting foolish sayings and songs in the dingy scout hall where my friend Christopher was molested by Mr Ferguson while trying to practise his trombone. It was not a promising association. I felt sure that any minute now I'd be called upon to support my team, leaping into the air and shouting 'Bush Babies! Bush Babies! We're the best!'

Somehow it took an awfully long time of aimless milling about for people to get into a circle. A strange mixture of anxiety and irritation was welling up inside me. I was after immediate catharsis – wasn't that what this was all about? – and it was taking half the session for these people just to stand still in the right place. But when the session finally began I wished it hadn't. Memories of first year drama flooded into my head as Marge the healing facilitator forced us to leap into the centre of the circle and introduce ourselves, accompanied by a physical attitude. It was dreadful. Waiting for my turn was like standing on the diving blocks waiting for the gun in a swimming gala. I wondered if I could cut my losses and leave right then, but I thought about Sally and stuck it out.

The session continued after what seemed like an eternity of sitting around miserably and sharing and eating doughy yeast-free crunchies. By this time I was convinced that I didn't belong there. I was the luckiest, most stable, in control, switched on, whole woman on the planet. The only other Sister who seemed even part-way normal was Iona, and she was there because she'd killed her husband. Lesson one: madness is relative.

We'd just finished our craft experience (fridge magnets and some rather cathartic finger painting) and were heading into yet another sharing spree when I started to feel I was coming unstuck. Marge quietly called me aside.

'Clementine, are you experiencing feelings of hostility?'

'What?'

'I sense a blockage in your healing process. Perhaps you should try to make more of an effort to integrate yourself into the rest of the group.'

Duly reprimanded, I returned to the group to integrate.

After what seemed like hours of gently regimented humiliation we finally got around to doing something that I enjoyed. We each had to concentrate on a negative emotion we felt strongly about and then write a story, which would 'smudge our aura' and purge us of that emotion. I was rather proud of my story, and by the time it came to reading out our offerings I was bursting with excitement. I leapt up and volunteered to share. Mine was a gruesome little tale of revenge with a particularly satisfactory and dramatic ending which I relished reading to my captive audience.

When I had finished there was a horrified silence, followed by ominous snuffling. Marge put on some music for the closing individual meditation. She called me aside again and took me into the sick-house green passage out of earshot while the others carried on. I felt like I'd been called to the headmistress.

'I can't have you here if you're not going to take this seriously, Clem,' she admonished in a measured, rational voice. 'Some of these people are a lot worse off than you are. It's not on to poke fun.'

I was mortified. 'I'm sorry. I really didn't intend to poke fun.' Then I tried to smile at Marge but it didn't work.

'Your main problem, Clementine, is that you are angry.'

This comment made me angrier still.

'Oh *well* ...' I couldn't help the sarcasm, though I knew it didn't do my image any good. 'I hardly needed to pay good money and to sit around making ugly fridge magnets to find *that* out!'

It was true. Everything made me angry. Everything from newspaper stories about child molestation to people who didn't put the milk back in the fridge was enough to make me feel homicidal. Marge continued, annoyingly unruffled.

'You are so angry that you can't see past it. You also have very low esteem at the moment.'

Thanks for nothing, I thought. I didn't need that rubbed in. I hadn't come to be insulted.

'What's your point?' I asked rudely.

'My point is that your hostility is being totally misdirected here. You're upsetting everyone and you're not helping yourself. Part of solving the issues is facing them in the first place and you seem reluctant to do that.'

I realised that she might actually be suggesting I leave. *Then* what would I do? I'd have to face myself on my own. Impossible. I made another attempt to mollify her.

'I'm sure it's helping, and I'll get over the anger, I just ...' I knew it sounded like begging. Marge was smiling at me but shaking her head.

'It's not the right environment for you, Clem. I think you need time alone to reflect. And I think you need some individual counselling before you're ready to work in a group like this.'

Jesus, was she actually suggesting I was *more* maladjusted than the rest of them?

'One thing you definitely need is to do something to get rid of all this anger.'

'What, like go on a killing spree?' I laughed mirthlessly. 'I was thinking more along the lines of writing. Why don't you try doing some more of it if you enjoyed it so much?'

Without warning the anger subsided and the tears came. 'I don't understand what I did wrong, Marge. I read them my story, that's all. Just like the others. I *liked* my story.'

'Your story traumatised them, Clem, and you know it. You deliberately went all "spooky" and gave people frights at the scary bits.'

'Isn't that how you're *supposed* to read a story?'

'I don't think I need to explain what I mean. Clementine, you've had a taste of what it's like to be down. Bear that in mind before you make jokes at other people's expense.'

She was right, of course, and she succeeded in making me feel guilty, but surely the very fact that I had been right down in the pits, one of the Seriously Depressed, meant that I was allowed to make jokes about them? About *us*? Like only Jewish people are really allowed to make Jewish jokes with impunity. The fact is, she had asked us to write about what was troubling us and my head was full of feelings of revenge against men. Frankly, I thought I'd exercised enormous restraint in my writing when what I really wanted to do was tear my clothes and pull my hair out screaming 'slice off dicks, fricassee his balls, sprinkle his own pubes in his sandwiches ....' So much for catharsis. Now that staying with the Sisters no longer seemed an option I was reluctant to leave. I braced myself and confronted the truth.

'Are you suggesting I leave?' I asked, biting my lip.

'For now, yes.'

'But what about the money? I've paid for the full course.' I was clutching at straws and I knew it. Marge smiled again, took some notes out of a little metal petty cash box she'd been holding all along and handed them to me.

And so I was expelled from the Sisterhood. Clearly there was a set way of alternatively healing myself that I had failed to observe, and cathartic rites of abandon happened within limits. It's a pity, really, that it came to a head because I read my story – just when I felt I had found a self-help strategy I'd been looking for. I crossed the road outside and waited some distance from the designated corner for Sally to pick me up on her way back from fetching the children from school. I didn't want to hang around with the rest of them once they'd finished meditating and I skulked about in the shadows like a friendless schoolchild, vulnerable, troublesome.

Iona was the first to emerge and she crossed the road towards me.

'I suppose you're going?' She looked quite shy for a murderess.

'I suppose so,' I shrugged.

'Pity,' she said.

'Thanks.'

'I liked your story. You should do more.'

'Thanks.'

Then Sally arrived in the station wagon, bursting with school projects, a mini-riot happening on the back seat as Rachel tried to detach Davey from his bulldozer. Sal calmly told Rachel to 'shut up and make space for Clementine'. She duly obeyed and I climbed in. Sally's serene authority amazed me. I waved at Iona out of the back window and shouted, 'Congratulations!' Then we drove away from the Sisters. Iona was still waving as we drove out of sight. She looked a bit confused, but she was smiling.

'Who were you talking to?' asked Sal as we drove home.

'That was Iona,' I answered. 'She killed her husband.'

'Iona *Parker*?' Sally seemed quite excited. She said her name as though I'd been hanging out with a celebrity.

'We don't know surnames.'

'It must be her. There can't be too many young women called Iona in Cambridge who killed their husbands.'

'So she's really a murderess?' I was quite impressed.

'Murderess? Well I suppose it depends how you see it. The story went that she accidentally brained her late husband with a chip pot one night when he was giving her her regular Saturday night beating in front of the TV. When the neighbours forced their way in the next morning they found him lying with his head in a pool of blood. Iona was still talking to him, drinking tea in front of the TV, watching the morning soaps. It caused a major stir as you can imagine. She's quite a heroine for the feminists.'

'She liked my story,' I told Sally.

'What story?' she asked.

And so I told Sally about my story and confessed to her that I'd been cast out of the Sisterhood. I told her that Marge had more or less said I was beyond her help. Then I treated her to bits of the Gospel according to Marge and catalogued my misdemeanours. She laughed, even if it was ruefully, and that's when I realised that the person I really needed to tell was Jack.

Confession

'Hello?' Jack answered, disguising his voice with a foreign accent in case it was someone he didn't want to speak to. It was an old trick of ours and I knew his repertoire of accents by heart.

'Hello Jack.'

'Oh my *God*, darling, it's *you*!' Jack boomed dramatically, changing back to his normal voice. 'I thought it might be someone asking for my third year marks. I've been so worried about you. You just dropped off the map, and Cruella de Ville in Paris wouldn't tell me where you'd gone.'

'I'm in Cambridge.'

'*Cam*bridge? What are you doing there?'

'Having a nervous breakdown.' I laughed, then my lips trembled all over the place but I managed to avoid a full-scale weep.

'What happened?'

I decided I'd just spill all the beans at once, hang out every bit of dirty laundry for his scrutiny.

'I'm a bit fucked up, Jack. I got knocked up by The Suit and ended up losing the foetus in a spurt of gore in a toilet on the ferry to England when I was coming with Maddy to get an abortion.'

It was so silent on the other end of the line I could hear the strange seashell sound of the international call. Finally Jack spoke.

'Please tell me you're not being serious. Why didn't you phone me?'

'There was nothing you could do. And I couldn't talk that time in Paris because Kurt was hanging around me like a bog fly listening to every word I said.'

Jack was quiet for a moment, and when he spoke his voice kept cracking up.

'I just feel dreadful that I was carrying on as if everything was okay, cheerfully drinking cognac or grumbling about marking while you were ... Are you all right, Clemmy?' He sounded stricken, as though he were about to burst into tears himself. I'd have expected all this sympathy to make it very difficult not to start blubbing all over again, but my tears all seemed to have dried out.

'It's okay. Happens to lots of people, I suppose. Well ... perhaps not in the same way with the food poisoning and falling off bikes and getting your dress cut off you by a stranger as the prelude ... I was just unlucky.'

'What did the bastard Suit do about it?'

'The bastard Suit didn't know. Maddy came over to bring

me to England so we could sort it all. She's been amazing. Then I miscarried on the ferry anyway. Then Angus came over and I was horrible to him and I have one less friend in the world. Now all the shit's over, touch wood, and I just have to get my head straight again.'

'Jesus, what an *annus horribilis*, my darling girl. I know this might sound unbelievable but I'm almost lost for words. Are you going to go the shrink route? You can have mine if you come home, he's a real sweetie.'

'Actually I've decided to try this kind of healing workshop thing ...'

'Yeeeess?' Jack's voice rose with inquisitive scepticism. He was trying valiantly not to scoff. I wasn't quite sure where to start.

'I don't know where to start,' I confessed.

'Oh come on, darling. Run it by me,' Jack coaxed.

'Well Sally, my sort of aunt, told me about it. It's a kind of series of art therapy workshops for women only.'

There was a moment of silence from Jack. Then he cleared his throat and took a deep breath. 'I'm absolutely not passing any judgement on what the rest of the Sisterhood goes in for, Clementine, but are you really sure it's the right thing for you?'

'I'm not going to tell you about it if you're all judgemental,' I teased.

'You're quite right. And I'm an ancient old fart, a relic from the era of shock treatment and Valium. I'll shut up.' And he did.

'It's really quite interesting,' I said, and embarked on a brief, straight-faced description of the session, without filling him in on the ending.

Jack digested this in concerned silence, clearly unconvinced.

'So it's working for you, is it?' he asked me finally.

'Well yes, in a way.'

'And you're going again?'

'No, I think I can say in all certainty that I won't be going again. One session was quite enough for me.' Then I burst out laughing.

'Oh thank God, sweetie, I was beginning to fear I'd lost you to the New Age aliens.'

'On the contrary. I seem to have been expelled from the Mother ship.' I explained the sorry state of affairs. 'I'm such a disaster, Jack. Even the maladjusted won't have me now.'

Jack ignored my little wail of self-pity. 'I am sorry to have been right in my misgivings,' he said, not sounding sorry at all, 'but you simply don't belong there. Those are not the only Sisterhoods, thank God. Places like that are for frustrated, unattractive women who hate the world and have no style. They are clubs for angry spinsters in hair-shirts, Clem.'

'It wasn't a spinsters' club, Jack. Several of the people there are married.'

'Jesus Christ. Can you *imagine* what it's like being married to a hair-shirted spinster?'

'I think by definition you can't be married to a spinster. It's a contradiction in terms.'

'Of course you can, darling. Try not to be so literal! You just don't belong there. It's like a shoe that just doesn't fit you, like in Cinderella. Except in this case of course you're Cinderella with an ugly little midget shoe, sweetie, don't get me wrong.'

I laughed. Jack was a dreadful bigot, but he knew how to cheer me up. He sighed deeply at the other end of the world.

'I can't wait for you to come home, Clemmy. Come and join me in my parlour for a whisky as soon as you are ready to take on the human race again.'

It was the most appealing invitation I could imagine.

Invitation home

The morning after my phonecall with Jack I went for a walk. I wanted to think about his invitation, about why the thought of going home had seemed so seductive, about whether I was ready. The ground was all crunchy and frosty and crisp and I stomped around in Sally's wellingtons, cracking the crusty surface and feeling like a child splashing in puddles. Suddenly I realised I felt better than I had in months. Perhaps this was it, I realised. Happiness.

When I got back to the house I found a note from Sally:

> *Gone to fetch kids. Need to talk to you urgently. Please be there when I get back. Sal.*

The note wiped the smiled off my face. Perhaps Sally wanted to expel me too? I wondered whether I had done something terrible inadvertently and was just standing at the phone table in this state of paranoia when the phone rang. I snatched up the receiver with a racing heart.

'Hello?'

'Clem?' It was Claude. But her voice sounded small and far away.

'Hello, Claude,' I replied, my voice still shaky with anxiety.

'Are you okay?'

'I'm fine. Sorry, the phone startled me, that's all.' I wasn't quite sure what to say. It was so long since I'd spoken to her. Where could I start? She felt so far away and apart from what I'd been through. I made a feeble attempt at a beginning.

'How was the conference?' I asked her.

'Oh fine. Fine. Too long.' Silence again. Disconcerting.

'How's Gran?' I asked her.

'Not great, I'm afraid,' came the small, tight voice. 'Apparently she had another little stroke recently and refused to speak anything but High Dutch for almost a week. Most inconvenient. It was very trying for the nurses.'

I couldn't help smiling. The old battleaxe; in her dotage and still managing to give everyone a run for their money. But it wasn't good news. Claude was silent for a moment. Then, very quietly, as if each word she spoke hurt her: 'Clem ... why didn't you tell me?'

So she knew. How? Maddy must have told her, I supposed. I could hardly blame her. But Claude knew and she sounded hurt; hurt, not angry, and even close to tears. I immediately felt guilty for having assumed she would reproach me or lecture me; that she wouldn't understand.

'I tried to phone you, Claude, but you had just left.' This suddenly struck me as highly significant. At the heart of my relationship with Claude lay a perpetual failure to connect.

'Maddy told me you were at Ben's and you'd had a rough time, so I phoned straight away. I got Sally, who told me you were out. She obviously presumed I'd know everything and simply mentioned it in passing. I don't even *know* Sally.'

'I'm so sorry.'

'No, Clem, *I'm* so sorry.' It went quiet on her end of the line again. 'Hang on,' she said, and I heard her blow her nose in the background.

'Clem? Are you still there?'

'I'm here.'

'Clem, I miss you very much. Can I persuade you to come home? It might be nice for you to come and see Mac,' she ventured tentatively. 'One never knows how long it'll be before it's too late to communicate with her at all.'

But I knew it was her own vulnerability she was confronting, even her own mortality. I was her daughter and she wanted me there. I just wished it wasn't so hard for her to say it.

'I'll try Claude, I promise. I'll see what I can arrange.'

Suddenly it felt like an invisible obstacle had been removed from my path. It was obvious that I needed to go home.

When Sally came through the front door I was still standing in the kitchen next to the phone, staring at it as though it were some kind of divine instrument of revelation. Her face fell.

'Clem, I've made a terrible mistake. I had no idea that your mother didn't know and I said something about the miscarriage.

I think she was terribly shocked. Oh God, I feel so awful. Maddy didn't even want to tell me about it, but I was so worried about you when you first arrived that she had to. And I never imagined you wouldn't have told your mother.' She looked stricken and stumbled over her words in her haste to confess.

'I know, it's okay,' I tried to console her. 'Claude just phoned and we've spoken. Really, it's fine. Don't worry.' I stepped forward to hug her and we stood there for a while. It was a strange reversal of roles to be reassuring her like this, especially now that I had decided I was going home. Eventually we released each other and she searched the drawers for some paper towel to blow her nose on.

'I just presumed she'd know,' Sally said. 'I hope you can forgive me.'

'Actually, I should thank you. I was dreading having to tell her myself and at least you've spared me that.'

Sally's guilt was not easily assuaged. 'I so wanted to be useful to you. To make it all better. And I feel like this mistake has cancelled out anything positive that I've done,' she said, miserably. So I told her just how much she and Ben had done for me; that because of what she'd told Claude she had asked me to come home, and that I was ready to go.

The next morning I went into Cambridge with Sally and booked my return ticket. Then I faxed Jack my flight details and asked him to fetch me. I told him not to tell anyone I was coming back; that way, I could take my time and re-warp to local conditions in peace.

On the way to the Cambridge train station the next Wednesday, Ben stopped outside the WH Smith. I wanted to buy a notebook for the plane. Sally and I chose one with a suitably anonymous black cover and a strokeable texture, spiral-bound and just the right size to be able to write in on one of those silly foldout aeroplane tables. She bought it for me as a goodbye present. I was touched to discover that Rachel and the twins had done drawings for me. There was a princess in a tower from Rachel – a princess with remarkably familiar electrified-looking dark hair, which Rachel had drawn with childish candour sticking out from her head almost parallel to the ground in wiry kinks. The twins had drawn me a trunkload of gory nature pictures, red in tooth and claw, each one telling an elaborate story. They told me the stories all the way into Cambridge, acting out the goriest sections gleefully until Ben growled at them good-naturedly to 'wind their necks in' or they wouldn't get their trip to visit Clem and the animals in Africa. Sally, the ever-practical, told them to choose one of their pictures each for me, since I couldn't take all of them on the plane.

Once I was waving to them all from the train I was already so far away. Home was so close I could almost taste it. Sally smiled like a Madonna and Ben shouted at me to come back soon. The twins leapt up and down, screaming that they wanted to go back with me *now*, which was very gratifying. Only Rachel remained remote, waving with a polite, guarded smile, no doubt waiting patiently to rejoin her Barbie collection or to return to the television. The train pulled out and I waved at them all until they had disappeared out of sight.

V

Return of the native

Return of the native

The aeroplane is a readjustment chamber. I open the notebook to the first clean, clear page and write my name in it. A woman with a curly-haired, caramel-coloured toddler sits down next to me and tries to install the boy in the seat next to her. She bumps the notebook. A long line of black ink trails from my name down the blank page.

'Sorry,' she says in a South African accent. And I love her and her boy and her flat vowels. And although I know she is apologising in advance, for the whole flight, rather than just for bumping my tray, I am flooded not with dread but with a strange beatific contentment.

The airhostess begins her banal magic show. She veils and unveils her props – life jackets, oxygen masks – with a practised series of flourishes. Everything down to the food and bedding is covered, concealed, curtained, boxed.

The little boy struggles against the constraints of the safety belt, then performs just as badly on his mother's lap. She must swear under her breath as she struggles to calm him, because the instant she gets him to stay still he begins with his monosyllabic chorus.

'Fuck,' he says, quite quietly at first so that I am not sure that he's said it. His mother ignores him. 'Fuck!' he says again, louder this time so that heads start to turn and I have to suppress a smile. His mother shoots me an apologetic look and tries to keep him quiet, but this only spurs him on. He begins to say it over and over again, increasingly loudly, delighting in the effect it is having. His mother begins to reprimand him, which throws him into fits of mirth. I feign great absorption in the in-flight magazine to hide my laughter. 'FUCK!' says the boy once more, with enormous gusto.

'Shut *up*, Grant,' says his mother. He shrieks delightedly at the reaction and continues to shout the word repeatedly and gleefully. I ponder whether a child that young could have

Tourette's syndrome. The woman next to them tries to ignore it and politely talks baby talk to him, and the mother is at her wits' end. Then a blank expression comes over the boy's face. He has forgotten the word, lost the key to instant attention. He lets out a series of little screams instead, then starts trying a range of similar words, but none seems to have quite the same effect. I smile at her. I'm ready to smile at anything. I'm going home.

Touchdown

No man ever steps in the same river twice, for it's not the same river and he's not the same man.
– Heraclitus, *On the Universe*

By the time we descended towards Cape Town every beatific feeling had drained away and been replaced by unbridled panic. A sour, sick feeling of dread was bubbling in my gut. I wanted to throw up. I wanted to parachute out of the plane and run away into the wilderness forever. I tried to emit psychic messages to the pilot, ordering him to divert the flight path, but he landed us neatly at Cape Town airport. He told us, in English and Afrikaans, that it was a thirty-degree day out there, and then mercilessly pumped elevator muzak at us while we tried to exit.

Jack was waiting for me at Arrivals. He let me fall onto his chest and wrapped me in a reassuring cloud of Gucci. 'I've brought reinforcements,' I announced, and handed him a packet clanking with duty free perfume. Then he whisked me away in his battered white Opel and made me (in my cheap Paris edition Jackie O's) feel like a celebrity shunning unwanted publicity instead of a reject and a failure who can't even do an overseas sojourn successfully.

Relaxing in the blissful peace of Jack's boudoir, his answering machine set uncompromisingly in answer mode, I felt suspended again between past and present, reluctant to look either in the face. Jack, dressed in some gorgeous flowing white linen outfit so that he looked like a camp Angel Gabriel, was ministering to my every need, plying me with whisky, telling me how startlingly pale and interesting I was looking. And all was well, until my mind drifted back to reality.

'What will I say when I see people?' I asked him in terror.

'You'll say you've just returned from Paris and you had a lovely time.'

'But what if they ask me how it was? What if they ask me why I came back?'

'Tell them whatever you want to. Tell them you were a TV presenter or a porn star and you couldn't stand being recognised in the *supermarché* any more. Tell them whatever you feel like telling them at the time. It's your business. You don't even have to tell them anything if you don't feel like it.'

I thought back to my attempt to fool Angus into believing my time in Paris had been nothing but drinking wine with Frenchmen outside churches in the sunset. What a dismal failure that pathetic fictionalised version had been, and how quickly he'd seen through it. I thought about Kurt glutting on the misery in my journals and I thought about Maddy and the secret she'd kept for so many years. Perhaps she had a point. Perhaps if I could just clear the static in my head I might be able to think about myself more clearly.

'I think I need to be out of town for a while,' I told Jack, as the idea began to form in my mind. 'Just for a few weeks.'

'You're not going to run away again, are you?' He looked genuinely worried.

I smiled. 'I'm staying. That's about as much as I *do* know for sure.'

Jack suddenly broke into a huge grin.

'What's so funny?' I asked.

'I've just remembered we locked your passport in my safe.'

Suitably reassured, he settled down with a whisky for a good *skinder*.

The next morning Jack woke me gently with a pot of herbal tea.

'I have a surprise for you,' he said. 'Stick your clothes on and prepare to feel a whole lot better.' Then he drove me down to René the Hairdresser. I was laughing as they decked me out in my plastic poncho.

'Be extra specially nice to her,' Jack instructed René, who rolled his eyes camply, suggesting that this really went without saying. René looked at my reflection in the mirror, sucking in his cheeks and posing as he smoothed my hair and visualised.

'I'm thinking straight, I'm thinking shiny. I'm thinking kind of Brooke Shields on a good day but with two separate eyebrows,' he said after a few moments of inspiration. 'How do you feel about that?' I smiled consent. He snipped and preened and stroked and flattered my hair into glamorous obedience. He followed its natural inclinations rather than trying to impose some foreign regime on it, and it worked. He fed me sparkling mineral water and sent me packing with a bottle of 'taming lotion' and some useful tips for ongoing minimal maintenance.

'I'll bring her back to you soon,' said Jack, winking. He had my therapeutic routine taped.

That night, when I was waiting for Jack outside the theatre, I accidentally met Kurt's new girlfriend. She was a sleek, well-groomed, fragile-looking Indian girl dressed for a dance class. She too was waiting, and we fell into conversation. She told me sweetly that she was impatient for the new man in her life to finish in the library because he'd promised to put up her bookshelf that evening. She started telling me about his work and I knew even before she told me that her boyfriend's name was Kurt. I panicked at the thought that he might arrive at any minute and stood up to leave. Before she could ask my name I said goodbye and went to wait at Jack's Opel, out of sight. I was incredulous: for all her quiet fragility (in fact probably because of it) she had him wrapped around her finger.

'What's wrong, Poppet?' Jack asked as soon as he saw my face.

'Nothing,' I said, forcing a smile.

Jack raised an eyebrow.

'Okay, I met Kurt's new woman.'

'Ah.'

'She didn't know who I was, we just ended up chatting on the steps ...'

'I see.'

I paused, somewhat mortified by what I had to report.

'He's putting up bookshelves for her, Jack, *bookshelves*. What exactly did I do wrong?'

'Maybe you've reformed him.'

'Maybe I can't do relationships. Maybe I'm just a bit of a dud in general.'

'Oh what crap,' said Jack. 'Fine, so you didn't do glamorous work overseas ... so you got knocked up by a seedy Frenchman. So what? You've passed Real Life 101 and you've got your whole life ahead of you. I think your failure has been a great success. I, on the other hand, am a man with a great future behind me. Count yourself lucky. And think of the stories you have to tell.'

Okay, I had 'come through'. But somehow I didn't feel I'd jettisoned much baggage along the way. It was time to do something for myself and I knew just what I wanted to do. I would go and hide out for a while; just until the static in my head cleared and I could think again. I would do a Greta Garbo and hole up like a hermit. Perfect! For the first time since I decided to come home I'd hit upon something I actually knew was the right thing to do, and it was thrilling to feel so decisive. But first I had to see Claude and Mac. No, in fact I *wanted* to see them. I got on the phone and booked another one-way bus ticket home.

A second homecoming

I arrived back in Grahamstown on the bus in the early morning.

Through the groggy-looking crowd I saw Claude waiting, standing alone and apart from the rest in front of the chemist, her expression touchingly anxious and expectant. A wave of protective love surged through me: it was unexpectedly wonderful to see her again.

Claude made me breakfast in the seventies pine-panelled kitchen. It had stayed the same for so long that fashion had come full circle and it had acquired a kind of retro chic cachet. Claude didn't press me for an account of my last few months. Instead, she talked about her work, about the recent ructions in the department; she gave me news of old friends. There seemed to be a mutual understanding that this was not the time to unburden, but it didn't feel like evasion either. I knew Claude had to go to work, but there would be more than enough time when she came home. I looked forward to a day of doing absolutely nothing.

'Do you have everything you need?' asked Claude, as she grabbed her workbag and was about to leave.

'Of course. Don't worry about me,' I said. 'I'm okay now.'

That evening, when Claude got home, I'd made us pasta. We ate dinner on our laps in front of the empty fireplace, companionably silent for a long time.

'I spent a year trying to live in England,' she said, apropos of nothing in particular. 'I hated it. I hated the contented, unchallenging lives they led ... I hated the smug, self-assurance of the people I worked with, the people "cultured" London seemed to be full of, the tried and tested second-handness of everything. I *tried* to like it, for Jimmy's sake, but after a year I told him I had to go home. So we packed up our life there and came back. He got irritated when I went to Black Sash meetings and came home raging about what was happening – as if I'd had the chance to get away from it and had spurned it – but I had no choice. The problems here made sense to me. They were real.'

I thought of Paris; the endless jousting, the food snobbery, the unwholesome sexuality, the smugly self-assured civilisedness, and was overwhelmed by a feeling of pride and gratitude for my mother. It felt like my turn for a revelation. I told Claude about my time there, about Yves. I told her about the baby that never was, and a strange look passed over Claude's face. 'I can't believe I could have been a grandmother. What a strange thought. You know, I actually quite like the idea.'

That started me off, and we fell into each other's arms and laughed at ourselves behaving like characters in an afternoon soap – except with more snot and less mascara.

The once and future queen

This was where the deceased lived.
– Graham Swift about the asylum in *Last Orders*

Mac had been moved to a frailcare section at Greenfields after her second stroke. As we walked down the passages to her room, we were flanked by rows and rows of finished-looking people who I felt sure would rather not be around any more. Granny Mac herself, once so formidable, lay swaddled pathetically, her frail body trussed up like a beef olive in the tastefully clinical floral bedspreads, attached to a tube and fussed over by Claude. How had she shrunk so fast? Could someone have turned the tube on the wrong way so that it sucked instead of fed? She seemed to be shrivelling into a pale, talc-scented relic as I watched. She noticed my arrival immediately and fixed me with a disarmingly direct stare, quite uncannily like Maddy's Laser Look. Claude took charge.

'Mac, Clem's back from France. You remember Clem?'

Mac's dark eyes popped open. 'Of course I remember my own fucking granddaughter. How's that Kraut boy of yours?' she barked at me, in what Claude later explained was now a very rare moment of lucidity.

'We've split up, Mac.'

'Good move. His eyes were too close together.' This was a

complete fallacy, of course. Kurt had attractively wide-set eyes, but I enjoyed the gratuitous insult.

Mac seemed inspired by her outburst too. She tried to sit up in the bedclothes and motioned to me to come nearer. 'One thing you must learn, girlie,' she said, probably having forgotten my name, 'is that that kind of man is good for bed but not for breakfast.' I nodded sagely and obediently and tried hard not to laugh.

'God, she's amazing! She gets ruder by the day,' I said to Claude once we were safely in the car and out of earshot.

'You think *that's* bad?' Claude sounded almost as if she were boasting. 'Last week some misguided but well-meaning nurse brought a priest to visit her. Mac had a long conversation with him, then, without warning, her patience ran out. She looked up at the priest and said "Well, it's been nice chatting, but let's cut the shit. What exactly are you selling?" The priest protested that he just wanted to talk to her and he wasn't trying to sell her anything at all. "Well, what did you come to talk to me about then?" she snapped at him. "I came to talk about the Lord," he replied. And Mac told him triumphantly that she'd known all along he was trying to sell *something* and he could piss off because she wasn't buying the Lord or any other of his miracle products.'

But I had been lucky with Mac that day. Mostly she was far away. Some days we couldn't reach her at all, and it distressed me terribly then to watch Claude coping. I couldn't stop thinking about my grandmother. Perhaps it was because her story would soon come to an end that I was suddenly desperate to hear more about the beginning, about her past. Or perhaps it was just part of piecing myself together.

'How did she end up being called Mac?' I asked Claude when we were driving home after one particularly dismal visit.

'It was after her first husband died. MacKinnon, my father. She'd never taken his surname – she stuck with van Zyl – but after he died, Clementina Johanna became Mac. As Scottish as haggis itself. She …'

'Wait a second!' I interrupted. '*Clementina* Johanna?'

'Yes. Surely you knew that?'

'But I thought I was named after the song.'

'Well you were, in a way. It was a kind of a compromise. Jimmy was after one of those utterly unpronounceable Irish saint names that mean something like "She who keeps her knees together" for you, but I put my foot down. And anyway, he liked the song. Where was I?'

'Mac became Scottish …' I prompted, still reeling with the discovery.

'Oh yes. So … Mac concealed her own identity behind a sporran of Scottishness and resolutely refused to speak Afrikaans again. Somewhere in her stubborn mind she was convinced it was the Dutch and their God, their whispers behind their hands and their superstition about lightning, that had killed her man. Once when I was little I said something about being Scottish in front of Mac's sister. Willemina scoffed "Scottish! What *kak*." Mac shot her a scorching look and we left Willemina's house immediately, even though we hadn't had tea yet. Willemina died three days later in a freak accident. Mac took it as a sign that God was calling it quits with her. She made her peace with Him and politely requested that they leave each other alone after that.'

We drove on in silence for a few minutes, then Claude slapped her forehead with her palm as if she'd just remembered something. 'Oh by the way, I have some good news,' she announced. 'Angus is coming back. He said you'd understand why. Something about the landscape driving him mad and that Maddy had been right; it was like being a sailor marooned in the calm waters. He sounded a bit pissed and kept on saying "undulate undulate" and talking about how boring and tame the English countryside was. He told me he'd had better conversations with Pepe than with any of the Oxford intelligentsia. Who is Pepe, incidentally? He said you'd know him.'

'He's our inflatable plastic sheep,' I said with a small laugh.

But the thought of facing Angus after our fallout in Cambridge filled me with dread. That was one subject I had not discussed with Claude or even with Jack, although it had been preoccupying me since I'd got back and discovered Angus was still in England. Although there were times when I had desperately wanted to know whether she'd heard from him I was too scared of hearing he'd said terrible things about me or, perhaps worse, that he wouldn't even mention me at all. It was all too complicated. I wanted to be a nun in a remote and impenetrable convent. Inviolate. Preferably lobotomised. Thought-less. It seemed like the ideal time for a retreat.

Before I embraced my hermit phase I had a phonecall to make. All this time with Claude had made me realise how much Madame Rouillard had done for me when I was really hardly capable of tying my own shoelaces, let alone coping with the problems that assailed me in Paris. I was happy to talk to her, this unlikely, temporary foster mother of mine, so far away in another hemisphere. I gave her Claude's number and address, and as she painstakingly repeated the unfamiliar words I could hear the espresso machine exhaling asthmatically in the background, the clink of china and glasses being collected and washed, the clients chattering in French. For a moment, just a moment, I actually missed that other life.

Retreat

Claude gave me her old laptop and let me borrow the Volvo. I eased it out of the drive and went to fetch the keys to the Moores' Kasouga beach house from Sylvia. Her husband, Phillip Moore, was a friend and colleague of Claude's, also in the English department, and they lived on African Street in one of the Victorian houses with a small *stoep* in front of the house and a garden nestled privately behind, where the children could safely be sent to play for hours while their parents laboured over marking and academic papers. A wind chime threw itself around wildly next to the front door and all around were signs of happy, well-adjusted living – a friendly dog, a wicker chair, a well-trimmed hedge bright with orange black-eyed Susans. Sylvia was well-groomed and glamorous, a little too glamorous for the wife of an academic in Grahamstown, and renowned for her hypochondria and her adulterous affairs with half of the faculty. Shortly after her marriage to Phillip, Sylvia, who'd had a teaching job at a local school, started developing various non-specific illnesses which necessitated that she give up her job and stay at home making herself beautiful all day – or so Claude, who was very fond of Phillip, had told me. She'd also told me that if I gave Sylvia any hint of my recent predicaments she'd be snuffling for details like a pig after a truffle. I reluctantly accepted her offer of tea and she ran me through the checklist for the beach house – alarm, water pump, electric switches, neighbours – while I obligingly drank my Lapsang Souchong and tried to focus on the instructions, waiting for a gap so that I could leave.

'The bathroom door is a bit tricky,' Sylvia continued. 'Phillip couldn't get it open for ages last time, and then when I was having a bath I got locked inside and had to let him in through the window ...'

I couldn't concentrate. I was desperate to get out of there, to get far away from Sylvia and her wind chimes and her predatory, intrusive curiosity.

'Are you sure you won't have another cup of tea? Or some chamomile? I find it so soothing, you know, ever since I've had ...'

'I can't. Really. I promised Claude I'd get there before dark.' I realised this was absurd. It was two o'clock in the afternoon and it took less than an hour to get there, but what other excuse did I have? Sylvia let me out, looking a little nonplussed, and I was on my way.

And then I was cruising towards the coast and the broccoli-treed hills of Kasouga in the old Volvo, cool and anonymous in my Jackie O's despite the gathering storm clouds.

Phillip and Sylvia's beach house was crowded with beds and stacked mattresses, evidence of a recent get-together (Scrabble card game scores, half-finished pictures on walls), and an assortment of antique furniture interspersed with oddments and cheap pine bunks. It was what Jack might describe as a cross between Calvinist simplicity and a gypsy camp, and I felt entirely at home there. I grabbed myself a beer to celebrate feeling cheerful. After a few seconds of attempting to twist off the cap I noticed it didn't *have* a twist-off cap, went in search of a bottle opener and produced, after much digging under the sink, some antique object vaguely resembling one which did the trick. Then, beer in hand, I found the key for the bathroom door, slid it into the lock and it worked first time.

'Ha!' I thought to myself. 'I am a pioneer-spirited independent woman who drinks beer on her own and can open doors men can't.' I shut the door again and decided to take my beer down to the sea.

There was a cold wind at the lagoon. A few fishermen were walking towards the beach, so I followed them, heeding Claude's advice not to walk alone. Apart from us, the beach was deserted. The wind blew at our backs off the dunes, bringing the sounds of the children playing in the campsite, the cicadas shrilling in the bush, the distant sound of cars. The unseasonable stormy weather made me think of fires, books, muscadel, thick socks, staying at home. It would previously have made me think of sex, sex with alluring men straight out of nineteenth century novels, but that was before I gave up sex for good, of course. It was also perfect weather in which to contemplate being holed up in a garret pretending to be a writer. I walked along the tideline, listening to the waves and watching the flurrying globs of foam skidding along the sand like footless cartoon mice in a hurry, until my extremities started to go numb and I headed home for a bath.

I grabbed the bathroom key and raced across the *stoep* to the bathroom door. I turned it in the lock but the door wouldn't open – it stuck at the critical moment. I tried again. No joy. I checked the label – right key – and tried again, but it still wouldn't turn. I was cursing and freezing and dying for a piss and it was dark. I darted out onto the lawn, hoicked up my skirt, pulled down my pants, pissed, rearranged my clothes, ran inside, and climbed into the bed, kicking and wriggling to generate some heat. I pulled my bag towards me by the strap and got out the vodka. Then I pulled a book randomly out of the crowded bookshelf, flicked on the bedside light, pulled the book under the covers, breathed hard to warm the space around me, and began to read, once again relaxing into the sheer indulgence of living someone else's life for a while.

The next morning I encountered a neighbour in the road. Well, *I* was in the road. He was in his garden, fenced off from the street, clearly in the midst of some elaborate *braai* preparations in his faded blue rugby shorts (it was a weekend, after all, I realised) and trying to untangle the Swingball, which was wrapped in a knot around the pole. He greeted me. My immediate reaction was to feign deafness and walk on, but then I remembered the issue of the bathroom door. It was a toss-up between being a hermit and having a hot bath sometime in the near future.

Chris was very kind. He wiggled the key around in the lock with his big freckled farmer's hand, and with admirable patience, and swung open the door to paradise. He invited me for drinks with his wife, Christine. No doubt they were a matching pair. Still, I felt mean-spirited when I declined. Instead, I lay in the luxurious bath, reading a recent copy of *Fair Lady*, revelling in the trivia of beauty tips and sex quizzes (rate your performance out of ten), and mentally vowing to start Exercise Programmes, Eat Healthily and Love Myself. I also decided not to wash my hair until I returned to Grahamstown since the beauty editor swore your hair 'went through its dirty cycle and then became clean again', doing wonders for its health. I lapped up all the 'new beginnings' advice, prepared myself to be a most willing fashion victim, and started to feel a lot better about life. I slept very well that night.

The jovial shouts of hordes of little boys woke me up the next morning. I climbed groggily out of bed, wrapped myself in a kikoi, and opened the door. Through the bushes I could see a steady stream of schoolboy legs pass by the entrance to the overgrown driveway as they proceeded down the dusty road past the house, herded forward by an occasional pair of adult legs and a gruff voice keeping them in line. A school party.

I had another bath (sheer bliss and indulgence), dressed, and walked down to the lagoon as part of my new exercise regime. The boys were trooping back from the beach to the campsite, draped in towels and flicking each other with mud.

'Afternoon ma'am,' said one little boy. I looked around for the 'ma'am' he was greeting but there was no woman but me. He'd walked on before I could greet him back.

'Afternoon, ma'am,' said another.

'Hello,' I said somewhat overenthusiastically to make up for not greeting the first.

I walked past the rest of them onto the sand and trudged up a sand dune to look at the view. On all the dunes were the long trails left by sand boards. I imagined them rubbing away at the boards with candle stumps just as I had at their age, anticipating the next ride, thinking nothing of the exhausting climb back up the dune each time. Then I went back and sat on the grass with Claude's laptop, expecting to pour words effortlessly onto the screen. Nothing came. I sat there until it got dark and I realised I was too tired and hungry to keep trying.

An arrival

The next day the words came. It was a revelation. I wrote all day, and was still lying typing into the laptop on the bed when the phone rang. I stared at it for a while, then realised it must be

Claude and picked it up.

'Claude?'

'Hello?' A man's voice. Angus's voice.

'Oh. I ... hi.'

'Wow. What a reception,' he said, playfully ironic.

'Hello Angus.' It threw me. I had almost forgotten that there was a 'rest of the world' to contend with and I wasn't sure I wanted to contend with it just yet. I tried in vain to read his tone of voice. What should I expect? I was terrified that whatever I said would make things worse than they already were. I wasn't ready.

'I'm phoning to tell you that I'm coming to take you out for dinner,' he announced.

Silence. I was relieved that he still wanted to see me, that he'd gone to the trouble of tracking me down and phoning me, but I couldn't help feeling pissed off that he'd never phoned me back in Cambridge; that he'd humiliated me by letting me stew.

'Is that okay?' Angus persisted.

'I'm sorry but I can't see anyone.'

'Oh. Why not?'

'I'm doing a sort of dirt experiment on my hair and I can't leave the house.'

'Well can't you wear a hat?'

'Oh fuck it, Angus, I'm trying to get my head straight in peace. Can't you leave me alone?'

'No.'

'*No?*'

'No. I don't believe it could be good for you to sit and stew in that house feeling sorry for yourself and I'm coming to fetch you whether you like it or not. We need to talk. So wash your bloody hair. Let's go and get a pizza and drink some wine. Okay?'

'But I ...'

He put the phone down.

'Arrgh!' I slammed the receiver down and threw myself back onto Phillip and Sylvia's bed. In all likelihood he was coming to reprimand me for my behaviour in Cambridge, but I was oddly thrilled and exhilarated by his bossiness and by the fact that I still mattered enough for him to go out of his way to find me. But then *why* had he never phoned me back? Had he been trying to punish me? I lay there pondering his motives for a moment then sat up and looked in the mirror. My hair, greasy and sand-encrusted, stuck to the scalp at the roots and frizzed out madly towards the ends. It looked like a fright wig. I groaned and flopped back onto the bed.

'Fuck him anyway,' I said out loud. 'I told him not to come.'

But I did wash my hair. It was a choice between principles and vanity, and vanity won. After all, I justified, I'd have so much more confidence standing up for my principles with clean hair. Once I'd bathed I sat dumbly in the garden staring at the hedge in the darkness, my mind drifting, incapable of doing anything except wait. But a strange thing happened. I found I had butterflies in my stomach. I was anxious as if for a first date. This was crazy! This was Angus I was waiting for, not some little fuck-bunny. I tried not to think about the dream I'd had about him, but images of the scene next to Sally's Aga came tantalisingly back to haunt me.

Eventually I heard the unmistakable sound of Angus's Beetle, louder than ever after driving all the way from Cape Town and Grahamstown, and my innards felt hot and liquid. The Beetle approached over the hill like an angry *brommer*, coming unstoppably towards me, until finally it bounced up the grassy milkwood-lined path and into the garden next to Mac's old Volvo. After all his bravado on the phone, Angus did not know how to greet me. He didn't know what to do with his hands. We stood smiling but apart, not quite sure where to look.

'You washed your hair,' was the first thing he said. And he grinned. Bloody hell. I shrugged dismissively.

'Did Claude tell you I was here?' I asked accusingly.

'No.'

'How did you find me?'

'Elementary, my dear Watson. Claude told me you were hiding out in Kasouga and didn't want to be disturbed. So I guessed you were at Phillip and Sylvia's and I got the number from them.'

'Very clever. Now what?'

'Should we go?' he asked. 'I can't promise good food, but the conversation will be scintillating.'

There was little choice, and we ended up at a little restaurant right on the beach at the pier in Port Alfred. It had once been a tiny beach café where we'd come in my childhood to use the toilet or buy sweets. I remembered tracing patterns in the windows, the glass sticky with sea air, buying Rev ice creams from the special freezer with its sliding glass lid and agonising endlessly over which of the brightly coloured offerings in the jars at the counter to choose – Wacky Wicks bubblegum, Fizz Pops, sweets that tasted fakely of apricot, Chappies or the niggerballs which changed from black to other colours as you sucked them. Claude had trained me to call them magic balls with the result that none of the other children knew what I was talking about. Someone had obviously gone to some trouble to turn the old café into what it was now, with its matching pink menus and tablecloths. I felt oddly protective. We sat down at a table. I couldn't quite look at Angus.

'Clem, it's me, Angus,' he said.

'I know,' I said, smiling faintly, 'that's the problem.' His hands were in front of him on the table.

'I wonder, do you only like bastards?' he asked me. 'I tell myself that's the case so that I don't worry about the fact that you clearly don't like me.'

'I *do* like you.'

'You know what I mean. I think the problem is that I've had it all wrong all along. Good women don't like good men, they like bastards. And I've decided that from now on I'm going to be a complete bastard.'

I rolled my eyes at him and smiled weakly.

'Hello, folks,' said the waitron, flashing her teeth and her beach bunny tan. 'I'm Kelly and I'm going to be your waitron for tonight.' Angus raised his eyebrows at me and grinned. 'Our specials tonight are a large pizza for R12.95, as well as calamari and steak for R22.95.'

It was so refreshingly gauche of her to say the prices. There'd been times during my stay in Paris when I'd desperately wanted to try the specials in restaurants but had been too embarrassed to ask the price and too afraid to order them without asking. Yves came, unbidden, into my mind. How scornful he would have been, how rude to the poor girl serving us with her neat exposed midriff and her cheerleader cheerfulness. I smiled at Kelly.

'I'll have a large pizza Siciliana,' I told her. I pronounced it Sisil-yarna. I snapped the menu shut and looked up to see Angus staring at me. He smiled.

'What?' I asked. 'What's funny?' I wiped my hand across my face and nose to check.

'Nothing. You've become a lot more … decisive or something, that's all.' He turned to Kelly. 'I'll have a large salami and green pepper,' he said, and smiled charmingly at her.

'Great,' said Kelly. She slapped our plastic menus together and departed.

'She is without doubt one of those waitresses who will approach you the moment you have loaded in a gargantuan mouthful of food and ask you how your food is,' said Angus. 'One day I'm just going to go ahead and answer and spew the mouthful all over the table as though it were perfectly normal.'

I laughed. Angus looked at me laughing as though something had just struck him.

'Clem, there's something I should have said to you a long time ago. I lo … I lo …' Oh my God. Surely he was not about to say Those Words? But if he'd intended to, he was too sheepish to carry on, and resorted instead to pulling a comic face, contorted as a desperate stutterer. I couldn't help smiling.

'I lo ... I lo ... I lo ...' he went on, drawing out the agony for comic effect. 'I lo ... I lost my heart in San Francisco,' he forced out eventually. 'There, now I've said it and I can't take it back.'

I let out a semi-stifled scream of irritation. 'You're pathetic. You can't even *say* it ... and what makes you think I want to hear this anyway? How could I ever take you seriously?'

'But I *am* serious, Clem. I've always ...'

'Rubbish!' But secretly I was excited, all over, by his flattering confession. Angus moved the candle to one side, leaned over the table and kissed me, quite comfortably, on the lips. Then he sat back in his chair, smiling. Something stirred ominously in my nethers. I sat absolutely still, startled by the unfamiliarity of these familiar lips and stirred by a tantalising hint of incest. I was mildly astonished to realise it was what I wanted. I *wanted* this man – this friend, housemate, and pet student of my mother's – to kiss me. I affected a startled, pissed-off look and he just grinned more broadly back at me. Suddenly I'd had enough of being coy. Thinking back, the men I'd ended up with were always the ones who'd been most insistent, and where had it got me? I wanted to take what I wanted without thinking. I wanted to do myself a good deed, just like Jack had suggested. I wanted Angus.

'I had a dream about you at Ben and Sally's, you know. About fucking you.' There, it was out.

'Really?' said Angus, looking surprised and delighted. 'Well I've dreamt about fucking you for the last four years, so you have a lot of catching up to do.' Jesus. A hot wave passed through my body just at the thought. My mind and body were in revolt against my status as secular nun. A delicious sense of discomfort was making me squirm.

'How did it happen?' Angus butted in on my imaginings. 'In the dream?'

'I dreamt you were fucking me over their kitchen table.'

It was Angus's turn to look startled.

'I find that a highly appealing idea,' he said, giving me a strange, heavy-lidded smile I'd never seen on his face before.

This was all happening so *fast*. 'Tell me, Ms Fynn-van Zyl, if that is what you were thinking, why didn't you just walk down the passage to my room and invite me into the kitchen with you?'

'Why did you just leave without saying goodbye?'

'You hardly behaved as if you wanted me around. And I thought I'd ruined our friendship forever by trying so ineptly and insensitively to seduce you.' That smile again. There was a small carnival happening in my privates by this stage. Then I remembered that he'd never returned my phonecall. That he'd left me stewing in Cambridge without a backward glance.

'Why did you never return my call?' I asked angrily. 'I went through hell with those snotty Oxford gatekeepers trying to get hold of you and you didn't even phone me back.'

'So it *was* you,' he said. 'I was desperately hoping it might be. The thing is, I never got the message.' I eyed him sceptically, sat back in my seat with arms folded defensively over my chest. Never again was any man going to bullshit me on these matters.

'Don't doubt me, Clemmy, it's true. I lent my jacket to one of the other South Africans for his interview because he didn't have one. Then, after our interviews, we went to the pub and got rat-arsed – not least, I might add, because I'd just totally ballsed-up my relationship with my best friend and annihilated any chances of romance with the woman I'd secretly lusted after for as long as I could remember.'

'Stop sucking up. What does this have to do with not phoning me back?' I asked mercilessly.

'I'm getting there … So I poured out my heart to this poor unsuspecting South African and bemoaned the fact that you hadn't phoned and that you probably never wanted to see me again. Suddenly, this guy started patting the pockets of my jacket, which he was still wearing, looking inside them all as if he had lost something. I asked him what he was looking for and he told me he'd picked up a message for me at the porter's lodge and put it into the pocket. It was gone. We searched through every pocket, even checking for holes in the lining, but there was no note. I asked him frantically who it was from, but he couldn't remember. I nearly throttled him. I was so desperate for it to be you who had called, but too terrified to phone in case it wasn't and I made things worse. The guy said he was sure the person would phone back if it was important, but you never did. Why didn't you try again, Clem?'

I stared at him across the table. 'Pride?' I suggested. 'The desire to hang onto a shred of dignity? But mostly fear. Don't forget I had already tried to phone you once and you never phoned me back. How was I supposed to know you'd loaned out your jacket and my message to some unreliable stranger? I just thought you didn't want to speak to me. And don't forget you were the one who ran away without saying goodbye.'

Fucking Angus

Sex with Angus was like slipping on a favourite pair of jeans you thought you'd lost then rediscovered. Like jeans that have taken a long time and a lot of weathering to fit you just perfectly and make you feel your most sexy. It was also surprisingly passionate, wonderfully tender and deliciously variable in mood and tempo.

The first time was a revelation. We lay in Phillip and Sylvia's cheap wooden bed afterwards, drenched in sweat and bright-eyed with astonishment, the sheets and blankets tangled around our feet. Angus was stroking my thigh, muttering sexily to me. 'Oh my gorgeous Clemmy. My luscious little Clam ... May I call you that?'

I was one big nerve ending. Silently I wrapped myself closer into his beautiful body and made myself at home.

'Remember when we first moved into the Soup Kitchen?'

'Mmm.'

'It was fun, wasn't it?'

'Mmm.'

'And then you took up with that pretentious fuckwit, Haus-

mann. GOD, how I regretted inviting him to that fucking dinner
... and in *our house*.'

Angus said the last as though it had been a case of adultery in
the first degree under his roof.

'And you took up with Tamara,' I reminded him.

'Do not mention that name. She is the only person in the
whole world that I actually refuse to speak to. Ever. You'll never
guess what's happened to her, by the way.'

'What?'

'She's become a Kumbaya kid.'

'A what?'

'A Kumbaya kid. She's found the Lord and started eating
meat again.'

The world was indeed a peculiar place.

'Maybe Tamara and Kurt were necessary formative experi-
ences,' I suggested, 'before the two of us could get it together.
Just like you were a formative experience for Tamara on the way
to finding the Lord.'

'Formative experience!' Angus spat. 'Think of all the *fucking*
you and I missed out on.'

And with that, we set to work making up for lost time.

Angus woke me up in the middle of the night.

'What's wrong?' he asked me.

'What do you mean?'

'You were shouting and thrashing around.'

'Was I?'

'Yes. You weren't doing me next to the Aga again, were you?'
He rolled me over, away from him and then pulled me towards
him so that we fitted like spoons. It was a while before he spoke
again.

'Do you think you could still love me if my name was
Cecil?'

'No, I think Angus is about as bad as I could tolerate.'

'Algernon?'

'Tricky.'

'And Dwayne? I mean it would make pillow talk difficult, wouldn't it. (Angus puts on high voice): "Oh Dwayne, Dwayne! Do it to me, Dwayne." '

But his name wasn't Dwayne. So we celebrated.

Angus was supposed to be at some kind of follow-up scholarship interview in Cape Town the next afternoon, but it was pretty clear that he wasn't intending to go, either to the interview or back to England to study. We lay in bed debating which excuse he should use until I finally got up and phoned the woman in the scholarship office. Angus lay in bed, smiling and watching me. I smiled back, then spoke into the receiver.

'Oh hello. Yes, I'm afraid that Angus Foot can't make his appointment today ... Yes, yes. No he's not up to it at all. You see he's having trouble breathing – largely because I'm sitting on his face.'

Angus sat bolt upright in bed, looking horrified. I let out a whoop of laughter.

'Only joking,' I screeched. 'The number was engaged.'

Happy returns

It felt so strange and so right to be driving back to Grahamstown with Angus's hand resting comfortably on my inner thigh. He had left his car at Phillip and Sylvia's so that we could drive back together since he protested that he wouldn't be able to fondle me if we were in separate cars. Also, I think he knew I shouldn't be left alone to ponder this thing, this Angus-and-Clem thing, which was happening so fast it felt out of control. The truth was I didn't want to be alone at all.

I had been sheepish about Claude seeing Angus and me together, but in reality she looked almost wistful.

'So you found her, did you?' she said with a satisfied matchmaker smile. Maddy emerged from the garden, incongruously dressed in chic city gear but wearing gumboots and an old floppy sunhat of Claude's, gingerly carrying a hose.

'Well *hellohhh*,' she said, eyeing Angus and me with raised eyebrows and a broad smile, sussing us out immediately.

'Hello Maddy,' I said, smiling pretty broadly myself. 'I presume you remember Angus?'

Later that afternoon Claude called me to the phone. 'Quick, Clem, it's international,' she shouted. Despite the fact that Claude now gallivanted around at conferences all over the world she was still remarkably panicky about the cost when someone phoned from abroad. She kept international conversations short to the point of rudeness, as a rule, and became flustered if the caller was kept waiting or the call went on for too long. I rushed through to put her out of her misery, my stomach sick with dread at who it might be.

It was Serge. He'd got my number from Madame Rouillard and eventually tracked me down at Claude's. He was worried about me, he said, and Yves wouldn't tell him what was going on. There seemed no point in hiding it any more, and I found I could talk quite rationally when I told him what had happened. It was only when he expressed his genuine distress that I had to brush away a lone hot tear.

'All alone, *chérie*?' he asked, sounding distraught. 'Why did you not come to me? You must know I would have helped you. And Yves? Where was Yves?'

'I didn't tell him then, Serge. I was too scared. I told him after it was all over.'

Serge was silent as he digested this.

'How is he?' I asked quietly.

'Yves? He's pretty miserable, actually, but it does him some good. He's been seeing a lot of Antoine, being nicer to Anne. Oh, and Véronique's getting married to some boring rich guy.'

'Poor him,' I said. 'Let's hope they don't breed.'

Serge laughed. 'I miss you Clémence. I wish you had phoned me.'

'I miss you too, Serge. Thanks for everything.'

A week later there was an envelope from Normandy bearing an interesting reinvention of Claude's address written in Serge's casual scrawl. Inside the envelope was a collection of photographs of all of us in Caramany, which Patrice had taken. I looked happy. Here I was, lying on the grass with Inge reading Stendhal, sitting on the beach talking to Serge with my knees drawn up under my chin and my arms around them, me mock-charging Sebastian with a log while Robert and Yves watched with amusement and even admiration in the background. Perhaps I had not been such a complete failure after all. I came to a postcard of an apple-cheeked Normandy maiden bearing a basket of matching rosy apples. On the back of the postcard was the touching legend *'Je t'embrasse de mon big banane.'* I embrace you with my big banana. I think it was Serge's stamp of approval.

Once Serge's letter had started me rooting around in my past, I threw myself into the process with unexpected energy and commitment. I would have to go back to Cape Town soon, to find a life and a job, and Angus had to get back within the next few days. It was time for me to launch into some mental and physical spring-cleaning. The trunk in my old room at Claude's was waiting for me. I snapped open the catches and released into the air the smells and ghosts of my younger selves.

I stood blinking stupidly at the contents of the trunk and realised with a mild shock that what had felt both so current and so eternal just one year ago was already the distant past. It was confusing, this sudden feeling that you were a long way from your starting point when you hadn't even realised you were moving in the first place. It was a happy kind of sadness, and I started sorting with a vengeance, remembering with a hint of a smile how Maddy had sorted out my packing in Paris and quietly proud that I could manage quite okay on my own now. I unpacked the relics – jerseys, books, essays, letters and the photos of Jimmy, some slightly singed, which I'd saved from Claude's inferno all those years ago – with an attitude both tender and pragmatic. And in doing so I knew I was getting a foretaste of the end of something.

Mac gives the nod

Despite being a devoted atheist, Mac had always held a Christmas and Hanukkah celebration in the past. So on the twenty-fifth of December we drove to Greenfields to continue the tradition, the car loaded with a sawn-off pine branch, several boxes of Christmas tree decorations, gaudy Hanukkah candles, Christmas pudding, brandy butter, chicken-mayo sandwiches (a nod towards turkey), a few bottles of hooch, and some rock hard and completely inedible koeksister-like confections drenched in syrup which Maddy had made as a 'gesture' to Judaism and insisted on calling teiglach. We also brought three cans of Gillette shaving foam (Normal Skin) to make snow for the pine tree. It was thirty-three degrees Celsius. The nursing staff had come to expect a certain degree of eccentricity from Mac's clan, and judging by their reactions to our activities they were not disappointed.

Angus had insisted on coming with us, and Mac was obligingly lucid when we introduced him.

'Ah, Angus. Good name. Good Scottish boy. Keep him away from the golf course,' she said in a growly whisper. We made tea and attempts at conversation, during which Mac seemed to doze off. Then suddenly, without warning she opened her eyes and surveyed the room. Her penetrating gaze rested on Angus. 'If I were you I'd pick that one,' she said quite clearly to Claude. It was a bizarre and rather awkward benediction.

After we had left Greenfields and I no longer felt I was inhaling death and talcum powder and other substances I didn't want to think about, Angus told me about an aunt of his who'd had Alzheimer's. 'Sometimes she didn't recognise her husband Richard,' he explained. 'She'd had another husband before him who'd died many years earlier and whose name had been

Rodney. When I was visiting her one day and Richard left the room Aunt Alice turned to me, still a cunning old bat despite being a few sandwiches short of a picnic, and whispered quite anxiously "Does Richard know about Rodney?" '

I laughed, grateful for his attempts to lighten my mood. 'Angus, promise me that if I ever get like that you'll make them give me strychnine.'

He smiled at me, teasing. 'Oh come on, Clem. It might be good for a laugh. I could wheel you out of the cupboard to entertain our ancient guests on a Saturday night.'

'Ha ha,' I said. But I rather liked the thought of growing old with Angus. Then my thoughts strayed back to Mac. 'It's really hard, you know. Sometimes I'm not even sure whether she notices me, whether she realises I'm there.'

'Well she certainly noticed *me*,' Angus gloated.

'Don't get too swollen-headed, honey,' I reprimanded him. 'You were the only male in the room.'

I only saw Mac once again after that. This time it was just the three of us with her – Claude, Maddy and me. It was a warm summer's day and we'd bundled her into the car in her blankets and gone for a drive along the coast to Kenton. Mac looked, apparently vacantly, out of the window for a long time while Maddy talked and Claude and I sat thinking our separate thoughts. Suddenly Mac turned to Claude:

'You know, Jo'burg's got a lot better since they brought the sea here,' she said with evident satisfaction. It was very funny, really, but none of us laughed. It was the last thing I heard her say.

Return to the soup kitchen

Vladimir: To have lived is not enough for them.
Estragon: They have to talk about it.
– Samuel Beckett, *Waiting for Godot*

The doctors said they had no way of knowing how long Mac would live – it could be weeks or months. Claude said she'd phone me if I needed to come back, and she told me to take the Volvo. The next day we put the Beetle on the train and Angus and I drove back to Cape Town in the Volvo in time for the New Year, pottering happily around the passes and stopping to snog in lay-bys like teenagers. I was ecstatic to get back to the Soup Kitchen. In Angus's absence the transients had realised that their food and drink source had dried up and they'd moved on. The last of the housemates had moved out at the end of the academic year and the house was ours. We locked the front door behind us with twin sighs of relief, and lit candles since the electricity had also been cut off while Angus had been away and so, joy of joys, had the phone. New Year was spent in semi-darkness and in splendid isolation. We hid out in the house, and when we were bothered by knocking one morning Angus made a big unwelcoming sign for the door: *Soup Kitchen closed for business until further notice*, it read. We ventured out only to get the phone and electricity reconnected and to collect takeaways and black rubbish bags. Then we pitched all the detritus from all over the house into the black bags and had sex in all the rooms just because we could. In one of the rooms, recently vacated by a Goth computer-programmer called Vic, Angus set up a desk with Claude's old laptop so that I could write. Perhaps, if I tried hard enough, I could exorcise my imperfect past.

I didn't want to go out for fear of meeting someone I'd actually have to speak to. And I was so happy secreted there with Angus that he virtually had to force me outside 'for my own good' in the end. I'd spent so much time dreading meeting Kurt, but one of the first times I left the house I ran into him, quite literally, outside the café. I'd planned to meet him at some very much later stage, suitably worldly, groomed and glamorous, but sadly, as it happened, I'd slipped out in the middle of the night in a pair of ancient tracksuit pants to fetch some ingredients for our late-night cooking spree. I smelt of fried garlic and my hair was rolled into a hair band and fastened like a dog turd on top of my head. It was a brief and awkward meeting during which I managed (despite my appearance) to make a fairly creditable pretence of being in control of myself. By the time I arrived back at the Soup Kitchen, minus the groceries, I was a wreck. Angus opened the door and I fell apart.

'I hate him so much!' I roared.

He did his best to console me and to calm my rage, but I could tell he was angry and hurt that Kurt still had such an effect on me. He convinced me that I had to steel myself and fetch the bag of belongings I'd apparently left at Kurt's 'as part of my reclaiming of my past'. To ensure that I went, Angus 'gallantly' frogmarched me to Kurt's house. As it turned out, when we arrived Kurt was out. The fragile Indian dancer opened the door, and there was an awkward moment as I owned up to being Kurt's ex-girlfriend and apologised for not telling her that day outside the theatre. But she was charmingly unfazed: 'Small world,' she said with a pretty smile. 'He still hasn't put up my bookshelves.' Angus talked charmingly and non-stop to her about Nijinsky for a quarter of an hour and I waited with increasing desperation to leave in case Kurt came home.

'You didn't have to be *that* charming,' I said as we left. But the truth is that Angus liked people. He was sociable. He talked to people in queues and talked overly loud in shops to entertain the shoppers. I loved him, I realised. It had dawned on me that I'd fallen in love with him, slowly but surely. It was not an experience I'd had before. Angus, my old friend, was a revelation.

Only once we were safely back at the Soup Kitchen did I open the bag we'd fetched from Kurt's. Inside was a strange assortment of items, namely:

- one pair unfortunate looking undies (grey, once pink)
- one plastic handbag with broken strap: contents – tissues (used)
- beginner's guide to Foucault (highly embarrassing relic of days spent trying to understand what Kurt was saying –

would disown it but name in front a dozen times while bored and practising signature. Also highly compromising notes in margins: excruciating)

- several well-read Jane Austens (hah!)
- three stiffy disks with my third year essays on them (thank God Kurt despised computers)
- two files
- one pair rather disgraceful *takkies* (dirty socks still stuffed inside them)
- one Bluffer's Guide to Feminism (unspeakably awful)
- one Cosmo with page on 'Coping With Problem Hair' turned back and well-fingered (tried not to think of Beautiful Indian Girl's sleek and well-groomed bob)
- head part of chicken costume from fancy-dress party

I was sitting blushing furiously with humiliation all on my own in my study when Angus came to the door, hesitated outside and knocked.

'May I come in?' he asked. You had to love him. He was so determined to be better than my previous intrusive journal-reading lover who sniffed out my secrets and used them to flavour his own works of art.

'Of course. You don't have to be *such* a Sensitive New Age Guy.'

'What are you doing?'

'Humiliating myself.' I showed him the contents of the bag and he burst out laughing.

'I wouldn't worry, Clam. The Dancing Girl probably makes him re-watch *Fame* and *Flashdance* every Saturday night and thinks they're the best movies she's ever seen.'

It was an unlikely scenario, but an extremely comforting one.

'I'll bear that in mind,' I said.

I ditched everything except the Austen novels into a black rubbish bag without a backward glance, and with an immense feeling of achievement and satisfaction I settled down and reread *Northanger Abbey* in one sitting.

An ending

It turned out that I'd come back just in time for Mac. A few days after we'd pottered back to Cape Town, she slipped into a coma. She died quietly in her sleep the same night with her hands folded over her chest somewhat defensively and an expectant smile on her face, which was hugely disconcerting for the nurses who found her. She was alone, and I think that she'd planned it that way. I even suspected she might have struck a bargain with the rather unspecific Almighty I'd sometimes heard her admonishing when she didn't know I was listening.

When someone dies, the last thing you said to them always seems so flawed and pathetic. When Claude told me Mac was dead I couldn't help thinking about the last time I saw Jimmy. We'd argued because I didn't want to go and bath and be on my own when he and Claude (so obviously, in retrospect) needed to talk. How does one orchestrate a last meeting if you never know it's going to be the last? What does one say? The day Mac died, Angus and I drank to her at dinner. I thought I was fine about it all, that it wouldn't affect me. In fact I felt heartless that night when instead of crying myself to sleep over my lost grandmother I got drunk with Angus and lay in bed telling him wicked stories about her. It was only the next day when I bumped into a mere acquaintance in the supermarket and burst into floods of tears when she asked me how I was (an awful scene requiring the use of almost a whole toilet roll taken straight off the shelf) that I realised how much it meant. The poor woman looked quite disturbed. She had hardly expected to elicit such an answer with her bland question. I apologised and stumbled home, half-blinded by tears, realising with a pang of guilt as I walked through the Soup Kitchen gate blowing my nose that I'd inadvertently stolen the toilet roll from the shop. It made me smile. Mac would have approved of a little pragmatic shoplifting.

Once I'd calmed down I took stock. I realised I'd come far enough to finish writing it out and move on. So I made my last pilgrimage to the laptop in Vic the Goth's old room.